THE THREE PARTISANS

THE THREE PARTISANS

A Novel

JEAN-YVES PITOUN

UNION
SQUARE
& CO.

NEW YORK

This is a work of fiction. Names, characters, businesses, events, and incidents are the products of the author's imagination. Any resemblance to actual persons, living or dead, or actual events is purely coincidental.

ISBN 978-1-4549-5806-2
ISBN 978-1-4549-5807-9 (e-book)

Library of Congress Cataloging-in-Publication Data is available upon request.
Library of Congress Control Number: 2024042773

Union Square & Co. books may be purchased in bulk for business, educational, or promotional use. For more information, please contact your local bookseller or the Hachette Book Group's Special Markets department at special.markets@hbgusa.com.

Printed in Canada

2 4 6 8 10 9 7 5 3 1

unionsquareandco.com

Cover design by Jared Oriel
Cover art by Arcangel: Roy Bishop (street), Simon Mulcahey (planes);
Shutterstock.com: Here (texture); Trevillion: © Shelley Richmond (man)
Interior design by Kevin Ullrich
Photos on pages 467–469 courtesy of the author

For my children, Cathy and Christopher,
and my brother, Arnaud

PROLOGUE

"WHATEVER YOU IMAGINE, IT WILL be a hundred times worse."

Men and women who have been in combat rarely talk about it except to each other. How could anyone possibly understand what they went through?

I grew up in southwest France in a town at the foothills of the Pyrenees, a place where rugby is a religion and a rebellious spirit a badge of honor. Every Sunday my father and I went to the stadium where we met his comrades from the Résistance. After the games, we crowded into the Café des Sports. The owner was a friendly redhead with green eyes and a dazzling smile, who always left her counter to kiss my father when we came in. The windows were misty, a huge mirror on one side and walls decorated with yellowed Toulouse-Lautrec posters. The air smelled strongly of Gauloises cigarettes. They drank Pernod, I drank grenadine. They talked, I read comic books. Soon they forgot I was there.

I heard stories about fighting in the Tunisian desert, prisoner of war camps in Italy, Royal Air Force and US Air Force units in England and, of course, about the Résistance. I heard about blowing up jails, attacking trains, and smuggling allied aviators to Spain through the mountains. I heard about the women they had fought beside and how brave they were. I heard about the exploits of people I knew and of others I had never met. Two names stood out—Janine Dumas, a Frenchwoman who headed the escape line whose name was always mentioned with utmost respect, and Captain Mike O'Keefe, my father's Irish American brother-in-arms from Chicago who seemed to me bigger than life.

I also learned my father was Jewish, but I was not. It upset me: I wanted to be exactly like him. I was only five, but I remember how they all would laugh and tease each other. Then, they'd grow silent, light cigarettes, tilt their empty glasses, and eyes shining, stare into space.

Much later I understood that many of the men and women they talked about had been killed. On those Sunday afternoons my father and his friends were mourning their lost comrades. The memories were sharp, the wounds still raw, but this was how they healed.

Years later, carelessly thrown into a drawer in my parents' home, I found black-and-white photographs taken during memorial services after the war. A dozen men and women in their Sunday best; in one photo, I could see front and center standing next to my father a tall attractive woman who wore a look that conveyed passion and fortitude, a look that only someone able to love fiercely could bear.

Most of what follows is true.

I

JANINE DUMAS SHIVERED. SHEETS OF rain were falling outside. She pulled the collar of her raincoat tighter around her neck and hissed to herself: "Why am I always so cold?"

Glancing wearily at the empty fireplace, she scrubbed her shoulders and paced the farmhouse's main room. It was bare save for a seed company calendar on the wall opened to October 1942 and featuring a picture of the fall harvest. She rubbed her hands and stretched her back muscles the way she used to do in warm-up exercises before ballet. How she had loved dancing. She caught her reflection in the grayed mirror above the dresser and saw, for a fleeting moment, her past self.

No time for such frivolous distraction today. She snorted at the memory and turned away from the mirror. She did not think of herself as beautiful, but she was, with dark, liquid, hazel eyes that sparkled with intelligence, yet today were filled with worry. Peering into the hallway, she glanced at the young American airman sitting on the floor, staring straight ahead. A nineteen-year-old bombardier with the US Air Force, his B-17 had been shot down over Normandy. Or so he said. Freddy Griffith was his name; he was the only survivor out of a crew of ten.

Feeling her gaze, Griffith raised his callow face from the *Farmer's Almanac* he was reading and glanced around. "Do you live here?" he asked and immediately raised his hand in apology. "I know I shouldn't ask. They told us at briefings. If we're rescued not to ask names or where we are . . ."

Janine breathed in the farm smells of cured meat and cold ashes and shook her head. "No, I don't live here."

"Right. You don't look like a farmer's wife," Griffith said with a grin.

This almost made Janine smile. She was a dentist and practiced with her father in Toulouse, one of the largest towns in southwest France.

"You're the first person I met who speaks English," Griffith said. "I want to thank you. I know you're all taking big risks to help me."

The US Air Force briefed him well, Janine thought. Yes, this was risky, very risky. She had been smuggling shot-down allied airmen to Spain and the British base of Gibraltar for over two years and had seen many resistance organizations decimated by Vichy France's police and by German intelligence.

The previous night had been typically wearing. Janine had taken the omnibus from Toulouse, changed trains twice, and slept poorly. Her papers had been thoroughly checked as she crossed into German occupied France and she was now in the heart of Brittany, dreading the decision she might have to make. Something was not right about Griffith. His identification papers said he was born in Del Rio, Texas, and that he had trained at a base in England, but when he was put in the presence of an American pilot who came from the same base, the man claimed he had never seen Griffith before.

The pilot attested that Griffith spoke with a definite Texas twang. And MI9, the British Directorate of Military Intelligence in charge of escape and evasion, had confirmed that Griffith, a navigator from the 8th AAF bomb group based in Polebrook, had indeed been shot down on September 21 over Cherbourg.

Still, when Griffith was asked about his life in England, his responses were vague. When asked for the names of the pubs outside the base, he responded that he was a member of the Mormon

Church and believed in abstinence. Also, he didn't know that "lorry" was the term the English used for truck. Perhaps he was just not curious. Some people were like that. They go to foreign places, avoid interactions with the locals, and just stick to what they know.

Janine knew that the German Luftwaffe trained agents to pose as allied aviators. They were provided with the identification papers of captured allied airmen who had been ordered to strip down before being shot on the spot. Then a Luftwaffe agent of similar height would put on his clothes, down to the socks and skivvies, and roam the countryside until picked up by the Résistance. For the job, they recruited young Germans who had grown up in the United States and returned to Germany during the Depression, when Hitler was calling for all true Aryans to return to the motherland.

She glanced again at the young aviator flipping through the *Farmer's Almanac.* Still a teenager, he looked awkward in his French civilian coat, too tight around his shoulders. This Griffith had gone through a harrowing experience, Janine thought. His plane had been shot down and his crewmates were dead. He had been cooped up in attics and cellars all over Brittany for weeks. He was obviously in shock and entitled to memory lapses. *Of course he is an American airman!* Janine made up her mind. If everything about Griffith checked out, she would take him to the Spanish border herself.

The war years had been hard on Janine. She had been devastated by the loss of her husband, a pilot in the French Air Force, who was killed in June 1940, a few days before the birth of their daughter, now two years old. She was heartbroken but determined to find a way to help the allied cause. Her chance came when she learned that a pilot from her husband's outfit was helping rescue stranded British airmen. She got in touch with him and began to organize smuggling runs across the Pyrenees. When that pilot was caught and executed, Janine took the full measure of what a dangerous undertaking this was, but the airmen kept coming and they had to be helped. Janine rebuilt the network, but constant worrying was now an integral part of her life.

The sound of footsteps made her turn and Loïc Briant walked in. In his late twenties, with a broad rugged face and short-cropped hair, he wore blue overalls pushed into rubber boots under a fisherman's coat. They had worked together for months, and she felt safe in his presence. Very safe, and Janine felt bursts of absurd love for him at times—they trusted each other with their lives but she was a doctor from the city, he was a farmer, and the distance remained. Loïc's father had been killed in the trenches in 1916. His mother had died, and his brother was a prisoner of war in Germany. He lived alone and ran the family farm all by himself and did it well. Loïc was a rarity, a Protestant in a Catholic community. At the outset of the war, he had responded to the deacon of his church's call to help a group of German Jews and Spanish Republicans escape a French detainment camp before the Vichy government turned them over to the Nazis. Protestants in France had a history of resistance born from centuries of Catholic persecution. Fighting the oppressor came readily to them.

Loïc nodded to Griffith, then ambled to the window to stand beside Janine. He kept his left hand in his coat pocket. Janine knew his arm was shriveled by polio and that Loïc was ashamed of it. The polio had kept him away from the army, but also from finding a wife.

"What did he say?" Janine asked.

"Agfa," Loïc replied.

A shadow crossed Janine's face. "Are you sure?"

"Of course I am sure. I made him say it three times." Loïc's eyes twitched shut periodically, a nervous tic betraying more irritation than anxiety. "They're waiting by the bridge. I'll take care of it."

"Have you ever?"

Loïc shrugged off grimly at whatever was going on inside him. "First time for everything."

Janine stared at the rain outside. When she joined the Résistance she had been forewarned that one day she might have to do the unspeakable and not expect others to do the dirty work for her. "No, I'll handle it," she said.

Loïc glanced at Griffith and whispered, "I can't let you do this. Let's talk outside."

"No. Go get the horse ready."

"This is wrong."

Janine clenched her teeth, pushing away a feeling of foreboding. "It's the way it has to be."

Loïc shook his head like the stubborn ox he was. She was the leader of the line and he had always respected her decisions, but he could not uphold this one. And now he was angry. "I can do this better than you," he insisted.

"It's my responsibility," she said.

Loïc's face darkened as he walked to the door. "I'll hitch up the cart," he announced, louder than necessary.

"We'll need coats. It's still raining," Janine said.

"I keep them in the barn."

Janine waited for the door to close, then she turned to Griffith. "All right, young man, let's go."

Griffith closed the almanac and looked up eagerly. "Where are we headin'?"

"South. How's your Spanish?"

"Rusty," cheered Griffith with a big smile. "Oh, jeezus! That's great! I can't wait to get back. Everybody's been real nice, but I'm startin' to go nuts. Hell, at the last place they wouldn't even let me look out the windows. Oh boy, that's good. Thanks a bunch."

Janine had learned British English in school, but now with the arrival of American airmen, she felt she had to learn the language all over again. *Nuts? Thanks a bunch?*

They hurried across the muddy yard and into the barn. Loïc pointed at oilskins hanging on pegs amid hats and rubber aprons. They put them on, pulling the hoods over their heads, and moved toward a horse-drawn cart. Loïc adjusted the harness and then stuffed tufts of hay into the horse's ears.

"What's he doin'?" Griffith asked.

Janine shook her head. She had no idea. Loïc caught the exchange and glanced at the dark sky. "Thunder . . . *Boom, boom,*" he explained, and pointed at the horse's head. "Cheval, scared crazy."

Griffith understood that, smiled, and helped Janine climb into the cart where she huddled on the backbench. Griffith sat beside Loïc, who slapped the reins over the horse's back. They wheeled across the yard and onto the road. The animal broke into a gentle trot. It was raining hard, and Janine shivered in her oilskin.

While she had known that Griffith's papers issued at Fort Bragg, North Carolina, were authentic, she had needed to be certain about the photograph on those documents. So she had asked for one final verification: a chemist working for the underground had developed a method to test photographic paper and determine if a picture was printed on Ilford paper made in England, Kodak paper made in America, or Agfa paper made in Germany.

Agfa, Loïc had said. "Griffith" was a German spy.

Janine had never killed anyone. She had never so much as slapped someone's face. She remembered Résistance fighters talking about executing spies—it's easier to hate people if you only see the back of their heads. "Take a deep breath and do what needs to be done," they had said. Janine stared at Griffith's nape. This was a nineteen-year-old kid. She feared him and felt sorry for him, but she could not hate him. As the moment approached her terror grew. She considered all the reasons why she should not do this—they had made a mistake, there had to be another way. Maybe they could lock him up somewhere. But this boy, whoever he was, had met many helpers in the last few weeks. If she let him go, they would be arrested and tortured. A few would talk. Twenty or thirty men and women would die or be deported because of this.

They crossed a narrow bridge onto the road, which snaked into a grove. This was the place. This was where it had to be done. Suddenly, she knew she could not kill this man. *Do the unthinkable!* she was told. The absurdity of it all infused her with unexpected strength. Janine pulled a 6.35-millimeter revolver from under her oilskin but felt suddenly compelled by the need for one last test.

"Wurdest du in Bremen ausgebildet?" *Were you trained in Bremen?* she asked casually in German.

"Wie?" Griffith responded automatically. A terrifying instant later he swung around, saw the gun, and lunged for it. He was well trained. Janine fought back furiously but his powerful arms pinned her to the wagon's bench as he grabbed her gun.

Two shots rang out.

The German's body sagged into Janine's arms. She pushed back and watched in horror as it rolled onto the floorboards. Loïc had fired point-blank into his head. Thanks to the straw the horse had not reared, but the detonations had frightened a flock of birds that was now screeching and soaring into the sky. Loïc stopped the cart and put down his revolver.

They were both stunned. Blood was everywhere. They watched the body shake violently as life emptied out of it.

"Oh, God," Janine whispered.

A whistle rang out and two men walked out of the woods. Breton farmers, one middle-aged, one young. Father and son probably.

"The hole is already dug," the father said.

They slid a burlap bag over the German's head and carried him away. Hard rain pouring, dirty pink water streaming down the floorboards. Loïc scooped a handful of straw and cleaned the blood off the bench, then he stepped ahead and removed the plugs from the horse's ears.

Janine hauled herself to the cart's front bench. Her face was drenched, she was trembling. Loïc climbed back aboard and with more straw, wiped the blood off her oilskin. He thought about taking her in his arms to try to comfort her. He was just about to but could not find the right way. Janine sat there, staring straight ahead, and the moment passed.

Loïc clucked his tongue, and the horse resumed his trot. Turning back, Janine caught a glimpse of the two farmers working deep in the undergrowth. She knew they would undress the body before dropping it into the grave. Civilian shoes and clothing, especially in large sizes, were scarce and expensive on the black market. Those would be cleaned and used again, hopefully on a real allied airman next time.

"I had to make sure they were right about the photographic paper," Janine said, giving in to an overwhelming need to justify her actions.

"Your stubbornness almost got us killed," Loïc said.

"He was my responsibility," she replied, not giving an inch.

They rode in silence. Loïc fumed to himself. He should have stood up to her. Killing was a man's job. He had slaughtered pigs, sheep, and cows all his life. True, killing a man was different. Gruesome. Horrible, but his job, nonetheless. He shuddered, then felt Janine's hand on his arm.

"Thank you, Loïc," she murmured.

He was still angry but grateful for her touch.

Janine held his arm tighter and breathed in his musky smell. Hay laced with sweat. She wanted to embrace him. She wanted to bury her face in his shoulder. She wanted his powerful arms wrapped around her body. She did nothing.

"You can cry, it's all right, you know," Loïc said.

"I never cry."

Loïc's nervous tic flashed again as his eyes twitched shut a few times. "Well, I do. No shame in that."

Janine looked down at her hands and forced herself to stop trembling.

"Push it away," Loïc said. "What just happened."

Janine nodded, determined to do so and failing miserably. "Get going. I don't want to miss my train."

"You're picking up airmen in Limoges?"

Janine nodded. "Griffith was supposed to be part of that convoy."

Loïc clucked his tongue again and the horse picked up the pace.

Janine closed her eyes: *a deep breath and do what needs to be done.* She had not been able to.

2

ROBERT LEVY HATED THE PLACE where he was born. A knotted feeling weighed on his chest every time he came home to Kherrata, a small town perched high up in the Atlas Mountains of Eastern Algeria. The local population consisted of six thousand Muslims, three hundred Europeans, and about two hundred Jews, Robert's family counted among the latter. Snow had come early that year, and a dirty white layer covered the hills. Their street, the main thoroughfare, was one of the few paved roads in town. It was Shabbat, so the Jewish-owned stores were closed, and the street was empty.

Robert worked as a mechanic in a car repair shop in Sétif, twenty miles away. He visited home rarely but tried to return for religious holidays. A few days was all he could take before his mother's disapproval and "greater plans for her oldest son" started to take their toll. He always wore his suit for the occasion. Lean, almost six feet tall, with a tanned face and dark curly hair, he displayed an ever-present smile that added to his air of self-confidence.

When his parents' friends, the Zeitouns, appeared in the middle of the afternoon for coffee, Robert got more than an inkling of what else his mother wanted. He joined his father, mother, sister, and three brothers: all sitting at the big dining room table facing Joseph Zeitoun, his wife, their daughter Arlette, and her two young brothers.

Robert's father was in his early fifties but looked older. A rubber seal, hiding a dead eye, blackened the right lens on his glasses, a memento of World War I. Under this severe exterior, Robert knew there was a gentle soul who fretted constantly about the war and the future of his children. He wore his gray suit with the rosette of the Légion d'honneur adorning the lapel of his jacket. For his heroism during the Great War, he had been awarded the highest French decoration a soldier could receive.

La mouquère, the maid, served everyone, muttering under her breath, "Je n'aime pas les Zeitouns, c'est tout." *I don't like the Zeitouns, that's all.* Of course she didn't. Joseph Zeitoun owned a clothing factory. They were so rich as to be detestable in her view.

La mouquère had a soft spot for Robert; she thought he was the best-looking in the family. Yet she knew he was also the unhappiest. For the past three years he had lived with an ear glued to the radio, fiddling with the dials to get the latest news from the war. There was mostly bad news, with Adolf Hitler's armies occupying Western Europe, part of the Soviet Union, and North Africa.

But lately there had been a glimmer of hope, extraordinary news censured by the Vichy government, but known to all. In June, the Free French in Libya had confronted Rommel's German forces at Bir Hakeim and inflicted heavy casualties on the German panzer and Italian Ariete tank divisions. The term "Free French" was replaced with "Fighting French" by Winston Churchill himself. With this opening in mind, Robert was determined to join the fight.

In the typical fashion of North African Jews, Joseph Zeitoun was talking about everything but the reason for the visit. Robert's father had bought and renovated a two-story building up the street. It had a shop on the ground floor and an apartment upstairs. "Wouldn't this be a wonderful opportunity," he murmured, "for the Zeitoun and Levy families to go into the retail business?"

In 1940 the pro-Nazi Vichy government had passed the loi Carré, an anti-Semitic law that took away the French nationality from North African Jews and forbade them from working in the French administration. Tens of thousands of Jewish civil servants lost their jobs and since then, all government positions were now closed to Jews. The older Levy had decided that his son should go into business.

That was not all he had decided. Robert looked across the room at the Zeitouns' daughter Arlette, a pretty, young woman with dark hair and almond eyes Robert had known all his life. She caught Robert's gaze and returned a friendly glance.

As a first-born son in a Sephardic Jewish family, Robert was expected to be the guardian of tradition. But rebellion was in every fiber of his body. He spoke French and fluent Arabic, but when at ten years old he was told that in addition to French school, he had to attend Hebrew school, he ran away. The entire community was in an uproar until his father found him a week later hiding out with Arab shepherds up in the mountains. His mother had beat the living hell out of him and the rabbi managed to cram enough Hebrew into his stubborn head to get him bar mitzvahed.

Now, except on the high holidays, Robert never stepped foot in a synagogue. He forgot his Hebrew and replaced it with the English he learned listening to American blues, jazz, and BBC news bulletins. English would be his key to the outside world, his gateway to freedom.

Across the table, Arlette whispered to her mother, who exchanged a few words with her husband before muttering a reluctant "oui." Arlette winked at Robert, who stood up and followed her. Once out of the room, she took Robert's arm, and they stepped outside. A Renault Monaquatre sedan was parked in front of the house. A beautiful automobile with charcoal fuel tanks on the roof, it was Arlette's father's car, and an extraordinary luxury in such a place.

Arlette led Robert to a granite bench on the sidewalk. "You've got to get us out of this," she said. "If you don't come up with a bright idea today, you'll end up with a wife."

"You don't want to get married?"

"Not to you."

His face flooded with relief, he looked at her with smiling eyes. He didn't want to marry her, but he liked her.

"What they're discussing in there is for you to become a shopkeeper and for us to be married before Tu B'Shevat," Arlette continued. "And that's in less than four months. They hope I'll have a calming influence on you. They also expect me to be pregnant by summer. A couple of children and he'll settle down. You know how they think."

"I certainly do," Robert said.

"They want to resolve this today and announce our engagement next week. Once they do that, it's sealed. Then it'll be a question of honor. I don't want to be an abandoned bride."

"They should crawl out of the Middle Ages."

"You go tell them that."

"They'll be furious and will make your life miserable."

Arlette nodded emphatically. "Yes, but you'd do that too."

Robert smiled grimly. She was right.

Next to them on the sidewalk, a bicycle was tied to a rack with a heavy chain. Arlette followed his gaze to the hamstrung vehicle. "Your father padlocked your bicycle."

"I can pick that lock," Robert said. He dug into his pocket and pulled out a fat roll of bills tied with a rubber band. "I'm going to Algiers."

"Where did you get all that money?" Arlette asked.

"My job at the repair shop."

"We both know that's a lie. You sold hashish again!"

Robert shifted nervously under Arlette's disapproving look. "How do you expect me to get out of here?" he asked.

Arlette sighed and stood up. "Fine! You explain *that* to our families."

"It'd be easier if I just left."

"Easier for you but not for me," Arlette said, pulling Robert toward the house. "Do you know how angry my father's going to be? Well, make sure he's angry at *you.*"

Robert waved a gallant hand toward the door and followed Arlette. Entering the dining room Robert flashed a huge smile. He opened his arms and marched up to Arlette's father. "Mr. Zeitoun, Arlette and I have been talking and there is something I need to tell you, but first I have to kiss you."

Arlette's father glanced at his wife for approval and stood.

"God has answered my prayers," Robert's mother whispered as she watched Robert and Joseph Zeitoun kiss on the cheeks several times.

"Mr. Zeitoun, I'm honored. You're willing to give me what is most precious to you—your daughter, the apple of your eye. She's beautiful and much brighter than I am. Mr. Zeitoun, she deserves better. I can't marry her. That would be a crime. And she doesn't want to marry me either, she thinks I'm a bum."

"She'll do what I tell her to do," Joseph Zeitoun said.

Robert's mother held her forehead and cried. "My son, you want me in my grave?"

"Mother, there is a war and I want to join."

"To get yourself killed!" his father barked. "You are not twenty-one yet. I decide what you do."

"In America, boys under sixteen are lying about their age to enlist in the armed forces," Robert said, turning to his father. "Dad, you and I have talked about this. You know we have to fight."

"In what army? You aren't even French! Look at me," he said, flipping his hand by his dead eye. "You saw how they treated me. I was awarded the Légion d'honneur yet now the Vichy government's anti-Semitic laws decide I am no longer French."

"It's the Vichy government, Dad. They're traitors."

"They hate Jews!"

"That's why we must fight them."

"And you're going to fight them," Charles Levy asked, raising his chin, "all by yourself?"

"The Free French are in Libya, the British in Egypt. The war is coming to us. Dad, you taught me that there are two kinds of Jews, the ones who whine and the ones who fight. You were in the trenches for four years. It's my turn to fight."

"Come here," Charles Levy said, standing up and taking Robert in his arms. "It's different this time."

"Yes, it's different! It's worse. All we hear about is Jews rounded up and shipped away." Robert kissed his father. "I'll be fine. Like you, Dad." With welled-up eyes he turned around and walked out.

"You're letting him go?" Robert's mother yelled as the room exploded into turmoil.

Robert's father raised his arms to calm everyone. "At his age, I didn't want to get married either. My father, God bless his soul, put some sense into me."

This was news to Robert's mother, but she quickly refocused on the crisis at hand. "Robert, come back inside!" Turning to her husband, she wailed, "He's not coming back."

Robert's father sat down, put his lips together, and let out a disparaging *pfuu*. He spread his hands and looked at Joseph Zeitoun. "I was a heartache to my father. My son is a heartache to me."

Outside, a car engine whined, coughed, and came to life.

"Is that my car?" Arlette's father asked, patting his pockets. Now the roar of the Renault Monaquatre's eight cylinders filled the room. "He took my keys!" Joseph Zeitoun said as he rushed out of the room.

The Renault was already moving. Joseph Zeitoun ran after his car but was forced to give up. Charles Levy didn't even try. He shook his head, looking sadly after his son. The children were jumping up and down in excitement. The women were crying. It was all so upsetting.

Shifting gears, Robert spotted their maid in the rearview mirror waving happily. "Kan allah fi eawnik, Robert!" *May God be with you, Robert!* she shouted.

3

LIEUTENANT MIKE O'KEEFE OF THE British Royal Air Force Eagle Fighter Squadron felt relaxed as his plane soared over the thin layer of clouds covering western France. His unit was escorting bombers back from a raid over Germany and soon they would return to base.

A Chicago native, Mike was part of the early wave of idealistic young Americans who had enlisted in the RAF while the United States was sitting on the sidelines. The isolationists in Congress refused to help Britain. Mike was one of the top pilots in his unit, with eleven kills and tallies drawn on the side of his aircraft to prove it.

The pulsing throb of German radar drumming in his headset cut short his high spirits. *Bam, bam, bam!* Suddenly, all around him the sky filled with puffs of black smoke hanging in the air like paint splashes. *Babablam!* His Spitfire shook as the whole cockpit shattered and the top of his instrument panel shredded into pieces.

Whuuu! Mike fought back overwhelming panic—*breathe, breathe, breathe!* He checked the formation of bombers a thousand feet above and focused on what was left of his instruments.

The crisp English voice of Peterson, his wingman, came over the intercom. "O'Keefe, I think you're hit."

"I'm all right," Mike answered.

Mike reduced speed to lose altitude. He tapped the gauge dials. The engine coolant indicator was edgy—*not good.* He cleared his throat to steady his voice. "Left coolant line's shot. Right one's holding."

"Excellent," Peterson said.

Mike felt intensely cold suddenly. He looked up and spotted a gaping hole in the panel above him. Then he looked down—there was another hole in the floor. Shrapnel had speared the underbelly of the aircraft and blasted through the cockpit between his legs. Mike pulled his knees up and shook his feet. His pants were soaked with blood.

"Damn!" He pulled off his glove with his teeth, unzipped his flight suit, and searched for his cock.

"You all right?" Peterson asked.

Mike pulled up his hand. His fingers were covered with blood. He wiped it off on his pants. "Krauts almost blew my nuts off."

"I know young ladies who'd be all torn up about that," Peterson said.

Well, yeah—Mike pulled up the talisman he wore around his neck and kissed it. A gorgeous dark-haired nurse had given it to him. It was one of her black stockings tied up with a stick of lipstick and a lock of her pubic hair—his good luck charm. He hoped to God that the thing worked—*don't let me down now, sweetie!*

"Bailing out, old chap?" Peterson said.

"No POW camp for me. I'll be fine."

Mike checked the instruments, trying to steady the wire of fear jumping inside him. The aircraft's lifelines shut down one by one.

"Coast's still miles ahead," Peterson said.

"Engine's holding well," Mike lied. "Give me some room."

Mike glanced at Peterson's plane moving away—*good-bye, friend.* His Spitfire's engine could explode at any moment, and he had made sure his squadron mate would stay at a safe distance. He now squinted at the shimmering surface of the North Sea ahead. That water was home—*almost.* The condition of his aircraft made him an easy kill. He scrutinized the sky, searching for enemy fighters who often waited for exhausted crews on their way back from missions, but the sky above remained empty—*in their barracks eating sauerkraut.* The engine began snarling with a deadly rattle. The temperature gauge plunged into the red and the oil pressure raced toward zero.

"Flames coming out of your engine," Peterson said, the unflappable tone of his voice hiding his concern.

The fuel tank was in the front of the aircraft between the engine and the cockpit. If it caught, it would trigger a flamethrower aimed at Mike's face and barbecue him.

"I'll bail out over water."

"I'll stay with you to get a position."

Still far ahead, that water. The engine now clattered like a box of broken tools. At two hundred miles an hour he was traveling over three miles a minute. One more minute would make the difference between capture and freedom. Of course, there was the possibility of the engine exploding—*then my cock would be the least of my problems.*

Mike began counting. "Six, seven, eight, nine . . ." The sound of the engine was heartbreaking. He counted louder. "Twelve, thirteen, fourteen . . ." When flames blazed out and circled the fuel tank, he jettisoned the canopy and pulled the harness. *Whoosh*—he was hurled into a windstorm. Drawing himself into a ball to produce as much forward motion as possible, he found his mind flooded with thoughts of that nurse in the hotel room in Brighton—the taste of her lips, the softness of her skin. He counted five seconds and pulled the ripcord. The parachute cracked open, the straps between his legs snapped tight, and a colossal jab of pain shook him as he shouted at the top of his lungs.

Floating fifteen hundred feet over the water, Mike spotted a couple of ships ahead and watched his plane crash into the sea.

The glacial water of the North Sea hit him like a gigantic slap. His whole body stiffened but he managed to snap off the harness of his parachute and float to the surface as his wingman made a low pass and tipped his wings to signal he had radioed his position. Bobbing in the waves, Mike decided the cold salty water would shrink his blood vessels and cauterize his wound—*my cock is all I think about.*

No German planes or ships today. English fishermen picked him up. They gave him a blanket and plied him with whiskey. A civil patrol car waiting at the port took him to a coastal hospital where a doctor cut through Mike's flight suit.

"Where am I hit, exactly?"

The doctor adjusted his glasses and took his time. "Pecker's in one piece if that's what you're wonderin' about."

The doctor had never seen such bloody luck. The shrapnel had lodged below the left testicle a quarter of an inch from the femoral artery. He maneuvered Mike into a prone position and provided a shot of morphine. The doctor removed the shrapnel—a jagged-edged thing the size of a shilling—and applied a bandage to the wound.

"Want to keep it?" he asked, holding up the nasty metal item in his tweezers.

"Yes," Mike answered. "I'll put it in with my good luck charm."

The doctor watched him pull up a black stocking talisman from his shirt's collar and shook his head.

"I wouldn't mess with it if I were you. That thing worked brilliantly."

This was sound advice. Mike nodded, and the doctor dropped the shrapnel on the surgical tray. As he got another morphine shot, Mike felt the medicine surge through his body and a smile broke into his perversely optimistic face. He actually felt *good.* Handsome with a broad Irish forehead, he looked older than his years; hardship had tilled furrows at the corners of his deep blue eyes. This was a man thoroughly unimpressed with himself.

With his tall, thin body wrapped in scratchy blankets, he was loaded into a home defense ambulance that drove him back to the base that night. When they finally rolled on to the gravel in front of the main building, the morphine had worn off and Mike was in serious pain. The back door of the ambulance swung open. With the cold night air enveloping him, he opened his eyes to stare at Peterson's pale English face.

"Just in time for pints, mate. How do you feel?" he asked.

Mike sucked up hard to control the misery overtaking his lower parts. "Fresh as a daisy," he answered.

The driver looked at Peterson, who had already grabbed the other end of the stretcher. "Go easy," the driver said.

They lifted the stretcher and carried Mike into the building.

"Family heirlooms in tip-top shape, I hear?" Peterson said.

"A millisecond later . . . ," Mike winced, "I'd be in line for the lead castrato's job at La Scala."

"And what a loss of a beautiful Irish tenor that would have been!" Peterson said.

A nurse met them on the way to the infirmary. Mike remembered her from visits to mates on her ward. She was the kind of woman who took the war personally. Caring for so many severely wounded men took its toll—she looked older every time he saw her.

They transferred Mike onto a bed. He was cold and sweating at the same time. Fever dancing in his eyes, he watched the nurse prepare his morphine shot—*yes, that.*

"Luck of the Irish. O'Keefe, you're buying next Sunday," Peterson said.

Mike brushed him off as he felt a cold wave washing away the agony. The pungent opiate taste suffused his mouth. This was heaven.

"If you need anything, the bell's right above your head, dear," the nurse said.

Mike glanced at the switch dangling on the electric cord as the nurse walked to the door.

"Shall I leave the light on, dear?" she asked.

"Yes, please."

She knew. Pilots were full of bravado during the day, but night was another matter. The terror of air combat came back to torment them with nightmares that shook them to the bottom of their souls. Lights were better left on.

4

JANINE BOARDED HER TRAIN IN RENNES, the capital city of the Brittany region. All private automobiles had been requisitioned by the German military, so public transports were always crowded. Their train stood in the station, and it was dark when two Wehrmacht supply trains finally clattered by. In the pale half-moon light, Janine could discern the snouts of big guns lunging out from under camouflage covers and anti-aircraft battery stations still in their wood frames. She counted twenty-eight cars on the first train and twenty-six on the second. Armaments to build up the defense on the Atlantic wall, she figured. *This war will go on forever.*

After French dental school Janine had continued her studies in Germany and learned more than dentistry. She witnessed Kristallnacht in the fall of 1938, when the Sturmabteilung, the SA paramilitary forces, and German civilians carried out a pogrom against Jews throughout Germany. The city's largest synagogue was looted and scorched a block from her school. She watched male office workers take off their jackets, roll up their sleeves, and in murderous fury attack Jewish store windows with sledgehammers while well-dressed women applauded and couples held up their children so they could see the Jews getting what they deserved.

Non-Jews were not exempt from the madness, either. People whispered about assassinations of political opponents and the establishment of euthanasia programs to eradicate the physically or mentally disabled. She never forgot those days. So Janine fought the Nazis her way. Training a pilot took a lot of time and resources. Smuggling allied airmen back to England so they could fight again was crucial to the war effort. Janine focused on efficiency. She had learned from the Germans.

When the train began moving, she sat by the window staring at the raindrops running down the tempered glass. The morning killing weighed heavily on her. She wished she could crawl into a hole and hide until the end of the war. And her thoughts drifted to her dead husband. There were nights when she woke up dreaming they were making love. She was lonely and knew she could not live this way forever, especially as she kept meeting determined men whom she shepherded from trains to safe houses, across towns and mountains. From time to time, there was a special one with that fire burning inside. Courageous, but never foolish or unkind. He followed orders but could not be pushed. Janine kept her distance, but those encounters left her wanting. And then there was Loïc.

She changed trains at Le Mans, switching from one dark green second-class car to another. Janine glanced at the other passengers. Nobody looked back. Since the occupation, people had stopped looking at one another. Because of strict rationing, everyone was constantly searching for food, clothing, and heating fuel. All anybody wanted was to stay out of trouble and take care of their families.

There was shame, too. The Catholic Church said this humiliation was the consequence of the country's self-indulgence. The French had turned away from God, embraced easy pleasure, and given up duty and sacrifice. The war was punishment. Women were denounced for not having had enough children—*not enough children, not enough soldiers.* Frenchwomen were being blamed for losing the war. One and a half million French soldiers were now prisoners of war in Germany and the country had been split in half. The northern zone and the whole Atlantic coast were under German occupation and the south, "la zone libre," was under the reactionary government of Maréchal Pétain, that fought the Resistance and collaborated with Germany.

Idly checking the cuffs of her jacket, Janine discovered specks of dry blood on her sleeves. She tried to rub them off, to no avail. Loïc was now on her mind. His vigilance had saved her life. She knew he was attracted to her and hated herself for using it at times. He trusted her, did not question her, and took risks just because she asked. But Loïc was no fool. He understood danger and had been helping escapees long before she joined the Résistance. He was shy. And after the killing, he had wanted to show his affection, but she had sat there, cold as ice. *So he's a farmer. A little prudish bourgeois you are. You're more enamored of him than he is of you.*

Janine worried about informers. In December 1941, a spy had infiltrated an escape line operating along the eastern border of France, smuggling aviators from Lille to Lyon and Marseille. More than a hundred helpers had been arrested. Fifteen were executed by firing squads and four were beheaded. The others were sent to concentration camps. The French and Belgian underground had struggled for months to identify the informer but came up with nothing. So it was safe to assume that *he* or *she* was still at it, had joined another line, and was busy shuffling escapees across the country, all the while identifying helpers and safe houses. *Has our line been penetrated?*

The train pulled into Saint-Pierre-des-Corps station. Janine stepped down from the train and walked the length of the platform past a group of SS officers getting into the first-class car. They were smug and entitled, joking among themselves. Now Janine was angry. They had an expression for the occupation. "Wie ein Gott in Frankreich leben." *To live like a God in France.* And they did. One of the conditions of the armistice was that the French had to pay twenty million Reichsmarks per day for the cost of the occupying German army. This bled the French economy dry while the Germans could buy anything they wanted—first-class travel, high-class prostitutes, black market restaurants, and fine clothes for their wives back in Germany.

Janine entered the stationmaster's office. The attendant behind the desk ignored her and she stepped into an adjoining room. Janine's uncle stood as she closed the door. Tall, distinguished, with thick salt-and-pepper hair and piercing blue eyes, his handsomeness had not faded with age.

"Good evening, Paul."

This was not his real name. Janine's uncle had changed aliases several times since the beginning of the war, and now carried papers identifying him as Paul Turenne. Even in private, Janine called him by his current nom de guerre.

"Bonsoir, petite."

Her name never changed. He had called her "little one" since she was a baby. Her mother's older brother, Turenne was an accomplished surgeon who had taught obstetrics at the Faculté de médecine de Paris.

Janine had been precocious in school but also restless; she found sex early and became pregnant. Abortion was illegal and carried a five-year prison sentence. It was performed by "faiseuse d'anges," angel makers, often in precarious sanitary conditions. Janine had the good sense of confiding in her uncle, who was infuriated but performed the procedure at great risk to himself. Keeping the episode private created a special bond between uncle and niece. And today he worked with the British Intelligence and financed the escape line, while Janine smuggled aviators.

The last couple of years had been harsh on Janine's uncle. Elisabeth, his wife of thirty-five years, had founded one of the first Résistance networks. She was caught and executed by the Nazis in 1941, but Turenne had kept up the fight. People were arrested or disappeared, and others stepped in to replace them. It was a brutal cycle.

"What happened in Brittany?" Turenne asked.

He already knows. "We had a mole," Janine said.

"Who took care of it?"

"I tried but couldn't. Loïc did it."

Turenne's face aged suddenly, an eerie transformation. "Any thoughts about what's going on?"

"Somebody's watching us," Janine answered. "This is their third attempt at infiltrating the network."

"We've got to be tougher on the people up north. They need to be more careful."

"They could not have spotted this one. He was very good."

Turenne looked at his watch and pushed a satchel toward her on the table. "Blank identification papers under the seams."

"We're running out of money."

"I know." Turenne extracted his wallet out of his breast pocket and pulled out a wad of cash. "That should carry you over."

Janine turned away and slid the cash in a pouch fitted over her brassiere. Her uncle had sold his private clinic when he retired. She knew his personal funds were almost gone. "We owe you a lot of money." She said.

Turenne shrugged that off. "There is good news. The British consul in Bilbao sent word. Churchill himself has approved funding. He's got money for us."

"Finally."

"I'm going to Spain next week," he said.

Janine opened the satchel and transferred the contents of her bag into it.

"There is someone I want you to meet." Turenne stood, took ahold of the connecting door's knob, and added. "Suzanne is the train conductor who escorts aviators from Belgium to Paris. She works with Résistance-Fer and fought in Spain. You should know each other. Just in case . . ." He didn't finish his sentence, but Janine did it silently: *Just in case I get caught.*

When Turenne opened the door Janine was surprised. She expected someone older. Twenties, petite, with intense dark eyes, Suzanne wore a French Railway conductor's uniform and kept her hair in a bun. Holding each other's gaze, the two women appraised one another and shook hands.

Turenne headed for the door. "You know what to do." No: au revoir, *see you again.* It brought bad luck. The war made everyone superstitious. Turenne was gone and Janine suddenly felt a stab of foreboding—*he is going to get caught. I'll never see him again.*

"You were in Spain," Janine said.

"My husband is a Spaniard; we met in France and joined the International brigades in '36. I've been working underground operations since I was eighteen."

The trust between the two women was immediate. They quickly set up passwords and how to arrange contacts. Suzanne left first and a few minutes later Janine headed for the platform, where she boarded the train for Limoges.

One hour later they stopped at the checkpoint between the German-occupied and non-occupied zones. "La ligne de démarcation"—the border cutting France in half and dividing the North from the South. Janine knew the controls were thorough and her heart was pounding as she stepped down onto the platform. A talented artisan had made the satchel Janine carried and the documents were hidden between the inner layers and in the double bottom. That bag had made it through several checkpoints, but Janine had added an extra precaution. She opened the satchel for the gendarme who assiduously searched it, but when he found a pouch filled with soiled cloth menstrual pads, he closed it quickly. Janine carried the pouch for that purpose. It always worked.

She reboarded her train and at dawn they pulled into Limoges. Janine stepped down onto the platform and walked to the Café du Depart. The room was frigid and only half full. She ordered at the bar and took a table. The waiter came over and made a show of pouring hot milk into a cup before setting it in front of her. As he finished, he glanced at three young women sitting by the bar. Janine nodded and paid with a ten-franc bill. The change came in coins out of his waistcoat pockets.

Janine drank slowly. Hot milk was the signal. A priest sitting in a booth looked up from a breviary and gave her an inquisitive look. Janine acknowledged him. The young man sitting across from him was half hidden behind the pages of a newspaper. She did not bother to find the others, but she could almost *feel* several pairs of anxious eyes staring at her.

When the public address system announced that the train for Toulouse was entering the station, people stood and gathered their bags. Janine finished her milk and headed for the door with the priest following her. Four young men wearing sturdy French clothes arose and mingled with the crowd staying away from one another. Janine joined passengers streaming down the underground passageways and the first airman appeared beside her. They exchanged a glance and moved on side by side. Behind them the three girls from the bar cut through the crowd, each joining an airman as the priest headed out of the station. No words exchanged, no visible rendezvous—a well-rehearsed ballet.

Janine's man was older, a pilot she thought. The train slid beside the platform and the people on the quay rushed the cars. Sharp words were exchanged, but it all worked out somehow. When Janine and her pilot climbed into the train, the three airmen and their new "dates" did the same.

"Attention au départ."

The cars jerked and the train got under way. Janine found seats for her and the pilot and indicated he should stay put. She stepped out and checked on the other airmen in crowded compartments separated from the corridor by glass doors. Her first couple was quietly holding hands; the second shared a newspaper and they were reading, each holding a page. The third airman was grinning; his girl held his arm tight and was whispering in his ear.

She came back and sat across from her pilot, who raised the collar of his jacket and closed his eyes. Probably fed up with having to always fake being asleep, Janine thought.

"Tickets, s'il vous plaît." The conductor clicked his ticket puncher against the doorframe. Janine's pilot barely opened an eye and handed out his ticket. The conductor clipped it and handed it back. "Merci, Monsieur." The airman thanked him with a nod and went back to sleep.

"Identités, m'sieurs-dames."

Everyone sat up straight as two French policemen checked passengers' papers. This time the pilot looked up, his ID card ready. The policemen checked each photograph, paying particular attention, it seemed, to the women.

"Merci, mesdames."

And they were gone. The women exchanged looks—*they're looking for women now?*

Janine remained calm but a new worry gnawed at her. Were the Vichy police aware that escape lines were using women to escort allied aviators?

When they arrived in Toulouse, the sun was up. Janine and her pilot stepped onto the platform with the boys and their girlfriends following at a safe distance. She made sure everyone passed through control and then headed down the steps of a public restroom. She walked by the Dame Pipi—the washroom lady, knitting behind her desk—and opened a door leading outside.

A postal worker had backed his truck against the building and opened its rear doors. The pilot shook Janine's hand and climbed aboard. The airmen showed up one by one. Janine shook hands with each before they climbed into the truck. The mailman closed the doors and drove off—if all went well, those aviators would reach Spain in a few days.

Janine dropped a bill in the Dame Pipi's dish. The woman muttered a thank-you but never looked up. Reaching the top of the stairs, Janine spotted the girls boarding the next train out of town. In a few days they'd be on another transfer on a different line. Their routes were constantly changed to not attract attention. If arrested, Résistance-Fer would immediately give the alert; their contacts would go underground and sadly the girls would be left to fend for themselves.

Janine walked out of the station and found her bicycle chained where she had left it. She had been another person—a person who had never attempted to kill anyone—when she fastened that chain three days ago. She unlocked her bicycle, wheeled over the Canal du Midi bridge, and rode into the city. She lived in a good part of town, a neighborhood of solid bourgeois buildings with old-fashioned carriage gates. She turned into the rue du Taur, stopped halfway up the street, and carried her bicycle inside a building. The wall by the entrance was lined with the plaques of professionals with offices on the premises: a lawyer, an obstetrician, and two dentists. The largest plaque read: LOUIS DE GUILHEM, JANINE DUMAS, CHIRURGIENS-DENTISTES, 4IÉME ÉTAGE, GAUCHE.

The apartment was silent and again, eerily the same as she had left it. Janine was glad everyone was still asleep. She had never felt dirtier and took a bath, thoroughly soaping and scrubbing when she found dried blood on her legs and arms.

The family was up when Janine walked into the kitchen. Anna, an older version of Janine, was obviously relieved her daughter was home safe. Her father, Louis, wore his dentist's smock. In his early fifties with a round face and thin brown hair, he smiled a little sadly. As Janine kissed both of her parents, little Emma entered the room and ran into her mother's arms.

"Mommy, where were you? I missed you."

Janine hugged and kissed her daughter. "I missed you too, sweetie. Have you had breakfast?"

"I want to sit on your lap."

They began to eat. Janine spoon-fed Emma until the little girl changed her mind. "I want to eat by myself."

Janine let her go reluctantly. Emma finished her meal and slipped off to play.

Louis caught the exhaustion in Janine's face and squeezed her hand. "I'll take your patients today."

Janine nodded; then, looking at her mother, said, "I need to talk to Dad."

Anna acknowledged her daughter and slipped out of the room. Even within the family, they shared information only on a need-to-know basis. The fear of breaking under torture was always on their minds.

Janine opened the satchel and emptied its content onto a chair. "From Paul," she said.

Louis got a razor blade from a drawer, sliced the satchel's stitching, and removed the blank ID cards hidden inside. Janine pulled out her money pouch and pushed the wad of cash on the table.

"Good, we'll be able to pay the guides," Louis said.

The doorbell rang. They heard Anna shuffle along the corridor and the door open and close. Louis hid the money and documents under the morning paper before his wife appeared to announce: "Your first patient is here."

Louis stepped to the sink and washed his hands. Janine picked up her clothes and toiletries and left the kitchen. Halfway down the corridor, she pushed a door open. Her room mirrored her disarray, with books on the floor and clothes draped on the back of every chair. She wearily dropped her belongings on the dresser, undressed, and got into bed. *Thou shall not kill*—the blood, the gun, the slumped shape of the dead man. She remembered reading that when you killed someone, fragments of your victim stayed with you. She could still hear his voice—*"Wie?"*—and even smell the sickeningly sweet metallic scent of his blood.

For the first time since the death of her husband, Janine cried.

5

ROBERT ARRIVED IN SÉTIF LATE in the afternoon and drove to a Renault garage where he gave three hundred francs to the mechanic to refill the charcoal fuel tanks and drive the car back to Kherrata. Arlette's father would be furious he'd borrowed it; a full tank might help soothe his anger.

Robert entered the train station, where he learned that the express to Algiers was expected two hours late. He walked across the street to a café Maure—an Arab café. The place was dark, with few customers. Robert ordered goat cheese, bread, and lemonade and played games of dominos with old men who spoke in quick, raspy Arabic. They never talked to him but instead complained to each other about the war, the weather, and *ce merdeux Israélite*—that Jewish shithead—meaning Robert, who played dominos better than they did. They assumed he was cheating but couldn't figure out how.

Robert caught his train and the next morning he was in Algiers. The difference in climate was staggering; it felt like summer. The place had that stark mixture of wealth and poverty common to colonial cities. The European neighborhood was clean, its streets lined with palm trees. The Casbah hung on the hills above the European quarter, its dirty white walls shining under the morning sun. Arabs in robes and burnooses ambled along the sidewalks. Every square inch of vacant wall space was plastered with posters of Maréchal Pétain.

Robert took a trolley, got off on the edge of the Spanish district, and proceeded to the butcher shop of his friend Eli Choucroune. Eli's father was a shochet, a ritual slaughterer. He owned and managed the

Jewish slaughterhouse while his son ran the shop. It was not a good arrangement. The two argued constantly and Eli had no interest in being a butcher. He was a musician who played the piano, jazz mainly. He and Robert had met in Sétif a few months before. Eli had wanted to try hashish, Robert had sold him some, and they became fast friends. Eli had invited Robert to stay with him if he ever came to Algiers. The shop was crowded but when Eli spotted Robert, he hurried from behind the counter and led him outside, away from his father.

"You're getting here just in time. This place is about to blow up. Where are you staying?"

"You said you'd put me up."

That afternoon, on the third-floor landing of a working-class building near the Casbah, Eli opened the door of his apartment. The place was small but the bed was made and the place was clean. There were a few books on the shelves and a Boisselot upright piano next to the window.

"That's your bed," Eli said, pointing at a rolled-up mattress standing against the wall.

They dragged it to the center of the room and unrolled it onto the floor. Eli pulled blankets and pillows from a dresser and handed them to Robert, who tried the mattress and looked satisfied.

"So, what's the big news?" Robert asked.

"The Americans could arrive any moment. The underground got a confirmation."

Robert darted Eli a doubtful look. "There is an *underground* here?"

Eli appraised Robert and made up his mind. "It's mostly us Jews. I'm in touch with people who plan to disrupt communications during the Allied landings. We'll need to get into official buildings and since you're a mechanic and good with tools, we could use you."

"Disrupt communications, how?"

"There is a meeting tonight. Do you want to come?"

Robert felt his gut tightening. "Why not?"

***

That night, Robert and Eli went to the Hotel Alletti in the heart of the European quarter. A luxury establishment with a bar famous for harboring the most expensive prostitutes in Algiers. There were already customers sitting at tables and booths in groups of three or four. Robert and Eli stood by the entrance, not daring to enter, but the maître d' waved them over and led them to a table.

"We're waiting for Mr. Chouraki," Eli murmured. "He owns the largest department store in Algiers. They say he works for the American secret service."

This description felt a bit extravagant to Robert. Then Chouraki appeared. The man was chubby and looked comical in his straw hat and rumpled white linen suit. He was with a tall gentleman in a tailored suit and there was a flurry of whispers. People elbowed each other and the whole place went quiet. Chouraki and his companion got drinks from the bar and moved from group to group. When they stopped by their table, Eli stood and introduced Robert. They all shook hands. Chouraki was eager and congenial, his companion the opposite. Stern and clean-shaven, with a narrow face and receding hairline, he definitely did not look French. He never said a word but watched and listened intently. Robert felt he was trying to measure the strength of their commitment.

"Robert, do you have any military experience?" Chouraki asked.

"No. But I'm a pretty good shot."

"What kind of gun?"

"Hunting rifle, double barrel."

Chouraki glanced at his companion. "Just as well. That's all we have." There was a silence; then he added in a voice heavy with resentment, "We were promised weapons but they didn't arrive."

The man in the gray suit did not react but he was clearly held responsible for the foul-up.

"Robert is a mechanic and he's good with tools," Eli said eagerly.

"That's a useful skill," Chouraki said.

"What am I expected to do?" Robert asked.

"We have a postal worker who will get you inside the central post office," Chouraki explained. "He'll show you to the second floor."

"What's on the second floor?"

"The switchboard controlling the telephone lines for the entire city of Algiers. We need to cut those lines to compromise communications on the day of the landings."

"Vichy officials won't be able to talk to the military," Robert said.

Surprised, Chouraki took a hard look at Robert. "Exactly."

What am I getting myself into? Robert thought. An insurrection planned by a middle-aged department store owner. His companion looked shrewd, though.

"Are you with us, Robert?" Chouraki asked.

Robert steepled his fingers. Every fiber of his being was screaming: *Don't do it!* He clasped his hands. "Of course."

"Good," Chouraki said. "The signal will come through as a personal message from the BBC. We'll let you know."

They excused themselves and moved to the next table. Robert followed Eli out through the lobby and watched groups of young men walk into the bar, get their orders, and become replaced by others.

"The man who did not talk. He's American," Robert said.

"Have you ever met an American before?"

"No. But he shakes hands exactly the way they do in gangster movies."

Eli laughed and moved his arm around Robert's shoulder. "You're a smart guy and you didn't let Chouraki bully you. At the end he practically begged you to join."

"And I did." Robert grinned. "Now we'll see how smart I am."

6

LA POULE D'OR, IN THE heart of Pigalle, was a place for true connoisseurs. It had an air of decadence that fit the mood of the times. Turenne was a habitué and here Janine's uncle was known as Monsieur Paul, a man rumored to be wealthy and well connected. These days people were respected and feared not because of who they actually were, but because of who they were perceived to be.

The crushing defeat and the occupation had reshuffled the decks. Fanatics, opportunists, and the perpetually dissatisfied had risen to the top. They conspired, settled scores, made money, and abused their newfound power. Turenne was a master at adapting to this nasty, fickle world and had the accoutrements to prove it. On his right was a blonde with hazel eyes and on his left, a redhead with emerald-green eyes. Both attentive to Monsieur Paul's slightest whim.

Onstage, girls were finishing their cancan routine au naturel—*in total nudity*. This was not one of those overpriced establishments off the Champs-Élysées where champagne was sipped in crystal flutes and German officers would take their wives. There was no pretense at La Poule d'Or. The women were available and the range of services provided was limited only by money and imagination. The clientele was mixed: German military, Spanish diplomats, Swiss bankers, Gestapo officers, French collaborators, thugs, and black marketeers of various origins felt at home here. They were all part of an international demimonde brought together by mutual business interests and a shared taste for exotic pleasures.

Turenne kept an eye on the dark red curtains separating the lobby from the main room. His appointment was late and in this line of work that was always a cause for concern.

The owner came over, squeezed Turenne's shoulder, and smoothly slipped a document in his pocket. "Luftwaffe, the usual source."

"Thank you. Not too crowded tonight."

"Slow." The owner glanced at the tables occupied by Nazi officers in black uniforms with death's head insignia. "That war in the East must be getting worse. The SS are all leaving."

"The Soviets will roll right over them," Turenne said.

"Let's hope so." The owner patted Turenne's shoulders and moved on.

Just then Turenne spotted his rendezvous slipping through the curtains, blowing on hands numbed by the November chill—*finally*. His man was in his thirties with a friendly face and a twinkle in his eye. Even in these dark times, this face said, life should not be taken too seriously. He appeared to consider underground work to still be a thrill. Half British, half French, he had been a liaison officer for the British General staff and found himself isolated behind the German lines during the retreat but managed to send home intelligence about the German buildup of defense infrastructure. He had recently joined the escape line and shown himself particularly adept at smuggling airmen across the country.

For his new identity, he had picked the aristocratic name de Lacoste and was passing as the disgraced son of a respectable family. He and Turenne worked closely but refrained to meet in person. They used La Poule d'Or as a mailbox to communicate and at times share intelligence that Turenne passed to the British secret services.

De Lacoste found his way to the bar, ordered a drink, and lit a cigarette. Turenne pulled a timepiece from his breast pocket and threw him an irritated glance. De Lacoste took a drag off his cigarette and shrugged: *I'm here, aren't I?* He downed his drink, threw a bill on the counter, and walked away. When he stepped back into the lobby, the hatcheck girl watched him approach with anticipation.

"Bonsoir, Monsieur de Lacoste."

A surreptitious exchange: de Lacoste was handed a thick envelope he quickly pocketed while slipping a pinup magazine to the hatcheck girl, which she made disappear under the counter.

"Stay safe," de Lacoste said and headed for the door.

Seconds later he was in the street hurrying away from the club. When he reached the Boulevard de Clichy, he spotted a black Citroën parked at the curb with two men inside. "Merde!" He turned around, tapping on his head as if he had forgotten something, and retraced his steps. The hatcheck girl looked up as de Lacoste walked back into the club.

"Police outside. Les flics," he whispered. "Tell Monsieur Paul to go out the back!"

The music was reaching its finale in the main room and patrons began streaming into the lobby. The hatcheck girl raised the folding board of her counter and was about to step out when Turenne appeared with a woman on each arm. As they made their way through the crowd, Turenne shook hands with a Luftwaffe general.

"General von Arnim, es ist mir immer ein großes Vergnügen." *General von Arnim, always a pleasure.*

The general acknowledged him with a nod and whispered, "Zwei Frauen? Ich gratuliere!" *Two women? Congratulations!*

"Haelt mich jung." *Keeps me young*, Turenne said.

Von Arnim laughed, stood at attention, and turned to Turenne's companion with the alluring mane of red hair. "Mademoiselle Lucile."

He clicked his heels and bent over to kiss her hand. She pursed her bright red lips and smooched his face, leaving traces of lipstick on the corner of his mouth. The general wiped it off and sniffed the lipstick on the back of his hand, smiling in fake ecstasy.

"Another Prussian in love with you, Lucile," Turenne said.

"He likes to spank me."

Turenne cocked an eyebrow, but she reassured him. "I deserve it and he pays well."

Turenne led his ladies to the cloakroom where they produced squares of cardboard with numbers on them.

"Monsieur Paul . . . ," the hatcheck girl whispered as she handed over his coat.

Turenne put on his coat and checked the pinup magazine in the inside pocket. He did not hear his name. He dropped a bill in the tip jar, picked up the ladies' furs, and moved off.

"Monsieur Paul!" the hatcheck girl called louder.

But Turenne was now in conversation with the German officers. De Lacoste watched from the door and made a face. He thought about cutting through the crowd, bumping into Turenne, and trying to warn him—*no, too risky*. The rule was to never ever reveal they knew each other.

The hatcheck girl kept handing out coats and exchanged a distressed look with de Lacoste as Turenne and his ladies exited into the street.

It was raining outside. A fine Parisian mist that looks like nothing but drenches you to the bone. The girls wrapped themselves in their furs.

The doorman approached. "Taxi, monsieur?"

From a nearby doorway, de Lacoste watched the doorman blow his whistle but before the cab reached the curb, a black Citroën cut it off and stopped in front of Turenne and the girls. The blonde saw danger coming and ducked back into the club while a man who looked like an ex-boxer with a thick neck and crooked, flattened nose appeared, pulling the car door open and pushing Turenne and Lucile inside it. He wore a black leather coat: *German Gestapo*, de Lacoste thought as the woman protested.

"Mais enfin qu'est-ce que vous faites?" *But what are you doing?*

"Ta gueule, pute!" *Shut up, you whore.*

Not Germans, French cops, de Lacoste determined. They idolized Gestapo agents so much they dressed like them. The doors closed, the tires screeched, and the car sped away. De Lacoste watched helplessly—merde, merde, merde.

It was past midnight but Commissaire Boucher, head of the antiterrorist Special Brigade of the Renseignements généraux, was still at work in his prefecture police office across from Notre-Dame. With a bulldog's face and a square jaw, heavy bags under his eyes, and a drinker's purplish nose, he was one of the top officials tasked with enforcing Maréchal Pétain's collaborationist policies. The Germans were not the archenemy anymore; the real enemies were the Jews, Freemasons, Socialists, and Bolsheviks in the Résistance. In this brand-new era French and Germans worked in concert. Nazi secret police had only 2,900 men in all of France and relied on the 150,000 men of the French police to fight the Résistance. So, when the close rapport between high-ranking German officers and a well-to-do Frenchman caught the attention of the Nazi security service, they asked the French police to investigate.

Boucher put Turenne under surveillance and quickly determined they were dealing with a skilled underground operative. The man was constantly on the move but rarely met anyone in the open. He traveled frequently to the Basque country, where he dropped out of sight, only to reappear several days later. This told Boucher that Turenne forayed across the Spanish border to meet contacts. All signs indicated Turenne was running an escape line and Boucher saw this investigation as his chance to satisfy his German colleagues and advance his career. And there was also the issue of money. On the first of every month, a Geheime Staatspolizei motorcycle courier delivered to Boucher an envelope filled with cash that tripled his commissaire's salary. The war was making him rich.

His telephone rang and Boucher picked it up.

"Be right down," he said and hung up. "Let's see what the son of a bitch has to say."

Boucher knew he wouldn't get much out of Turenne tonight. During the first session, you instilled fear and then it was just a matter of time. It was between sessions, dreading the next interrogation, that the resolve would crumble. Boucher was a squat, forceful man. Even at this late hour, he wore a shirt and tie under a freshly pressed double-breasted suit. From a drawer, he pulled out a truncheon and headed for the door, past a recruiting poster on the wall proclaiming: POLICE NATIONALE—POLICE D'ÉLITE. It featured French policemen wearing uniforms modeled after German ones with flat caps, jodhpurs, and boots—collaboration was everywhere.

Three floors down to the basement, Boucher found his men smoking in the hallway. Inspector Franjou had been an amateur middleweight contender in his youth. "He didn't want to come down. We had a little round," he said, kissing his fist.

His partner, Inspector Lenoir, was older. He had a narrow, bony face, with thick white hair cut short, military style. "Blank ID cards and German documents inside his coat pockets. They're on the desk. Also, his wallet and a big chunk of change."

Boucher glanced at Lucile cuffed to a radiator at the end of the hallway. "That's his girl?"

"One of them."

"Have your fun with her and kick her out in the morning," Boucher said.

The inspectors smiled. "Thank you, Patron."

Boucher pushed a door open. Turenne sat in a windowless room, cuffed to a metal chair bolted to the cement floor. He was bleeding from his mouth and nose; his left eye was swollen and almost closed. He winced every time he took a breath—broken ribs probably.

"Who're you?" Turenne snapped with all the arrogance he could muster.

"Commissaire Boucher, Brigade Spéciale anti-terroriste."

Boucher—Butcher, perfect name for the job, Turenne thought, eyeing the truncheon dangling from the leather strap on the policeman's wrist.

Boucher caught his glance and raised his arm. "You know what this is?"

"Un nerf de boeuf." *A bull's cock*, Turenne said.

"Stretched and dried. Hard as steel," Boucher said, slapping it into his palm.

"Why am I here, Commissaire?"

Boucher seemed about to reply but instead swung his nerf de boeuf so that it cracked against Turenne's shins with tremendous force. The pain was excruciating. Turenne screamed helplessly.

"Hurts, doesn't it?" Boucher said with feigned concern. Moving to the desk, he checked the wallet and pocketed the thick wad of bills, then flipped the magazine open. The pages had been replaced with sheets of blank ID documents.

"For allied aviators, right? Fill up with a French-sounding name and put in a picture." Boucher now unfolded a document bearing German military letterhead. The Poule d'Or manager had slid it into Turenne's pocket.

"And intelligence you're smuggling to the British," Boucher said. "You've got a good operation going."

"It's not what you think."

"No?" Boucher smiled. "Enlighten me."

Turenne whipped his chin to indicate the German document on the desk. "This is part of a classified German counterintelligence operation."

Boucher nodded as if impressed. "Classified, huh? So, you *cannot* tell me about it."

"Call General von Arnim . . . He'll vouch for me."

Boucher pretended he had not heard correctly. He put his hands on his knees and leaned over, bringing his right ear close to Turenne's mouth. "General von who?" he asked.

"General von Arnim. Commander-in-chief of Luftwaffe France."

"He's a friend?"

"He is."

Boucher shook his head. "Von Arnim is not a friend. But you want him to be because you run an escape line and you want to find out about the Luftwaffe's intelligence operatives." The commissaire was impressed and he showed it. "Got to hand it to you. It's risky collecting information this way." Boucher stood up and almost as an afterthought swung his truncheon.

Turenne bellowed in agony. "You're . . . wrong," he finally managed to say.

Boucher took the chair behind the desk, lit a cigarette, inhaled, and stretched his legs. "I know about people like you. You make money on contracts with the military, socialize with Nazi officers, and even work for them at times. You're a respectable French businessman who speaks German and pretends to believe in a national socialist Europe," Boucher said, raising his head to blow out a mouthful of smoke. "You parade around surrounded by women but you're no pimp. You're the head of a very efficient Résistance network. What were you before the war? A lawyer, a doctor?"

"Sold insurance," Turenne lied.

"Really? I pictured you in something more . . ." Boucher smiled, playfully searching for the right word. ". . . lucrative. A banker perhaps."

"To be a banker you need the right connections. It'd have been easier if I were a Jew."

Boucher burst out laughing and stood. "You run an escape line that smuggles British spies, allied aviators, *and* rich Jews."

A phone rang next door—a quavering persistent ring. Again, Boucher leaned forward with his hands on his knees and stared into Turenne's face.

"You're a smart man. Whatever you did before the war, you did it well." Boucher sighed and continued. "This war is lost. We've got to rebuild Europe with Germany at our side against the Bolsheviks. The Nazis are not perfect, but the other side is worse—rather Hitler than Stalin, I'd say." Boucher straightened up, grumbling at the sound of the phone still ringing next door.

Turenne took a deep breath and whispered in a tired voice, "I'm not a terrorist and I agree with you. This country has to be rebuilt from the ground up."

"There you go, we think alike."

"I work with German army intelligence, ask them."

Boucher knew Turenne was bluffing. The Abwehr would never respond to a request from a French policeman working with the Gestapo. The Abwehr was military intelligence; the Gestapo was a political organization. German military officers had only contempt for the secret police.

Boucher stepped back. The phone next door was clearly annoying him. "How stupid do you think I am?" he shouted, his face crimson with anger.

The nerf de boeuf swung wide and hit with tremendous force. Turenne lost consciousness. His last thought was that he would never walk again.

1

SINCE THE KILLING IN BRITTANY, worry had overwhelmed every aspect of Janine's life. Denunciations were rampant. French police controls were more stringent while the number of downed airmen grew every day. Janine and her father shared adjoining offices and practicing dentistry had become difficult. The Germans seized most of the medical supplies manufactured in France. Arsenic and ether were impossible to find, so dental surgery and pulling teeth were now carried out without painkillers. "We're back to the Middle Ages," Janine said.

Every morning at 8:00 a.m. she stepped into the waiting room. A dozen people were already there. Janine picked up the clipboard where patients wrote their names. They were seen on a first-come, first-serve basis and latecomers spent hours waiting. She was about to call her first patient when a name on the list made her heart jump: Mademoiselle Victoire. Dread spread inside her like weeds. She put down the clipboard and stepped into her father's office.

"Mademoiselle Victoire left a message," she said.

Louis took a short breath, hiding the worry unsettling his face. "I'll take care of your patients."

Minutes later Janine stood on a crowded tram heading for the train station, bracing herself for the bad news she knew would come. Victoire was Suzanne's code name. She would only call a meeting for something important. Janine knew the Communists didn't trust outsiders and she guessed she was being followed. As the tram reached the train station, it started to rain. Janine stepped off and opened her umbrella. A voice behind her made her turn.

"Madame, vous avez oublié votre journal." *Madame, you forgot your paper.* An older man handed her a newspaper and disappeared into the crowd.

They are thorough, Janine thought. They made sure she had not been followed before disclosing the meeting's exact location. She crossed the street, found shelter in a doorway, and opened the newspaper she had been handed. On top of the second page, written in cursive, were the words: *Objets Perdus—Lost and Found.*

Inside the station, she found the Objets Perdus desk and the receptionist pointed at a door—*they even know what I look like*. This made Janine even more anxious as she entered. Suzanne, in her Railways conductor's uniform, extended her hand.

"Good morning, comrade," she said, half in jest, half in earnest.

Fights grief with humor, Janine thought, shaking the proffered hand.

"Turenne has been arrested," Suzanne said.

The words hung there. Hope against hope, Janine for an instant wished she had misheard.

"It happened two days ago."

"The Germans?" Janine asked.

"No. The French police."

"Is that better?"

"No. When they're done with him, they'll turn him over to the Gestapo."

"They work hand in hand?"

"They do," Suzanne said. "The French police are now in charge of internal surveillance. Last year they created a Special Brigade to fight the Résistance. Commissaire Boucher is in charge of that. He's the man who had Turenne arrested."

"Is Turenne being interrogated?"

"Of course. And you should disappear for a while. Turenne will resist as long as he can to give you time to get into hiding. But if he breaks down, he might tell them everything he knows."

"He's strong. He fought in the First World War."

"It's not a matter of strength. Some people can endure torture, others cannot."

The meeting was over. Suzanne was getting ready to leave and Janine desperately wanted to keep her there, know more, something, anything.

"Any way your people could help Turenne?" she asked.

"Is that a request?"

"Yes."

"I'll pass it along." Suzanne buttoned her jacket. Reading the distress on Janine's face, she added, "Those who fall are replaced. That's the way it is for us too. For every comrade caught, we get three new volunteers. The numbers are on our side."

"Turenne is a hard man to replace."

A dour smile etched along Suzanne's lips. "Sometimes a strong woman will do, comrade."

The words ricocheted through Janine—the *meaning* of those words. Her uncle was gone. She now was expected to run the escape line all by herself. "I hope I can be that strong," Janine said.

"Turenne said you were. Get in touch if I can be of help. I travel free," Suzanne said, pointing at the SNCF logo on her uniform.

Janine took the night train to Bayonne to be smuggled into Spain the following day. Freezing rain battered the car. She shivered the entire way with a hard-knotted feeling in her chest. The year before when the head of the line had been caught and executed, Turenne had filled in, helping with money and contacts. He guided her and she relied on him. Now the whole weight of the escape line was on her shoulders. She was anxious, frightened even, but there was no choice. She had to keep going.

A strong woman will do.

8

MIKE KEPT RELIVING BEING SHOT down over the channel but couldn't really remember how he had survived. His wound was healing but he knew he was a different man than before his near-death experience. After his stitches had been removed, he applied himself to walking without crutches and was soon strolling along the corridors smuggling flasks of whiskey to his wounded comrades. One morning he was thrilled to wake up with an erection and decided to "celebrate himself" as the saying goes. It did not go well. The gush spurt out of control; the aftereffects were unpleasant, and he got a stern lecture from the nurse changing the bed sheets.

"Give the *bloody Muppet* some rest!" she had said.

Mike was eager to get back to combat but missed his father and America. The US Eighth Air Force had established bases in England and since the summer, Americans in the RAF were joining the US Air Force. All were looking forward to tripling their pay and getting American food instead of English rations, and Mike hoped that signing on with the US Air Force would alleviate his longing for home.

When the doctors declared him fit for active duty, his RAF mates threw him a going-away party. He played the piano and had a good voice; he sang "Too Blue to Cry," drowning his nostalgia in a drinking binge that cost him a full month's pay. He had been with the Royal Air Force for over nineteen months. How could he leave his screwball British brothers and the boisterous squadron brawls?

The next morning, he woke with a headache that felt like his brains were coming apart. Since dawn, he had listened to the roar of squadrons taking off. The barracks were deserted and Mike hated that emptiness. It reminded him of the nights he'd spent waiting for friends to return from missions—and the morning realizations that they would not. He cleaned his bunk, packed his bag, and headed for the station. An hour later he was in London, stepped out of Victoria Station, and, his headache still bothering him, walked into a pub for a beer and fish and chips. As so often happened, the owner wouldn't let him pay.

"Your money is no good here," he said while customers within earshot nodded in approbation. Two women raised their glasses in his honor. Mike thanked them all. He had seen time and time again how grateful the English people were to the Americans who had come to Britain's rescue in her darkest hour. A RAF uniform and an American accent would get you drinks, theater tickets, dinner invitations, and the adulation of English girls.

English girls! Mike was more than a little anxious about his manhood. He longed for a woman's body against his, but doubts lingered about the little limping devil—all sails inflated one minute, dead calm the next. *You'll be fine. It's all in your head.*

Despite the war, or perhaps because of it, there was something intoxicating about the city. Bars were filled every night with people determined to enjoy themselves. The women were looking for a good time and wanted it right away. The Sherman Club was one of many similar places that had popped up since the beginning of the war. It featured a small band and a dance floor lined with tables, dreadful food, good liquor, and outrageous prices.

Mike looked around; he liked women who were elegant and self-assured. You had drinks, danced, made love, and then you were back in the cockpit of your Spitfire. Some details stayed with you—the softness of her lips, the mound of her sex, the taste of her skin. The band finished a number and as the lights came up Mike spotted a lovely woman sitting at a table with a group of people. She saw him too, waved shyly, and stood. Now he remembered her. She had been engaged to one of his squadron-mates who had been killed during the summer. *Oh God, no!* Mike was in no mood for condolences. He tried to slip away but she was already heading toward him. She approached and Mike could see her eyes filling with tears. He kissed her on the cheek while she timidly rubbed the lapel of his uniform. He did not need to ask how she was. Misery was all over her face. The music had started again, and he was thankful that they could barely hear each other. He mumbled how sorry he was for her loss. She had heard he had been shot. Was glad he was alive. When they reached the bar, drinks appeared. They gave up talking and drank. The band began playing Benny Goodman, "I Would Do Anything for You." The lights dimmed and couples moved toward the floor.

"Would you like to dance?" Mike asked.

She looked down and nodded. Her body was firm and after a couple of awkward dances Mike's sense of rhythm came back and he held her tighter. They had more drinks and went back to the dance floor for a series of British-style foxtrots during which partners had to maintain body contact at all times. A spirited Charleston and she was ready whenever he was. They took a cab to her place, a small apartment near Piccadilly Circus.

Mike's worries faded as they began to make love. For the first time in weeks, he stopped obsessing about his manhood. Between rounds of lovemaking, they sat in bed smoking. The imposed blackout rendered the city outside ghostly and silent. They stared into the darkness and every time one of them took a drag on a cigarette, the tiny red flare lit up the room.

Thinking about it later, Mike felt the encounter had been sweeter than expected. They had wanted tenderness and mending and they both had gotten that. But it had just been an encounter and he knew something was lacking. He had nearly died the month before and now he wanted more, much more—to wake up in the morning watching the face of the woman you adore. Bring her coffee in bed. Laugh with her, eat with her, have children with her. Mike felt a fiery need to embrace life and to be in love.

At oh-nine hundred Mike reported to the US Army Air Force headquarters, off Westchester Square. There, he filled out stacks of paperwork and picked up a uniform. The brass had taken over the upper floors of a grand, nineteenth-century building. The hallways were piled with crates stacked six feet high. The US military had brought over half the country with them. Desks, chairs, file cabinets, Smith Corona typewriters, ink, paper, carbons, even good old American toilet paper. It all felt a bit excessive to Mike, but this was America all right.

The Air WAC secretary sitting at a desk looked up as he approached and pointed at the open office door in front of her.

Mike walked in to face Colonel John T. Topor sitting behind an oversized cluttered desk. The man was stout, his shirtsleeves rolled up, his white hair cropped short. He wore a fruit salad of ribbons and medals, none of them combat related. Mike knew the type. Topor was a career Air Corp officer who had flown training missions all his life and was now too old to fly in combat. He, of course, would resent smart-ass pilots like Mike with inflated egos and disdain for the chain of command.

Mike saluted. "Good morning, sir."

Topor raised his head and pointed at the file he was reading. "University of Chicago. Must be pretty smart."

"Very smart, sir."

Topor ignored the wisecrack. "A stint at Fort Beauvoir, army engineering?"

"I was searching for my calling, sir."

"Aren't we all?" The colonel sneered. "It says here that you qualified as an acrobatic flyer. The government paid for that?"

"No, sir."

Those were nightmarish days. When Mike joined the University of Chicago Civilian Pilot Training program, he discovered that he suffered from severe motion sickness, so he took acrobatic flying and trained relentlessly, concentrating on the spins and rollovers that made him the sickest. He'd vomited so much, he'd lost twenty pounds in a few weeks. But he conquered the nausea and acquired skills that had proved invaluable in combat missions.

"Must have cost a pretty penny to take all those lessons. Your family loaded or something?" Topor asked.

"I had some savings, sir," Mike answered, knowing where this was heading.

"From what, running a gambling joint? Are you related to ward alderman Thomas O'Keefe?"

"Yes, sir. Loved by his constituents. Never misses a parade. Might have more medals and ribbons than you, sir."

Topor closed the file. "A well-connected ornery little bastard you are. You'd make your alma mater proud."

"Thank you, sir."

Topor signed a document, stapled it to a few others, and handed the papers to Mike. "You're assigned to the 105th US squadron based at the Salisbury Air Force base. You're to report there before eighteen hundred hours today."

"Yes, sir." Mike took his orders, saluted again, and walked out.

"Well-connected," Mike mumbled as he stepped into the street. Hell, he had been well-connected all of his life. And the war had freed him from that in a way. In the RAF no one cared who his father was. It was a relief, though Mike was proud of his dad. There had been hard times—the family was dirt poor during the Depression.

His mother managed to feed them by selling vegetables at an outdoor market where in winter the wind would chill you to the bone. She caught pneumonia and died when Mike was six. His father got involved in bootlegging, fended off a couple of attempts on his life, and endured a stint in federal prison.

After Mike's mother had died, O'Keefe senior kept his son close. He cooked their meals and did not remarry for years. Mike grew up idolizing his father and the men working for him. Amiable men comfortable with brute force, they made sure Mike knew how to take care of himself—how to handle a man with a knife, fire a handgun and a rifle, and even a Thomson submachine gun. He had fond memories of those days.

When the prohibition ended his father made a smooth transition from bootlegging to politics and was elected alderman. His dad was now in the patronage business. He did favors and got favors in return. Sometimes money changed hands; other times it was goods and services, jobs, or government contracts. Mike had no interest in his father's brand of politics and the war had allowed him to escape that world. But now as he joined the US Air Force, it had come up again. It did not matter where he went; *the connection* always caught up with him.

The next day, Mike began training on the brand-new Lockheed P-38. A superb aircraft, well-armed and fast. Getting used to the American military was more difficult. It was bureaucratic and run strictly by the book. Truth was, the Americans were green; war was a novelty to them and their officers had no interest in learning from the RAF—*we do things our way*.

Still, at times Americans and Brits worked together and Mike was grateful to be chosen to be part of a secret joint British-American mission with a surprising destination—Gibraltar! The Rock! He was thrilled to be back in combat.

9

ROBERT COULD FEEL PALPABLE ANXIETY in the streets of Algiers. Women lined up in stores to buy all the cooking oil available, parents kept their children out of school. Rumors were rampant—the government was about to be overthrown; the French Navy would fight the invasion but not the French Air Force. No one knew where it would happen but it was clear the Allies' arrival was imminent.

Eli related to Robert the rumor that the invasion would be carried out by American troops on British ships. "I hate the Royal Navy. I despise those bastards."

"Mers-el-Kébir?" Robert asked.

"Yes, Mers-el-Kébir," Eli said.

Robert understood. After the invasion of France in June 1940, French naval units in Brittany took to the sea to avoid German capture and sailed for Mers-el-Kébir, a naval base on the coast of Algeria. Fearful the French fleet would be used by Germany to invade England, Churchill had sent the British navy to blockade the base. The admiral in command had ordered the French fleet to sail to England or the port of Martinique. The French admiral had responded that his orders were to stay put in accordance with the terms of the Franco-German Armistice signed the week before.

Astoundingly the Royal Navy opened fire. At first the French sailors waved cheerfully at their British comrades, believing this was the start of a joint naval exercise. It was not. The British sank the entire fleet, killing over thirteen hundred sailors. The event was a godsend for the German propaganda machine. Newsreels featuring French sunken ships and sailors' bodies floating in the water ran for months in movie theaters all over France. French outrage over the betrayal of their British allies had many disastrous consequences. The first and foremost, recruitment for the Free French movement plummeted.

"I was there!" Eli said. "In the early evening, we heard navy guns and then gendarmerie cars with loudspeakers drove through the streets asking for good swimmers. We bicycled to the harbor and we could hear men crying in the water. We swam out in the darkness and found bodies, lots of them. Some were just pieces, corpses without heads or arms or legs." Eli paused and shook his head. "We rescued six sailors. Two of them died before we could get them to a hospital. At dawn the beach was littered with hundreds of bodies. It was awful!"

One thousand miles north on the south coast of England, Mike sat in the cockpit of his plane waiting for orders to take off. He couldn't wait. But he had to wait. On the runway, the fog was so thick their departure was delayed five times. Mike kept pestering the weather officer who finally lost patience:

"Settle down, mate, it's so thick out there, even the bloody seagulls are walking."

They finally departed and sneaked in tight formation down the French, Spanish, and Portuguese coasts and a few hours later touched down on Gibraltar's narrow airfield. It was pouring rain and Mike got drenched on the ride from his plane to the mess hall. They got greasy Spanish omelets for breakfast and a few hours' sleep in damp quarters. It was now obvious the next big action would be taking place somewhere near the Mediterranean. An enterprising navigator from Minnesota had set up a betting pool. Mike put ten dollars on Greece.

"Algiers," said the British major who briefed them.

They looked at the maps and studied the route and of course, the British major had skipped over how much of a gamble their mission was. They would be crossing the Mediterranean without the certainty of a safe place to land. If something went wrong, by the time they reached the Algerian coast they would be too low on fuel to return to Gibraltar. Mike, who was miffed about losing his bet, could not resist needling him.

"To clarify a point, sir. If the airfield is not secured by the time we get there, we'll have to crash-land in the desert, right?"

"Right," the major answered, in an impeccable Oxbridge accent.

They took off an hour later. Gibraltar had been a disappointment and Mike had caught a cold. He was running a fever and kept sneezing into his air mask. It was a moonless night but he could discern a thin ochre line that he knew was the coast of Morocco. He glanced out at the aircrafts flying in formation around him, sneezed again, and rubbed his good luck charm—*Africa.*

In Algiers, two hundred young men crowded the basement of Monsieur Chouraki's department store. Some carried weapons—everything from double-barreled hunting rifles to nickel-plated ladies' purse revolvers. Robert held a sawed-off shotgun on his lap and patted the box of shells in his pocket. He knew the gun's shortened barrel made it useless at a distance farther than fifteen feet, but perhaps it would scare someone. Eli carried a revolver and kept checking to make sure the safety was still on.

"Leave it alone," Robert said.

At the front of the room, the two men they had met at the bar of the Aletti Hotel stood next to a large Phillips radio set. Chouraki, in another rumpled suit, was fiddling with the dials as his companion watched. They had learned, as Robert had guessed, that he was indeed an American and was rumored to be working for US

Intelligence. Eli chuckled when Robert nicknamed him "Bogart," after his favorite movie star.

Chouraki raised a hand, put a finger over his lips to ask for silence. He turned up the volume on the radio and they all heard the opening of the BBC Radio program: "The French speak to the French!" The broadcast started with coded personal messages, each having meanings to various resistance groups. "La villa est silencieuse"—*The villa is silent.* "Il fait froid sur le Mont Blanc"—*It is cold on the Mont Blanc.* "Allo, Robert, Franklin arrive!"

Chouraki raised his fists in celebration. This was the message he was waiting for. "The Allies will be landing in Algiers at midnight!" he said.

Two hundred backs straightened at once. Robert's heart pounded in his chest. He leaned over to Eli and whispered, "Allo Robert arrive. It's for me." The joke felt flat.

Glancing at "Bogart," Chouraki raised his hand again and said, "General Eisenhower has confirmed that no British troops will come ashore, only Americans."

Robert turned to Eli, who nodded with satisfaction, and they all began moving out. As he had guessed at their first meeting, their mission was to cut off communications between the pro–German Vichy officers and their troops positioned on Algiers' beaches. That meant taking over power stations, telephone switchboards, and making sure Radio Algiers stayed silent. They hurried toward the city's main Postes et Télécommunications office. Five stories tall, it was a magnificent revival of Moorish architecture modeled after the Alhambra palace in Granada.

"Here is our man." Robert pointed at the entryway. It was dark but the red burning tip of a cigarette was clearly visible in the shadows.

"Marx," Robert said.

"Lenin," a voice responded.

Robert wanted to laugh. These were the passwords the members of the postal workers' union had insisted on. A mailman stepped out and unlocked a heavy sculpted wooden door. "Follow me," he whispered. They climbed the marble staircase to the door of the exchange. It was massive with heavy deadbolts. The mailman inserted keys in the locks, turned them one by one, and pushed the door open.

They faced a huge room that housed an enormous telephone exchange with hundreds of plug boards.

The mailman gave them a two-finger salute. "Good luck, comrades." And he was gone.

"It's gonna take forever. How do they say we should do this?" Robert asked.

Eli unfolded a piece of paper and read the instructions: "'Clip the right wire on the connector. Leave the left one alone. No need to cut the same line twice.'"

They had a colossal amount of work ahead but just knowing that others were doing the same in post offices all over the city was exhilarating. Yet it was tedious and they quickly ran out of steam.

"We've got to pace ourselves," Robert said.

Set, snip. Set, snip. They found their rhythm and learned to change hands so their muscles wouldn't cramp up. They moved to the third aisle when Robert froze—he had heard something. "Police?"

They listened as a sound in the distance grew into the high-pitched wail of a siren. Cars roared by, then blaring horns and trucks. Robert found it unnerving. "Can't people get any decent sleep in this town?"

"It's twelve thirty," Eli said.

"So?"

"The allied landing was supposed to start at midnight."

This made them anxious. They went back to work, snipping wires as fast as they could. Three more aisles to go, then two, then one. Their shears got dull, the skin on their hands blistered, and the blisters bled. Sirens again. Approaching fast.

"You think that's for us?" Eli asked.

"Nah. We're small fish."

Robert was wrong. The vehicles stopped outside. They heard the thumping sounds of doors opening and closing. Then a voice amplified by a megaphone.

"This is la Police Nationale," it boomed. "This building is surrounded. Put down your weapons and come out with your hands up!"

Robert and Eli ran to the window and watched police vans lining up.

Fear coursed through Robert like electric wires. He glanced at Eli. Maybe it was the light but he was pretty sure Eli's face had turned gray.

A French officer stood in the middle of the street holding a megaphone. "You have one minute to come out," he announced. Then, he handed the megaphone to his deputy and stood there, his arms akimbo.

"What if they don't show up?" Eli asked.

"Who?"

"*Who?*" Eli asked, incredulous. "*The Americans!*"

"You heard the message 'Robert arrive.'"

"What if *Robert* got delayed or won't come until next week?"

"They *will* show up," Robert said, determined to believe in what he was saying. "Let's finish the last aisle."

In the street, the officer took up the megaphone again. "An explosive charge has been placed in front of the main gate. It'll detonate in one minute and we'll storm the building. My men are authorized to shoot at will. This is your last warning."

A gendarme ran back from the gate uncoiling a wire as he went.

"The roof," Eli said.

They dropped their shears and raced for the stairs, grabbing the banister to launch them into a spin at every turn.

Babablam! The main door blew open several floors below. Acrid smoke rose, filling their noses and eyes. Coughing and crying, they bolted onto the terrace and ran to the edge just as, down in the street, the police commander blew his whistle. The gendarmes rushed the building.

"They'll shoot us, you think?" Eli asked.

"Probably," Robert said, pointing at the roof. "Let's try the gutters."

"It's too steep, we'll fall off."

Out of nowhere a sharp whistle and boom. A salvo exploded in front of the governor's palace across the street. The detonation was so powerful the post office entrance disappeared in a cloud of black smoke. Another whistle and second salvo tore a huge crater into the gardens with rocks, branches, and mud battering police vans and armored vehicles. The policemen broke ranks and ran back to their vans with more police now rushing *out* of the post office. Eli stared at the dark sea sparking with the discharge of artillery rolling in quick succession. "Battleship guns," he said.

"How do you know?"

"It's like Mers-el-Kébir. I'll never forget that sound."

The police fired a few more desultory shots at the building and drove off. Farther away navy guns pounded continuously.

"Those Americans are showing up just in time."

"Saving our butts."

Suddenly, deep booming filled the air and shook the ground.

"What was that?" Robert asked.

"Coastal guns. The French navy is shelling the Allies!" Eli said.

"Those assholes!"

"Payback for Mers-el-Kébir."

Coastal line batteries rolled into action with a heavy continuous drumming. Popping out of the darkness, Algiers' tallest buildings shone in silhouette against the bright phosphorus explosions.

They coughed their way down the stairway thick with smoke and slipped into the street. The noise was deafening. They ran to an observation point overlooking the city and watched hundreds of ships dotting the gray sea—a staggering sight, remote, yet menacing.

As the sun rose, they were able to make out the activity on Algiers' main beach. There, armored carriers were rolling off landing barges crammed with American soldiers. Standing on the coastal highway, less than one hundred yards away, French infantry troops were just watching.

"Look," Eli said, pointing. "French troops are not fighting."

"It worked."

"What worked?"

"Cutting communications. What we did," Robert said. "They have no orders, so they watch."

Still, they could hear heavy gunfire. "They're fighting somewhere!"

They ran down toward the harbor where the acrid stench of cordite filled the air and the cracking of machine-gun fire was deafening. They doubled up, ran to a fortification wall, and peeked over.

It was real war down there—a half-sunk British destroyer blocked the entrance of the harbor, and a second one was on fire and listing badly. Columns of water rose from the sea as shells fell around her.

"Merde," Robert said.

The docks were a killing field, with disembarking US soldiers under French marine fire. Bodies littered the pavements. Medics carried the wounded on stretchers dripping with blood. Eli sank to the ground under the cover of the parapet with tears in his eyes. "French killing Americans! That's crazy."

"The Americans are surrendering," Robert said.

Down below, US troops had raised a white flag. French colonial troops screamed out a battle cry and rushed down to disarm them, collecting watches, wallets, and other valuables as they went. And the mayhem continued. Robert and Eli watched French officers run over and order the troops to return the valuables to the prisoners. Chaos on top of chaos. Many men were wounded and now they had to line up to get back their watches, gold chains, and wallets.

Within minutes the fighting at the harbor turned around again as a droning noise blanketed the city. Like a swarm of bees, allied aircrafts blasted the coastal batteries overlooking the bay and the whole situation changed instantly. Now, French Vichy officers were ordering their men back in formation.

"They're giving up," Eli said.

French troops marched out, leaving behind American prisoners who suddenly were prisoners no more.

Mike saw operation Torch from above. As his squadron descended over the Algerian coastline, he had a good view of the beaches. No traces of fighting, just barges on the sand and troops moving inland. He spotted a jeep parked on the side of the road with maps spread on the hood and civilians gesturing at the driver asking for directions. *Oh, God!* Mike thought. They'd spent months preparing for the invasion and they got lost the moment they moved inland.

A minute later Maison Blanche airport appeared ahead of him. Mike led his squadron toward the airfield and touched ground. As he taxied on the runway he glanced at the French, American, and British flags flapping in the wind. His fever was gone. The mission had been a cakewalk.

Mike was later told that the French officer from the Armée de l'air commanding the detachment protecting the airfield had been informed in advance by the OSS of the allied landing. He was a seasoned officer and knew that in any group of men you always had at least one overzealous imbecile who could get a lot of people killed. So he took the precaution of not issuing ammunition to his troops. When US forces appeared at the Maison Blanche airport entrance, the sentries saluted and raised the gate.

It was November 8, 1942. Robert had seen action and it had left him disheartened. The carnage at the harbor was seared in his mind. Hundreds of American soldiers shot by French marines—real men down there, real dead, real wounded. Robert was ashamed and it did not make him feel any better to learn that French forces defending the port had been wiped out as well. French soldiers sacrificed to their officers' twisted sense of honor and sacrosanct respect for the chain of command.

Unfit for company, Robert declined an invitation to dinner at Eli's parents' home and spent the evening walking the deserted streets. Algiers was the first major city in the western hemisphere to be freed, but no one was celebrating, almost no one. Turning a corner, Robert heard the faint sound of a melody in the distance—a capsule of gaiety in a dead silent town. A group of American soldiers in front of the Governor's Palace were blowing on harmonicas and singing "When Johnny Comes Marching Home." Robert watched them, the music offering a solace for his dark mood; he even caught himself humming along: *"Hurrah! Hurrah!"*

10

WITH HIS FACE SWOLLEN AND his pants caked with blood, Turenne had been tortured several nights in a row but had not talked. When Obersturmbannfüher Karl Lindinger, head of the Paris Gestapo, learned that Turenne was doubtlessly running an escape line, he demanded that Boucher turn him over summarily.

Boucher had no choice but to comply. "Their turn to have fun with him," he had said.

Turenne was now cuffed to the back door handle of the same Citroën he had traveled in a few nights before. Detective Franjou sat next to him and Lenoir was behind the wheel. They headed for the German secret police headquarters on the rue des Saussaies.

As they turned into the rue du Faubourg Saint-Honoré, Lenoir slowed down. A fire engine pulled by two horses was attempting to make a U-turn with a fireman attempting to guide the frightened horses out of the way. Traffic had come to a standstill. The instant the Citroën pulled over, its doors swung open.

Whush, whush, whush!

Shining straight razors slashed the policemen's hands, arms, and legs. They yelled, attempting to fend off their assailants. Franjou's thigh was slit from knee to waist.

Turenne recoiled, watching blood squirt through the policemen's ripped clothes. In the front, a dark wiry Catalan, with a beret pushed down to his eyebrows, yanked Lenoir's gun from his holster, dragged him out of the car, and cut his suit from shoulder to groin. Lastly, looking for a final touch, the Catalan neatly sliced off Lenoir's earlobe.

"¡No pasarán, cabrón!" *They shall not pass, asshole!* The anti-fascist slogan of Spanish Republicans.

In the back, Franjou was yanked onto the sidewalk as he frantically patted his wounds to stop the bleeding. He tried a boxer's stance but his assailant slapped him hard and took his gun.

"The keys, monsieur, please," the man said in a harsh working-class accent, a match for his stained dark blue factory worker's overalls. Franjou pulled out the keys. The man grabbed them and kicked the policeman so hard, he landed spread-eagled on the sidewalk.

"We're friends," the man said, sliding on the back seat and uncuffing Turenne. "Get down on the floor and close your eyes, comrade." His name, Turenne would later learn, was Jacquet, and the man behind the wheel, Cervantes. Moving his ruined legs carefully, Turenne scrunched down and managed to fit on the floor between the seats. In the front, the Spaniard had already pushed the car into gear. The Citroën climbed onto the sidewalk, bypassing the fire engine, and tires squealing, flew off the curb, the shock absorbers thumping loudly. They drove for a while until Turenne heard the sound of a garage door opening and closing.

"Keep your eyes closed," Jacquet said. "The less you see the better." Turenne got out of the car and felt a strong arm fastening around his waist to help him walk and then a sudden movement of the floor told him where he was—an industrial elevator, going down. Subway workers, Turenne guessed. When the elevator stopped, the apparatus locked into place with a sharp clang.

"You can open your eyes now," Jacquet said.

Turenne watched an iron door slide open, revealing an underground storage vault and farther back, the lights of a subway repair station. A man in a suit and tie came into sight—thirties, painfully thin, he stuck out his hand. "Proust," the man said.

Turenne nodded. It was the fashion in the underground for people to take the names of famous writers. They shook hands, moved past discarded machinery, and sat down on crates. Proust offered Turenne a cigarette and when the offer was declined, lit one for himself.

"We are FTP," he said, picking a speck of tobacco off his tongue.

"I figured that."

FTP, Franc-Tireurs et Partisans—the armed wing of the French Communist Party. Turenne noted the accent, Hungarian or Polish . . . and Jewish. There were lots of Jews in the French Communist Party. They had immigrated to France in the 1920s, fleeing pogroms and dictatorial regimes. Struggling to survive was second nature to them, so when the Résistance came into being, they were the first to join.

"I owe you my life," Turenne said. "Thank you."

"You needed rescuing," Proust said, blowing smoke as if gratitude was out of place.

Turenne knew better. The FTP was not a charitable organization. Its operatives were hard men. They took tremendous losses—*no time for tears* as the saying goes. They had rescued him for a reason.

The next day in Toulouse, there was another message from Madame Victoire and Janine met Suzanne at the train station, where she was told Turenne had been freed.

"How is he?" she asked.

"He has been tortured. He could barely walk. I cleaned and bandaged his wounds. He will need medical attention. We smuggled him to Marseille last night. He said he had contacts there." Then

Suzanne handed an envelope to Janine. "It's from Turenne," she said. "He and Proust discussed an arrangement."

"What does he want?"

"For the BBC to broadcast the names of French policemen fighting the underground and remind them that they'll be held responsible after the war. Turenne wrote down the names."

"I'll try," Janine said.

"It's not a request. We know you can get it done," Suzanne said. "There is something else. More difficult."

"Yes?"

"Plastic explosives. Composition C-4, RDX, cyclonite. It comes in bulk drums, twenty-five kilos. Four drums and a hundred blasting caps. The British can get that for you."

"Exceptionally difficult," Janine said.

"Tell me something I don't know."

Janine looked up at Suzanne with newfound respect. "That man Proust, tell me about him."

"He fought in the International Brigade in Spain in '37. That's where I met him. A man of his word if you keep yours."

"Was Spain as brutal as they say?"

"Worse. Exactly how it's going to be here."

"Another civil war?"

"Yes. French against French. As you can see, it has already started."

Janine shook her head as if trying to negate such calamity.

"There is something else. The police inspectors raped the woman Turenne was with. She was released and has volunteered to work for the escape line."

"Can she be trusted?"

"Turenne vouched for her. Lucile is her name."

Janine nodded. "Good, we're short of escorts."

II

JANINE WATCHED GERMAN ARMORED VEHICLES roll into Toulouse as she bicycled to the train station that morning. A depressing sight, in response to the Allied landings in North Africa, the German Army was invading southern France. The free zone was no more and smuggling allied aviators would be even more difficult.

The next morning, she was in Spain meeting with the British consul in Bilbao. Franco's police kept the British consulate under surveillance, so they met in the examining room of a Spanish dentist she had known before the war. With his Sherlock Holmes mustache and hair parted to the side, the consul looked every bit like the Englishman he was. The two trusted each other but it had not always been the case.

Their first contact had been in the winter of 1941 when Janine had appeared in his office with three RAF pilots who had been shot down over Holland. She was so young, the consul was skeptical, but the RAF men treated Janine with great respect. So, he listened as she described how airmen were moved hand to hand down toward the Spanish border. They had to be fed and provided with civilian clothes. Train tickets had to be purchased and Basque guides had to be paid. Janine told the consul that her uncle had been financing the escape line but was running out of money. They needed help.

"We will work *with* you but we will not work *for* you," Janine had said. "We'll bring the airmen to Bilbao. You will reimburse our expenses. We will share no information and take no orders. We take all the risks, we run the operations our way or we don't do it at all."

The consul was riled by the typical Gallic attitude, but week after week, the escape line kept delivering British airmen and the diplomat used his meager consulate resources to reimburse her for the expenses. He too was running out of funds. After months of pressure and numerous testimonies from rescued RAF aviators, the purse strings were finally untied and the funds arrived through the diplomatic pouch.

"We're being commended by the prime minister's office," the consul said. "Every time a 'presumed dead' aviator reappears on his RAF base, it lifts morale."

"Raises morale? I never thought of that," Janine mused.

"Allied aviators now feel if they are shot, they've got a chance."

"I'll let our people know," she said.

Janine then related the news of Turenne's escape and the consul was at first elated, then distressed to hear about his condition. The French police were scouring the country searching for him and every hospital was on the lookout for a patient fitting Turenne's description.

"Could British Intelligence help Turenne out of Marseille?" Janine asked.

"They are a difficult bunch but I will ask."

And there was the FTP's demand for C4 plastic explosives. The consul doubted he could convince the very anti-communist British war department to provide weapons to people taking orders from Moscow.

"Put conditions on delivery," Janine said. "Demand that they blow up a facility out of RAF's reach."

The consul liked Janine's hard-boiled approach. Her uncle's arrest had not deterred her, quite the opposite. He handed Janine a satchel containing half a million francs and stacks of forged ration tickets. "We'll get more. I'll keep on the pressure."

The meeting was over. He held out his hand, but Janine did not shake it; instead, she reached out and kissed him on both cheeks. "Thank you, thank you," she said, then turned and headed out the door. The consul stood there, stunned. The gesture had affected him more than he would ever admit. He knew he would do everything in his power to help that impossible woman—*cette femme impossible.*

12

THE PARIS GESTAPO CHIEF HAD been enraged by Turenne's escape. He had berated Boucher for his incompetence and the whole French police for failing to dismantle allied airmen escape lines. German intelligence estimated that over 50 percent of the aviators shot down over Europe were rescued by the Résistance and smuggled across France to Spain. Airmen, once back in England, would get new aircrafts and return to bomb more German cities. Lindinger wanted results and threatened to suspend Boucher's stipend.

Boucher was upset and humiliated. He never expected for the Résistance to attack his men in full daylight in the middle of Paris. And there was the gloomy subject of money. He had been investing wisely and was becoming wealthy but needed the Gestapo's money to keep flowing. He had to find ways to mollify the Germans. So, when he received an anonymous letter describing a Spanish Jesuit priest at Saint Crick's college ferrying allied aviators, Boucher suspected the clergyman was part of Turenne's escape line and decided to handle his arrest personally.

He had arrived in Poitier that morning and commandeered a car and two gendarmes. The informer's letter described the priest waiting at the Poitiers Buffet de la gare with his airmen until female escorts led the aviators to a train for Toulouse. The letter also accused the priest of unnatural acts with young boys, but Boucher ignored that. Informers often smeared their victims and accusations of deviant sexual behavior were common.

Saint Crick College was an austere place with gray walls, narrow windows, and classroom doors, which opened directly into a cloister. Upon arrival Boucher dashed across the courtyard accompanied by the Father Superior and his two gendarmes. Unshaven and encased in a black leather coat, Boucher looked menacing. It wasn't just his hatred for Turenne and his fellow terrorists; Boucher despised the place. He loathed Jesuits with their elitist education and holier-than-thou attitude, especially this smug Father Superior with his black soutane, purple collar, and heavy silver crucifix. The prelate had initially resisted Boucher's requests, but having read the search warrants, he had reluctantly complied.

"Slow down, my son, I'm not getting any younger," the old man complained.

"Where's Father Valencia's classroom?" Boucher snarled, quickening his pace.

"He's in room eighteen. I'm taking you there now, commissaire." The clergyman stopped to catch his breath. Boucher watched two boys run into the building ahead of them—*he's slowing me down to give him time to get away*.

"What do you want with him?" the Father Superior asked as he struggled up the stairs. "He's one of our best teachers. The archdiocese is very pleased with him."

"I'll bet."

Those Jesuit bastards were corrupting the entire Catholic Church. Boucher reached room eighteen and stormed inside. The classroom was empty but for a lone student writing at his desk.

"Where's Father Valencia?" Boucher demanded.

"He's in the music room," the student said.

The Father Superior intervened. "No, he is not! At this hour he tutors the *novitiati*—the novices preparing for their initiation."

Boucher focused on the student. "Where is the music room?"

Realizing his mistake, the student closed his books and edged toward the back door. "I . . . I don't know," he muttered, looking terrified.

With a whip of his chin Boucher ordered the gendarmes to block the back door. "You don't know where the music room is?" he asked, with more than a touch of amusement in his voice.

"Father Valencia is in study hall," said the Father Superior. "I'll get him for you."

Boucher ignored the old man and concentrated on the student, moving toward him, massaging his fist. Fighting tears, the boy desperately wanted to stand up to the policeman.

"The music room is at the end of the arcade, last room to the right," he whispered, bending his head in shame.

Boucher shoved the Father Superior aside and ran down the stone passage until he reached a door conveniently labeled SALLE DE MUSIQUE. He turned the knob. It was locked. He grabbed one of the gendarme's rifles and butted the lock.

Blam! The door swung open, revealing Father Valencia and three students, one of whom tried unsuccessfully to turn off a radio receiver. Boucher handed the gendarme his rifle and turned up the volume. The announcer's voice could be heard over the static of German radio jamming. "Radio Paris ment, radio Paris ment, radio Paris est Allemand." *Radio Paris lies, radio Paris lies, radio Paris is German.*

"Listening to the BBC? Is that part of your novices' training?" Boucher asked. One of the gendarmes gave a snort of laughter.

"Round them up," Boucher said.

"The boys too?" the gendarme asked.

"Especially the boys."

The gendarmes forced everyone out. The novices were eighteen at most, little more than children, with short-cropped hair and bodies thin as reeds.

"What do you want with them?" Father Valencia protested. "I was the one listening to the BBC. Leave them alone."

"You corrupted them, Father," Boucher answered.

"Yes, and I alone should be punished for it."

"No worries. You will be."

The gendarmes pushed Father Valencia and the trembling novices out of the room, ahead of a smug Boucher.

13

IN ALGIERS ROBERT, ELI, AND the french who had helped the Allies during Torch were singled out by the American military and encouraged to attend English classes run by an officer who had taught English as a second language in Arizona. Robert signed up. He enjoyed being around Americans. He loved their get-the-job-done attitude. They even set him up in business. They sold him cartons of Lucky Strikes cigarettes that he resold in individual packs on the black market. Soon Robert was making more money than in his hashish dealing days. But he felt empty: *I'm just back to my old tricks.*

Eli was dubious when Robert announced he wanted to enlist in the French Africa Corps. "The US Army will equip us and we'll be trained by French foreign legion officers," Robert said. "We'll fight the desert war beside American and Commonwealth troops."

"They say it's a blood bath in Tunisia," Eli said.

"War is chaos; always is," Robert replied. "Do you want to be stuck here for the rest of your life and work for your father in the butcher shop?"

Eli shook his head. No, he did not.

Eli and Robert enlisted in the French Africa Corps just before Christmas. On a camp near the Tunisian border, they learned machine guns and hand-to-hand combat, to kill with knives or bare hands, and to survive in the desert for days with little food and water. Soon they crossed into Tunisia. Their mission was to hunt down German patrols. If they encountered superior forces, orders were to hit and run, switching to guerrilla tactics.

One hundred and twenty men were moving two abreast. They marched at night and rested during the day. *We're making history*, Robert told himself, but the thought did not hold. The straps of his backpack sliced into his shoulders and the continuous rain chilled him to the bone. "Making history" was supposed to be glorious. This was vile.

They now advanced on the djebel, a vast expanse of deserted hills covered with sand and rocks. It occurred to Robert that guerrilla tactics on this terrain was absurd—*hit-and-run with no place to hide or local population to provide shelter.*

On the tenth day, they heard the first echoes of battle. The Allies were attacking the Wehrmacht installations in Ferryville, twelve miles ahead of them. When the wind turned, they could smell wave after wave of burning chemicals, melting iron and fuel oil. After a final grueling march, they arrived in Sedjenane and flopped onto the ground amid a symphony of bitching and swearing. Robert and Eli grabbed their shovels, made themselves dugouts, and set up their machine gun.

After dinner, Eli pulled up the prayer shawl he wore under his uniform, covered his head, and prepared for the evening prayer.

"You want to say Shema with me?" Eli asked.

Robert was too embarrassed to admit that he didn't remember the prayer's words. "Say it for the two of us," he said.

Eli began to recite: "*Sh'ma Yisrael Adonai Eloheinu Adonai Eḥad . . .*"

Robert listened, his thoughts wandering, gloomy thoughts mainly—how his lack of religious fervor had saddened his father.

As the yellow light of daybreak emerged, Robert scrutinized the desert. It was serene again and exuded the honey mint smell that came after the rain. It was a staggering feeling to be on the front line, knowing that the enemy was out there, somewhere.

Later that day, a German reconnaissance plane flew overhead. They had been ordered to hole up and not shoot. Robert could see the black swastika on the tail and the pilot was taking his sweet time photographing them. But orders were firm, no firing!

"We should've shot down that plane. Now, they know where we are, our strength, defensive positions, everything," Robert said, fighting a knotted feeling in his chest. *We're cannon fodder.*

They expanded their dugouts into trenches, filled sandbags, and piled them up at the edges of the gun pits. Then they practiced moving from hole to hole. Robert manned a machine gun and Eli fed him ribbons of bullets.

Nothing more to do but wait. Eli lit a cigarette, drank some wine, and handed the canteen to Robert, who shook his head.

"You don't drink, you don't smoke. What're you, a Muslim?"

"I wonder at times," Robert said.

Eli took a drag of his cigarette. "Whatever happens, please don't tell my father you saw me smoke on Shabbat."

"Can I tell him about the pork?"

"What pork?" Eli smiled, but there was worry in his voice.

"All that American meat and beans you have been eating right out of the can, what do you think it's made of? Kosher pork?"

"It's made with beef! And I didn't touch the fried bacon!"

"That's big of you."

Eli wiped his mouth with the back of his hand. "Those beans were good."

"That's religion for you," Robert said. "Bunch of old farts who can't shit, eat, or fuck anymore sit around discussing what they really miss. Then they decide *you* can't have it."

Robert and Eli chuckled and slapped hands, eliciting disbelieving looks from their neighbors—*these two are crazy.*

At dawn, they were attacked from all sides. Shells, mortars, and tracer bullets zigzagged toward them and exploded in the olive groves.

"That's what happens when Jews eat pork," Robert told Eli as they crouched low in their dugout. "Now we're all paying for it."

Squinting into the distance, they could see a column of tanks advancing with a line of trucks following behind.

"Panzer Mark IV's." Robert sounded in awe.

"How do you know?" Eli asked.

"Didn't you ever see those German propaganda films about Rommel's *Afrika Korps*? Those are the tanks."

Eli peered out of their dugout. "Amazing machines."

"Yeah, yeah. And deadly." Robert pulled Eli back. "Stay down."

Barely a mile away the tanks were now slowing down to let the trucks move ahead of them—a military ballet, efficient and sinister.

"Troops are getting off the trucks," Eli said.

Dust rose above the desert as boots hit the ground. Then the tanks moved ahead again, leaving the trucks behind.

"And now troops are marching in the shadow of the tanks," Eli said.

An experienced war machine was closing on them. They could hear the whining of tank engines and the drivers switching gears. It was spellbinding. Then, a few hundred yards away the tanks foundered on swampy ground and German troops raced for cover at the base of the hill. They were so close Robert and Eli could hear the clanging of their weapons and canteens.

A German platoon ran straight at them. "Here they come!" Robert cried.

"Shoot at will!"

Robert swiftly gauged his sights and fired. The Germans fired back. *Crack-crack*—bullets flew, bouncing off rocks, raising geysers of sand all around them.

Whoosh. Shells whistled overhead. Robert kept firing and could feel his scalp tingling under his helmet. His skin crawled and became amazingly sensitive. *All those bullets, one of them is going to find me.*

Eli stared at the field, shrieking with excitement while expertly feeding Robert bullets. "Keep shooting, Robert! Keep shooting!"

Crack-crack-crack. The machine gun had become red hot from continuous firing. German troops leaped up to fire, then dove for cover in waves of eight or ten. Robert tried to time his firing to their movements.

"Are we hitting anybody?" he asked. "Seems like there're fewer of them after each dive."

"I see more of them!"

Then Eli spotted German infantry setting up mortars. "Let's get the hell out of here."

They had practiced the move many times, but today they looked like chickens fleeing the coop. First, they started out in the wrong direction. Then Eli realized he had left the tripod behind and stumbled back to get it. Robert dropped the machine gun, caught it at the last second, and seared his hands on the sizzling barrel. They had settled into their new hole when Robert discovered he'd left his canteen behind.

"Merde." He climbed out but Eli grabbed his ankle.

"You stay right here," Eli said, pulling him back.

A loud whistle and a mortar shell exploded on the spot they had just left. *Babablam!*

"You see that?" a terrified Robert asked.

"Yep. Those bastards are good!"

Robert's burned hands stung like hell. His entire body was shaking and the deadly dance continued—set up, fire, move, set up again. They were getting better at it when the smell hit them.

"What's that?" Robert asked.

"Death," Eli answered.

The stench of cordite, blood, and human excrement was overwhelming. Bodies lay torn apart. Dying men screamed, their intestines unraveling on the sand. Robert kept firing while throwing up—*don't look, damn it!*

Keeping a cool head, Eli picked up the ammunition belt. "We've got to move."

They zigzagged along the hill and found themselves in their initial dugout. It was now a small crater stinking of steel and gunpowder.

At midday, the German troops retreated. Robert and Eli sat in their hole. Robert was shaking. He could not control himself. Eli seemed serene but both kept to themselves. They drank water but could not eat. A soldier crawled from hole to hole passing orders. "Attend the injured. Bury the dead."

They helped the medics move the wounded to the makeshift infirmary. Robert was stunned by how much they cried as they were carried. Next they attended the dead who until this morning had been sons, husbands, and brothers. Dragging and pushing dead comrades and body parts into ditches was pure horror. The temperature rose and the stench became unbearable.

"Guerrilla tactics!" Robert spat. "Fucking brass in Algiers should be shot!"

The German offensive had stopped but the tanks were still stuck in the mudbanks and French gunners began lobbing shells at them. It was a precision exercise that required a direct hit on the tank turret. Every time this happened, cheers came out of the holes. Robert and Eli watched German soldiers jump out of tanks with their bodies on fire. They rolled on the sand, trying to put it out. Seeing a tank being hit was fun; watching those men die was not.

And things got worse. In a cacophony of whining diesel engines and spinning tracks, the tanks managed to extricate themselves from the swamps. The instant they reached hard ground, another assault began. Robert fed the ammo belt while firing his machine gun. Eli was up on his knees firing his rifle with great accuracy. He shot a couple of infantrymen before Robert pulled him back.

"Let's move."

More men were dying. The yelling was deafening. Blood-soaked patches of sand. One of the foreign legion officers who had trained them lay on the ground. A mortar shell had blown off both of his legs and blood gushed from the stumps.

"Medic!" he called. "Medic!" Then, he looked at Robert and said: "Merde!" This was his last word.

They set up in a new hole, swarms of tracing bullets from the tanks crackling around them. Eli was up firing his rifle.

"Get down, damn it!"

Eli dropped down. Robert aimed and fired but after a few rounds the chamber clicked empty. "Bullet belt's stuck!" he shouted.

Eli was on his knees. Robert saw a telltale paleness washing into his face. "Where are you hit, Eli?" Robert shouted over the roar of the battle. "Show me!"

Robert checked Eli's chest. "I don't see any . . . ," he began hopefully. But then he rolled Eli over and spotted a gaping exit wound just above the shoulder blade and, rolling him back, a smaller hole below the rib cage where the bullet had entered.

"Eli! I told you to fucking stay down!" Robert shouted. Eli's eyes remained open, staring at the sky. A stick grenade spun above them and landed in the trench. Robert dove for cover.

Babbam!

A hail of steel and rocks flung Eli's corpse several feet in the air and Robert watched his friend's body bouncing against the side of the trench.

"Oh, God."

Robert crawled over and pulled the prayer shawl from under Eli's army fatigues. He wrapped Eli's head in it and kissed the forehead through the cloth. His eyes filling with tears Robert cradled his friend's head in his arms. *Why did I talk you into this?*

The battle still raged around him. Machine guns rattled and tanks fired continuously. An aircraft roared overhead; Robert looked up—the Luftwaffe. *Perfect. They'll finish us off.* Then he took another look. This was a fighter airplane with a star painted on the tail—*an American fighter!* It was firing at the tanks. Tracer bullets focused on the aircraft but the pilot kept flying over them, concentrating so much firepower on the armored column that the German infantry raced away from their tanks.

"Yeah, run away, you bastards!"

Two legionnaires crawled in beside Robert. "Viens avec nous." *Come with us*, one of them said.

Together they ran toward the tanks now unprotected by infantry and fired their rifles point-blank through the observation slits. It was easy, actually. When Robert fired his first shot, he heard the driver scream inside. It didn't bother him as much the second time. They stopped several tanks in a matter of seconds and the legionnaires turned around and raced back up the hill. Above them, the American plane was slaloming between tracers with smoke coming out of its engine. Robert fired in one last tank and followed the legionnaires. Running back, he found himself in the path of the crashing American fighter plowing through sand and stones. Flames gushed from its ruined engine. Robert could see the pilot engulfed in smoke struggling to open the canopy and, in desperation, smashing his fists against the glass. Robert ran toward the plane. The pilot pulled out a revolver when Robert climbed onto the wing.

"How do you open it?" Robert shouted, gesturing at the cockpit. The pilot pointed at a latch on top of the fuselage and Robert popped the canopy open. The man's face was covered with black soot. His eyes looked unnaturally large. Robert slid his arms around his chest and pulled him up. They swung on the edge of the cockpit, shuffled out on the wing, and jumped. The pilot shouted in pain as they landed. Then, he grabbed Robert's arm and leaped forward, yelling.

"Get away, fast, fast!"

As they sprinted away Robert felt a prickly burn on his left thigh. A shell whistling above them hit the aircraft. They rolled into the ditch cradling their heads as the plane exploded into a fireball.

"Fire won't last . . . almost out of fuel."

The plane's ordinance exploded in spurts. Fuel poured into the sand and the smoke turned black. The pilot checked his burned arms and chest and turned to Robert.

"Thanks for getting me out," he said. "Name's Mike."

Mike's eyebrows and eyelashes were charred. That's why his eyes looked so big, Robert realized. "Name's Robert."

Mike tried to extend his hand but stopped, wincing in pain. Then he took a closer look at Robert.

"What's up with your leg?"

Robert looked down at his left leg. It was soaked with blood.

"Can you move your toes?" Mike asked.

"Oui."

"You feel your cock?"

"Cook?" Robert asked.

Mike grabbed his own and Robert hurriedly plunged his hand down inside his pants. "Oui, yes," he cried.

A grin spread over Mike's face. "You're fine."

Robert sighed but the relief didn't last as German voices around them shouted: "Hände hoch! Hände hoch!"

German soldiers aiming rifles surrounded them. Mike and Robert raised their arms expecting to be shot but an officer appeared and ordered them out of their hole.

The wounded lay on the ground in front of a large tent emblazoned with red crosses. Inside, surgeons worked on the German wounded at four operating tables. The only surviving French medic bandaged Mike's hands and spread sulfate on his chest, arm, and neck. Robert's wound was deep; the medic patched it as best he could.

As they lay side by side, Mike whispered, "I saw you fire in those tank slits."

Robert shook his head, not understanding. "Slits?" he asked.

"Shooting inside the tanks."

Robert got it. And shook his head. He could not believe he had actually done that. "It was easy."

"Easy? That took balls. The Germans caught the two guys you were with and shot them," Mike said, cocking his fingers to mimic a cold-blooded execution.

"Merde," Robert said, then turned his head to the side and studied Mike. "Why are you here?"

"I was hit during the raid over Bizerte. My plane was pissing fuel and I knew I wouldn't make it back to base, so when I ran into you guys, I thought I'd score a Panzer or two before bailing out." A brief laugh triggered a spasm of pain. Mike's face was friendly but blistery and strained with misery.

"Are you hurting?" Robert asked.

"My eyes are on fire . . . Get me my flask."

Flask. Robert knew that word. He pulled a flat stainless container out of Mike's aviator jacket and helped him drink.

"Thanks," Mike said. "Whiskey, help yourself."

Robert shook his head, then screwed on the top and put the flask back where he found it.

"You don't drink?"

"You need it more than I do," Robert said.

A German officer appeared and in an atrocious accent announced, "La guerre est finie pour vous." *The war is over for you.* He sounded envious.

"Today was my first encounter with the enemy," Robert told Mike.

"You went after tanks with a rifle on your first day?"

"Yes."

"And you got hit." Mike's blue eyes twinkled sardonically. "It's like losing your cherry and getting the clap on your first fuck."

Robert did not get it. He tried to smile but winced instead.

Night was falling and it was bitterly cold. They lay on cold ground, shivering and hungry. Food was distributed to the Germans. The French wounded asked for water, were ignored, begged, and finally got some. The nightmare started when medics laid blood-stained tarps on top of them. That tarp stank of blood. The smell was repulsive and got worse as time went on. All the wounded, Germans and French, were moaning. Some cursed, others prayed, many were delirious. Robert was in serious pain. A bullet had been lodged in his thigh since morning and his whole body shook with fever. Animals were howling not far away. The colder the night the louder the howling.

"What's that?" Mike asked.

"Hyenas," Robert said.

"Scavengers?"

"The smell of blood brings them."

"Oh, Lord." Mike sighed.

The hyenas' barks sounded like hysterical human laughter. Robert tried not to think about Eli's body lying on the field but became convinced he could hear men shouting and fighting the beasts.

The smell of blood was now so powerful, men were throwing up. Mike had passed out. Robert could not sleep. He was drenched with sweat yet bitterly cold. Temperature dropped below freezing and the stinking wet tarp turned into a sheet of ice. Robert didn't know if he was awake or dreaming. His father's face appeared before him whispering: "*Please, son, don't get yourself killed.*" Robert felt tears running down his cheeks. He didn't want to break his father's heart.

His dad had read him stories as a child, shown him how to fish and hunt, and instilled in him a sense of pride and decency. He had given him the greatest gift a father could give—*he taught me to believe in myself.* Enlisting had been the right thing to do. A certitude inspired and fostered by a strong and gentle soul up there in the mountains of Kabyle. *Dad was wounded too, he's with me.* And for an instant, Robert actually *felt* his father's presence.

The night went on. Trucks pulled in, their engines' diesel fumes triggering an epidemic of coughing and groaning, reopening wounds and causing the reek of blood to become even more powerful. Robert heard voices while German wounded were carried from tents to trucks. At long last, the tarp cracked and was pulled off. Robert sucked in the cold morning air and stared at the paling sky. The stench abated. He could breathe. He was alive. He turned to his new friend.

"Mike?" No answer. Robert shook him gently.

Mike grunted and asked, "How do you feel?"

"Good," Robert answered. "You?"

"Same."

They held still. The slightest move triggered jolts of pain rippling through their bodies.

Mid-morning, Robert, Mike, and three-dozen French wounded were crammed into open trucks. The torture started when the vehicles began jolting over roads damaged by bombs. With each pothole men moaned and those in better shape slammed their fists on the truck's cabin. By the time they entered Ferryville several men had died. The trucks slowed down when they reached the center of town where a large crowd welcomed them, shouting: "Les soldats Français qui sont venus nous libérer."

"What're they saying?"

"They cheer the French soldiers who came to free them."

"We sure look like liberators," Mike said.

Arabs in burnouses ran alongside the trucks handing out cakes. Robert snapped up a handful and stuffed several in his mouth, so famished his hands were shaking. "*Macroutes*," he said clumsily, feeding Mike, who couldn't move his bandaged hands. They devoured the cakes made with shredded dates, still warm and tender under the crust. Nothing had ever tasted so good.

"These people are Tunisians?" Mike asked between bites.

"Yes. They have the reputation of being the most hospitable people on earth."

"We've come to the right place," Mike said.

Along with the food, people shouted questions. How big was the allied army? Did they have tanks? Destroy cities? Rape women? Steal food?

"All of the above," Mike said after hearing Robert's translation.

The trucks stopped at a guarded airfield and rolled to a hangar where the Vichy French Red Cross had set up shop. There the living were carried off and those who had died during the trip were left outside. When water was offered, Mike drank liters of it. Robert only needed a couple of glasses. Their wounds were cleaned, sprayed with sulfate powder, and re-bandaged. A nurse put a cloth strip over Mike's eyes.

In the afternoon Tunisian medics carried them aboard a plane with a large red cross on its side and laid them in bunks stacked three high alongside the cabin. The engines roared to life and the plane began vibrating. Robert could hear grumbling above the sound of the rotors. There were a few more bumps as they sped along the runway and then all was smooth and easy. Robert closed his eyes—*much better than that fucking truck.*

A couple of hours later they were flying over a city at the foot of a mountain from which rose a plume of smoke.

Mike pushed up the cloth over his eyes.

"Naples," he said, looking through the small window near his bunk.

"How do you know?"

"That's Mount Vesuvius, down there."

In the fading light the plane descended toward the sea. Robert listened to the landing gear whining and locking into place. He closed his eyes, bracing for what was coming. *BABABLAM.* The plane bounced on the tarmac, triggering an explosion of anguished cries. The revving of the engines drowned the clamor and they taxied toward a hangar.

Robert fought his own waves of pain, reminding himself: *The moment I stop hurting I'll be dead.* He tried to focus on a pleasant memory—Arlette. *I should have married her. We'd be in bed right now, her warm body against mine. What's wrong with being a shopkeeper?*

14

JANINE HAD BEEN SHAKEN BY Father Valencia's arrest. The moment they heard, the waiter of the Café du Depart in Limoges went into hiding and Janine changed her appearance. She now wore her hair in a prim bun, donned a hat with a veil, and sported glasses. Her new identification papers stated that she was a lawyer born in 1909, making her thirty-four years old. This affluent-looking woman traveled first class. In those troubled times, rich meant pro-Vichy, pro-government, and pro-German. The gendarme at Police Control in Nimes was clearly intimidated by her ID identifying her as a member of the Paris bar. He barely glanced at her briefcase and waved her through. *I should have gone into the law*, Janine thought, idly. Everybody hates dentists.

With the Germans now occupying the entire country it was even more dangerous for her to travel, but the demands of the escape line were unremitting. Janine had been in Nimes for two days and her rendezvous had not yet shown up. They had agreed to meet at the entrance of the Roman amphitheater, which turned out to be a poor choice. The place was overrun by German soldiers touring the ruins and guides barking into loudspeakers, thrilling the crowd with tales of gladiators fighting to their death and Christians being thrown to the lions. The rule was that if someone did not show for a meeting, you'd come back twice at the same time. On the third morning Janine found herself surrounded by a twittering contingent of German army nurses in starched blue uniforms and white hats.

When she moved away from the amphitheater, she caught sight of a man in a dark suit crossing the street.

"Good morning, comrade," Proust said.

They strolled down the sidewalk talking like old acquaintances. "You were supposed to be here two days ago," Janine said.

"I was busy. Good news from the Russian front. The entire German Sixth Army surrendered in Stalingrad four days ago."

Janine digested the news. "Are you sure about this?"

"Yes. One million German casualties. The Red Army has cut Germans' access to the oil fields in the Caucasus."

Janine kept on walking. *What if this is true?* she wondered, feeling a spurt of optimism. *Maybe this war will not go on for another ten years.*

Pedestrians walked by. Proust waited, his face weary. "So, what did the rosbif decide?"

"You mean, the *English*?"

"They turned us down?" Proust asked, bitterness ringing in his voice.

"They did not. They sent twice the amount you asked for," she said.

He raised an eyebrow. "What do they want done with the other half?"

"We'll get to that. But if you take it, you owe them. You break your word, you're dead to them."

Proust buried his fists in his pockets. "And when do I get it?"

"Now," Janine answered.

Proust was impressed but did not show it.

"Your turn to follow me," Janine said.

She turned into the first street. Proust turned into the second and proceeded to the next corner, where he spotted her ahead of him standing in front of an empty jewelry store. The shop window behind the metal grate was shattered and the floor was covered with broken glass. Display tables topped with black velvet had been tossed around and painted Stars of David covered the walls.

Janine walked into a passageway lined with trash and unlocked a door. Proust followed her inside and both waited for their eyes to get used to the darkness. Janine located a wall safe, produced two more keys, inserted them into the locks, and turned them simultaneously. She pulled the heavy steel door open and pointed at a stack of bags piled inside. The script on the sides read: *Plâtre Lafarge*—Lafarge plaster.

"Four hundred pounds, almost two hundred kilos."

"What about blasting caps?"

Janine tapped her foot on a wooden box on the bottom shelf. "In there, along with the wiring."

Proust unsealed a bag, scratched off a tiny piece of plastic explosive, tasted it with the tip of his tongue, and nodded in appreciation.

"Cyclonite is poisonous, you know that?" Janine said.

"Not in very small doses. Gives you a hell of a kick, though. Keeps you awake for a whole night."

"You want it?" Janine asked.

"What do they want us to do in return?"

"Blow up a weapon's manufacturing plant."

"Why not the Eiffel Tower while they're at it?" Proust snapped.

"Don't take it. Just walk away."

Proust snarled—*like I have a choice.* "Give me those keys."

Proust locked the safe and slid the keys into his pocket. Then, he looked at Janine. "We've got bad news from Poitiers."

"Yes."

"Father Valencia talked. He told them about you and how you get in touch with him. I was in Galicia with him in '37. He's a courageous man, but he had no choice."

"Did he give names?"

"No, just your description, but I assume you took care of that. He also told them about the hot milk signal you use at the café in the train station. Don't think badly of him."

Janine looked down at her feet. "I don't."

"They tortured his novitiates in front of him. They used tables."

"Tables?" Janine asked.

"Very popular with Franco's henchmen in Spain. They stripped the kid naked and laid him on two tables with his testicles hanging between the edges. Then they forced Valencia to watch as they pushed the tables together."

"They're monsters."

"They are. The older novitiate died," Proust said gravely. "He was eighteen. When they started on the second boy, Father Valencia talked."

15

"ANOTHER TRUCK," ROBERT GROANED, WATCHING a green Fiat army truck pull up on the Naples' airfield tarmac. The wounded were carried aboard and the body of a soldier who had died during the flight was left behind.

The trucks started up and the torture resumed. The roads were in terrible condition and Naples was one loud, colossal traffic jam. The Axis forces and the general population were competing for space and the military did not always win. Mike's face had turned bright red. He could not open his eyes. "I can't see anymore," he said.

Robert stared at the tarpaulin above his head, dreading the next pothole. When it hit, he passed out only to regain consciousness and ride in misery before fainting again. After what felt like forever, they entered a cluster of ancient gray buildings. Men climbed aboard the moment the trucks pulled over. They seemed to be French POWs. Robert was only half-conscious but understood that they were in a hospital. His pain was intense. He could not imagine it ever going away. Perhaps he would die. That'd be all right. At least the misery would stop. He saw ancient frescos on the walls as he was wheeled through archways and corridors. Finally, amid white tiles and bright lights, the sweet, nauseating scent of ether.

He woke up in a huge room with a cathedral ceiling. Morning light flooded through windows above rows and rows of iron beds, all of them occupied. Men wearing brown cotton pajamas were limping on crutches or sitting on beds. Robert realized he too was in a bed wearing brown pajamas. The pain in his leg was there but if he stayed put, it was bearable.

"God damn it!"

Robert knew that voice! It was Mike in the next bed, unrecognizable. His arms and torso were bandaged and his head was encased in a metal brace. His whole face was covered with gauze, leaving just a slit for his lips, crimson red and peeling.

"Where am I?" the slit asked.

"In a hospital for allied POWs."

"Am I blind?"

"There is medicine over your eyes."

"Hurts like hell. What . . ." Inhaling deeply, he tried to move his hands but gave that up. "What . . . does the medicine look like?"

"It's black like dry mud."

The image of RAF friends recovering at the Cardiff burn center flashed through Mike's mind. They had looked like mummies covered in brown plaster. Crystal something, they called it—*Crystal violet.* He heard a woman speaking Italian and Robert answering in French. "They give me shots?"

"Yes, every three hours. Morphine," Robert said.

"When was the last one?"

"Un'ora fa." *One hour ago.*

Mike moaned. *Two more to go.* Another sharp swell of pain overtook him. He despised it, tried to squelch it, and failed.

Robert watched Mike shiver and knew he'd been lucky. The bullet had been removed from his thigh. He had been told that he would be able to walk in a few days. Mike's condition was more serious. Badly burned skin had been peeled off from his hands, arms, and torso. The corneas of his eyes had also been burned and were being treated. Through the windows Robert could see a row of flags emblazoned with swastikas flapping in the wind, an unpleasant reminder of who was in charge.

Mike was tossing in his bed. The next morphine shot came none too soon. When the nurse pulled out the needle, Mike stopped shivering. The metamorphosis was welcome but eerie.

"Talk to me," Mike murmured.

"We're in a convent converted into a hospital. The nuns run the place. They care for the wounded, clean the floors, bring food, they do everything."

Mike mumbled. "Guards?"

"The guards are Italians but the nuns are in charge. You want to stay on their good side. Even the guards are afraid of them."

"I like nuns," Mike said. The morphine was working beautifully and he fell asleep.

For dinner, they got a bowl of soup filled with macaroni. A nun sat on the edge of Mike's bed, crushed the pasta on a plate, and fed him. After months of sleeping on hard ground, Robert could not get used to a mattress. In the middle of the night, he grabbed his blanket, slid onto the floor, and slept.

It was still dark when he woke up to the sight of a nun with a wrinkled face and a white cornette. She was waving an angry finger at him and whispering in high-speed Italian, insisting that he get back into bed. When he was settled, she pulled down his pajamas to check his injury. Robert was self-conscious being naked in front of a nun but it did not seem to faze her. Then, she leaned over and wrote an *I* with a pencil on top of the headboard and produced a small crucifix on a chain she insisted he put around his neck. Robert tried to protest but got a lengthy lecture that left no doubt about how much trouble he would be in if she caught him without that cross. "Circonciso. Medici Italiani. Circonciso. Medici Italiani eclusivamente," she kept whispering.

He understood. He was *circumcised.* The *I* meant *Italian*. He was to be checked by Italian doctors only—never German doctors.

Later that morning, she came back to give Mike his morphine shot and told Robert she was the convent's Mother Superior. Although Mike's wounds were on his face, arms, and chest, she pulled down his pajamas and put an *I* on his headboard.

"You're Jewish?" Robert asked after she had moved on.

"Mike O'Keefe. Does that sound Jewish to you?"

"But you're circumcised."

"Yeah, so?"

The Mother Superior reappeared and gave Mike a crucifix and a lecture in Italian about wearing it at all times.

"Sono Cattolico," he managed to say.

"Esatto!" *Precisely!* Finally, she had one who was a decent liar.

When medical rounds started the Mother Superior led the doctors—two Italians and one German—through the ward. There was no question of who was in charge. She chose the patients to be examined and by whom.

A couple of weeks later, a middle-aged Italian doctor removed the bandages covering Mike's face and carefully cleaned off his eyelids.

"Apri gli occhi."

Mike opened his eyes and winced, blinded by the light he had not seen in so long. Then, he turned his head, looked at the ceiling, the other beds, and finally at the doctor.

"I can see. Thank you, Lord."

He grabbed the doctor's arm. "Grazie, dottore." *Thank you, doctor.*

"Prego," the man answered.

Now that Mike was able to eat, drink, and smoke by himself, Robert became the Mother Superior's personal aide. He walked on crutches but doing things for other people helped him. He fixed the hospital generator and tuned the nuns' ancient Fiat. He repaired the stoves in the kitchen and fixed broken locks, which made the guards nervous. He could tell the old woman liked him. What she didn't like was the war. She often raised a finger and made pronouncements in Italian: "Men are stupid and war is a failure of civilization." She'd point at the SS training camp across the road, at the wounded prisoners, at the Italian guards.

"Tutte bestie." *All animals.*

Every week POWs received Red Cross packages and Robert, who missed sweets, bargained hard to trade his cigarettes for chocolate. His fellow POWs came from all over the world—British, Americans, New Zealanders, South Africans, even Nepalese Gurkhas. Most spoke English and Robert's fluency improved. He learned a version of the language clipped to the essential:

"Let's go."

"Name's Robert."

"Grab some chow."

"Sonsabeeches."

"Go to hell."

"Keep your big nose outta this."

"Goose-stepping bastards."

And the ever essential: "Fuck you!"

Spring brought balmy weather and uncertainty. Men needing no further medical attention were being moved to POW camps in Germany, Robert and Mike among them. Robert had emotional good-byes with his few surviving friends from the Corp Francs still in recovery. The Mother Superior gave him a pocketful of food and pinned a fifty-lira bill to the inside of his jacket. Robert thanked her in pigeon Italian. She nodded briskly, turned on her heels, and walked off down the ward.

"Tutte bestie."

16

LOÏC PACED THE DECK OF a fishing boat heading toward the French coast. He had left his farm in Brittany the week before and so far, the trip had gone smoothly. Shielding his cigarette with the palm of his hand, he braced himself against the freezing wind. It was a moonless night; the clouds were low and the water pitch black. He had not seen Janine since the killing of the German spy, and he missed her. He reminisced how she had nested up against him that day, then brought himself up short: *She's a city woman, a doctor. She isn't for you.*

The appearance of the ship captain was a welcome distraction. A typical Basque fisherman—strong and surly with a pale face and skin taunt over high cheeks. He borrowed Loïc's cigarette to light his own.

"Is it always this cold?" Loïc asked.

The red glare of his cigarette briefly illuminated the captain's watchful eyes. "Worst weather in fifty years. God's punishment for the war."

A flickering light appeared off the starboard bow.

"A ship?" Loïc said.

"No. That's the San Sebastian lighthouse. The other boats will show up soon. We'll all enter the port together, so it'll look like we're back from fishing." The captain took a drag of his cigarette. "How're they doing down there?" he asked.

"Surviving."

Barely. The stink of fish and oil fumes belowdecks had done their worst. Out of the nine allied airmen crammed into the hold, five were seasick.

"One of them can't see?" the captain asked.

"A pilot. His plane exploded when he parachuted out. A Belgian doctor removed every piece of metal in his body, but he couldn't help with his eyes. So the poor fellow is blind."

"We'll take him off the boat last so he doesn't slow the others," the captain said, then pointed at the sea. "Here they are."

A line of trawlers appeared out of the darkness. The captain went inside to stand beside the helmsman. The trawlers slowed down. They edged portside and joined the lineup. Loïc could now see the twinkling lights of Saint-Jean-de-Luz and Ciboure ahead with the dark shadow of the Pyrenees Mountains looming behind. He was relieved the trip was almost over. They were short-handed and forced to smuggle larger groups of escapees at one time. Bigger groups meant increased risk and a growing sense of dread.

A few miles away in the coastal village of Ciboure, Janine looked out at the dark ocean from her hotel room window. It was bleak out there. She rubbed her face and forced herself to cheer up—*today I'll see Loïc*. She felt a deep affection for Loïc. Perhaps more; her emotions fluctuated. At times they had an erotic tinge that flustered her.

Janine's mood lifted a bit. The day before, in the confessional at the local church, a priest had slid her half a postcard featuring a statue of Joan of Arc, a code that meant de Lacoste would be joining the line in the southwest. She had never met him but knew he was half-British, was in contact with British Intelligence, and had worked closely with Turenne in Paris. She was pleased, they badly needed experienced operatives like him. The muffled sound of a foghorn made her look out. Outside, fishing boats were clearing the mouth of the Nivelle River and veering toward the port. Janine put on a Canadienne jacket and left the room.

Prosper waited at the bottom of the stairs. He was a round man with a gray beard and dark intense eyes behind thick-rimmed glasses.

He had fought with the International Brigades in Spain and now shepherded airmen's border crossings. They shook hands and hurried toward the harbor.

At the loading dock, Loïc had joined the fishermen forming lines to unload their catch. Forty- to sixty-pound tuna were passed man to man to carts on the wharf. Loïc kept an eye on his airmen popping up on deck to be smuggled off on rowboats. A woman appeared, carrying jugs of wine and speaking in rapid Basque to the fishermen.

"Someone is watching us," the fisherman next to Loïc said, jerking his head toward a man standing on the dock. "No one knows who he is."

The man wore a raincoat and smoked a cigarette. "Is he Basque?" Loïc asked.

The fisherman chuckled—*no, not even close.*

At the stern of the fishing boat the blind airman was now being led down to a rowboat. Two men helped him. They were careful but his transfer had to be conspicuous to the man on the dock.

Janine and Prosper waited on the north side of the port. They helped the men off the rowboats and led them to a stone building across the street. When the boat carrying the blind man arrived Janine leaned forward.

"I'll guide you. There are a few steps here," she said, taking his hand. They reached the top of the stairs, crossed the street, and entered the building, where airmen crowded the hallway.

"Keep moving. It's safe in here," Janine called.

"How far is Spain?" asked a freckle-faced British airman.

"Five miles to the border," Janine answered.

Several men grunted in satisfaction. Janine set the blind pilot at the door. "Stay here, I'll come back for you," she said, before pushing through the crowd into the room beyond. She lit candles, revealing a vast chamber with tapestry-covered walls and a monumental fireplace.

"It's bloody cold in there," someone said.

"Want to go back to the boat?"

A few chuckles but no takers.

"What's this place anyway?" an Australian voice asked.

"This is the house where a Spanish princess stayed the night before she married the king of France, Louis the Fourteenth," Janine said.

"The last room she saw before losing her friggin' virginity!" whispered an airman with a cockney accent. "Sure hope the Spanish princess was hot-blooded."

"She was!" Janine said, getting into the humor of the tale. "She gave him nine children."

Several men laughed and everyone felt better.

Prosper stepped over and said, "I will take you inland tomorrow and turn you over to the guides who will smuggle you into Spain. Sleep as much as you can. You'll need your strength. It'll be a hard journey."

Janine picked up a blanket from a pile on the floor, walked back to the sightless pilot, and handed it to him. "Here, stay warm. Where are you from, Lieutenant?"

"Bournemouth, ma'am, on the south coast of England," the pilot answered, wrapping himself in the blanket.

"You are not going inland with the others. We'll smuggle you to Spain aboard a truck."

"Thank you." The pilot nodded; then, surmising that Janine was about to leave, asked, "Ma'am. Do you know anything about my condition? A Belgian doctor explained it to me, but I couldn't understand what he said."

"You'll be in a British hospital in Gibraltar in a couple of days."

"Yes, but will I see again?"

Janine had no idea. "Yes," she said. "Of course."

"Are you sure?"

"That's what I have been told," Janine lied. What this man needed most was hope.

The pilot searched for Janine's hand and shook it. "Thank you, ma'am. I don't even know your name," he added eagerly.

"It's better that way." Janine squeezed the man's shoulder and left.

At the port, the last tuna had been unloaded and Prosper climbed aboard the trawler. He, Loïc, and the captain conferred about the man still watching from the dock.

"Something has to be done about him," the captain said.

"He's getting on his bicycle," Loïc replied.

The captain rolled a couple of knives in a piece of burlap and picked up a heavy walking stick. Minutes later they rowed across the basin and anchored on its south side where they waited at the edge of the road. The clicking of bicycle wheels soon resounded in the distance and out of the morning mist the rider appeared, his raincoat flapping in the wind. Loïc walked toward him with the stick, casually beating the rhythm of his pace. The man on the bicycle raised his head; Loïc ignored him but at the last second shoved the stick between the bicycle wheel sprockets. The man shouted and flew over the handlebar, landing hard on the pavement. The captain and Prosper threw a burlap bag over his head and roped his wrists with a fast fisherman's knot. The man protested loudly until Loïc kicked him hard and shut him up.

Later that morning, Prosper led Janine inside a house and down a flight of stairs.

"Is he German?" she asked.

"He doesn't sound French."

Janine dreaded the prospect of another cold blood killing. When they reached the basement, Loïc stepped up and blocked her way.

"This time I'll take care of it myself," he said.

"Who is he?"

"He won't say," Loïc answered. "I roughed him up. He talked nonsense about a Monsieur Paul in Gibraltar."

"He said what?" Janine reacted. Monsieur Paul was one of Turenne's aliases. "Let me talk to him."

"I don't want you involved," Loïc said, his face reflecting strong resolve.

Her botched-up performance with the German spy still sharp in her mind, Janine put a hand on Loïc's arm. "I might know who he is. Loïc, let me in, please."

Loïc opened the door grudgingly. Their man sat on the floor, a burlap bag over his head.

"Who are you?" Janine asked, closing the door behind her.

The prisoner tilted his head, angling his ear toward Janine. "Did you get my postcard?"

"What postcard?"

"The one with a picture of Joan of Arc."

An incensed Janine dug out a folding knife, flipped it open, and cut the ropes. "How can you be so stupid?" she shouted as de Lacoste tore the bag off his head.

"Those Basques are crazy!" he hissed, his face bloody and crimson.

"You're the one who is crazy!" Janine yelled. "We were doing a transfer and you thought you could watch and nothing would happen?"

"I was looking for you! I've got three British airmen with me. I don't know what to do with them. All the hotels are closed."

"And that couldn't wait until tomorrow?" Janine hollered.

"They're on the beach." De Lacoste's anger was now diluted by the absurdity of the situation. "I stuck them inside one of the sheds where they store chairs and umbrellas," he said, wiping his bloody nose with the back of his hand. "They are *not* happy in there."

Janine waved him off and opened the door. "He's safe."

Loïc and Prosper filed back into the room.

"You shouldn't be so nosy," Loïc said.

De Lacoste jumped up, enraged. "You bastard!" he spat, lunging at Loïc. "Did you have to hit me so hard?"

"Hey, hey, hey!" Prosper hollered, keeping them apart.

Later that day, a bandaged de Lacoste joined Janine in the back of a café. There was bread, Basque sheep cheese, and wine on the table.

"How did you get Turenne out?" she asked, filling their glasses.

"We smuggled him out of Marseille aboard a Portuguese trawler," de Lacoste said. "He's in a Gibraltar hospital now."

Janine's face showed palpable relief at the news. "Thank you for that." She sipped some wine and said: "I was told you have been in France since the beginning of the war, and you knew that nurse near the Belgian border who got caught?"

"Yes, Louise," de Lacoste said in a bitter voice. "We were together for over a year. The Gestapo found a wounded Canadian pilot in her attic," de Lacoste said, getting emotional. "She was arrested, and I never saw her again." He tilted his head and added, "I wanted to go back to England but my bosses in London were pleased with the *splendid work* I was doing. They had very few bilingual agents in France, and they felt I'd be more useful here."

"They forced you to stay?" Janine asked.

"They *asked* me to stay."

Janine sat back. She knew how dangerous staying was. The Germans treated British spies even worse than *résistants*. They were tortured for weeks before execution.

"Any idea how the police found out about Turenne?"

"He was denounced. The checkgirl and I tried to warn him that cops were outside but we couldn't get to him." De Lacoste shook his head, getting emotional again. "They beat him up pretty bad. He could barely walk when we put him on that boat in Marseille."

Janine gauged de Lacoste. The man had worked underground for almost three years and had survived. Even managed to get her uncle out of Marseille, quite an accomplishment.

The gasoline truck's engine idled as the driver kept the engine warm. Prosper helped the blind RAF pilot climb aboard and lay down behind the seats. "You'll be in Bilbao this afternoon. Good luck."

Prosper watched the truck swerve onto the road. Another irony of war, the United States supplied Spain with gasoline to insure Franco's continued neutrality. The Spanish government had of course pledged the aid would not be re-exported to the Axis powers, but Franco owed Hitler for his support during the civil war and allowed trucks loaded with American gasoline to cross the border in the dead of night to supply the Panzer divisions in southwest France, with border guards under strict orders to wave them through. Many British and American wounded airmen benefited from this arrangement. A young pilot, native of Bournemouth, on the South coast of England, was the last of them.

17

THE TRAIN RUMBLED NORTH TOWARD ROME, Milan, and Germany. Mike, Robert, and another hundred POWs sat in crowded passenger cars under Waffen SS control and were not allowed to speak with Italian civilians. It hardly mattered—their fellow travelers looked disheartened and unwilling to talk anyway. The temperature was high for May and the sun shone fiercely on the parched countryside. The German presence, barely visible three months ago, was now overwhelming. Mike and Robert watched endless military convoys pouring down the peninsula on every north-south roadway.

Robert kept an eye on the guards who had trained machine guns at the end of each car. If a prisoner attempted to jump out, he'd be cut down before reaching the ground. Their train now crossed the outskirts of Rome and Robert glanced at the sky. He could hear the drone of airplanes. "An air raid?"

"Not for us," Mike said. "The Vatican is in Rome. It's the capital of Catholicism. The city is off limits to aerial bombing."

"How sweet. You Catholics don't bomb each other."

They were still some distance from the stazione di Roma Termini when whining brakes blended with wailing sirens and the sound of anti-aircraft batteries going into action.

"Looks like someone changed his mind!" Robert said.

Civilians aboard the train started screaming, a deep primal howl of hysteria and fear. Bags went flying. Desperate men, women, and children rushed to the doors and jumped out. Once on the track, they ran with pandemonium exploding around them. The SS guards remained in control. They flushed the POWs out and with a few well-placed rifle butt blows kept them in line. Bombs detonated inside concrete structures and blasts bounced around so fiercely it was impossible to tell where the explosions were coming from. Suddenly a voice barked in Arabic. "Ameucheoueu!" *Let's run!*

Robert shouted back: "Mazal hall, djaihine!" *Too early, you idiots!* Mike was about to follow, but Robert grabbed him, hissing. "Stay put."

Three Moroccan prisoners ran and two Brits followed. The SS guards calmly aimed and shot them. When they came level to the wounded men crawling on the tracks, the guards finished them off with bullets to the head. Robert grimaced. Mike looked away.

The bombing intensified as they reached the station. Terrified civilians swiped across the main hall stampeding toward the shelters. Parents lifted children above their heads to keep them from being crushed. The surging crowds overwhelmed the SS guards and prisoners and everyone was dragged along in a colossal human tide.

Robert yelled: "Zorka, seu'fa louokteu!" *Now, you go!*

POWs scurried off in different directions. Paralyzed by the crowds, the guards raised their weapons, but firing was useless.

"The handrail," Robert shouted, grappling against the panicked mob. Dragged sideways, Mike fought his way through a deluge of heads and shoulders but managed to grab Robert's extended arm to be pulled toward the banister at the edge of the shelter's entrance.

Their German sentry, less than ten feet away, ordered them inside. "*Schnell!*" he shouted. Arm extended, he aimed his rifle. Someone popped his elbow. The gun discharged in the air. The sentry lost his footing and was dragged inside the shelter by the crowd. Mike and Robert clung to the handrail. Their haversacks were torn off their backs. Coat and shirt buttons popped off as they edged against the surging mob. Crouching down, they burrowed against a sea of legs and feet *away* from the shelter.

When they reached the end of the ramp the crowd thinned. They ran toward the tracks. Bombers continued to batter the city. The ordnance's whistling was deafening. They ran and ran until behind them the bombing subsided. They had lost all their belongings. A small piece of the Mother Superior's fifty-lira bill still hung on the safety pin inside Robert's lapel. No water; their canteens were gone. Their scorched throats turned raw. Water became an obsession, but they kept running along the tracks heading north.

"When we marched into Tunisia, we had nine straight days of rain. I had never seen that much water in my life," Robert said.

"Did you need to tell me that?" Mike groaned.

Robert raised a hand and tilted his head. "I hear dogs." He knelt and pushed his ear against the rail. "A train's coming." He stood and pointed at smoke in the distance.

"Is that for us?" Mike asked.

"Of course it is."

No place to hide but a round tower next to the track.

"The roof," Robert said.

They circled the building, climbed the ladder embedded in its concrete side, and lay flat on the roof, panting. A locomotive pulling an open freight car was approaching. It moved slowly, keeping pace with sentries and dogs out checking the tracks.

The convoy stopped right under them. They could see inside the open car crowded with recaptured men. The engineer climbed on top of the locomotive and gaped at Mike and Robert.

"Buona sera." *Good afternoon*, he said softly.

The man swung the thick pipe hanging from the side of the tower and pulled a lever. Mike and Robert exchanged a look at the sound of the gushing water filling the locomotive's tank. They were lying *on top* of a water tower. Mike saw the smile forming on Robert's lips—*not funny, you son of a bitch.*

Down below, the dogs had picked up their scent. They yelped and sniffed the track feverishly. When they approached the water tower, the engineer pulled the engine's exhaust valve, spewing hot steam on both sides of the locomotive. The dogs leaped away. When they returned, they whined and sniffed around aimlessly. The engineer had washed away all traces of Mike and Robert's scent. In the open car, the Moroccans bickered in Arabic about their chances of jumping the guards and commandeering the locomotive.

"Klappe halten!" *Keep your mouth shut!* A guard raised his gun and fired inches above the Moroccans' heads. That calmed them down. Then it was quiet except for the locomotive's wheezing and gushing water. Mike and Robert recoiled as the engineer climbed back up and pulled on the pipe. But the man simply returned to his machine, unlocked the brakes, and the locomotive puffed away. It was barely out of sight when Robert and Mike pulled off the roof planks, cupped water with their hands, and drank frantically. Then they took off their clothes and rolled into the tank.

"God has got a sense of humor," Mike said.

They walked all afternoon and at dusk reached a marshaling yard where cars were being cranked up a hill and rolled down to their assigned track. Shivering now in the night air, they waited for the light to turn off in the point man's station. When it finally did, they sneaked out onto the tracks and checked the destinations on the side of the cars: Munich—Frankfurt—Dusseldorf—Stuttgart—Hamburg. At last, jackpot! A tank car with the STANDARD OIL torch logo and a sign that read VIA FRANCIA. They knocked on the tank—it sounded empty. They climbed up the rungs of the ladder on the side and unlocked the hatch, recoiling at the acrid smell inside.

"Wine," Robert decided.

"In a Standard Oil car?" Mike asked, sounding dubious.

"This is war. Clean it up. Reuse it."

They moved down a metal ladder and walked around inside. There was a small pool of wine in the middle of the sloped floor. Mike dipped a finger in and tasted it. "Not bad."

"Right vintage?"

"It'll do," Mike said, having another slurp.

"You've been locked up for too long."

Exhausted and hungry, they lay down under the open hatch. Robert fell asleep. Mike relived the day. Robert had saved his ass again. That morning in the station he had picked the right time to run: *I would have followed the first attempt and I'd be dead.* He tossed, turned, slurped a little more wine, and fell asleep.

A loud clang woke them. The car was rolling; they raced up the rungs and looked out. It was dawn and their car was now part of a moving train. Mike glanced at the yellow sun rising behind them and extended his arm to the right.

"Heading north, my friend," Mike said. He grabbed Robert's head and rubbed it playfully with his knuckles. They laughed. They had escaped and were heading toward France—*this war was fun.*

The train stopped often in the open countryside. It was spring and orchards were loaded with apples, peaches, and apricots. They were not perfectly ripe yet, but Robert and Mike did not mind. At every stop, they ran into the fields and came back with armfuls of fruits. The sun was warm and the country lush. Freedom was the most amazing feeling in the world.

"It's like being on vacation," Mike said from his perch on the moving car. "We should have brought bathing suits."

As if responding to his words, the train cleared a hill and suddenly provided a view of the sea. They stood on the ladder, shoulders out of the hatch with the wind in their faces. It was the Pentecost holiday and beaches were crowded with Italian families. They could see people sunning themselves, kids playing in the surf. The train swung gently. Mike pointed out a port city in the distance with cranes striking up and out like huge storks. "Genoa," he said.

"How do you know?"

"Pilots memorize a lot of maps."

"Did you fly Spitfires in the RAF?"

"Yes. That's a great airplane. It has a wide canopy, you can see 180 degrees around, which is great for dogfighting."

"Dogfighting?"

"That's when you go around and around trying to keep the enemy from getting on your tail," Mike said, twirling his fingers. Then he cocked his thumb, mimicking a gun. "You want to kill him before he kills you."

"Right," Robert said, cringing at the predicament.

"You're fucking terrified but in the thick of it the adrenaline kicks in. At times there are dozens of airplanes all buzzing around like wasps trying to sting one another." Mike looked up, reminiscing. "And after the kill, when you've watched your enemy spin down and crash, you get high. There is nothing like it. You go from being scared stiff to wanting to get back to it right away."

"I wouldn't like it," Robert said.

"I always said a prayer at takeoff and landing," Mike said. "You think you get used to it, but every time you're as scared as the time before."

"I heard about you guys," Robert said, glancing at Mike with renewed fondness. "The BBC had a program on American pilots who came to help the British when nobody else did. You liked being in the RAF?"

"Yes. Great people. Best fighters in the world. It was an honor, a great honor," Mike said, conscious those days were not always that idyllic. "There was a shortage of pilots, so we were constantly dispatched to attack enemy fighters. There were days when we never got more than three hours of sleep. We prayed for bad weather so we could sleep." Mike paused, stricken by a sudden sadness. "And of course, we prayed for all those friends who never came back."

"But you always did," Robert said.

"I was shot over France. I parachuted into the North Sea. English fishermen picked me up. I was lucky."

Robert was impressed by how Mike made it all sound so unremarkable. "What did you do before the war?" he asked.

"I went to college and worked for my father."

Robert glanced at Mike, appraising him. "Your father's wealthy?"

"He did well. Made his money selling liquor when it was still illegal."

Robert turned, really interested now. "Like Al Capone?"

"You know about Al Capone?"

"Of course I do. So, how was it?"

"My father and I were close. My mother had passed away when I was a kid. I loved that my dad was involved in bootlegging. It was nifty." Mike's face turned thoughtful. "There were bad times too. Several of my dad's friends were killed. I used to wait for him at night, standing beside my window in my room. I worried about him all the time."

"How old were you?"

"Eight, ten." Mike frowned, remembering.

"But your dad is not doing that anymore?"

"Right. When the Prohibition ended, he got into politics. He got married to a younger woman, became respectable, and had four more children." Mike smiled at the thought. "We were poor when I grew up and all of a sudden, we had maids. The summer before I enlisted, I was invited to every elegant party in town. Let me tell you, those rich kids are soft. No fight in them. I cleaned them up at poker and stole their girlfriends."

"Being the son of a gangster was more fun."

"Yes," Mike said. "My father knew it too. He said to me once, 'If Prohibition happens again, you and I are going into the bootleg business together.'"

"What did your father say when you enlisted?"

"He didn't like it. He could have stopped it, but he didn't." Mike sighed and added, "Everybody knows my father. He is an important man. If you're his son everybody thinks you're a big shot."

Robert appraised Mike. "But you wanted to be more than just your father's son?"

"Right," Mike said, surprised at Robert's sensitivity. "Anybody would."

"Not me!" Robert exclaimed, turning his face into the wind. "A rich father. Going to parties. Meeting all these girls. I'd have no problem with any of that!"

Mike laughed. "Well, what about you? You enlisted?"

"I had to get out there, my mother was about to marry me off."

"That's funny."

"Not to me." Robert positioned his fingers half an inch apart. "I was this close to end up being a shopkeeper in a shithole town up the Atlas Mountains for the rest of my life." He shivered at the thought. "Do you know Jewish people in America?" he asked.

Mike shook his head. "I grew up in an Irish neighborhood. Went to Catholic school, and I hate to say it, but the clubs we went to were closed to Jews."

"No Jewish friends?"

"You're the first one."

Robert liked that. "You're my first gentile friend."

Mike's face suddenly changed. "Get out of my way!" he cried as he quickly climbed out of the tank, scrambled down the rungs, and pulled down his pants, just in time. A stream of brown liquid splashed onto the side of the tracks.

"I told you not to drink that wine!" Robert shouted, enjoying the sight of Mike holding onto the ladder with his butt hanging over the tracks.

"It's not the wine. It's all that fruit. We haven't eaten fresh produce in months."

Suddenly Robert too felt unwell. He climbed out in a hurry and the two of them spent the evening trading places on the ladder. By nightfall, weak and exhausted, they lay down inside the car and slept.

A change in the rhythm of the wheels woke them up. The train was slowing down. Robert sprang up and looked outside; it was still night. A sign flashed by, and Robert's heart drummed in his chest. He jumped down and shook Mike.

"Limoges, we are in France!"

"How do you know?"

"*Limoges capitale de la porcelaine.* That's what the sign said."

"Limoges China, expensive stuff I hear," Mike said.

For Robert, this was an extraordinary moment. He had dreamt about France all his life. Growing up in the French colony of Algeria had been like being the illegitimate son estranged from the ancestral home. *I am in France!* Robert wanted to jump out and run and shake people's hands. Suddenly everything made sense: the post office in Algiers. The battle of Sedjenane. The hospital in Nocera. The bombing of Rome. He had been on a path to this place and now here he was. The train came to a stop on a sidetrack. It was still dark when a railway worker moved along the train, holding a swinging lantern: checking the brakes, hitting their metal plates with a hammer. *Cling—Cling—Cling . . .*

Robert jumped down on the track, frightening the man.

"Putain de merde!" *Holy shit!* he cried, hand on his heart, watching Robert, then Mike, climb out of the hatch.

"Prisonniers français?"

"Oui," Robert answered.

"Venez avec moi." *Come with me.*

Clearly, fleeing POWs were not uncommon in this train yard. The man led Robert and Mike across tracks to a workshop. He pointed at a framed picture of Maréchal Pétain on the wall and dismissed it with a rude gesture. He cranked up a wall phone and spoke into it: "Deux gosses, un français, un amerloque."

Mike looked to Robert, who translated. "Two kids, one French, one American." Robert didn't mention the man had used the slang word for *Yank.*

The railway man hung up. "Restez là." *Stay here*, he said, then shook their hands and left.

"Is he going to get help?" Mike asked.

Robert spread his hands, meaning *I hope so.*

"I'm starving," Mike said.

Robert pulled out an apple and handed it to him. Mike shook his head. He finished his wine, propped his legs on a chair, and went to sleep. Early-morning light filtered through, and Robert wanted to see more of France. He climbed onto a stool and looked out the transom. He could see a street next to the tracks lined with buildings painted bright colors—pink, yellow, green. A woman opened a window, shook out bedsheets, and left them on the railing. On a bridge over the tracks, a man rolled by riding a bicycle. *Everything is so clean and peaceful here.* But would France welcome him? Robert recalled stories about massive arrests of Jews in Paris orchestrated by the French police. A sound at the door made him jump off his stool.

"Bonjour, messieurs."

A woman wearing a French Railway uniform walked in. Her name, they would find out later, was Suzanne. After ascertaining their nationalities, she questioned Mike about life in England. What was the price of beer in pubs? His favorite brand? Did he prefer pale ale or real ale? What were bus fares in central London? Then, she turned to Robert and asked about their time as POWs in Italy. What was the name of the hospital in which they convalesced? What did it look like? Who ran it? How did they escape? When were they in Rome exactly? She seemed satisfied with their answers and Robert mentioned they hadn't had any solid food in days.

Suzanne nodded and said, "Come with me."

She guided them out of the station and led them to a commercial street with businesses still closed at this early hour. They passed by a store with a COIFFURE DAMES sign swinging above the entrance and entered the door adjacent to the shop. There, they headed along a hallway to a patio with a French door where another woman was waiting for them. Her name, it transpired, was Charlotte.

"Welcome to the finest hair salon in town," Charlotte said. An attractive woman in her late thirties, she gave them a preoccupied smile and a firm handshake when they entered her kitchen. As they would learn later, Charlotte regularly sheltered allied aviators and was Suzanne's sister.

"Il faut enlever vos vêtements de camp," Charlotte said.

"We need to get rid of our clothes from the camp," Robert translated.

They undressed, stood awkwardly in their skivvies, and were handed pants, shirts, sweaters, and jackets that fit them well enough. In the meantime, Suzanne was pulling cheese and salami out of the icebox.

Charlotte had whipped shaving cream in a bowl and was now flourishing a hand razor sporting a thin, lethal blade.

"Asseyez-vous." *Sit down*, she said, pointing at a chair by the sink.

"She's going to shave us?" Mike asked incredulously.

"Frenchmen your age don't wear beards. You stick out," Suzanne said.

After expertly sharpening the blade on the razor strop, Charlotte mixed hot and cold water in a pail. Robert elbowed Mike to go first. Charlotte draped a steaming hot towel on Mike's face and lathered his cheeks. His eyes rolled madly, following the steel blade screeching dangerously along his cheeks. When Charlotte dried Mike's face with a cloth, he rubbed his skin, surprised by how smooth it felt.

Charlotte turned to Robert and said, "Vous avez fait passer votre copain en premier, comme ça si je lui avais tranché la gorge vous vous seriez sauvé."

"She making fun of you?" Mike said.

Robert translated stoically. "I made you go first, so I could run away if she cut your throat."

"The lady's right. You're a sissy."

Robert winced at the feel of the hot towel but relaxed at the coolness of the shaving cream. At the table, Suzanne had cut thick slices of bread and made tartines with butter and saucisson. She handed one to Mike.

"Thank you," he said and began to eat ravenously.

Robert was hungry but Charlotte steered his chin away from the food and said, grinning: "Soyez patient." *Be patient.*

When she completed her task, Robert rushed to the table. There were tartines ready for him. He shoved food into his mouth and nodded a big "merci" to the women, then took a drink to push the food down.

Suzanne stood and pointed at the cellar door. "There are cots for you downstairs. A man will come tonight with ID papers. Good luck."

Suzanne kissed her sister and headed out.

That evening Charlotte came down to the cellar with a man who spoke English with a British accent and introduced himself as de Lacoste. He told them they would be smuggled aboard a convoy of French wounded POWs coming from Germany. These men were too sick to work, so the Germans sent them home. The repatriation was meant to be a show of goodwill, but for every POW sent home, two Frenchmen of military age had to go work in Germany. "La Relève," *the relief*, they called it. It was a clever ploy; healthy young men *relieving* sick prisoners of war who crowded infirmaries in POW camps.

Out of an envelope came military discharge documents and identification cards, which Charlotte attached to Mike and Robert's lapels with safety pins. Mike was told that he had been shell-shocked and had lost his ability to speak. If people talked to him, he was to show them the card pinned to his coat. Robert was handed a pair of crutches and thanks to his recent experience, had no trouble using them convincingly.

"POWs who get sick during the trip are routinely taken off these convoys and put in French hospitals before they can move on," de Lacoste explained. "Your medical papers say that you suffered from dysentery and spent two weeks in a hospital in Dijon. The nurses won't know who you are. Don't talk to French prisoners. There will likely be German informers among them."

"When is the train showing up?" Robert asked.

"Tomorrow afternoon. It'll take you to Toulouse; I'll be waiting for you there inside the terminal by the ticket counters. Good luck." De Lacoste shook their hands and left.

18

SOMEONE MUST HAVE TALKED. GESTAPO surveillance of ports was now unrelenting, and Janine had halted the smuggling of aviators aboard fishing ships. So Loïc was back to land routes. He rode his horse-drawn flatbed filled with manure, with the heat from the sun making it stink like hell. Two American aviators were hidden under the stench.

As he reached the top of a hill, he scrutinized his village—two dozen houses clustered around a church. There were three airmen hidden in the village school. De Lacoste had brought them over the night before. Loïc didn't like the man, yet he had to admit that he was good. Every month, de Lacoste deftly smuggled two and sometimes three groups of airmen across the country. Counting his two airmen on the flatbed, five Americans would be on their way to Toulouse that night.

The Gestapo was paying huge rewards to the French milice to track down allied aviators. That paramilitary organization acted as the armed wing of the Vichy regime and was just as brutal as the SS. Since the killing of the German spy in the fall, everything and everyone looked suspicious to Loïc. And today something *felt* wrong, so he brought the cart to a halt. The village looked as it always did, and then it hit him. It *looked* normal but did not *sound* normal. Today was Thursday, kids were out of school on Thursday—*they should be running around. Where are the kids?* Feeling the wagon at rest, one of the airmen lifted his head from under the manure-covered tarp. "Are we there?" he asked.

"No. Down, down," Loïc said, gesturing with his hand. The aviator's head disappeared. *Still, something wasn't right.* Loïc turned the horse around, *away* from the village. They had barely traveled five hundred yards when the roar of an engine made him look back. A black Renault had appeared at the top of the hill. Loïc reached down and pulled a Mauser handgun and a couple of candlestick German grenades. The Renault was approaching fast and came up right behind the flatbed.

Gunfire cracked. A milicien standing on the Renault's running board had fired his machine pistol into the manure. Then, bullets splintered the cart's planks and Loïc felt a burn on his right side. He slid under the bench, armed a grenade, and dropped it onto the road. It bounced between the wheels of the flatbed, rolled on the pavement and under the Renault.

Babamm!

The milicien was thrown off, riddled with fragments. The car rose several feet in the air, crashed, and caught fire. Loïc fought to rein in his horse, but the animal bucked, panicked by the explosion, tipping the flatbed into a ditch and exposing the airmen under the tarp. Loïc rolled onto the road, blood spurting from wounds on his neck and shoulder. The Renault's horn bleeped continuously. A milicien crawled out of the back and attempted to open the front door to pull the driver out, but flames were engulfing both sides of the car and the driver disappeared behind a wall of fire.

A truck pulled over and soldiers jumped out. The road, so quiet minutes before, was now alive with miliciens and German soldiers. By the flatbed, one American airman made the sign of the cross and knelt beside his comrade killed by the milicien gunfire.

A milice chief pulled a bleeding Loïc up by the hair and forced him down on his knees. "Proud of yourself, asshole? Aviators were found in the school and now every man in the village is being deported," he said, pointing at the two approaching army trucks crowded with French farmers.

They were Loïc's friends and neighbors. An older man in the back wore the tricolor mayor's scarf across his chest and WWI medal on his jacket. He saluted Loïc with two extended fingers in the shape of a *V* for *victory*.

"Courage, Monsieur le Maire!" Loïc shouted.

"Courage à toi aussi, Loïc!" the mayor answered.

When the trucks had faded in the distance, the milice chief stepped behind Loïc and shot him twice in the head.

Janine was in between patients when she received a coded telegram informing her that Loïc had been summarily executed. Leaning against her office wall, she slid down on her heels and descended into abject misery: *I recruited Loïc. I'm responsible.* Grief and self-hatred coursed through her like poison. *I convinced Turenne to finance the escape line. I brought misery to everyone I know.*

She did not share the news with her parents. That evening at dinner, Emma felt her mother's distress and insisted on sitting on her lap for the entire meal. After putting Emma to bed, Janine walked into her room, lay face down on her bed, and cried her heart out.

19

ROBERT HOPPED ON HIS CRUTCHES next to Mike as they crossed the main hall of the Limoges train station. They were escorted by Charlotte wearing a Red Cross armband. At the checkpoint Charlotte waved off the German sentries. "Croix Rouge, laissez-nous passer." *Red Cross, let us pass.* Her hatred of the Germans was monumental. The sentries moved aside. She gave them a curt nod and muttered, "Racaille."

Mike shot Robert a questioning look.

"Scum," Robert whispered.

They went through an underground passageway and up onto the departure area where they became aware of the crowd staring at the next platform. Two German soldiers were guarding a middle-aged couple. The woman was crying as her husband tried to comfort her. A frightened young man stood beside them. His suit was too small, his hair reddish blond—*a British airman.*

"Les malheureux." *Poor wretches,* Charlotte whispered, watching them.

Now French miliciens in blue uniforms were shoving their way through the crowd. Robert, Mike, and Charlotte watched as they handcuffed the pilot and slapped the woman across the face. When the husband tried to intervene, they turned on him and punched and kicked him so ruthlessly that Charlotte shouted, "Ca suffit!" *Enough!*

A milicien turned to the crowd, pointing a finger and daring the person who had spoken to step forward. In the silence that followed the hapless couple was dragged away.

"Who're those guys?" Mike whispered.

"La milice," Robert said. "Pro–German French paramilitary. They specialize in fighting the Résistance."

"Traitres et racaille." *Traitors and scum*, said Charlotte uncomfortably loudly.

The train pulling into the station was a relief. As grateful as they were for her help, Mike and Robert had grown weary of Charlotte's audible hatred of the enemy. Their papers were checked, and they climbed aboard. A nurse led them along a corridor lined with compartments crowded with sick ex-POWs on bunks stacked three high and were shown to two empty bunks. Robert lay down and fell asleep as the train departed. Mike tossed and turned. All those broken men around him brought back the memories of the base infirmary and the misery he had experienced there. He pushed those thoughts away but now the beating of the French couple at the station flashed through his mind—*you don't see how ugly this war is from the cockpit of an airplane.*

Giving up on sleep Mike stepped into the corridor and sat on a flap-seat watching nurses move in and out of the compartments, dispensing water and medicine. One of them smiled as she walked by. She had a luminous face with brown eyes under dark, shiny hair. Mike lit a cigarette and gazed out at the darkening countryside, the horizon a pink line in the distance. A movement startled him. The pretty nurse had taken the seat beside him.

"Comment ça va?" *How are you?* she asked.

Mike took a drag of his cigarette and looked away—*you're shell-shocked, remember*. The nurse checked the card on his lapel.

"Are you English or American?" she whispered.

Oh fuck! Mike thought. *Now what?*

"You smoke like in American movies," she explained in a low voice. She made sure no one was watching, then took Mike's cigarette and made a scissors motion with her fingers. "Not like this." She held the cigarette between her thumb and index finger. "Like that." She took a puff and let the cigarette dangle from her lips.

"Try it."

Mike held his cigarette as he had been shown, then let it hang casually from his lips.

"Good, now you're smoking like a true Frenchman." Then she checked Mike's right hand and turned it side to side. "I'll be right back."

She left and Mike let out a weary sigh. *She's gonna get a guard.*

But the nurse came back alone with a cotton cloth and a bottle of yellow liquid. "This is bleach to clean the stains," she explained as she scrubbed the nicotine off his fingers. "Those are a dead giveaway that you are American or British because of how you hold your cigarette."

It was taking her a while to remove the stains and Mike had never felt so awkward.

"Now, that's much better," she finally said, looking into his face.

"Thank . . . you," he muttered.

The train moved through the outskirts of a city and was slowing down. "Go inside," she whispered.

The train entered a station and came to a stop as Mike went back to his bunk. *Now she'll call the cops*, he thought, lifting the window blind and looking outside expecting to watch the nurse wave over one of the sentries on the platform. But no one got off their car. Most passengers on the platforms trudged alone. No more cheerful good-byes or happy reunions these days.

"Regarde ce qu'il y a de l'autre coté." *Look at what's on the other side*, someone said.

Mike, Robert, and several POWs stepped into the corridor and watched heavy military presence across the track. German soldiers with dogs lined up on the platform with Gestapo men in leather coats standing behind them. A freight train entered the station. It stopped opposite their windows, blocking their view of the platform. It was made up of cattle cars and the nearest were only a few feet away. They could see fingers between the planks. People were crying inside, begging for water.

"C'est qui ces gens?" *Who are those people?* someone asked.

A nurse lowered a window, and the stink of human refuse filled the corridor.

"Fermes ça tu veux!" *Close it up, will you!* someone shouted.

"There are women and children in there," Robert said.

Just then their train began to pull out of the station and rolled past all those cattle cars filled with people begging for water.

"Merde," Robert muttered as he went back to his compartment and crawled into his bunk. Those were *Jews* on that train. So the wild stories he had heard in Algeria were true. By the smell of it, those people had been in those cars for days. Where were they being taken? What would happen to them when they got there? Robert felt a surge of despair rise inside his chest. The rabbi of the synagogue in Sétif had talked about entire Jewish communities massacred in Poland and buried in mass graves. It had seemed so outlandish at the time. It still did. And yet those men, women, and children packed like animals in an endless line of cattle cars were real—victims of evil staring at him.

Mike was also shaken as he returned to his spot in the corridor—*what the hell is going on here?* In 1941 he had watched thousands of British children packed aboard evacuation trains to escape German raids in the cities. Those trains were overcrowded and chaotic but nothing like what he had just witnessed. The pretty nurse returned to the seat beside him.

"Are you an aviator?" she asked.

Mike nodded and the nurse smiled ruefully, rolling her wedding ring around her finger.

"My husband was killed last winter. American planes bombed the factory where he was working."

Mike froze. "I'm sorry."

"We lived in Saint-Nazaire. It's a port on the Atlantic coast."

"I know where that is." Even as he said it, Mike realized he shouldn't have. He had escorted bombing raids to Saint-Nazaire. There was a U-boat submarine base there and shipyards working for the Kriegsmarine.

The nurse looked up, her face showing anger and sadness. "When you release your bombs do you ever think about the people on the ground?"

Mike bit his lips. "No, we don't," he admitted. "We worry about anti-aircraft fire and hitting the target."

"But you know you kill a lot of civilians."

"We do. We do try to avoid it . . . we really try . . ."

"We hate you, you know," she said. "We scream at you when we hear your planes coming."

"I didn't know."

They were silent, then suddenly she asked, "Would you do something for me?"

"Of course."

She stood and led him to a small room stocked with medical supplies. In peacetime this was the train conductor's booth. She closed the door and turned to him, demanding. "Take me in your arms."

Mike edged away, nervous. "Are you sure?" he asked.

"Yes."

He opened his arms. She held him tight, pushed her forehead against his chest, and cried.

"Hold me closer," she said.

Mike wrapped his arms around her.

"You didn't lie to me," she sobbed. "You're an American. Americans killed my husband but now Americans are fighting to free us from the Nazis."

She buried her face in his shoulder. "When I think about Americans, I want to think about you." She took a deep breath. "Do you understand?"

Mike wasn't sure. "Yes," he said.

She wiped her eyes and stood up straight, in control again. "I have to get back. I'm getting off at the next stop. Two men are sick, I'm taking them to the hospital in Toulouse."

They walked back into the corridor where Robert was now sitting on the flap seat. "Had a good time?" he asked, not looking at Mike.

"It's not what you think," said Mike, sitting down. "Her husband was killed in an American bombing raid."

Robert sat up. "She knows who you are?"

"Yes." Mike shook his head. "She isn't gonna do anything."

"How do you know?"

"I know."

They sat silently side by side, swaying slowly with the movement of the train.

"You should have stayed in your bunk."

"I should have."

Mike pulled out a cigarette, looked at his fingers, and put the cigarette back in the pack. "She cleaned the nicotine stains off my fingers. Dead giveaway that I was American, she said."

Robert raised his head, his anger gone. "I didn't know about that."

"Neither did I."

A few minutes later, they were both asleep, Robert's head drooping against Mike's shoulder.

"Look at those men," an older nurse remarked as she passed by. "They look so hard when they're awake, but the moment they fall asleep they look like children."

An hour later the train pulled into Toulouse station. Red Cross workers on the platform helped two sick POWs step down from the car and laid them on stretchers while Mike's nurse—whose name, it transpired, was Nanette—held up their IV bottles. When Mike stepped onto the platform, Nanette wiggled her fingers at him. He raised his unstained fingers and thumbed up. She nodded and headed off alongside the stretcher-bearers.

The stationmaster blew his whistle and the train started rolling. Leaning on his crutches, Robert joined Mike and they followed the stream of passengers toward the terminal.

20

ROBERT AND MIKE HAD BEEN waiting anxiously inside the Toulouse terminal for over an hour. They had watched the POWs and the nurse drive off in a Red Cross ambulance. The station had emptied, and they felt conspicuously out of place standing next to the ticket counters where de Lacoste said he would meet them. Robert could not take it; he stepped out and spotted de Lacoste standing across the street.

"What is he doing waiting out there?" Robert wondered.

They walked out of the station and noticed several police vans lining the sidewalks. Clearly de Lacoste had not wanted to run that gauntlet. Two gendarmes pointed at Mike and Robert and waved them over.

"Soldats français?"

"Oui," Robert answered.

"Vos ordres de démobilisations." *Discharge papers.*

A gendarme stood in front of Mike and snapped his fingers.

"Tu comprends pas le français?"

Mike got that: *You don't understand French?*

Hopping sideways on his crutches, Robert stepped between Mike and the gendarme and raised his chin. "Un peu de respect pour un grand blessé ça vous arracherait la gueule?" *Would it kill you to show proper respect for a gravely wounded war veteran?*

The gendarme stood his ground and snapped his fingers. "Papiers."

Robert handed over his own papers and took an envelope out of Mike's pocket. The gendarmes checked the documents, glanced at each other, and gave them back.

"Minute."

Two plainclothes policemen stepped over. Out of the corner of his eye, Robert could see de Lacoste moving *away*. One flic took the papers, the other stood in front of Mike and read the tag on his lapel.

"Fais voir tes mains." *Let me see your hands.*

Mike stood there frozen, working hard to control his panic. *I'm shell-shocked. Don't know what he wants.* The cop grabbed Mike's wrists and checked his fingers.

"Tu fumes?" *You're a smoker?* he said.

"Tu vas nous donner des cigarettes?" *You gonna give us cigarettes?* Robert asked.

The cop ignored him. "Regardes ses mains," he told his colleague.

The other cop checked Robert's fingers. "C'est bon."

"Circulez," the cop said.

"Pas de cigarettes?" Robert called, his voice mocking as the policemen walked away.

"Don't taunt them," Mike whispered.

"Cops only respect strength."

"That was close."

"Yeah. Your nurse saved your ass." Robert leaned on his crutches, and they moved across the yard toward de Lacoste, who had raised his chin just enough to indicate they should follow him.

Despite the scare at the station, Robert soaked up the spectacle of French life. This was his first time walking through a French city. There were no natives here and you could not tell by the way people dressed whether they were rich or poor. The town was pleasant and untouched by the war. They crossed a bridge over the Garonne River and Robert could feel the cool mist created by the current. He had never seen a river so wide, nor water so green. *Water!* The vision of Jews in cattle cars begging for water speared his heart. He could feel the rage inside him. This beauty before him had a nasty underbelly. German soldiers in groups of two or three strolled around like tourists, and the cops patrolled the station—*danger was everywhere.*

De Lacoste led them into a commercial street and inside the narrow entrance to a hotel. Then he leaned over the counter and took a key from the rack. The owner sat in her kitchen reading a newspaper and didn't bother to look up.

"The lady isn't curious?" Robert said.

"If she's ever questioned, she never saw you," de Lacoste replied.

They climbed to the third floor where de Lacoste pointed at the end of the hall. "The toilets are there," he said, unlocking a door.

The room was furnished with a double bed, two chairs, and a small table upon which was a package wrapped in newspaper.

"Food for you," de Lacoste said, pointing. "Someone will come to talk to you. Except to go to the toilet, do not leave this room." He slid the key in the inside of the lock and was gone.

Robert pulled the curtain aside and looked out the window overlooking a courtyard crowded with garbage cans. "We could jump if we had to."

"And go where?"

Good question. Robert sat astride the chair and wedged his chin on top of his fists. He was away from everything he knew, in a country he had dreamt about all his life. But that deportation train had shaken him to the core.

Mike sat on the floor with his back against the wall. Robert stood and began moving back and forth. "Settle down," Mike said.

"We've got to find a way to get back to combat."

"We will." Mike slung his legs up on a chair and winced. The wound in his groin was several months old but it flared up at times.

"Put your feet up and wait till it goes away." That's how his father who had come back from the Great War with a wounded knee had dealt with it—*strong and unflappable, my father.*

Mike remembered how after enlisting he had kept the decision to himself. His father had come to his room with a bottle of Irish whiskey and glasses.

"So, you quit your job to join the Royal Air Force," Tom O'Keefe had said, filling the glasses.

Mike was impressed. "How did you find out so fast?"

"The British Consul called asking if I wanted him to hold off your papers. A rash decision maybe?"

"The RAF needs pilots. I am a good one."

They drank in silence. Mike's father looked down and swirled the whiskey in his glass. "I enlisted to fight in the Great War against my father's wishes. Now I understand how hard it was for him," he said, taking a sip. "I was expecting it anyway."

"You were?"

"You can't stand working for me."

Mike looked up, surprised. "You know that?"

"You're my son. I raised you. I know how you think."

"So, you approve?"

"Hell no!" Thomas O'Keefe growled, refilling his glass. "War's a terrible business. There'll be a time after a day's fighting when you'll want to hide in a corner and cry. Done it plenty of times myself."

They drank for a while. Thomas O'Keefe rested his elbows on his knees and looked at his son. "We've been through a lot, the two of us."

"I wouldn't trade those years for anything," Mike said.

"You were all alone when your mother passed away."

Mike winced at the memory. He was six years old, and his father was in jail.

"You and I came through, Dad," Mike said.

"We did." Thomas O'Keefe finished his drink. "Why don't you think about your enlistment for a day or two?"

"I've made up my mind, Dad."

"Yes, you have. I'll miss you, son."

"I'll miss you too, Dad."

Thomas O'Keefe stood, patted his son's shoulders, and walked to the door. Mike could see tears in his father's eyes.

Both were asleep and a knock made them jump. Mike scrambled up while Robert got off the bed and opened the door.

"Good afternoon," said the woman standing there. She shut the door and turned the lock. They stared at her in astonishment. She was young and pretty, wearing a classic summer skirt, white blouse, and dark blue blazer. She picked up a chair, moved it to the center of the room, and set her leather bag on the floor.

"My name is Janine and I need to talk to you separately. So, please, sir, stand by the window," she said to Mike. Then, setting a chair opposite hers, turned to Robert. "You sit here."

Startled and amused by how she was ordering them around, Mike and Robert did as they were told. Pulling out a notebook Janine turned to Robert and, speaking in a confidential voice, asked, "What is your name?"

"Robert Levy."

"Where were you captured?"

"Sedjenane. In northern Tunisia."

"And then?"

"We were both wounded and sent to a hospital in Italy."

"Where in Italy?"

"Nocera, south of Naples."

She made a note and raising her voice for Mike's benefit asked, "Let me see both your wounds."

Robert stood and pulled down his pants to show the deep cicatrix on his left thigh. Mike opened his shirt and exposed his chest freckled with dark red scars.

Janine tried to hide that she had always been partial to men with broad shoulders. Mike caught her appreciation, opened his shirt wide, and made a little curtsy.

Janine kept a straight face and turned back to Robert. "So, you escaped from Nocera?" she asked.

"No, we were part of a POW convoy being transferred to Germany. There was an allied raid on the train station in Rome and we escaped in the confusion."

"And then you made it all by yourselves from Rome to Limoges?" she said, a note of disbelief in her voice.

"Yes," Robert replied. "In an empty tank car."

"No food? No water?"

"We picked fruit in orchards on the way."

"That's quite a story," Janine said.

"When you got a squad of SS after your ass, you get creative."

Janine did not smile but her eyes crinkled with sympathy. "Let me talk to your friend."

Robert stood, walked to the window, and jerked a thumb over his shoulder, implying that Mike should take his place.

"That hospital in Italy, is that the one with the church across from the entrance with the two big towers?"

Mike glanced at Robert but caught himself and said firmly, "There was no church, just a chapel in the hospital."

"Then it must have been the POW hospital near the Fiat tank factory?"

"There was no factory."

"What's your name, sir?"

"Michael Thomas O'Keefe, rank Captain, serial number 0-301121."

"Where were you based, Captain?"

"I'll only give you my name, rank, and serial number," Mike said and with a sly smile added: "Geneva convention rule."

By the window, Robert rolled his eyes.

Janine watched Mike's bemused face and gave him a Gallic *pfuu.* She opened her bag, pulled out a dentist's headlamp, and set it on her forehead. "I need to examine your teeth."

"You're a dentist?" Mike asked, impressed.

"You don't have women dentists in America?"

"Not that I'm aware of," Mike said and then added, his voice gently mocking, "Don't hurt me, please."

"I won't if you are a good boy," Janine responded in the same tone.

Mike chuckled and opened his mouth. Janine checked his fillings, paying particular attention to a molar in the back.

"You were in the RAF before joining the Air Corps?"

I'm not answering that, Mike thought. Janine was so close he could smell her perfume along with plain soap and the lovely scent of her skin.

"You can close your mouth." Janine removed her headlamp and dropped it in her bag.

"How did you know I was in the RAF?" Mike asked.

"You've got a very low serial number. So, I assume you enlisted early, then one of your fillings doesn't match the others. One in the back is the work of a British dentist. A sloppy job, actually. You should get it fixed."

"You were looking for German fillings."

Janine watched Mike, gauging him, amused. "Lucky you, you don't have any."

Mike held her look. The woman's strength of character overpowered her physical attractiveness and out of nowhere he felt a disconcerting need to embrace her. A man's hug. To protect her against the whole wide world.

"I'll be back this evening. Do *not* leave this room," she said.

And she was gone. They listened to her footsteps in the corridor, a knock on another door, the whisper of a conversation, and the sound of that door closing.

"Other escapees," Robert said.

"Impressive lady," Mike muttered.

"Frenchwomen get to you, don't they?" Robert said.

"Well, yeah. They're beautiful and they keep rescuing us."

Back in the street, Janine unlocked her bicycle and rode away. The wind felt good on her face. She had been in the depths of despair since Loïc's killing but those two had lifted her spirits. Robert was resourceful and clever. He must have been the one who pulled off the escape from that deportation train. And that American pilot was brave. Enlisting in the RAF in 1940 took guts. Airmen casualties were frighteningly high at the outset of the war, but he had survived, promoted to captain even. *Don't hurt me, please,* he had said, teasing her. Cheerful and inquisitive, her husband had been like that.

Two hours later Janine was back. This time she closed the door and leaned against it.

"All right," she said. "You'll stay in Toulouse until we can get you safe passage and proper identification documents."

"We'll be staying here?" Robert asked.

"No. You'll be staying in my home. It's also our dental office. A lot of people come and go. You won't attract attention there and you'll meet my parents and my daughter. The man who picked you up at the station will be coming to get you. We need photographs for your ID papers. He'll take care of that."

She left, closing the door behind her.

Robert and Mike looked at one another. "She's hiding us in her home?" Mike asked.

"That's what she said."

De Lacoste showed up around four and led them into the city's commercial center. Kids were coming out of schools and the sidewalks were filling up with mothers and their children. To make sure they weren't being followed, de Lacoste stopped often at storefronts and checked the street in the window's reflection. In one of these store windows, Robert noticed a sign that read ENTREPRISE FRANÇAISE next to a photograph of Maréchal Pétain.

"What's that?" Robert asked.

"It means the owner is *not* a Jew," de Lacoste said.

Robert took that in and noticed that many store windows displayed the same sign. De Lacoste led them to a department store where they waited to have their pictures taken. Three German soldiers were ahead of them. They were looking at an album but could not decide what size pictures they wanted. The photographer got impatient and moved Mike and Robert ahead. It made them both nervous, but the Germans did not seem to mind.

The photographer adjusted the light and raised Mike's chin.

"I love James Cagney," he whispered and added in French, "Un petit sourire!" *A little smile!* The flash bleached Mike's face for an instant and then Robert took his place.

"Un petit sourire!"

They didn't manage much of a smile. Still the photos would do the job. They were taken back to their room and told to wait to be picked up.

Hurrying away from the hotel, de Lacoste was looking forward to his evening. With so many Frenchmen away fighting the war or being POWs in Germany, France was paradise. He had girlfriends in every city on the escape line. Along with the sex came the added benefit of a place to stay. It was safer than checking into a hotel where you were required to fill out a fiche de police—telltale forms that were delivered to police stations every morning. Out of habit, he scanned the sidewalk and a man wearing a black leather overcoat caught his eye. Only Gestapo men and French cops would dress that way on a warm day like today. De Lacoste stepped into a store and felt his heart pound in his chest as he recognized the man walking by. He had a thick neck and a boxer nose—Inspecteur Franjou, the policeman who had arrested Turenne at the Poule d'Or in Paris.

"Merde, merde, merde." De Lacoste followed Franjou, who turned at the end of the street and took a table on the terrace of the café across from the hotel where Robert and Mike were staying.

The French police know about the hotel. De Lacoste slipped through the café's side door and sat in the back. He watched Franjou order a beer and pay the waiter, who extracted change from his vest pocket. De Lacoste knew the routine—you always paid when you were served so you could leave in a hurry. De Lacoste ordered white wine and paid. Franjou's presence spelled disaster for the escape line. And it got worse. Minutes later a middle-aged man walked out of the hotel with Mike and Robert in tow. De Lacoste guessed this was Louis de Guilhem, Janine's father. On the terrace, Franjou stood, finished his beer, and followed them.

From bad to worse.

De Lacoste tagged along and it was not easy. Janine's father was checking for a tail in store windows and at times the group turned around and headed back in the direction from which they had come. Yet Franjou had an uncanny ability to predict those moves and always vanished in the nick of time. When they reached the Place du Capitole, de Lacoste realized Franjou was being led to the heart of the escape line. Louis entered a building just as Janine was coming out. Father and daughter exchanged a few words and Louis beckoned Robert and Mike inside.

De Lacoste watched Franjou take in the entire incriminating exchange. After Janine had walked away, Franjou crossed the street, read the professional plaques on the side of the building's entrance, and headed off. De Lacoste pulled out his revolver, armed it, and slid it into the pocket of his jacket. Scanning the street, he spotted a young woman who had just stepped off her bicycle and was lifting her child out of the baby seat. In a split second he was behind her. Grabbing the handlebars, he jumped on the saddle.

"What are you doing?" she cried.

"I'll bring it back!" de Lacoste yelled over his shoulder as he pedaled away.

The woman started to scream, then remembered her baby and only stamped her foot in rage as she watched her bicycle disappear. De Lacoste caught up with Franjou, who was now in the Place du Capitole heading for the velo-taxi stand. He wheeled toward him and was a few feet away when he raised the revolver in his pocket and fired through the cloth. Two dry cracking sounds rang. Franjou staggered forward and crumpled to the ground with people looking around trying to figure out where the sounds had come from. De Lacoste got off his bicycle and solicitously helped Franjou sit up.

"What happened, bud, you fell?"

"They shot me," he mumbled. His eyes wide with terror, he touched the blood coming out of his mouth. Passersby took only furtive looks before scurrying away.

"I'll give you a hand."

"Thank you," Franjou whispered.

De Lacoste leaned over, pushed his gun against Franjou's heart, and fired point-blank. The sound was muffled this time. A shudder went through Franjou's body, and he lay still. De Lacoste stood over him shaking his head.

"This man is not well," he said to a couple of women who stopped to stare at the bloody mess; then he picked up his bicycle and rode away.

Inside the apartment, Louis introduced Mike and Robert to Janine's mother Anna, who was carrying a little girl in her arms. "This is Emma," she said.

"Hello, Emma," said Mike.

Emma put her head on her grandmother's shoulder and stuck her thumb in her mouth as they traversed the tastefully furnished apartment.

"You'll be in Grandma's old bedroom," Anna said. "It might not be to your taste but at least the bed is comfortable."

Grandma's room was crowded with a canopy bed, an armoire with mirrored doors, a dressing table, and an armchair. On the wall hung a large cherrywood cross complete with a sculpture of the martyred Jesus. Anna walked to the dressing table equipped with combs and brushes and tipped up the adjustable oval mirror.

"If you want to work on your hair . . ."

It took Mike and Robert a moment to realize she was making a joke.

"Make yourself comfortable," she said, pleased with her sly humor. "We'll have dinner in a few minutes."

It had been so long since either of them had been in such elegant surroundings. Mike looked around for a place to settle and finally picked the edge of the armchair. Robert glanced at the crucifix on the wall and sat on the bed.

"Would you do it?" Robert asked.

"Do what?"

"Put your whole family in danger to save complete strangers?"

"They better be worth saving," Mike said.

The cork came out with a loud pop of a gun being discharged. Louis lifted the bottle clinched between his legs and filled the glasses, when they heard the front door opening and closing.

"*Maman!*" Emma left Anna's arms and ran to the hallway.

Janine came into the room, embraced Emma, kissed both sides of her face with utmost affection, and picked her up.

Moved by the mother-daughter tenderness, Mike became shy and looked at his hands.

"Something happened on the place du Capitole," Janine said, taking a seat. "The police are everywhere."

Emma wriggled in Janine's arms and pointed at Mike.

"Papa."

"Non, ma chérie." She pointed up. "Papa est au ciel." *Daddy is in heaven.*

Anna bit her lips. Louis concentrated on pouring the wine and passing out the glasses. Mike and Robert exchanged an uneasy glance.

"To freedom," Louis said, holding his glass aloft.

"To freedom," everyone answered, clinking glasses and taking a sip.

The dinner conversation was in French. Robert got tired of translating and Mike was left to his own thoughts and was free to fixate on Janine sitting across from him.

Half amused, half flustered, Janine could feel the radiance of Mike's interest. *Just another handsome aviator*, she thought.

After dinner Emma lifted the piano lid and with two fingers played the first few notes of "Twinkle, Twinkle, Little Star."

Mike looked up. "May I?" he asked, indicating the keyboard.

"Of course," Louis said.

Janine shook her head—*not a good idea*—but Mike was already beside Emma. He finished the melody and began playing Irish lullabies. Emma put a thumb in her mouth and swayed to the music. When it ended Emma elbowed him and said, "Une autre." *Another one.*

And Mike played "Minnie's Yoo Hoo." Emma knew that one and followed along. Janine rose and stood by the piano. She watched Mike's fingers fly across the keyboard and couldn't help wondering what those strong, beautiful hands would feel like, not pounding those keys, but on the small of her back. The second Mike finished the piece, Janine pushed away the longing and hoisted Emma up from the bench.

"Encore! Juste une autre!" the little girl protested. *One more!*

"It's way past your bedtime, young lady."

Mike turned on his bench and with the others watched mother and daughter disappear down the corridor.

Robert was in bed fast asleep. It was night outside and Mike had heard Janine's parents move to their room a while ago. Glancing into the hallway he could see light coming from the dining room. Janine was still up. Mike put an unlit cigarette between his lips and bravely headed down the corridor.

With her elbows on the table and resting her chin on one hand, Janine was smoking and reading patients' charts. She looked up as Mike walked in.

"Sorry to bother you. I'm out of matches," Mike said, forcing a smile.

Janine handed him her cigarette. Surprised by the intimacy of the gesture, Mike lit his own from the burning tip and gave it back.

"You can't sleep?" Janine asked.

"Nope," Mike said, taking a seat.

"Same here. The war has made an insomniac out of me."

"Your daughter has a great ear for music." Mike pointed at the piano.

"Yes, and if I had let her, you'd still be at it. You play beautifully, by the way."

"My father taught me those lullabies when I was a kid."

"A good man, your father."

And they sat there smoking, barely mindful of one another. Mike was intimidated. This woman was tough, fighting for her country in very dangerous ways, and at the same time gentle and warmhearted.

"From what I could make out during dinner, I gather your husband passed away," Mike said in a reserved way.

"Yes. He was a pilot in the French Air Force. Shot down two months before Emma was born. Now she thinks every new man who shows up is her father. I miss him very much."

"That must have been a difficult time. I'm sorry."

Janine nodded a thank-you and looked up. "What about you? Are you married?"

Mike shook his head. "I guess I haven't met the right woman yet."

Janine took a long look at him and smiled. Then she leaned over, stubbed out her cigarette in the ashtray, and asked, "How much longer will this war go on, you think?"

"The Allies are in Sicily. Landing in Europe will happen next year. Lots of fighting still ahead of us, though."

"It'll get a lot worse before it gets better."

"Yes. But we will prevail." Mike nodded forcefully. "We'll obliterate those Nazi sons of bitches."

Janine picked up tobacco from a pouch, deftly rolled a cigarette, and borrowed Mike's to light hers. "I like your optimism."

Again, Mike appreciated the intimacy of the gesture. They sat there in silence as if they had known each other forever. The cuckoo clock striking the hour shook them out of their reveries.

Janine gathered her files and stood. "I've got patients early in the morning but you . . . you can sleep late," she said, squeezing his shoulder as she passed.

She was gone and Mike remained there, her gentle touch still flaring through his body.

The next day, Janine came to Mike and Robert's room and explained that they would be leaving for Spain in a few days. Two girls would meet them at the train station and take them to Pau, a city in the foothills of the Pyrenees. Janine handed them their identification papers complete with the photographs that had been taken the day before.

"Also, we'll get you new clothes."

"What's wrong with the ones we have?" Mike asked.

"If someone notices that you are wearing the same shirts and jackets in the ID pictures, they'll know that your documents were recently made."

Mike was impressed. "So many ways to get caught."

"Survival is all in the details," Janine said.

Mike looked at her and understood with a sudden tightening of his chest that Janine was much more than a helper. "You're running this whole escape line?" he said, immediately realizing he shouldn't have asked.

Janine did not answer, did not even look at him, just mentioned that security controls had suddenly increased in the city and their departure might be delayed.

That evening, after he had played lullabies for Emma and everyone had gone to sleep, Mike hoped that Janine had stayed up. He found her reading in the dining room. She looked up as he walked in. "Out of matches again?" she asked, poking fun at his excuse from the night before.

"No. I just enjoy your company."

Feeling a flush rising on her cheeks, Janine took a drag of her cigarette. "I do too."

Mike nodded with pleasure. "Why have security controls increased all over the city?"

"The police are on edge. A policeman member of the special brigade fighting the Résistance was shot on the Place du Capitole yesterday."

Eyebrows rising, Mike took that in. "There is a *special* police unit fighting the Résistance?"

"Yes."

"And the underground is killing those cops?"

"As many as they can, yes."

Mike tilted his head, remembering his childhood days and the mob killings in the streets of Chicago. "What about those miliciens? They look pretty nasty."

"They go after them also. We're in the middle of a civil war," Janine said, waving the cigarette smoke away in front of her face. "Tell me, how is life in London with all the bombings?"

"German air raids killed thousands and leveled entire blocks, but people never complain, never lose faith. They've even managed to keep their sense of humor."

"That is real strength."

"It's survival. You can't get up in the morning and look at British weather without wanting to kill yourself or make a joke. So, people with a sense of humor have multiplied while the others have sunk into despair and disappeared."

"The law of evolution at work," Janine chuckled.

"Right," Mike said, pleased to have managed to cheer her up. "Could I borrow a smoke?"

Janine pushed her tobacco pouch across the table and laughed watching Mike fail miserably at spreading the loose-leaf tobacco on the thin sheet of paper.

"Let me help you," she said, filling the paper with tobacco, moistening the shiny edge with her tongue, and rolling the cigarette.

"You're good at this."

"Practice makes perfect."

Mike smiled, lit up, and they were silent again. How would it feel to hold such a woman in your arms, he wondered. She could not be seduced, but after she had made up her mind, she'd be the most single-hearted lover.

"Where are you from in America?" Janine asked.

"Chicago."

"Do you have family there?"

"Yes. My mother passed away when I was young. My dad remarried. He's got young kids. I've got three half brothers and sisters."

"How old were you when you lost your mother?"

"I was six," Mike said, forcing a smile. "Yesterday, when you came home, you were so tender with your daughter. You reminded me of my mother."

Janine smiled but Mike detected private worries somewhere in her smile. "Was your mother sick?"

"She caught pneumonia. She was in the hospital, and I went to see her every day after school. One afternoon, the nurse came out of her room and told me my mother was dead," Mike said, taking a long drag of his cigarette.

"Your father wasn't with you?"

"Nope." A sad smile etched along Mike's lips as he ran his fingers through his hair. "I wanted to kiss my mother one last time, but the nurse wouldn't let me. The bedsheet had already been pulled over her head."

"And you were so young." Janine blew some smoke and added in a low voice, "Emma's dad was gone before she was born."

A smile passed between them. A sense of fellowship, and Mike felt again an overwhelming need to take her in his arms.

"Do you miss home?" Janine asked.

"A bit. But I'm glad to be fighting." Mike hesitated but went on. "Robert and I are eager to get back to combat but we wonder if we could be of help to the Résistance here?"

"No," Janine said firmly, stubbing her cigarette. "Get back to the Air Force." And with a smirk added, quoting him: "We need you to obliterate those Nazi sons of bitches."

Mike watched Janine, feeling those dark eyes could read his every thought. Glancing at the cuckoo clock, he asked: "Patients early in the morning?"

"Yes," she said, moving around the table and as she had done the night before, squeezing his shoulder as she passed. "Try to get some sleep."

21

NICOLE AND LUCILE HAD LITTLE in common. One had been raised in a working-class family in a modest provincial town; the other came from Paris and a more bourgeois upbringing. What they shared was an intense hatred for French collaborators.

Nicole was eighteen; she had recently graduated from secretarial school and began applying for positions in business and administration. A few months before, through a relative in the Résistance, she had joined the escape line and started escorting allied airmen across France. Her father was prisoner of war in Germany and her mother had taken a German officer as a lover. Nicole was outraged by her mother's betrayal. The relationship between the two was so strained they barely spoke.

Lucile had barely recovered from spending two hellish nights in the basement of the Renseignements Généraux office in Paris. Police inspectors had raped her repeatedly while she could hear the screams from Turenne being interrogated a few doors down. The ordeal had transformed her. She had been a prostitute since she was sixteen, but no more. The day after she was released, she shortened her hair, trimmed her nails, stopped wearing makeup, and dressed as ordinarily as she could. The Résistance provided her new identity papers and she moved to Toulouse where she was put in touch with Nicole.

Lucile was vague about her past and only mentioned that someone she had worked for in the Résistance had been arrested and she needed to get away from Paris.

Nicole had less to hide. Her mother was a slut, she missed her father dearly, and when the German officer spent the night, she left the house early so she wouldn't have to run into him in the morning. The man brought over coffee, chocolate, and brandy to the house, but Nicole refused to touch any of it.

"Coffee, chocolate, and brandy! Are you crazy? Steal the stuff," Lucile said when she heard. "You can resell it for a fortune on the black market."

They laughed. Nicole could feel shrewdness in Lucile and found it reassuring. Their first mission together would take place the following Sunday and they went about the business of escorting allied airmen across France. It was not easy, even odd at times. You had to pretend to be the aviator's girlfriend. You made much of him, held his arm, and kissed him on the cheek but you couldn't talk. Even if they spoke a little French, their accent was so bad it could get you both arrested. But this was how Nicole had chosen to fight, honor her father, and rebuff her mother.

"Any of those airmen good-looking?" Lucile asked with a grin.

"Some are," Nicole said. "You feel how strong they are although they rely on you completely. I took a really handsome one once; I wanted to ask him a million questions but there was no way. It's an act. You pretend knowing them, but they are complete strangers. That's the part I hate the most." She shrugged and left it there.

"And we have to keep an eye out for the police," Lucile said, the memory of her sojourn at the Renseignements Généraux basement in Paris fresh in her mind.

"Always watch out for men who are well dressed," Nicole said.

Janine, Mike, and Robert hurried through the rainy streets of Toulouse when the bells of the cathedral announced the end of morning Mass. Parishioners streamed out of the church and the three found themselves caught in a sea of umbrellas. They reached the station and stood on the bridge across from the entrance. Janine kissed Robert and turned to Mike, who put a hand on her arm. She was about to say something, but he spoke first.

"When the war is over, I'll come back for you," he said, his voice thick with emotion. Then he reached out; her coat was half open and he zipped it up for her.

A tender gesture. Janine gave him a certain look—*I'll never see you again, but that's kind of you to say.* She raised her face, put a hand on Mike's cheek, and kissed him on the lips. "Watch yourself, Captain," she said tenderly. Then she turned around, crossed the street, and disappeared.

Robert and Mike took a table on Le Café de la Gare's terrace and paid for drinks with money Janine had given them. They knew she would be watching until they had made contact with their guides. It did not take long. Two girls wearing colorful spring dresses under raincoats approached their table, smiling shyly. "Robert, Michel?" they asked.

"Oui," Robert said.

They stood and Nicole and Lucile kissed them.

"You are French?" Nicole asked Robert, who nodded.

"Tu as fait bon voyage?" Lucile asked Mike.

"Oui," Mike answered, agreeing to whatever she'd said.

"Come with me," Nicole said, taking Robert's arm.

They walked to the ticket window where Nicole purchased tickets. She carefully counted her change before dropping it in her coin purse. As they headed back, she caught Robert glaring at the German guards patrolling the station's main floor.

"Don't worry about the Germans. It's the French we've to watch out for."

"French police?"

"And French informers. The Germans pay them rewards. They're everywhere," Nicole said. She motioned to Lucile and the four of them crossed the main hall. Lucile held Mike's arm and talked, handling both questions and answers. Mike could not understand most of it but got into the spirit of the masquerade.

"Seems like she's known him forever," Robert said, watching the performance.

"It's her first trip. She is nervous."

Robert watched Nicole closely, observing how she checked people on the platform and led them away from those she deemed treacherous, mainly men wearing suits—possibly police detectives.

They boarded the train and found an empty compartment. As soon as the train began to roll, Lucile opened a paper and started to read. Mike sat upright, lost in thought, reminiscing about Janine's kiss on his lips—*watch yourself, Captain.*

Nicole and Robert chatted. She said little about herself, but did mention that she had applied for a secretarial position in Pau, the city they were headed to. He liked Nicole's thick brown hair gathered off her forehead, her striking oval face, and her mouth always close to a smile. He was disappointed when she pulled out a book. He would have preferred to get to know more about her but understood her caution. The less he knew, the better. So he turned to the scenery. He still couldn't get enough of France—the lushness of the countryside, the villages and farmhouses so well maintained. He had left Algeria only four months ago, but it now seemed to belong to another life with no connection to his present existence. They arrived in Pau in the early afternoon. The girls led them away from the control line and through the platform entrance of the Café de la Gare.

They moved past pool tables and the bar and stepped into the station courtyard without passing the controller.

"The fewer people see us, the better," Nicole told Robert.

Outside, the air was warm. Pau was a lovely town lush with greenery and flower gardens. They walked across an avenue lined with palm trees that reminded Robert of Algeria. He glanced at Nicole—*I'd like to live here with her.* Irritated at himself, he snorted a tense chuckle—*tomorrow you'll be in Spain.*

They boarded a funicular that took them three hundred feet up to the Palais des Pyrenees. Though it was late spring, the mountains, clearly visible in the distance, were still covered with snow.

"Freedom's on the other side," Mike said, staring at the view.

"A hell of a fence," Robert replied.

They headed toward the center of town. Streets became crowded, and Nicole turned even more vigilant. With a quick gesture she told Lucile that she and Mike should walk a few paces behind.

Nicole's words resounded in Robert's head: *Don't worry about the Germans. It's the French we've to watch out for.* Sensing Robert's unease, Nicole briefed him—the rendezvous point was the Café Navarre on Place Reine Marguerite. If something went wrong, they should get back to that café. As they walked along, she pointed out streets and monuments so Robert would remember how to get there.

Lucile, hanging on Mike's arm, had resumed her chatting. *These girls are risking so much to save us,* Mike thought, remembering the French couple caught with the British airman in the Limoges train station and how the milice had beaten them up. How many girls back home would take a chance like this? he wondered.

Prosper waited on tables on the terrace of his café. He was in a good mood. He had learned that the blind pilot he had smuggled into

Spain aboard a gasoline truck was in a hospital in Gibraltar and would recover his sight. He swung his dishtowel over his shoulder and, spotting Nicole, swiped the top of an empty table. They took seats. Still on his guard Robert leaned back in his chair and took in the friendly atmosphere of southern France—*this place is beautiful, but informers are everywhere*. Mike grinned at Robert and opened his hands—*we're on vacation again*.

Prosper set glasses and a water carafe on the table. "Take them to the bus station at the Palais des Pyrenees and put them on the three o'clock Transports Palois Réunis bus to Mauléon and report back to me." Then he slipped a couple of berets to Nicole. "Make sure they wear those."

Mike's eyes lit up when he saw the carafe. He filled his glass and drank the contents in one gulp. Prosper shivered. "Only Americans drink that much water. Even in the trenches in the middle of winter."

On the way to the bus station Robert learned that the town of Mauléon was twelve miles from the border. There, they would meet guides who would smuggle them to Spain. Nicole pulled out the well-worn berets and the girls enjoyed fitting them on their companions' heads at exactly the right slant. At the bus station every man wore a beret like theirs. Farmers stood around the red bus talking and laughing. When the driver spotted Nicole, he glanced at the German sentries standing on the sidewalk, pointed at Robert and Mike, and snapped his fingers.

"Pas de bagages, montez. Mettez vous au fond." *No luggage, get in the back of the bus.* And to Nicole he whispered, "C'est dangereux. Tires toi." *It's dangerous. Get out of here.*

The girls kissed Robert and Mike and wished them good luck. The bus was still empty. They moved to the back and sat down.

"These girls have more balls than lots of men I know," Mike said, watching Nicole and Lucile walk away.

The bus filled up. A priest came aboard accompanied by two men, both tall with dark blond hair, clearly allied airmen who like them had been attired with berets. Farmers' wives climbed aboard, pushed bags onto the racks, and took their seats. Robert nodded to the farmer sitting next to him. The man nodded back and looked away. *He knows who I am.*

The two German sentries took the seats behind the driver. The bus started and at first Robert and Mike sat stiffly staring at the soldiers' backs but after a while they got used to their presence. The bus stopped often, and as they went on, it emptied slowly. After an hour or so they stopped in front of a village church where the priest exited along with his airmen.

Back in Pau, disaster was in the making. Nicole and Lucile had returned to the Café Navarre and found it surrounded by miliciens keeping a crowd of onlookers at bay. Feeling tentacles of fear spread inside her, Nicole worked her way through the crowd. She could hear the miliciens inside the café smashing glass and wrecking the place. She stood there transfixed as now furious shouts resonated and an incensed Prosper was walked out in handcuffs and pushed into a car.

Nicole recoiled with fright while feeling a hand pulling her back. It was Lucile whispering, "Let's get out of here."

Later that afternoon, the girls were on the train back to Toulouse. Nicole was in shock. She had delivered quite a few airmen to Prosper. He was a good man. He knew about her mother and had offered to help her find a job in Pau. "What are they going to do to him?" she worried.

Lucile was reflecting on her attempt to live a normal life but had been quickly reminded there was no way to escape this war. "If we had arrived half an hour later, we would have been caught," she said.

Nicole winced; she had not even thought of that. At least Mike and Robert were far away by now. And the thought of Robert made her sigh—talking to him had felt good. He was a good listener, and she was pleased by how he memorized her instructions and kept an eye on how she navigated the streets. She could tell he was impressed and wanted to know more about her. Suddenly, looking at Lucile, Nicole said, "You're right, we could have been caught today." Then, she looked away, trying to keep her thoughts to herself, but finally asked, "Do you have a boyfriend?"

Lucile smiled. "Not at the moment, no." Then added, wanting to tell a little bit of the truth, "But yes, I've had boyfriends, you?"

Nicole shook her head. "All the boys my age are fighting in the war or prisoners in Germany."

Out in the country, the bus had stopped at a crossroads and the driver signaled to Robert that he and Mike that they should get off and they did. There was not a house in sight. They watched the bus roll away and sat on the grass at the edge of a cornfield.

"What if no one shows up?" Mike asked.

"We start looking for fruit trees."

Mike cocked his thumb at the field behind them. "There's corn right there."

"French people don't eat corn. That's animal feed."

"I'm American. I'll eat anything."

"Here comes our savior."

They got on their feet as a farmer riding a tandem bicycle and holding the handlebar of a second bike wheeled over. It was a difficult way to ride but the man was good at it. He pushed the bike toward Mike, who caught it.

"Put these on," he said, handing out pant clips.

After they had fastened the clips around their pant cuffs, Mike mounted the bicycle and Robert climbed onto the tandem behind their guide. At first pedaling was easy but soon the road began to climb, and Mike started puffing and sweating. Robert had the advantage of sharing the effort with the guide, and he called to Mike, "You smoke too much. You should get some exercise instead of sitting in a plane all day long."

"Fuck you."

Farms dotted the landscape. The bells on the sheep and cattle roaming the verdant pastures echoed in the distance. An hour later they rolled down a hill and took a side path, bounced on uneven terrain, and reached a barn at the edge of a pine forest.

"Bicycle fini," their guide said.

"About time," Mike said as he slipped off the saddle rubbing his butt.

The guide led them inside the barn. A young couple stood in alarm as they entered. The man was perhaps thirty, his wife younger. They looked prosperous and were dressed for an excursion in stirrup pants and hiking boots. The woman wore a long coat, which she kept on despite the warmth. They exchanged a few words. The couple was Dutch, from Rotterdam—*Jews*, Robert thought.

The man left with his bicycles and a new guide arrived. He had the distinctive features of the Basque with high cheekbones and olive skin. The two blond airmen who were on the bus with the priest were with him. When Mike moved to shake their hands, the Basque guide stood in the way and grunted a short speech, which Robert translated.

"They are Canadians but the less you know the better. Don't exchange names. Don't try to find out where you are. When you get to Spain, you can talk all you want." The guide went on and Robert kept translating. "He's the boss. If you can't keep up, he'll leave you behind and get you on his way back. The hills are patrolled by Grenzschutz and Gebirsjager—troops from Austria, experts at mountainous terrain. Noise is our biggest enemy. Do not talk and walk as silently as possible."

Night fell and the temperature dropped precipitously. The path narrowed and began to climb. An hour later, thirsty and gasping for air, they stopped to drink from a stream and refilled their bottles. In a whisper, the Dutch woman asked how long they would have to keep climbing. The guide responded that they were still in the foothills and had not yet reached the mountains. Then he herded them back on the trail.

Later they reached a farm, and the guide went ahead alone. They sat on the ground and stretched their sore muscles. Mike took off his shoes and massaged his feet. Robert glanced at the Jewish couple. The woman looked exhausted, and her husband helped her lie down. Her coat fell open and Robert realized she was pregnant. She caught his look and gave him a pleading glance, putting a finger on her lips. Robert reassured her with a nod. *She'll never make it*, he thought.

The guide returned and led them to a barn next to the farmhouse. They had become so sensitive to noise that when the door creaked, they all cringed. A man came to them from inside. He held a flashlight with his hand over the lens, letting a few pink rays filter through his fingers. Their eyes got used to the darkness and soon they could make out people sleeping in the hay.

The man pointed to a ladder leading to a hayloft. Robert, Mike, and the Canadians climbed up. The Jewish couple found room downstairs. The woman curled up and her husband put his coat on top of her.

Mike and Robert were falling asleep amid the ambient snoring when the guide's head popped up. "Who was in Tunisia?" he asked.

They raised their hands, and the guide beckoned them over. They wanted nothing but sleep but followed him across the yard to the farmhouse. Inside they shook hands with the farmer, his wife, and their two daughters and son, who were all sitting around the fireplace.

"Please sit," said the farmer. He and his son stood, gave up their chairs, and pulled over stools. The older daughter handed them cups of hot chicory with milk and frangipane, a soft cake sprinkled with sugar.

"Maybe you'd rather have wine?"

"No, this is good," Robert said.

Mike and Robert drank their chicory and ate their cakes. The fire felt good on their faces. When they'd finished eating, the daughter brought them fresh slices.

"You were in Tunisia," the farmer said.

"Yes."

"Our sons are in North Africa."

The youngest daughter stood and came back with two framed photographs, which she handed to Robert and Mike.

"This is Oscar, and this is Ernest."

Young men, wearing Foreign Legion uniforms, with strong faces like their father. Robert could see that the photographs had been taken in a studio in Pau just before they shipped overseas.

"Maybe you met them?"

As Robert translated, they realized that the whole family had stayed up to ask *that* question. They looked at the pictures, carefully this time. They could feel their hosts' anxiety thick in the air. Mike shook his head.

"I'm sorry but we don't know them," Robert said.

"Ernest was in Syria and joined the Free French. He fought in Libya and in Tunisia. How was it when you were there?"

"It was pretty bad in February and March," Robert admitted.

The son now spoke up. "One of Ernest's friends was wounded and sent home. He told us that Ernest was in Bizerta at the end of April."

"Then his chances are good," Robert said eagerly, glad to share the positive news. "The Germans surrendered there in May."

"Are you sure?" the wife asked.

"Yes."

The farmer pulled out a month-old newspaper. "It says in here that Rommel's army is regrouping for a new attack."

"Regrouping is the word the Germans use for retreat. They surrendered on May ninth in Tunisia," Robert said. It did not mean that their son was alive, but it gave them hope.

"Oscar was in Oran."

Mike recognized the town's name and jumped into the conversation.

"I was there. Good place."

All present turned to Mike.

"We were told American troops shot French soldiers," the mother said.

"That's ridiculous. Don't listen to German propaganda," Mike said with Robert translating. "Foreign Legion troops gathered in Oran while I was there. They joined the American Fifth Army."

"The British Navy killed thirteen hundred French sailors at Mers-el-Kébir in 1940," the mother said. "We saw the photographs in the papers. That was not propaganda."

"The English were our allies and they massacred French sailors. The Americans could do it too," the son said.

"No, no, no!" Mike said, shaking his head in frustration. "This could never happen."

"There were no executions of French soldiers?" the father asked.

Robert could feel Mike's anger rising. He was speaking softly but a blue vein had risen on the side of his neck. He straightened up and looked the farmer in the face.

"I'm a captain in the United States Air Force. I give you my word of honor that no American troops would ever be involved in the killing of surrendering French soldiers."

Robert translated and the mother twisted her apron between knotted fingers and stared at Mike, fervently hoping he was telling the truth. Her eyes swelled, she turned to her family and made the sign of the cross. Her husband and children followed suit and their voices rose.

"Je vous salue Marie pleine de grâces, le seigneur est avec vous . . . Bienveillance de Dieu pour les hommes."

Mike joined in, "Hail Mary, full of grace, the Lord is with thee . . ."

They looked at him with astonishment, exchanged startled glances, and resumed praying, all feeling viscerally connected by the invocation.

"Vous êtes bénie entre toutes les femmes. Et Jésus, le fruit de vos entrailles, est béni."

"Blessed art thou among women. And blessed is the fruit of thy womb, Jesus."

It was the same prayer, the same rhythm only in different languages.

"Sainte Marie, Mère de Dieu, priez pour nous pauvres pécheurs, maintenant et à l'heure de notre mort. Amen."

"Holy Mary, mother of God, pray for us sinners, now and at the hour of our death. Amen."

If Mike's pledge had not convinced them, the shared prayer had. The farmer stood and gave them both a happy, piston-like handshake. They could feel that he wanted to embrace them but did not dare. The boy also shook their hands, and the women kissed them, moistly, on each cheek.

As they were about to leave, the mother wrapped the rest of the cake and gave it to Robert. She took Mike's hand and looked at him, her eyes brimming with tears.

"Je vous crois, Monsieur le Capitaine, merci."

"She believes you and she thanks you," Robert translated.

Back in the barn, Robert mulled over how Mike had recited a Catholic prayer with those farmers. It was a bond he wished he could share. He tried to recite the Birkhat HaGomel, the blessing said after surviving danger or captivity. But "Barukh ata Adonai Eloheinu, melekh ha'olam . . ." was all he could remember before he fell asleep.

Robert woke up with a start. It was still dark. He had heard something. Or not. Maybe it was just his stomach bothering him. He listened intently but could not pick up anything above the snoring. He crawled over to the hay-loading door that slid sideways and squealed as he inched it open. Robert stuck his head out. The mountain ridges were visible against the dark sky. Not dawn yet, but he could feel it coming. For a moment, he was back in the mountains of Kabyle with his shepherd friends who always slept with one eye open, on alert for sheep and cattle thieves. Robert concentrated but all he could hear was the pounding of his heart. *La boule à l'estomac*—still the knot in his stomach was winding tighter. Something was wrong. That sixth sense wired into his gut had never failed him. He moved back inside and shook Mike awake. "Let's go," he said.

Mike groaned. "Don't you ever fucking sleep?"

"Something's not right."

Mike sat up and rubbed his eyes. He had never seen Robert so anxious. "You want to wake up the others?"

"No time."

Robert moved to the loading door and leaped out. Mike followed. They ran to a cornfield with stalks rising higher than their heads. The earth was soft, and they advanced stealthily between the rows.

"Where are we going . . . ?"

Robert put a hand on Mike's mouth. They could hear the soft shuffling of the wind stroking the corn stems—*except there was no wind.* Shrieking birds rose from the field and rustled up into the brightening sky. Robert pulled Mike down in a furrow. The shuffling got closer and then *they knew*. They *heard*, rather than saw, boots marching toward them two rows to the right and one row to the left—German soldiers combing the cornfield walked right by them. After they shuffled away, Robert and Mike crawled to the end of the furrow and up the embankment. In the strengthening light, they now could see a black sedan and two army trucks rumbling up the unpaved road toward the farm. Miliciens exited the car and pointed at the buildings. A loudspeaker barked and all hell broke loose.

Soldiers jumped out of the trucks and kicked down doors. Within seconds the farmer and his son had been separated from the women, pushed against a wall, and shot. The rattle of machine-gun blasts echoed in the hills. From their perch, Robert and Mike could see that the soldiers had small frames and Asian features.

"Cossacks," Mike said.

In the farm's courtyard the Basque guide spun around a hay cutter and rammed it into a group of soldiers, impaling three of them on the rusty blades. Then he fired his pistol and wounded a couple more before falling under a hail of bullets. The Cossacks were enraged. They rifle-butted the escapees into the yard, separated the airmen from the others, and beat the civilians. The pregnant Jewish woman and her husband were kicked mercilessly. She went down on her knees, vomiting blood. Flamethrowers came to life. The Cossacks set the buildings on fire and ran into the burning barn to free the cows and sheep. As the frightened animals ran for the fields, the Cossacks machine-gunned them, laughing uproariously. The farmer's wife sat beside her dead son and took his head in her arms. The daughters cried as they cleaned the blood from their dead father's face.

Soldiers now dashed to the edge of the field to slaughter the few surviving sheep. Loud cheers accompanied each kill. Mike and Robert lay on a ridge overlooking a path. A soldier ran below them and stopped. They could hear him chuckle to himself. The Cossack's delight triggered a murderous rage in Robert—*that bastard.*

Mike turned and realized Robert was sprinting toward the Cossack. The man swung around a second before Robert slammed into him. They rolled in the dirt. Robert's hands clenched his throat, digging his nails into the flesh, strangling him. Another Cossack appeared. Mike leaped onto his back and brought him down. The man was so scared he soiled himself, sobbed, and begged. Mike hit him in the face with a rock and kept on hitting until the head was a bloody mass of flesh and bones. He stood and threw the rock away as the stink of warm blood, sweat, and shit hit him all at once.

He leaned against a tree and threw up. Then, overcoming his repulsion, he seized the soldier's gun, ammunition, and grenades and ran to Robert, who was still on top of his man. The Cossack was slobbering profusely but Robert kept squeezing until he was certain he was dead. "The prick was laughing," he said, wiping the man's saliva off his hands and onto the soldier's uniform.

"We've got to get out of here," Mike said, grabbing Robert's shoulders and helping him up. Gunfire from the soldiers shooting the sheep was still crackling in the distance. Mike removed the Luger from the soldier's holster and collected clips of ammunition. "Take that." He pushed the gun inside Robert's belt and stuffed cartridges in his pocket.

"That was stupid," Robert said, looking at the mangled bodies. "They'll find them and come after us."

"What's done is done. Payback for killing those farmers."

The smell of ashes and smoldering wood followed them as they raced through a beech forest. They reached a clearing and stopped to catch their breath, fighting the stitches in their sides. In between the trees they could still see the burning farm. A German ambulance had arrived, and medics were working to free a man from the hay cutter blades. They could hear him screaming.

They found a trail and followed it. Now below them, a horse-drawn fire engine was climbing up toward the burning farm while the miliciens' car and the German trucks and ambulance rolled down.

They reached a stream. Robert knelt on its bank and rubbed his hands with mud. "I've got that bastard's blood under my nails," he said, smelling his fingers. He scooped another large dollop of mud and scrubbed some more. Finally satisfied, he rinsed his hands and face. "I lost my mind. Good you got me out of there."

"Got pretty riled up myself," Mike said, washing his hands and face. Then he stood and looked toward the rising sun, orienting himself. "Spain is south."

Robert tilted his head toward the farm below. "That's the direction they'll expect us to take."

Appreciating Robert's shrewdness, Mike nodded. *North then.*

When they reached another clearing, they took a last look at the place where they had killed and nearly been killed. All that remained was white smoke rising above the ruins. They continued trudging north. All around them cows and sheep grazed in pastures. At midday they reached a paved road. They followed it downhill until they arrived at a crossroads where three people waited. Next to them a road sign read: PAU 21 KM.

"Are you waiting for the bus to Pau?" Robert asked.

They nodded. They were middle-aged locals—two men and a woman. Robert noticed the way they glanced at him—*they know who we are.*

The bus pulled over and the driver rolled the door open from inside. This was not the same driver as the day before, but again two German soldiers sat behind him in the front seats. Expecting the worst, Robert and Mike climbed onto the bus—*all they have to do to get reward money is to call the guards.* Nothing happened. The locals took their seats. Robert paid their fare with the last of the money Janine had given him and pushed Mike toward the rear as far away as possible from the sentries.

Back in Pau they walked to the Café Navarre. It was closed and guarded by miliciens. Robert questioned bystanders and learned that Prosper Navarre had been arrested and taken to Toulouse. The Germans were looking for two terrorists, one Jewish, the other American. It was rumored they had made it to Spain and the Guardia Civil was looking for them on the other side of the border. When Robert told Mike what he had learned, Mike gave a rueful laugh.

"Yesterday we were with pretty girls on vacation. Today we're on the most wanted list."

They had no contacts and very little money and soon they would be hungry again. The ravenous curse, Mike called it. In normal times you did not think much about food; in wartime you became obsessed with it. Hunger could torment you, weaken you, and kill you as efficiently as a well-placed bullet. They returned to the bus station to try to find the driver from the day before. Robert talked his way into the office of the Transports Palois Réunis and found the room where drivers and conductors waited for their shift. Their man was not there. Not knowing what else to do, the morning massacre playing over and over in their mind, they walked.

"I hate this goddamn town," Mike said.

"It's a beautiful place."

"That's the problem. If it were ugly, at least it'd fit the circumstances."

"Is Chicago an ugly town?"

Mike shrugged. "Some of it is."

"And that's where the violence happens?"

"Happens all over the place. When it's hot and humid in the summer, it feels right for people to slaughter each other."

"But here, it's too pretty for that?"

Mike clenched his jaw. "Exactly."

After a while they found themselves at the train station; it was as if their feet had done all the thinking.

"Janine and her family are in danger," Mike said.

"Why do you say that?"

"The day we got to her place, a cop from a unit fighting the Résistance was shot nearby. The owner of that café in town who took care of us was arrested and the Cossacks showed up on our way to Spain. Can't all be coincidences."

Robert gave a hesitant nod. "We've got to get back to Toulouse and warn her."

"We don't have enough money for train tickets."

"You've never traveled without tickets before?"

"No, I have not."

"You've lived a sheltered life, you know that?"

The next train for Toulouse was not scheduled until morning. It had started to rain and the station waiting room was not safe. They walked into the rainy night and into a public park. There, Robert broke the lock of a tool shed and let them inside. It stank of manure, but at least they were out of the rain. Mike found a stack of burlap bags and spread them on the floor.

Laying down Robert felt something inside his jacket and pulled out a package wrapped in newspapers.

"What's this?"

He unfolded the paper, revealing a piece of flattened pastry.

"The cake from the lady with the sons in North Africa."

They stared at it like a relic from a time long past. That woman's whole life was now shattered. Her husband and son were dead. Her farm was destroyed. *And all because she tried to help us*, Robert thought.

Mike cringed, remembering his anger when she had asked if American troops shot surrendering French soldiers and how she had kissed him after the prayer. "Je vous crois, Monsieur le Capitaine, merci."

Robert split the cake in half as equitably as he could. They ate off the open newspaper, making sure they did not miss any crumbs.

Mike recalled his father's warning: "Whatever you imagine, it'll be a hundred times worse."

He was right, of course. They lay down on the burlap and went to sleep.

22

COMMISSAIRE BOUCHER HAD RECRUITED INSPECTOR Franjou out of the municipal police in 1934 and trained him in the art of dismantling terrorist organizations. They had shared countless meals, hotel rooms, and even a few women, so when he identified his body in the Toulouse morgue, Boucher cried. He had dispatched Franjou to Toulouse to investigate tips about hotels sheltering aviators and in so doing had sent him to his death—shot in broad daylight in the crowded town center and apparently no one, *no one* had seen anything.

Boucher wanted revenge. So when he received intelligence from his Gestapo source that Prosper Navarre in Pau was part of an escape line, Boucher immediately had him arrested and transferred to Toulouse where he insisted on handling the interrogation himself. It was brutal and it went on all night. Waterboarding did not break Prosper. Electrical torture seemed promising, but they had to give it up when Prosper nearly died of a heart attack. The nerf de boeuf turned ineffective as Prosper lost consciousness after each blow. When Boucher doused Prosper's beard with lighter fluid, Inspector Lenoir tried to intervene. "You're sure about this?" he asked.

"I am," Boucher said, flicking his lighter.

Wooff! Flames engulfed Prosper's beard. The old man yelled at the top of his lungs. "Son of a whore!" and went on screaming until Lenoir threw a bucket of water in his face. Prosper's skin was now bright red and blistering, most of his beard was gone, and his dark blue bloodshot eyes looked enormous.

"Je t'emmerde." *I shit on you*, Prosper mumbled and he began to recite the Lord's Prayer. "Our Father, who art in Heaven . . ."

"He's religious," Lenoir said, taking a step toward Prosper. "Do you want a priest?"

"Yes," Prosper whispered.

Lenoir glanced at Boucher who, against his better judgment, nodded. Two uniformed policemen took over. They uncuffed Prosper and he collapsed on the floor. They each grabbed a leg and dragged him out of the room, along a corridor, and into a cell.

Sucking their cigarettes, Boucher and Lenoir waited at the bottom of the steps when a clergyman in a black cassock appeared. He glanced at the trail of blood on the floor and said nothing. He was about forty-five with a sallow face and deep scars on his left cheek. Lenoir pulled the cell door open. The priest took one look at Prosper lying on the floor and turned to the policemen.

"May God forgive you for this."

Boucher raised a fist and shouted: "Shut up, you queer!"

Lenoir pulled Boucher back. "Ignore him, Commissaire. The Father doesn't understand what we're dealing with here."

"I want to be alone with the prisoner," the priest said.

Lenoir turned to Boucher, who shrugged. The priest stepped inside and pulled the cell door closed behind him.

"Let's get you up," the priest said. He helped Prosper to the cot and put his hand on the old man's heart. "God bless you, my son."

Prosper stared at the priest, noting the web of scars on his face and the shriveled ear on one side of his head. "Thank you for coming, Father."

"You're welcome, my son," the priest said and then, touching his ear, he added, "I can't hear on my left side. I was wounded in the Ardennes in '17. I was an army chaplain."

Prosper's breathing had turned into a hard wheeze.

The priest made the sign of the cross. "In nomine Patris, es Filli, es Spiritus Sancti. Amen. Pater Noster, qui es in caelis, sanctificetur . . ."

Prosper could not follow the recitation. "I need . . . extreme unction . . . ," he murmured.

"I know, my son." The priest laid a piece of cloth on a stool, lit a candle, and with extreme care opened a jar of oil. Then he dipped his thumb into the oil and traced a cross on Prosper's forehead.

"Through this holy unction and His own most tender mercy may the Lord pardon thee whatever sins or faults thou hast committed."

"Amen," Prosper whispered.

"You have been freed from your sins, the Lord will save you and relieve you."

"Amen," Prosper murmured, tears rolling down his cheeks. Tears the priest gently wiped with the cloth.

"You've done well, my son," the priest said. Then he whispered, "I wish there were more Catholics in the Résistance."

"Traitor scums, those cops," Prosper said.

"Forgive us our sins as we forgive those who sin against us."

"I can't forgive those pricks!" Prosper whispered.

The priest glanced at the cell door. It was still closed, and no one was watching through the lucarne. "If you want to pass on a message, I'll do it for you," he whispered.

Prosper took the priest's hand, gathering his strength. "There is a Judas among us in the escape line," he hissed.

"A traitor who informs the enemy?" the Father asked.

"Yes."

"Do you know who it is?"

Prosper shook his head. "Tell them I didn't talk," he murmured.

"Tell whom?"

Prosper closed his eyes. The priest asked, "Someone in your family?"

Prosper's huge eyes shone with ferocity. He lifted his head and studied the clergyman's face. Taken aback, the priest put his hand on Prosper's chest. "Prosper Navarre, I'm your brother," he whispered.

Proper leaned back and began talking in a low murmur.

The Father leaned over and put his good ear next to Prosper's mouth. He listened to his whisper and then nodded. "I'll make sure she gets your message."

Prosper suddenly sat up, staring at the priest with horror—the certitude of betrayal exploding in his head. "You're one of them!" he shrieked, grabbing the priest's neck and squeezing as hard as he could. The cleric could not unlock the large hands at his throat, but he managed a squeal that brought Lenoir and Boucher over. The clergyman's face was crimson red, and the policemen could not pry him from Prosper's deadly grasp. Boucher stepped back and kicked Prosper hard in the ribs, breaking his hold. The priest sucked in air and stumbled away coughing and hacking.

Boucher stood above Prosper and sneered: "Fighting to the end, hey?"

"Scum of the earth you are," Prosper growled.

The priest took off his cassock in the restroom, hung it on the window knob, and changed into a gray suit. He slid his gun into the holster under his arm and turned back into the police inspector he was—Fernand Lazare, recently promoted for outstanding action against the Résistance. Standing in front of the mirror, he prodded the purple skin around his neck when Boucher and Lenoir appeared in the doorway.

"He's dead," Boucher said.

"Not a moment too soon." Lazare raised his shirt's collar and carefully knotted the tie high enough to hide the bruises on his throat.

"Did you get anything out of him?" Lenoir asked.

"Yes. He asked me to tell Doctor Dumas that he had not talked."

Boucher snapped his fingers, thrilled. "Bingo."

"He also said that they had a traitor on the line."

"Who?" Boucher asked.

Lazare shook his head. "He didn't know."

"You were perfect, Lazare," Lenoir said.

"I know," Lazare replied, wincing as he loosened his tie.

Boucher shifted his stance so he could gaze at Lazare's face in the mirror. "I was listening from the hallway. You know all the rites and prayers. Did you study for the priesthood?"

"I was a choirboy but that's as far as I went."

"Why did he get so mad at the end?" Boucher asked.

"You had told me the head of the escape line was a woman. So when he said Doctor Dumas, I responded that I would tell *her*." Lazare added with a cringe, "Then *he knew*."

"The bastard was sharp until the end," Boucher said.

Lazare grinned. "Yes. But he endured his beating for nothing and died with a bad conscience."

23

ROBERT WATCHED THE EXTRA POLICE and German sentries patrolling the Pau train station. "All that security wasn't there yesterday."

"Something's up," Mike said.

Robert led Mike away from the main hall, opting for the route Nicole had shown them. They entered the café, walked past the bar and the pool tables and, avoiding all controls, strode across the platform to climb aboard the waiting train.

"Looks like you've been avoiding cops all your life," Mike said.

"I have."

And now there was the question of traveling without tickets. Robert was confident. "In Algeria it only works in first class, but here people look more trusting," Robert said, glancing at the passengers as they moved along the corridor past half-empty compartments. "It's easier when the train is packed, though."

"Should we get off?" Mike asked.

"No."

The train was already moving anyway. The next car was filled with German soldiers. Mike took a step back, but Robert brazenly marched on. The soldiers were in good spirits, talking, smoking, and obligingly stepping out of the way to let Mike and Robert shuffle by.

"Going home on leave," Robert whispered.

They moved through first class. Robert checked the toilets. Both were vacant. In the next car, a man came out of one just as they got there.

"Merde."

They forged ahead with Mike feeling increasingly unsure about the scheme. "Maybe there is another way. We've got guns. We could rob someone."

Robert rolled his eyes. As they reached the next car, a lady in a pillbox hat with a severe look on her face stepped into the toilets. She turned on the red OCCUPÉ sign; Robert waited a minute and knocked on the door.

"Ticket, s'il vous plaît." No response. Robert knocked harder. "Ticket, s'il vous plaît."

The lady's voice came through the door, clearly irritated.

"Glissez-le ticket sous la porte, madame, s'il vous plaît." *Madame, please slide your ticket under the door.*

Robert knocked again and the ticket slid under the door. He picked it up and handed it to Mike. "Find us good seats."

Mike moved ahead. Robert found another occupied toilet and got another ticket just as the conductor appeared in the corridor. Retracing his route, he crossed paths with the lady with the pillbox hat. She was complaining loudly. Mike sat in an empty compartment in the last car.

"There's a lady out there who wants to have a word with you," Robert said.

"Should be ashamed of yourself. Steal a sweet lady's ticket while she sits on the commode," Mike said. "Have you ever been caught?"

"Yes, with the other trick on a train that does many stops where you get off and reboard to avoid the controller. The man wised up and nailed me."

"What happened?"

"I'd run away from home. They took me off the train and sent me back. A gendarme took me to my grandmother's house. She was used to getting me out of fixes and knew how to handle my mother."

"How old were you?"

"Twelve."

"You'd have done well in my neighborhood."

"Maybe I'll move to Chicago someday," Robert said.

"You could work for my father. You'd be good at it."

"Ticket, s'il vous plaît." They were both startled at the sight of the conductor—*click, click*. The man punched their tickets. "Merci, messieurs."

They watched him go. Mike pumped his fist—*all right.*

"What does that mean?" Robert asked.

"It's a celebratory gesture. It means well done."

Robert pumped his fist, but it felt clumsy to him. "We're still in the shit."

"Let's make sure Janine is safe," Mike said. "Then we'll climb those hills on those damn bicycles again, walk all night, and get to Spain."

"A born optimist you are," Robert said.

"No use being anything else."

Robert glanced at the mountains in the distance glistening under the morning sun.

"From your mouth to God's ears!" he said.

24

JANINE STOOD IN HER OFFICE preparing her dental instruments. She was anxiously waiting for Suzanne, who was due back from Bilbao with money and blank documents sent through British diplomatic pouch. They were struggling with an ever-growing number of escapees and Janine had asked for Suzanne's help. As a railway controller, she went through police controls with ease. Even Spanish controllers treated her as one of their own.

Janine could hear the patients in the waiting room. She was itching to check if Suzanne was there but feared jinxing it. At precisely eight o'clock she opened her door. The room was full. Every seat was taken, with a couple of men standing. Suzanne sat reading a book and Janine's heart lifted. She wished she could call her ahead of the others but did not dare. Patients' resentment was dangerous. The war had brought out the worst in people. The Gestapo paid huge rewards for information leading to the arrest of Résistance workers and spiteful people wrote denunciation letters. The underground controlled the postal workers' union, so the mail addressed to the Gestapo was read before being delivered. Doctors accused colleagues of being Jewish to take over their practices, mistresses reported that their lovers' wives were hiding British pilots, neighbors who had hated each other for years jumped at a chance for revenge. Snitching was a national disease.

When the information was accurate, the Résistance intercepted the letter and brutally murdered the snitch by paying him a visit as he sat with his family for the sacrosanct Sunday lunch. They would tie him up, cut his throat, and leave him to bleed to death. Most underground fighters refused to execute informants that way, so a handful of hardened men, mainly veterans of the Spanish civil war, took on the task. They accepted the brutality of professional insurgency and only had disdain for those who did not have the stomach for it. "La guerra es sangrienta y jodida." *War is a bloody fucking business.*

When Suzanne's turn finally came, Janine ushered her in and closed the door. The two women embraced. Suzanne pulled documents and cash out of her satchel and Janine hid it all in a laundry bag filled with soiled towels. Suddenly loud voices in the waiting room made them turn.

"Get in the chair," Janine said, switching on the drill.

Seconds later the door flew open. Two miliciens burst in followed by a man wearing a double-breasted suit.

"Commissaire Boucher," he said, aiming his gun at Janine's head. "Against the wall, please."

Janine could smell the alcohol on his breath. "I'm almost done," she said, running the drill inside Suzanne's mouth. The connecting door blasted open, and Louis stumbled into the room, pushed by two more miliciens. Janine turned off the drill and gave Suzanne a glass of water.

"Rinse."

Suzanne gargled and spit into a bowl. Janine pushed the laundry bag where she had hidden the money with her foot and turned to Boucher. "Where do you want me?"

He whipped his chin to indicate the wall. "You, out!" Boucher said, waving his pistol at Suzanne.

Suzanne hopped out of the chair. "Yes, sir," she said, picking up the laundry bag. Then, patting her jaw, she added, "Thank you, doctor. I feel much better." And Janine watched her walk out carrying a bag containing evidence that would have sent her straight to the firing squad.

"You're under arrest for terrorist activities and collusion with Anglo-American secret services, in clear contravention of the armistice between France and Germany," Boucher recited.

"That's ridiculous," Janine said.

"Yes! Your activities are ridiculous and useless. How many times does France need to lose this war?"

"Being a dentist is useless?"

Boucher waved his gun. "Out!" he shouted, leading the way through the reception room where waiting patients stood with their hands raised. Just then Anna came in with Emma in her arms.

"Leave my wife and granddaughter alone!" Louis's authoritative voice held the miliciens back for an instant. "Anna, take Emma to her room."

Anna turned back but Boucher pushed her forward. Then he swung around and pistol-whipped Louis across the face. Emma screamed as blood spurted out and trickled down her grandfather's face.

"Get them all out," Boucher ordered.

The family was pushed into the landing and Emma's cries echoed down the staircase.

"When will they be back?" a man asked, cradling his sore jaw.

"Find another dentist," Boucher said.

For Nicole the last two days had been a nightmare. After taking Mike and Robert to the bus in Pau and watching Prosper's arrest, she and Lucile had returned to Toulouse. In case of emergency Nicole had the address of a Toulouse dentist. Her instructions were to write her name on the patients' list as Mademoiselle Marchant and wait to be called. It was a hot day and having ridden her bicycle all the way from the suburbs, Nicole felt sweat trickling down her back. Reaching La Place du Capitole she noticed an unusual gathering of people and cars. She padlocked her bicycle and mingled with the onlookers as miliciens pushed a man and a woman wearing dentists' smocks out of a building. A lady followed them with a child in her arms. An older lady wearing a gray smock ran out waving her arms.

"I'm the concierge!" she cried. "Let me keep the child."

When the miliciens pushed her away, she shouted, "What do you want that little girl for?"

Murmurs of agreement and protest rose from the crowd.

"Let her have the child!" someone yelled.

"Frenchmen working for the Nazis are traitors!"

Boucher turned and faced the crowd. "Who said that?"

Nobody answered and Boucher raised an angry finger. "Those who collaborate with the Anglo-Americans *are* the traitors!" he shouted.

The concierge pleaded. "Monsieur, let me take the child. She's three years old. She does not collaborate with anybody."

Boucher shoved her away. "Go back to your hole!"

The old woman fell heavily but quickly got back on her feet. She brushed the dirt off her dress and crossed her arms, defiantly standing her ground.

"Thank you for trying, Madame Raymonde! Thank you!" the woman dentist said.

Nicole's heart sank. *That's the dentist I was supposed to see.* She retreated into the crowd and nearly cried out when she spotted Mike and Robert standing on the street corner a few yards away.

They had found their way back from the train station and now watched Janine and Louis being pushed into a Citroën as Anna and Emma were led to a police van.

Mike pulled the Luger out of his waistband and armed it.

"Are you insane?" Robert hissed.

"We'll hijack that car."

From across the street, Nicole watched Robert drag Mike away. Several people in the crowd saw the gun and heard the shouts in English. It was a miracle the miliciens didn't hear them.

Robert pushed Mike around the corner. "Put that gun away. This is not Chicago!"

Looking daggers at Robert, Mike slid the Luger back in his waistband.

"Now walk. Do *not* run," Robert growled.

"Those people saved our hides. They're being arrested because of us!"

"And dashing in with guns blazing would have helped?"

"We'd have scared them off, grabbed the wheel, and driven off with them in the back. By the time they got the van started we'd have been far away. It could have worked!"

"Could have!" Robert cried, furious. Automatically, he checked the street. It was empty. They kept walking, headed nowhere in particular. Robert heard a noise and glanced back; it was just a girl on a bicycle. He quickened the pace and turned around again. Something was wrong; the girl was riding too slowly but now she had picked up speed. Robert heard the brakes squeal as she caught up with them.

"Is that you?" she asked.

Robert was stunned. "Nicole, what are you doing here?"

"What about you? You should be in Spain."

"We couldn't get across the border."

"What happened?"

"Cossacks."

She knew what that meant. Dreaded troops, they came from Ukraine and enlisted in the German army for money. They were useless on the battlefield but good at terrorizing civilians. Nicole leaned over and touched Robert's shoulder. "Are you hurt?"

"No."

She put a hand on his cheek as she would a child. "Follow me."

They watched her pedal away. "An angel from heaven," Robert said.

Nicole stopped at intersections, waited for them to catch up, then rode on. She vanished at one point. They grew concerned, but she reappeared behind them minutes later.

"Smart way to check if we're being followed," Mike said. On and on they went, weaving through a working-class neighborhood—a boulangerie—a café at the corner—a grocery store—and a haberdashery.

Nicole stopped on the next block, chained her bicycle to a rack, and stepped through a doorway painted navy blue. The sign above it read: BAINS DOUCHE.

"Douche?" Mike asked.

"Shower, a bathhouse," Robert translated.

"We follow her in there?"

"You'd rather do something else?"

"Don't smart-ass me."

They were scared and hungry and the nasty mood was back. They stepped through the blue doorway and walked down a flight of steps covered with well-worn jute. The place was steamy and smelled of chlorine. White tiles with navy blue edges lined the walls. Nicole waited for them.

"I didn't know where else to take you." Nicole motioned toward the woman at the reception desk. "This is my aunt. She runs the place."

In the glaring light Nicole's aunt's face looked weary. Her blue smock showed large circles of perspiration under the arms.

"She doesn't want to know who you are," Nicole said. "She has five children, and her husband is a prisoner of war in Germany."

Mike and Robert thanked the aunt with a nod, but the woman looked away. Nicole handed Robert two towels and a key.

"This is for a private bathroom. Take a bath. You'll be safe here. I'll come back as soon as I can," Nicole said. "My aunt apologizes because she can't give you soap. You need ration tickets for soap, but here." Nicole self-consciously produced a bag of dark powder. "It's wood ashes. Not as good as soap but it works all right."

"We'll manage," Robert said, taking the bag.

Nicole pointed at a wall of doors. "Number eight." She was about to leave but remembered to say, "There is a timer. You get only one tub of hot water. So you've got to share." She smiled at the awkwardness of it all. "But you can get as much cold water as you want . . . to rinse off, I mean."

"Merci, Nicole," Robert said.

She raced up the steps. It was after six, less than four hours before curfew, and her options were few.

It was Mike and Robert's first hot bath in a long time. As water filled the tub, they took off their clothes and realized how filthy they were. They stepped in, got themselves wet, and rubbed their bodies with ashes.

"Take the right side, I'll take the left," Mike said. They lowered themselves down, slid their feet up on the edge, and lay head to tail.

"I saw a photograph in *Life* magazine," Mike said. "It showed newlyweds laying head to tail, a heart-shaped bathtub in a hotel in Atlantic City."

"I'm not marrying you."

Mike scrubbed. "Ever since we got to France, women have rescued us and taken care of us," he mused.

"Helpless and useless we are."

They lay for a while in water that had turned gray from dirt and ashes.

"It's getting cold," Robert said, pushing himself up.

They stood. Robert pulled out the plug, turned on the faucet and, shivering, they splashed themselves with cold water to rinse off the ashes ringing their calves.

"At least we got two towels," Mike said.

They toweled dry, put their clothes back on, and sat on the floor. Nervous energy spent, recent images tormented them—Emma and her grandmother being pushed into the police van—Janine proud and unbending thanking the concierge—the anguish on Louis's bloodied face.

"I barely know those people, yet they feel like family," Mike said.

Robert's eyes turned thoughtful. He knew instinctively where this was going. "What do you want to do?"

"Stay and fight," Mike said.

"Fight the Germans? The milice?"

"Yes. We get back in contact with the underground and join the Résistance," Mike said.

"Didn't Janine tell you to get back to the Air Force?"

"That was before. Now she needs help."

Robert wasn't so sure. "Okay."

"We're soldiers. We fight," Mike said, gently kicking Robert's leg.

"Right," Robert said.

"Good. We've got a plan," Mike said.

"Everything is perfect," Robert said. "We're cleaner than we've been in months and waiting for a pretty girl to take us out for dinner."

Mike leaned over and playfully pushed his fist against Robert's shoulder. "There you go."

Robert chuckled—he had just parodied Mike's knack for restoring confidence. They couldn't be more different, but providence had thrown them together—the fighter pilot and the private, the son of a wealthy American family and the scruffy Jew from Kabyle. Robert envied Mike's ingrained sense of hope—everything was possible and if things were wrong, then they could be made right—*join the Résistance*. He liked that.

Watching Robert, Mike sighed and rubbed his face. "I made a real fool of myself today. Anybody else would have run away, but not you."

"Going after that Cossack yesterday wasn't smart either. Now we're even," Robert said.

Nicole was spooked by all the arrests and took extra precautions. She rode twice around the block, slowing down to glance inside the café—only a few customers lingering over their drinks, nothing out of the ordinary. She chained her bicycle to a lamppost and stepped inside. The patron leaned over the zinc-topped bar, perusing a newspaper. The dog, asleep on the floor with his head atop his paws, gently moved his tail.

"I need to use your telephone."

Without shifting his eyes from the newspaper, the patron produced a Bakelite receiver and set it in front of Nicole. She dialed and let it ring three times before hanging up.

The patron brushed his thumb against his tongue and flipped pages looking for something to read among columns blanked out by censorship.

"How's your mother?" he asked.

"Same. We don't talk."

"Probably wise," the patron said; then, looking at the paper, he added, "A Gestapo official was shot yesterday. Listen to what *La Voix Catholique* has to say about it." He adjusted his glasses and read: "'We deplore the cowardly acts of terrorists whose goal is to compromise the order and tranquility that has prevailed in our city since the arrival of the German military. We ask the people of Toulouse to provide the occupation authorities with all the help necessary so that the perpetrators of this odious crime can be apprehended.'"

"Why do you read that trash? It only makes you mad," Nicole said.

The patron pushed the paper away. "My countrymen never cease to disappoint me."

The telephone rang. Nicole picked it up and said, "Les enfants sont revenus." *The children came back.* She listened and said, "Oui, je peux prendre un verre." *Yes, I can have a drink.* She hung up.

25

SUZANNE HAD HAD A HARROWING day warning helpers on the escape line about Janine and her parents' arrests. She had managed to distribute some of the funds and documents and there had been Nicole's call for help. Suzanne had never met her. At first, she was concerned about her youth, but there was a grit and determination about Nicole that were much older than her age. Suzanne trusted her instantly.

The two women turned up at the Bains Douche in a delivery van owned by a butcher who traded on the black market to feed men in the underground. Mike and Robert were happy to see her and of course, hungry again. At every turn skinned-hog carcasses swung on hooks above their heads.

"I see barbecued ribs," Mike said. Robert smirked. Their last meal had been the remains from the farmer's wife's cake the night before. Hunger was clawing inside their bellies and up their chests, paralyzing every muscle. The van finally backed into an alley and pulled over. Nicole opened the back door and led them down some steps into a butcher's basement with cold storage doors lining the walls.

"I have got to go," Nicole said. She kissed Suzanne, Mike, and Robert last, taking a little longer with him. "Be careful," she said, her eyes not leaving his as she stepped back. Then she carried her bicycle up the steps and Robert felt his throat tighten with gratitude as she rode away.

Suzanne watched Mike and Robert eat. They leaned over their plates and shoveled in food with trembling hands, eager for the meat in a stew made with peppers and tomatoes. Eventually their hands stopped shaking. They gulped their wine out of old amora mustard glasses and that too, helped. Suzanne pulled out pen and paper and questioned them about the debacle in the mountains. She asked about Prosper, the bus driver, the guides, the farmers, and the other escapees.

How many miliciens? What about the Cossacks? Was it a full platoon? As a train conductor she nodded in appreciation when Robert told her how he had stolen train tickets. When she was done, she reread her notes, folded the page, and wrote a list from memory. After unfolding the page, she compared the two, pulled out a lighter, and burned the pages over the sink.

Those two are smart, she thought. German border patrols were put on high alert the moment the Cossacks' bodies were discovered. The frontier was instantly sealed. Had they headed for Spain, they would have been caught.

"You'll be in the next convoy across the border," she said.

Robert glanced at Mike and then turned to Suzanne. "We don't want to go to Spain."

"And where would you *rather* go?" Suzanne asked with an edge. "We aren't running a travel agency."

Mike pushed his plate aside and leaned forward. "We owe it to Janine, her father, to you, and all your friends in the Résistance. We can be useful to you here."

"You'll just get in the way. Two more men to hide, two more mouths to feed."

"We're soldiers. We've been in combat. Robert's a born fighter with great instincts. I'm trained in the use of all kinds of weapons. I was also taught bomb disposal techniques and demolition."

"You learned that in pilot training?" Suzanne asked, incredulous.

"I did a stint at Fort Belvoir, Virginia. That's where the US Army trains recruits in sabotage and explosives."

"And we've got weapons," Robert said.

They stood and emptied their pockets, producing two Lugers, a knife, and four grenades. When they pulled out the ammunition, the bullets crackled merrily, rolling on the table.

"From the Cossacks in the mountains," Mike said.

Suzanne was supremely unimpressed, so Robert gestured to Mike: *Tell her.*

Mike took a sip of wine and smacked his lips. "I was raised in an Irish neighborhood on the south side of Chicago. My father was involved in . . . *illegal* activities," Mike said with a smirk. "I was his only son and his men taught me things. Weak points in a man's body, what to watch for if people are looking for you. The army taught me how to blow things up but the rest I already knew. There were constant turf wars between the Italian and the Irish mobs fighting for territories. It was a kind of urban warfare. What I'm saying is, urban warfare is what you're involved in here." Mike took another sip from his glass. "I think I could be useful to you."

The tale was outrageous, but it resonated with Suzanne. This American was describing a kind of combat she knew well—class warfare, strikes, turf struggle, communists fighting fascists. And those two sat there, watching her, obstinate and silent.

"There are people I need to talk to," she finally said. "We'll hide you here. It won't be pleasant."

"We don't care," Robert said.

But after a couple of days, they did. The pork butcher's attic was hot and stank with dozens of jambon de Bayonne and saucissons hanging from its ceiling. The hams were particularly bothersome, oozing greasy salt water that dripped on the floor, filling the room with the acrid smell of drying fat.

"A Jew drowning in pork fat, I am," Robert joked.

They fought to keep up their spirits, but the war gnawed at them. Mike was haunted by the thought of Janine, about how the world gave with one hand and took away with the other. Every day, they got water, food, and newspapers and Mike went through the delicate task of lowering their chamber pot through a trapdoor in the attic floor.

"Always knew bomb disposal techniques would come in handy," he'd say every time he did it.

26

MARGUERITE RICHTER LOVED HER LIGHT-FILLED office at Toulouse's Gestapo headquarters. Life had not always been easy for Marguerite, who was born in 1910 in Alsace-Lorraine, a part of France that had been annexed by Germany in 1871. She had grown up speaking German but when World War I ended and Alsace-Lorraine was returned to France, she learned French but never lost her accent. It got worse when her family moved to the southwest; there she was a schleu, a kraut. "Les étrangers devraient rentrer chez eux." *Foreigners should go home.* Marguerite heard it often.

She got married and had two children. In the factory where she worked, petty supervisors played favorites and female workers ignored Marguerite. She despised those people. Then the war started, and her husband was wounded during the Ardennes offensive. He lost the use of his legs and was now confined to a wheelchair. They were struggling on his disability pension and Marguerite's meager salary.

Since the Reich had re-annexed Alsace-Lorraine, Marguerite was a German national again and positions were available in the German information service. She was hired by Gestapo Sturmbannführer Erhard Kloss, who quickly appreciated her hard work and organizational skills.

"Very German," he told her one day. The ultimate compliment.

At first, she translated reports on civilian casualties of allied air raids—sensitive work as thousands of Frenchmen, Frenchwomen, and children were killed or wounded by bombs intended for French factories working for the German war effort. She accompanied her boss on air raid sites and was deeply affected by seeing a children's hospital destroyed during the Allied bombing of a nearby factory. Marguerite walked through ruins between rows of small beds reduced to twisted metal and watched as hundreds of small bodies wrapped in white sheets were buried in a mass grave. Allied aviators were monsters. She was determined to stop the massacre of innocents and help Germany win the war and bring about lasting peace.

That's when she started attending interrogation sessions. Most French working for the Gestapo had criminal records and abused their newfound power. The worst of them was a pimp named Montrose who had spent time in prison for nearly beating a prostitute to death. She watched him pee on a terrorist before running electric shocks through his body, explaining that the acid in urine made the body more conductive. It was just a matter of time before Marguerite got directly involved in strong-arm questioning. It began with the interrogation of a small-town mayor's wife—a member of the upper crust French elite Marguerite detested. The woman was so evasive and disrespectful that Marguerite lost her temper and slapped her. The woman broke down and after a few more blows, she revealed the location of a weapons cache. Marguerite had broken a couple of nails in the process but felt wonderful. More importantly, her boss was pleased.

"Just make sure sweet Marguerite doesn't get mad at you," Kloss had said.

It was common knowledge that women held up under torture better than men and Marguerite enjoyed the challenge. She knew they were obsessed with their looks and would always start by hitting them in the face. The prettier the woman, the better.

Marguerite had been studying Janine's file. Since the arrests had been conducted by the milice, her boss had insisted that Janine and her father be turned over to the Gestapo that was paying the Toulouse milice hundreds of thousands of francs every month. These were *their* terrorists. The phone rang. Marguerite picked it up. "Dankeschön," she said and hung up.

Her prisoner had arrived. She gathered her file and marched out of the room. It was hot in the building and in the summer, windows were left open in the hallways to create a breeze. Marguerite hurried along the corridor and spotted master interrogator Montrose who was half dragging, half pushing a man wearing a blood-drenched dentist's smock. *This must be Louis de Guilhem*, Marguerite thought. As they crossed paths, Montrose flashed Marguerite a cocky grin. Using the split second of inattention, Louis de Guilhem bolted for the open window.

"Merde!" Montrose caught the hem of Louis's smock, but the garment ripped, and they heard a scream and a thud when the body hit the ground three floors below. Looking out, Marguerite watched Louis's broken body on the sidewalk, legs splayed at impossible angles. The poor man howled in misery as two soldiers dragged him up the steps.

"Did he talk?" Marguerite asked.

"No, but it was just a matter of time. A dentist who can't take a little pain," Montrose chuckled.

Marguerite stood behind the desk and watched Janine being brought into the interrogation room and cuffed to a chair. She waited until the guards scurried out the door.

"You live an interesting life, Madame Dumas," Marguerite said, flipping through the thick file in front of her. "Most people swear they don't know why they're here."

Janine smiled. "Why am I here?"

A comedian, Marguerite thought. *Good, let's have a laugh.* "Did you hear that commotion outside when you came in?"

Janine smiled. "Yes, what was it?"

Marguerite smiled back. "Your father jumping out of a third-floor window."

"Oh my God!"

Marguerite opened the file and squinted to decipher her own handwriting. Janine found her silence unbearable.

"Is he dead?" she asked.

"No. But I could hear him cry. Lots of broken bones, I'm sure," Marguerite said distractedly. "He must have protected his head at the last second. Survival instinct, I guess."

Janine's eyes welled up as she tried to control the despair overwhelming her. Her kind, loving father's body crushed on the sidewalk.

Marguerite put her finger on a page. "Ah, Prosper Navarre! He told us about you. He was reluctant at first but he's now working for us."

Janine knew Marguerite was lying. Prosper had been wounded during World War I and again on the Aragon front in the Spanish Civil War. He might break down and talk under torture, but he would never work for the Nazis.

"You know Prosper Navarre, don't you?"

Janine had agonized over how to behave during this interrogation. She would not stonewall but mix truth and lies, giving as many useless details as possible.

"I don't know Mr. Navarre well," she said. "He was a friend of my husband."

"He told us you are running an escape line that smuggles allied airmen to Spain."

"How could I do such a thing? I'm a war widow. I've got a small child and I work full-time."

"We know. You and your father have one of the busiest practices in town. You make a lot of money."

"People come to me because I studied at Dusseldorf University. German education is the best," Janine said.

"It is, isn't it?" *The little bitch is clever*, Marguerite thought. "Monsieur Paul, do you know him?"

"Paul who?" Janine had answered too quickly. Marguerite picked up on it at once and Janine felt her attention sharpen.

"Also known as Pierre Fauchon or Germain Lecocq."

"I don't know any of these people."

"He financed the escape line until you got funds from the British."

"I don't know who that is." Janine was despairing to realize how much the Gestapo knew and at the same time stunned they were not aware that Paul Turenne was her uncle—*she's playing with me*.

"Loïc Briant was a friend, right?"

"I don't know who that is," Janine said, then angrily added, "I'm not who you think I am!"

"No, you're much worse," Marguerite snarled.

Janine's mind was racing. *They don't know about the German spy we killed.* Relief must have shown on her face, and it enraged Marguerite, who stepped forward and slapped Janine hard several times.

"You and Loïc Briant have been working together since 1941."

The blows became constant, punishing, bruising. When Janine fell on the floor still handcuffed to the chair, Marguerite kicked her mercilessly, aiming for her breasts and belly. Finally, she opened the door and motioned to the sentry outside.

"Get her up," she said.

The sentry pulled Janine up and set her back on the chair. Her face was bruised, and a trickle of blood ran from her mouth. Marguerite sat down, steepled her fingers, and leaned back in her chair, waiting for the sentry to leave.

"Loïc Briant was caught smuggling enemy airmen. He murdered two miliciens and was killed in the firefight. We know you visited him at his farm in Brittany."

Janine decided to give a little. "I've been to Brittany, but not on a farm."

"What did you do there?"

Janine bit her lips, hesitated, and said, "I had a lover in Rennes. I saw him a few times. It's over now."

"What's his name?"

"Philippe Degas." Again, she had answered too fast.

"Like the painter?" Marguerite asked, spotting the lie.

Marguerite closed Janine's file, seemingly distraught. "We'll talk again tomorrow. It'll be worse—you know that."

That night Janine was transferred to the political section of the Saint-Michel prison. When the cell door slammed behind her, she found herself in almost total darkness. The floor was damp, and the place stank of excrement and disinfectant. She felt her way around until she found the bunk with a blanket on top. She sat and after a while could make out the overflowing Turkish-style squat toilet in a corner. She wrapped her arms around her shoulders and shivered. Her dental smock was torn at the collar and several of the buttons up on the side were missing. She touched the cuts and swollen bruises on her face—*doesn't hurt that much.*

It seemed a lifetime ago when Commissaire Boucher and the milice had burst into her office. Her father was probably dead, and Janine's mind flooded with anguish about Emma and her mother.

"Stop!" Janine told herself—*stop thinking.* She stood and began pacing her cell, carefully avoiding the overflowing toilet. She walked for a long time and finally collapsed on the bunk to fall into agitated sleep.

27

BOUCHER, LENOIR, AND LAZARE HAD all received miniature coffins with their names engraved on the lids. Inside were notes instructing them to listen to the BBC's nightly broadcast to find out about their precarious future. Boucher didn't plan to tune in. Why should he listen to French traitor puppets of the Anglo-Americans?

"The more we know, the better we can fight them," Lenoir had countered. The men were holed up in an office smoking cigars.

Lazare, who had masqueraded as a priest, came into the room and took a chair, but refused the cigar Boucher offered him. With his short hair, pockmarked skin, and shriveled ear, he looked like a renaissance assassin—a petrified renaissance assassin, Boucher thought, somewhat amused.

The office was heavy with smoke when Lenoir fiddled with the knobs on the radio and the whining of the BBC overcame German jamming and filled the room with the familiar introduction. "Les Français parlent aux Français." *The French speak to the French.* Lenoir and Boucher puffed on their cigars and put their feet up on the desk.

"This is London. Tonight, we will report on the despicable actions of the French police. Two days ago, Commissaire Guy Boucher, the head of the anti-terrorism section of the Renseignements Généraux and Inspector Étienne Lenoir tortured a patriot to death. The man endured terrible suffering but did not talk."

The color drained from Lenoir's face. Boucher took a drag on his cigar and smugly blew away the smoke.

"Before he died, a priest came to his cell and introduced himself as an army chaplain who had been wounded and lost an ear in World War I. It was a lie. That priest is a police inspector who was wounded in a clash with the Résistance. He extracts information while hearing confessions from tortured patriots. He is knowledgeable about church ritual and gives dying men extreme unction. His name is Fernand Lazare."

"Bastards!" Lazare shouted.

"He is forty-eight years old and lives at 3, avenue Clemenceau in Toulouse. Tell everyone about the fake priest, tell everyone about the missing ear . . ."

Lazare jumped up and turned off the radio. "Those cocksuckers told them where I live. What about my wife and kids?"

"Calm down, Fernand," Boucher said. "We'll protect you."

"How? Terrorists are everywhere."

"We'll get you transferred."

"I don't want to move. I was born here. My parents live in Chatou, across the river. They are both over eighty years old." Lazare was shaking.

"We'll watch over them too."

Lazare slammed his fist on the desk. "I'm working to dismantle terrorist organizations. I'm acting under direct orders of my superiors, enforcing laws enacted by the French government under the authority of our chief, Maréchal Pétain."

Boucher raised his chin. "We never asked you to impersonate a priest."

"But you liked the results," Lazare hissed. "I won't sit on my ass waiting for the fucking Bolsheviks to wipe us out."

"Calm down, Lazare," Boucher said levelly. "We'll take care of you."

Lazare didn't trust this pompous ass commissaire from Paris. He jabbed an angry finger at Boucher.

"Fuck you."

The two men watched Lazare walk to the door and slam it behind him. Boucher drew on his cigar, formed an "O" with his lips, blew smoke rings out of his mouth, and poked one of them with his cigar.

"That son of a bitch has gotten us into trouble."

28

TWO BURLY FRENCH PRISON GUARDS escorted a cuffed Janine out of her cell. They marched her briskly down the hall, giving her no chance to talk to the prisoners watching from their cells.

"Hey, fatties, you afraid of a girl?" shouted a woman taunting the guards while leaning against the bars.

Another woman whispered, "Courage." Janine fought to hide the terror knotting her guts. *What courage? I'm not cut out for this.* She feared breaking down under torture. This had all happened so fast. At this time yesterday, her daughter was sitting on her lap, sharing breakfast. In her tormented sleep, she dreamt that she couldn't talk because her mouth was filled with pebbles and had woken up with her heart racing. She knew what the dream meant: She was terrified that her teeth would be broken.

They left the cellblock, and the guards led Janine through another building and out into a yard with a mature tree and a house that had once been the warden's residence. When they reached the door, Janine realized that her guards were reluctant to prod or even touch her. *Oh, God. They feel sorry for me.*

Once inside, she saw why. A truck battery and a coil of wire sat next to a metal garden armchair bolted to the floor. Janine was told to sit, and the guards cuffed her wrists and ankles to the frame. She gazed at the stove rusting against the wall and at the windows opaque with grease. This must have been the warden's family kitchen, she thought. Canisters lining a dirty shelf read: SUCRE, SEL, FARINE, PÂTES—sugar, salt, flour, pasta. There was also a cast-iron tub against the wall.

"Is this the kitchen or the bathroom?" Janine asked.

The guards ignored her. The older of the two heaved a sigh.

"Not proud of what you're doing today, are you?" she asked.

The man said nothing except with his eyes—*not proud. No.*

Janine strained to strengthen herself for what was coming—she would not show anger and would respond to threats and violence with kindness, and if possible, humor. Her only chance was to establish a personal relationship with her tormentors. Yes, that was it. But her hopes were short-lived as she realized those resolutions were absurd. *You can't strategize for torture.*

Marguerite walked into the room. "Good morning," she said cheerfully, dropping Janine's file on the kitchen table. *A busy woman with lots to do*, Janine thought. *And beating me up is first on her list.*

"I hope your memory has improved since yesterday," Marguerite said.

"Depends on what you want to know. I can remember a double abscess I drained six months ago but don't ask me the name of the patient. You know what's the worst about an abscess? It stinks. Ever smelled rotten eggs? Well, an abscess stinks even worse." Janine grimaced as if one was right under her nose.

"You think you're clever?" Marguerite asked.

"If I was, I wouldn't be here."

Marguerite looked at Janine with a mixture of anger and pity. "Who's your contact in Paris?" she asked.

"Contact for what?"

"Smuggling aviators to Spain."

"The only aviator I knew was my husband and he's dead."

Marguerite stood and gazed at Janine as one looks at a child who is lying. "This will be very unpleasant, and in the end, you'll tell everything I want to know. They all do."

"I don't know any aviators," Janine repeated. That was true—almost.

"The hard way? That's how you want to do this?" Marguerite asked.

"Of course not. I don't want you to hurt me."

"You give me no choice."

"But you keep asking questions I don't know the answers to. You're confusing me with someone else."

Marguerite slapped Janine hard across the face. Reeling from the pain Janine managed to keep her mouth slightly open to minimize the impact on her teeth.

"I know who you are! You lying bitch! Do you think I enjoy doing this?" Marguerite screamed.

"Perhaps. You tell me," Janine answered. As soon as the words were out of her mouth, she wished she hadn't said them.

Marguerite tore open Janine's blouse, yanked down her brassiere, and fastened metal clips to her nipples. "Is this what you want?" she asked.

"No!"

"What's the name of your contact in Paris?"

"I don't have contacts. I'm a dentist. A widow, mother of a three-year-old . . ."

A tight-fisted slap cut her off.

"Paul Turenne smuggled airmen through Limoges. Who are your contacts there?"

How does she know that? "Who's Paul Durenne?"

"Paul *Tu*-renne," Marguerite enunciated. "He was in Marseille this fall."

They know that too. Janine attempted to disguise her rising terror with a show of anger. "I've never been to Marseille, and I don't know that man!"

Marguerite filled a bucket of water at the kitchen tap and poured a generous amount of salt from the sel canister.

"Making pasta?" Janine asked.

"Salt water makes the shocks stronger," Marguerite said as she emptied the bucket over Janine's head, drenching her entire body and plugging the wires into the truck battery.

"Paul Turenne?" Marguerite asked, her hand on the switch.

"Don't know him."

The jolt of current was diabolically painful. Janine's teeth chattered uncontrollably and her whole body went into spasm. Her heart thundered in her chest as if it was about to bust out of her body. *I'm having a heart attack*, she thought. *Good.*

"Where is Paul Turenne hiding?"

"I don't know who . . . that is!"

The current crackled again, lasting longer this time, clips searing her nipples. Janine shouted, producing cries of misery that enraged Marguerite. Even after the current was switched off, Janine's body kept shaking, her heart pounding furiously inside her chest. She hoped to die . . . feared she wouldn't . . . *no heart disease in the family . . . all died of old age . . . or killed fighting the Germans* . . . Janine lamented as Marguerite stormed out of the room.

What now? Janine feared the worst and the worst is what she got.

Marguerite marched back into the room with Janine's daughter Emma in her arms. It took all of Janine's willpower, but she managed to break into a big smile.

"Oh, sweetie, how're you doing?" she asked, striving to look genuinely happy. "Emma, don't be scared. Mommy is all right. Is Grandma taking good care of you?"

"Mammie est partie!" *Mammie left!* Emma cried.

Janine tried to edge toward her daughter, but a painful electrical shock threw her body into spasm.

"Maman!" Emma screamed.

"We can't touch . . . sweetie . . . Don't worry this is . . . a game."

"*Maman, Maman, Maman!*"

Emma became hysterical. Her mother's contortions and refusal to take her were unbearable. Between jolts, Marguerite kept asking questions, but Janine kept talking to Emma.

"Don't look at me, baby . . . Close your eyes . . . Put your thumb in your mouth . . . Please, Emma, do it. Close your eyes!" Amazingly, Emma obeyed her mother. She stuck a thumb in her mouth, closed her eyes, and pushed her head against Marguerite's shoulder.

"Oui, Maman."

Marguerite instinctively patted Emma's head to soothe her as she would her own child. Then, realizing what she was doing, she turned the battery back on. Janine clenched her teeth and managed to remain silent, but she could not control the cuffs clicking against the chair.

"*Maman, Maman, Maman!*" Emma could hear the cuffs clicking and her mother's faint cries. She screeched hysterically. The nauseating smell of burned flesh suffused the room and Marguerite turned off the switch.

"You're sick! Sick! Take my daughter out of here!" Janine shouted. "How can you do this to a child? You're a monster!"

"*You* are the monster! You protect murderers who drop bombs on children's hospitals!" Marguerite yelled back. Then, still carrying Emma, she left the room. When the door slammed behind her, Janine collapsed into sobs.

In the next room, Marguerite sat Emma on a dusty mattress, but the little girl crawled toward the door crying, "*Maman, Maman!*"

Marguerite caught her and tried to cuddle her. "I know, sweetie, this is hard." She sang "Jesus Loves the Little Children" in German.

"Jesus liebt allekleinen Kinder,

Alle Kinder dieser Welt . . ."

But Emma kept leaning back, pushing away from Marguerite, who opened her purse and pulled out a bar of chocolate.

"Do you like chocolate?" she asked, her voice cloyingly sweet.

Emma took the chocolate and threw it away. "*Maman*," she cried, pointing at the door.

Marguerite put Emma down. "As dumb as your mother."

A polite cough—Marguerite looked up at Sturmbannführer Erhard Kloss standing in the doorway.

"Let me try," he said, stepping forward.

He opened a metal box filled with square Petit Beurre cookies and offered one to Emma. "Un Petit Beurre pour la petite fille?" *A Petit Beurre for the little girl?*

Emma shook her head and again pointed at the door. "*Maman.*"

Kloss closed the box. "This is no place for a child, Marguerite," he said, leaving the room.

Marguerite stood at attention. "Ja, Sturmbannführer."

29

PROUST HAD UNDERTAKEN TO SETTLE his debt to the British that morning. He now stood in a crowd of several thousand watching a funeral procession in Tarbes, a pro-Résistance town south of Toulouse, home of several aircraft manufacturers. He had not slept in days, and it showed. Soon he'd know if the ordeal had been worth it.

Around him men were somber, and women cried. A few days earlier the RAF had bombed a local factory that manufactured airplane propellers for the Luftwaffe. The raid had destroyed buildings and left huge craters in the yards, but the precision machinery used to calibrate propellers had been buried under debris and remained intact. The wreckage was cleaned up and production had already resumed. The civilian population had not fared so well. Bombs had fallen on the working-class neighborhood surrounding the plant. Over a hundred houses were damaged, eighteen civilians had been killed, and dozens wounded. The headline in the pro-Vichy newspaper *Le Semeur des Hautes-Pyrenees* read in big black letters: "*ASSASSINS BRITANNIQUES!*" Next came this state funeral for the victims. The procession was led by a band playing Chopin's funeral march, followed by eighteen flatbed trucks, each carrying a plain wood coffin adorned with a French flag.

Proust noted that the children's coffins were festooned with toys and stuffed animals—*nice touch*, he thought. The killing of civilians did not affect him anymore. He had seen the charred bodies of hundreds of men, women, and children after the fire-bombing of Guernica by the German Luftwaffe in '37. He thought the French were getting away cheap. No, the real damage was political. Thanks to the raid, the British appeared callous and incompetent. If Tarbes's population was to continue supporting the Allies, it was essential that the underground show they could act. Proust glanced at the city hall clock. It was 11:50 a.m. In a few minutes he'd know if they had turned things around.

He had used some of the explosives he had received from the British. Two communist workers had walked into the propeller plant doused with diesel fuel to hide the strong almond smell of the plastic compound tapped to their chests. Workers were searched at random but the two were not picked. Pure luck. They would have been shot on the spot if discovered—courageous those men were.

Proust and an Alsatian engineer had arrived in a car stolen from the Kommandantur. They flashed documents identifying themselves as German engineers sent from Stuttgart to inspect the damage and headed to the production floor where they behaved as if they owned the place. When a manager questioned them, they waved their papers in his face and shouted at him in German until he backed away. The Alsatian engineer, who had worked for DeWoitine aircraft, was an expert at calibrating propellers. He jimmied up the presses and placed the explosives in the heart of the locking mechanisms. Since the workers had been given an extended lunch break to attend the funeral, the fuses were set to detonate exactly at noon when the factory would be empty. They screamed some more at the plant manager, demanding to know why their expertise had been requested when the presses were in perfect order. The manager, who had not requested anything but was tired of being screamed at, apologized for the mishap. They left in a huff.

Success was crucial and Proust knew that the German reaction would be swift. Innocent hostages would be executed in reprisal. And then there would be more outrage from the population, and a rush of new recruits to the Résistance. Proust could not bear to look at the clock and when the bells of St. Jean's began to ring, his heart sank. Twelve o'clock and nothing—*they found the explosives*. He dropped his half-smoked cigarette and stepped on it. With tobacco so severely rationed, the man next to Proust looked at him as if he had lost his mind and picked up the cigarette. As he did, the first explosion echoed from behind the hill.

Seconds later, there was another one, louder this time. Startled, people in the crowd turned away from the funeral procession to look at the plumes of black smoke rising in the gray sky. The blasts kept coming every few seconds, perfectly timed.

Gendarmes ran to their vans and sirens came to life as they sped toward the plant. Fire engines rolled out of nearby stations. Men in the crowd stood still, nodding in satisfaction. They knew what was happening. A few furtively shook hands.

Slipping out of the crowd, Proust walked back to his hotel. At the beginning of the war, he had been buoyed by elation after each raid. Now all he felt was relief and despair at the relentless nature of the thing. He knew that he would now sink into a deep depression. These days it happened after every assignment, and he had resigned himself to wait it out. A colossal headache was crawling up his neck and settled deep behind his eyes. His stomach churned—*I smoke too much*.

His hotel would be a safe harbor for several days. Massive round-ups and pervasive identity checks would take place all over the city. Trains and buses would be watched. That was all fine with Proust, who did not intend to go anywhere. He just wanted to sleep. He had stocked his room with food and water and planned to hibernate until security measures abated. Reaching the quiet working-class hotel above a café, Proust took his key from the board and climbed to his room. He put his gun on the bedside table and took off his shoes. Removing his socks felt like an impossible task. He chewed some aspirin, lay down on the bed, and fell asleep.

Around dinnertime he awoke to rapid footsteps in the corridor. He listened to people rushing past his floor and heard the sound of a door opening and woman's voice on the upstairs landing. She did not sound happy. *Wrong floor*, Proust thought. He sprung up and felt for his shoes as his room door crashed open. Three Gestapo men slammed him against the wall and the beating started. He crawled on the floor, trying to protect his head. The blows kept coming. He tasted blood in his mouth. He heard his ribs crack. He was surprised by how much it hurt, and to his utter shame, he heard himself cry like a child.

They wouldn't let him put on his shoes and shoved him down the stairs. Curious heads popped out of rooms and retreated in a hurry at the sight of goons in leather coats dragging a man bloodied and bruised.

When they reached the street, the cool air felt good on Proust's ruined face. It did not last. The Gestapo men pushed him into the back of a black Citroën. Doors slammed shut and the car screeched away from the curb.

30

SUZANNE REMAINED IN TOULOUSE STRUGGLING to keep the escape line alive. She had also discovered she was pregnant. Both she and her husband Cervantes were overjoyed, but he had to stay in Paris where he worked as a subway technician while fighting in the underground. The separation was hard on them. Then the news of Proust's arrest and the rumor that he had died from a bullet in the back of the head in the cellar of a Tarbes police station filled her with penetrating sadness. To make matters worse, she was experiencing morning sickness with bouts of nausea that kept her in a dreadful mood.

When a source inside St. Michel's prison informed her that Janine's interrogation was conducted in the old warden's residence, she decided to act. The month before, the Résistance had successfully freed four men from a prison in Lyon by cracking a hole through the roof. All her life she had gone toward danger. She was skeptical about those two in the butcher's attic, but they had escaped the Germans twice. If there was a chance in hell that Janine could be rescued, she had to risk it.

An employee from the prefecture's building department smuggled out the prison blueprints and that night, she and Nicole drove Mike and Robert to a safe house. They both were eager for news and heartsick when they heard: Janine had been interrogated several times, her father had tried to commit suicide, and her mother Anna and daughter Emma had disappeared.

"Janine is being tortured?" Mike asked.

"Strong-arm interrogation, they call it," Nicole said.

Mike sank down under the weight of the news. "Those bastards."

The prison was built in 1853 but the warden's house had been constructed later. It was a stand-alone building on the south side of the facility with a church and a small garden behind the outer prison wall. They studied the blueprints and focused on the layout of the warden's house.

"Is there barbed wire on the roof?" Robert asked.

"Yes. Coils of triple concertina wire," Suzanne said.

"It's noisy to cut through that. We'll have guards all over us in no time," Robert said.

No roof then.

Nicole had slipped into the kitchen. Robert could see how she was intimidated by all that prison talk. Quiet yet resourceful—*she thought of hiding us in a bathhouse on the spur of the moment.*

A strong smell of coffee made them turn. Nicole was at the door, raising a pot while holding a pack of German Gollner Kaffee. "Coffee anyone?" she asked.

"Real coffee? Where did you get that?" Suzanne asked.

"My mother's German lover brings it to the house. I thought it'd be fitting to steal German coffee to keep you sharp while planning to attack a prison run by the Nazis."

They chuckled. Robert watched Nicole fill the cups. She was reserved one minute and resolute to the point of audacity the next. He couldn't help but be struck by the boundless attraction he felt for her. From that first day when they had walked out of the train station in Pau—*I want to live here with her*, he had thought.

"I need to go home. It's almost curfew time," Nicole said, picking up her coat and heading for the door. "I'll steal chocolate tomorrow." On her way, she kissed Robert on the cheek. "Be back in the morning."

"Be careful," Robert said.

"I will."

Robert watched her disappear. She was so down to earth, so normal. She liked him and was not afraid to show it. Everything in France was so different from the place he grew up.

Fortified by the strong brew, they went back to work. Mike measured the drawings and tallied numbers. The prison's external wall was twice as thick as the house wall. The builders had left a space in between to prevent humidity from seeping through. That was standard construction practice. Mike suggested blowing through both walls by laying one charge between the structures and another one buried at the foot of the wall.

"The trick is to use enough explosive to blow up the walls but not the whole building."

"And kill Janine on the other side," Suzanne said. "How much C-4?"

"For the house wall, two and a half pounds."

"And the prison wall?"

Mike studied the figures. "Twenty-four inches thick, ten pounds."

"Four and a half kilos. I can get that," Suzanne said. "And how will you set up that charge?"

"We'll bury it at the base of the prison wall. A couple of feet."

"Three feet would make me happier."

"Three feet it is." Mike glanced at Suzanne. "You've done this before?"

"Blew up a lot of stuff with dynamite in Spain. Never worked with cyclonite."

Mike and Robert looked at Suzanne with newfound respect. But then she raised a hand and rushed to the kitchen sink where she threw up. They watched her rinse her mouth and wash her face. "Something I ate," she said, waving off their concern. "Go on."

"We'll have to dig at night," Robert said.

"Yes. We'll need to use the church as a base," Suzanne replied. Feeling nausea rising again, she turned away, cupping her hand over her mouth. But after a moment, the discomfort faded. "Won't get any help there," she continued. "The parish priest is pro-Nazi. He proclaims at the end of each Sunday sermon that God is against the Communists and on the side of the new Europe, led by Adolph Hitler."

"We'll take care of him," Mike said.

"And we'll need a car," Suzanne said.

"My specialty," Robert said, cheerful at the prospect.

The next morning, Nicole guided Robert through the streets of Toulouse in search of a car. Many cyclists shared rides and they rode her bicycle with Nicole sitting on the handlebars, balancing between Robert's arms.

"We should race in the Tour de France like this," Robert said. He loved having her so close, smelling her perfume and feeling her shoulder pushing against his chest.

"I couldn't get you chocolate. My mother ate it all," Nicole said, turning to face him.

"That woman is awful." Robert grinned. "Are you still looking for a job in Pau?"

"Yes. I'll be there next week. Same trip we took."

She did not elaborate but Robert understood she would be smuggling more aviators and immediately he felt a clip of worry in his stomach—*be careful, please*. He did not say anything aloud.

They rode down to the city administrative district and found next to the prefecture a parking lot reserved for high-ranking French civil servants. Robert spotted a Peugeot gasogene four-door sedan with tanks of natural gas on the roof, a car he knew like the back of his hand.

"If something goes wrong, get out of here immediately. You understand?" Robert asked as they got off the bike.

Nicole glanced at the Nazi flag and the French and German sentries guarding the building entrance. She leaned over and held Robert tight in her arms—very tight, wanting to keep him there.

"Don't worry," he said as he saw her eyes brim with tears.

"I'm not worrying for myself."

"Don't worry about me. And you know what to do."

"I do." Her smile was genuine but so was the fear in her eyes.

Robert made sure she had a firm grip on the bicycle handlebars before he hurried away.

Nicole watched him leave to stand at the street corner where a uniformed policeman directed traffic. After a while, the cop stopped the traffic and pointed at Robert, signaling he should cross. Nicole's heart beat faster when Robert gave the cop a two-finger salute as if they saw each other every day. Then he strode across the parking lot to the Peugeot gasogene and stood against the driver's-side door with his hands down, looking up at nothing in particular. Nicole assumed he was fiddling with the lock and became convinced the policeman was watching him. After what felt an eternity, Robert pulled the car door open, got inside, and slid under the steering wheel. Waiting was unbearable but at long last Nicole heard the roar of the engine and saw Robert rise in the driver's seat, pushing the car into gear. She watched as the Peugeot moved across the lot, but when it reached the exit, the policeman extended his hand and ordered him to pull over.

Inside the car, Robert felt fear course through him. He wiped the sweat off his hands on his pants, thinking: *If I get caught, I'll never see her again.* Luckily, the cop blew his whistle, stopped the traffic, and waved at Robert to drive on.

Robert stepped on the gas and wheeled into the street. Glancing in the rearview mirror, he caught sight of Nicole climbing onto her bicycle. His relief intense, his dream and hopes burst out at once—he cared for her and she for him. He felt more French when he was with her. She had made a place in her world for him.

That afternoon, Robert and Mike drove to the church. When the clergyman's maid answered the door, Robert informed her that Monsignor Carlsbad, a German high prelate who was in Toulouse on an official visit, wanted to meet the Father and had sent a car for him. The maid was impressed. She had read about the Monsignor in the newspaper, where his photograph was featured on the first page—Robert had gotten the idea for his tale in the same paper.

Monsieur le Curé, she explained, was attending to his parishioners but would return for supper. She suggested they wait for him in the salon. Robert thanked her and said they would be back.

They settled on the terrace of a café across the street, ordered a carafe of wine, and watched the maid leave. As she had predicted, the priest, riding tall on his bicycle, showed up soon after.

Robert crossed the street. "Monsieur le Curé!" he called as the cleric got off his bicycle. Robert introduced himself and mentioned Monsignor Carlsbad. Before the priest could reply Mike pushed a gun into his ribs and helped him inside the Peugeot. All the locals saw were two polite young men escorting the local priest to an appointment.

Robert drove. In the back seat, le Curé protested loudly until Mike shoved him down on the floor of the car where he lay whimpering.

Suzanne waited for them on a bridge over the Garonne River. She climbed into the passenger seat and directed Robert to an abandoned factory leveled by allied bombing. They chained the priest to a twenty-ton metal press, brought him a bucket of water and a copy of the underground Résistance newspaper *Combat.*

"Think of it as a retreat, Father," Robert said. "Do some reading. The Allies are in Sicily and the Russians are pushing the Germans back into Poland. You might want to think over whose side God is really on."

"Petit con!" *Little jerk!* the priest spat at Robert's retreating figure.

Their next stop was a garage in the suburbs. The mechanic beckoned the car inside and closed the metal shutter behind them. They stepped out, shook hands, and watched him refill the charcoal fuel tanks. When he was done, he led Robert down into the inspection pit where they dragged out a crate marked VIGNOBLE FRONTON ROSÉ, which Robert carried up the steps and deposited in the trunk of the car. The mechanic brought out a bottle, lined up glasses, and poured. Suzanne covered her glass and motioned to her stomach—*digestive issues.*

The summer solstice was a hindrance. This time of the year nightfall didn't come until 9:30 p.m. and even then, the light persisted.

Robert sipped his wine and paced the room. Mike kept glancing at the clock on the wall and when he could stand it no longer, turned to Suzanne. "We've got a lot of work to do."

"We must wait until the neighbors go to bed," she said.

Fighting another bout of nausea, Suzanne felt a growing irritation—*these two better calm down or they'll get us killed.*

The street in front of the church was barely dark when they parked the Peugeot and slipped into the garden. Robert expertly forced the priest's lock and stepped into the house. Mike followed carrying the wine crate, which he swung carefully off his shoulder and onto the floor. Robert walked into the kitchen, where the priest's dinner was kept warm over a pot of steaming water, and turned down the heat. Suzanne closed the door, drew the curtains, and produced candles, which she lit.

Overlooking the garden, the house next door had a window hung with curtains that blew in the evening breeze, so Mike crawled out of sight to check the prison's outer wall—eighteen feet high and solidly built. Walking toe to heel, he measured the wall and dug into the grass with his shoe to mark the halfway point. Then he crawled back to the priest's house.

"Pebble stones and concrete. Twelve pounds of cyclonite should do it."

Robert pulled the lid off the crate with a crowbar and dug into the straw, delicately extracting explosives wrapped in grease paper next to tools, wires, and weapons.

"Got everything?" Mike asked.

Robert nodded. "C-4 explosive, two sets of wires and detonators, bolt cutters, four hand grenades, three Webley revolvers with ammunition."

"Use the grenades only if you have to." Suzanne was brusque. "They're hard to get."

Mike flicked a two-finger salute. "Oui, Chef!"

Suzanne's eyes narrowed. "You're getting on my nerves."

Mike raised his hands apologetically. "I just think we should all try to lighten up, that's all."

"Lighten up?" Suzanne snarled. "What do you think this is? Bastille Day with fireworks?"

"Enough!" Robert hissed. "Both of you."

Robert moved to the stove and filled plates with a bean stew. "Want to eat?" he asked Suzanne, holding one out. She shook her head. Her stomach was in no shape for any kind of food. Mike sat down and tasted the dish.

"That woman can cook. What's this?"

"Cassoulet," Suzanne replied. "White beans, tomatoes, duck comfit . . ."

Mike glanced at Robert and added, "Pork sausage and pork loin."

"My favorite," Robert said.

Watching them eat made Suzanne queasy—*how can they be hungry at a time like this?* She looked away and pulled the curtains back enough to check on the house next door. "Someone's there," she said. "They turned on the lights."

"Getting ready for bed," Robert said.

At last, the lights clicked off next door. They crawled across the garden and by the light of a half-moon began to chip out the cement in the prison wall. It was tedious work; their arm, shoulder, and leg muscles ached. They took turns but worked relentlessly.

"Kidnapping that priest was fun," Robert whispered.

"Yeah, you really got into it," Mike said. Using the chisel as a lever, he winced with effort as he removed a stone the size of his fist. Robert took his place, his face resolute, as if he wanted to tear out the concrete with his teeth. They took short breaks to drink "Nicole's coffee" that Suzanne kept making for them. They worked all night. It was a little after four in the morning when the hole was large enough for Mike to burrow his arm into the cavity.

"There is a space. It's filled with junk but it's loose," he said, pulling out handfuls of debris that, over the years, had filled the space. "And now I can feel the house wall."

Robert grabbed a shovel. A few minutes later there was a three-foot-deep hole at the base of the wall. Back in the priest's house, Mike unwrapped two C-4 cakes and tied them together. Then he cut another cake in half and kneaded it into a ball. Suzanne watched them from her chair, pulling the curtain aside now and again to check the window next door.

Mike buried the detonators in the C-4 plastic explosive and carried both charges outside. There he wedged the small one in the space between the walls and the big charge deep down against the wall foundation. Robert unspooled the wire across the garden and passed it to Suzanne through the kitchen window. The sun was rising; they went back inside, washed up, and yawned.

"Get some sleep," Suzanne said. "I'll wake you before Nicole arrives."

"Nicole is coming here?" Robert asked, worried.

"Yes. A contact inside the prison will let us know when Janine is taken out of her cell. Nicole will bring the message."

Robert grumbled at the news. He didn't want Nicole there. It was dangerous. He sighed but followed Mike into the priest's bedroom, where they split the blankets and went to sleep.

"As if they didn't have a worry in the world," Suzanne muttered. She listened—*and they snore.*

Suzanne didn't get much sleep. She was roused by the sounds of the prison rising and cringed at the thought of Janine waking up in jail knowing that she would be tortured again. Suzanne forced herself to swallow one helping of cassoulet. Minutes later, she rushed to the kitchen sink and threw up. While washing her mouth, she spotted Robert and Mike looking at her from the doorway.

"My mother was always sick when pregnant," Robert said. "That's what it is, isn't it?"

"I'm fine." Suzanne dried her face with a kitchen towel.

"Let's get moving," Mike said, picking up tools.

A knock at the door. It was Nicole with the news that Janine had been taken out of her cell. She stepped forward and kissed Robert on both cheeks.

"It's risky. Leave now," Robert said before following Mike outside.

Nicole stood there, confounded by Robert's surliness. She had been told that men changed personalities when getting ready for combat. Some would even gesture or walk differently. They became other people—*this is not the Robert I know.*

"Nicole, you must go," Suzanne said.

Before heading for the door, Nicole gazed at Robert in the garden, mindful she was witnessing something private and dangerous—*please don't get yourself killed.*

The wall blew up exactly as predicted. When a hailstorm of stones and gravel bounced against the house, Robert and Mike raced across the garden and disappeared into the black smoke bellowing out of the hole. A downpour from gushing pipes drenched them. The room was thick with fumes. They shoved a twisted bathtub out of the way. People were screaming. A guard appeared; Mike shot him. They stepped over his body and burst into the interrogation room. In all the smoke and confusion, they couldn't find Janine. They ran from room to room, before spotting a heap of a person—tied to the chair, their head slumped on their chest.

Mike hacked the chain holding the victim's wrists.

"Merci."

Mike looked up. The prisoner was a *man*, his face severely battered.

"It's not her, God damn it!" Mike shouted. "Where's Janine?"

"They took her away this morning," the man said.

Robert pointed at the hole in the wall. "Get him out!"

Mike cut the chains off the man's ankles and led him through the debris. Robert tossed out a grenade as he spotted a German officer leading a squad of guards into the house.

"Achtung Sturmbannführer!" A booted woman in a black skirt rushed over, snatched the grenade, dropped to her knees, and held the grenade against her belly.

"Nein, Marguerite!" the officer yelled. There was a muted explosion and the woman's body hurdled across the room. Blood splattered the wallpaper. Robert threw another grenade and rushed away as it exploded.

The prison siren started wailing as Mike helped his man toward the street. At the window of the house next door, a lady in her nightgown waved a French flag and shouted: "Bravo, bravo!"

Mike pushed his man into the back of the car and moved to the front. A stunned Suzanne looked at him. "It's you! Oh my God. I thought you were dead."

"Pretty close," Proust said. "They brought me here last night."

Robert slid onto the back seat as the two-tone *pin-pon* of police sirens clamored from every direction. Suzanne pushed the car into gear. The engine stalled. She pulled the ignition, the engine whined and whined . . .

"The choke," Robert said from the back. Suzanne opened her arms looking for the device. Robert reached over and pulled the knob. "There!"

The engine sputtered and caught. Suzanne wrenched the car onto the street. Robert let out a sigh.

"Do you know where Janine is?" Mike asked.

"The Gestapo is transferring her to Paris," Proust said. He rubbed his hair, his fingers like claws, hard on the skin. "I owe you my life."

Suzanne switched gears, triggering an ugly rattle from the transmission.

"Easy on the clutch," Robert grumbled.

As they pulled away from the mayhem inside the prison with its siren resonating over the whole neighborhood, Mike looked back. The lady in the nightgown was still fervidly waving her flag.

31

THE MOOD IN THE CAR was tense as they drove through town. Most private automobiles had been requisitioned for official use and one loaded with four civilians who looked nothing like local civil servants was bound to attract attention. Suzanne kept darting glances into the rearview mirror. Robert sat ramrod straight, a muscle in his jaw twitching every time the clutch creaked.

"Revolver?" Proust asked. Mike glanced at Suzanne and at her nod of approval, he slid a Webley to Proust.

"Merci." Proust checked the chamber and, keeping a finger on the trigger guard, held the gun nose down between his legs. Sirens wailed in the distance, and they all strived to appease the wire of fear inside them. A traffic policeman stopped them so kids in school uniforms could cross the street. The sirens were getting closer when the cop finally waved them on. They wheeled around the roundabout past a squad of miliciens who peered at them—*will they stop us?* No, the miliciens lost interest. Suzanne swerved into an avenue and stepped on the gas. They passed a fire engine roaring up the street in the opposite direction, then she took another right and swore under her breath—rows of German army trucks lined up the curb ahead of them.

"Merde."

Tension inside the car shot up. Suzanne downshifted and the car began to pass the convoy. The trucks sat idle. Their drivers stood by in groups of two or three, smoking and paying no mind to the Peugeot with its four hunched passengers.

"I thought I was finished back there," Proust said. He turned to Mike, grabbed his hand, and shook it.

Looking at Proust in the rearview mirror, Suzanne asked, "You were arrested in Tarbes?"

"Yes," Proust answered. "The Gestapo brought me over. They kept beating the shit out of me."

Suzanne drove north toward Paris and they settled in. Wherever Janine had been taken, they would go. They cruised between fields of yellow sunflowers blanketing the hills and watched the sun shine on carefully tilled land. It was hot. The car stank of sweat and overheated upholstery. They opened the windows to let in the warm fragrant air. Suzanne stopped at a village post office to make calls. When she returned Robert had taken her place behind the wheel.

"You don't like the way I drive?" she asked.

"You're hard on the clutch," Robert said.

Suzanne rolled her eyes and climbed into the passenger seat. "We've got a safe house for tonight."

They continued north. The countryside was verdant and beautiful. Proust kept glancing at Mike with curiosity. "What kind of explosive did you use?" he asked.

"C-4, RDX, cyclonite," Mike said.

"How much?"

"Five point seven kilos. Two charges. One fifth, four fifth."

"That's conservative," Proust said.

"I was worried about you on the other side."

Proust nodded in appreciation. "You set the small charge between the walls?"

"Right."

Robert listened to them talking shop and glanced at Suzanne—*do you believe these guys?*

"You used a pull igniter Mk3?" Proust was now asking.

"No, all I had was a switch Mk1. But it worked beautifully."

A thin smile worked its way onto Proust's pale lips. "An American saved my Communist ass. Who would have thought?"

"J. Edgar Hoover would be pissed." Mike grinned.

"Who's that?"

"Head of the FBI," Mike said. "A rabid anti-communist and world-class asshole."

Mike and Proust threw back their heads and laughed. It was contagious—Suzanne and Robert joined in. It did them good.

Proust asked to be dropped in Albi where Résistance-Fer would smuggle him back to Paris. It would be safer for all. They stopped at the train station and after meaningful handshakes, Proust got out of the car and they watched him walk away with a limp.

"They beat him up pretty bad," Suzanne said.

They kept on moving north, taking small roads through the Tarn and Garonne département. It was evening when they reached a house outside Tulle belonging to a local Résistance chief. The man was not there but his housekeeper was expecting them. Her husband got into the Peugeot and drove it away, east toward Carcassonne. If the car were ever linked to the prison escape, the French police and the Gestapo would be looking for them in all the wrong places.

The housekeeper fed them, and Suzanne was able to eat some soup. It reassured her—*I was just anxious*, she thought before falling asleep.

Robert and Mike settled into armchairs and popped their feet up. Neither could sleep. Robert could still smell the sour fumes of the gunpowder on his clothes. He kept seeing that woman screaming in German and picking up the grenade. He had heard about the SS motto of "absolute allegiance" but a woman committing suicide to save her boss? *Who are those people?* He pushed away the thought and a better one came to mind: Nicole so shy and beautiful stealing

German coffee for them. Then, bits and pieces of worry as he realized he had barely acknowledged her presence before the attack. *Did she kiss me?* Of course she must have. He couldn't remember. *Did I ignore her? What was I thinking?* He shook his head to push it all away, but it left him with a feeling of melancholy that blended with the tenderness he felt for her.

Back in town, Nicole had been in anguish all day. She was quite a distance from the prison when she heard the first blast and then gunfire and detonations. She knew she had to get away as far as possible, but she could not. She needed to know if they were alive or had been caught. Finally in midafternoon, she set out toward the prison with soul-sucking dread. When she got there the street was bloated with onlookers and police cars. The bar across from the church was doing big business. Nicole moved through the crowd realizing this was a stupid thing to do—someone might have seen her get into the priest's house and could recognize her. No one did but she learned that a woman whose window overlooked the church had seen people run into the street. The explosion had woken her up and no she did not remember how many they were or what kind of car they drove.

Nicole felt it was safe to go ahead with her last assignment. She found a mailbox and dropped an envelope addressed to the Toulouse archdiocese. It contained a note made of newspaper cutouts that revealed the bombed factory location where the priest was confined.

Suzanne, Robert, and Mike left the next morning in the back of a farm truck. At every stop another farmer or a village merchant shepherded them through the backcountry aboard horse-drawn buggies. In the evening they reached Limoges, where they hid in Charlotte's beauty salon cellar. Mike and Robert were surprised by how emotional they felt entering Charlotte's kitchen and being there again with Suzanne. A few weeks ago, they were just passing through, but it was different now. They were members of the French Résistance fighting beside these women. A brutal war this was, but they were proud to wage it. And there would be no respite: Proust had sent word that Janine was incarcerated at Fresnes prison outside Paris and suggested that Mike and Robert link up with him at a safe house in Paris, 14th arrondissement.

Few words were exchanged during dinner—the less said, the safer. Mike and Robert went down to the cellar where cots awaited them. The women stayed upstairs. Since the wave of arrests in Brittany, Toulouse, and Pau, Charlotte had lived in a state of heightened anxiety. But the news of Suzanne's pregnancy brought unmitigated joy. The two women kissed and laughed with tears in their eyes. Since the beginning of the war the sisters had sustained each other. Résistance was like a religion among communists, a commitment to be shared within the family. They despised their countrymen's submissiveness to German occupation: *They don't care. They're just waiting for the war to end.*

Charlotte's hatred of the Nazis was personal as there was the painful matter of her husband. "It's worse than if he were dead," Charlotte said with a grim smile, affirming the absurdity of existence. At first it was a good marriage. Her husband Maurice was a loving husband and a good father. He worked as a traveling salesman for a Cognac manufacturer and made a good income. Then he became involved in politics and developed a pathological hatred for those "socialist politicians who were leading the country to disaster." He'd come back from a business trip to Germany dazzled by how well that country was run and how hardworking its people were.

Maurice knew enough German to understand Hitler's speeches and found them electrifying. In 1941 he joined the Legion of French

Volunteers Against Bolshevism and enlisted in the German army. A few months later he was incorporated into the Wehrmacht and sent to the Russian front. When he wrote that he intended to come home on leave wearing his uniform, Charlotte begged him not to do it, to think of their son and how difficult his life would be if people found out his father was a Nazi. His leave was canceled, but Charlotte decided to send Daniel to boarding school in Dijon.

"In case of emergency you'll need to pull Daniel out of that school," Suzanne said.

"Why?"

"They'll use him to get to you."

"They would hurt him?" Charlotte asked.

"You wouldn't know what they're doing to him."

"They're that vicious?"

"Oh yes. You must be able to get Daniel and go into hiding at a few hours' notice. I'll get travel documents for the two of you."

The next morning, at the train station, Mike and Robert had an emotional good-bye with Suzanne. The war had a way of stretching time. They had only met a few days ago but felt they had known her forever.

"Good-bye, comrades," Suzanne said. "You didn't rescue Janine, but you freed Proust. It's all over the underground newspapers. The Résistance has stormed a prison and freed one of its own. It raises morale, more people are joining up, and that might be the most important thing of all."

They shook her hand. Résistance-Fer smuggled them to Paris. Proust had sent strict orders and their escorts treated them with subtle deference.

32

AFTER JUMPING OFF FROM THE third-floor window of the Gestapo office in Toulouse and crashing onto the sidewalk, Janine's father was kept in a cell for several days. He was delirious and his tormentors realized that further questioning would be useless, so they ordered the French police to take him to a hospital. If he survived, they reasoned, then they would have a chance to question him again.

Nanette was the nurse who examined him. She was a new hire at Toulouse Sainte-Marie hospital. She used to work on trains repatriating sick POWs but had trained as a scrub nurse and missed surgery. So when she heard a position was available in the orthopedics department, she applied.

The administrator explained to Nanette that half the facility was reserved for German military personnel. The French and German medical staff supposedly practiced wherever their expertise was needed, but the reality was different. German doctors had difficulty finding French nurses to assist them, and French doctors had trouble getting consultations from their German colleagues. Medicine was rationed for French patients but plentiful for Germans. Was she willing to work for a German surgeon who needed a scrub nurse?

The irony was not lost on Nanette. A few days earlier she had helped an American pilot conceal his identity by removing the nicotine stains on his fingers and now she was offered to work for a German doctor. She took the job.

The surgeon, Doctor Weiss, was a man in his early fifties with a thick mane of gray hair that reminded Nanette of the American actor Spencer Tracy, whom she had seen on screen before the war in *Captain Courageous.* Weiss had been wounded in World War I and walked with a limp. He spoke "surgery" French, so his vocabulary left little room for small talk. That was fine with her—the less interaction the better. Plus, he was a superb surgeon and Nanette considered herself lucky.

And she was proud of Doctor Weiss when a few days later the police brought a carpenter, said to have fallen off a roof. The man was in a coma, and she realized his wounds and broken bones were several days old. There were also suspicious bruises around his wrists. She had heard about torture, but this was the first time she had been confronted with the evidence of it. The man's chances of survival were slim and if he did survive, she feared he would be disabled for life. Nanette handed the patient's chart to Doctor Weiss, fully expecting him to pass it on to a French doctor. He checked the bruises and gently prodded the damaged tissue around the broken bones.

"Fell off a roof?" he asked.

"Yes."

He examined the man's hands. "Carpenter with hands of a concert pianist," he muttered.

He knows, Nanette thought, expecting Doctor Weiss to move on, but he surprised her again.

"Schedule surgery. Check blood type. We'll need lots of blood."

They worked in the operating room until past midnight. The man's hips had to be reset, then his legs, arms, and jaw. When they were done the patient was in a cast from head to toe and hoisted up in traction.

Two days later, Nanette found a note clipped to the patient's chart. It read: *Louis de Guilhem, dentist, tortured by the Gestapo.*

33

ON YOUR FIRST DAY IN JAIL, you always give your food away. Your cellmates are in much worse shape, and they need it more than you do. So on her first evening in Fresnes prison, Janine lay on her cot hungry and in pain. The burns from the electric shocks to her body had turned into nasty blisters filled with pus. Their smell told Janine that the infection was getting worse, although the stench was rampant. The whole wing reeked of rotten flesh from tortured prisoners. And there was the other torture, fearing for her daughter Emma, back in Toulouse, in the hands of that awful Gestapo woman.

Every morning at precisely seven o'clock, Janine and all the prisoners on her cellblock listened to the guards rounding up detainees selected for that day's questioning. If you had not been called by 7:15, you were safe for another day. The Germans were methodical. Intimidation came first. Every few days Janine got a new cellmate fresh from a torture session. All had been submitted to waterboarding and electrical torture. Janine was stunned to see how much a face could swell under blows. The women could barely open their eyes. Their first night was excruciating as their bodies came out of shock with every nerve quivering like a live wire. It was agonizing to watch such suffering, and that, of course, was the point.

The worst was Edith. She was in her twenties, painfully thin, and the mother of a six-month-old infant. She was negotiating a flight of stairs at a metro station with a baby carriage; a courteous German soldier offered a helping hand. She tried to refuse but he insisted good-naturedly. As they edged up the steps, the weight of the carriage surprised him and when he heard a rattling sound coming from inside, he checked and found a case of hand grenades under the baby's mattress.

Her tormentors had left her hanging by the wrists for hours. Both of her shoulders were dislocated, her upper arm bones pocking out from under the skin. She laid in unimaginable pain and Janine offered: "Perhaps I can help. Can you sit up?"

Edith managed to turn her body around and sit on the edge of the cot.

Janine cupped her elbow and gave her arm a sharp pull and a twist. Edith screamed. The left shoulder slid back into place and as if by magic the pain evaporated.

"Oh my God! Thank you," Edith said.

"Shall I try the other one?"

"Yes!"

But when Janine could not feel the shoulder bone on that side she hesitated. "I don't know about this one."

"Do it," Edith urged, her eyes closed in pain.

The pull and twist motion failed. Edith let out a heartbreaking yell. The ball of the bone was still out of the socket with every muscle in her chest twitching wildly. Janine loathed herself. She had torn Edith's shoulder ligaments and made it worse.

After Edith was taken away, Janine sank into despair. She could not sleep more than a few minutes at a time. She thought she had caught a lucky break when on the way back from the yard a guard hit her chest with his baton. She dropped like a stone and was carried to the infirmary where she fainted again as a nurse drained her mangled nipples and spread them with antiseptic. The reprieve did not last. After a few days, the infection was back.

"Janine Dumas!"

The cell door swung open, and Janine joined the other prisoners shuffling along the gangway to a courtyard where a prison bus waited. The vehicle was partitioned into cubicles built for one prisoner, but the detainees were so skinny, the guards crammed two or three women into each slot. Janine sat by a window and pressed her forehead against the glass. They entered Paris through the Porte d'Orléans and sped down through Montparnasse. It was a sunny day and Janine recognized the cafés. She even caught a glimpse of l'hôtel Royal-Bretagne where she and her husband had spent their honeymoon. They had eaten in restaurants, visited the sights, and then rushed back to bed in the middle of the afternoon. Afterward, they lay in bed laughing and arguing about the names of their children. They had wanted at least three, maybe four.

When the bus drove past the Invalides, Janine watched the long line of German soldiers waiting to visit Napoleon's tomb. This was one of the occupiers' favorite sights. As a special gift to France, Hitler had ordered the remains of François Napoleon, son of Napoleon and Marie Louise of Austria, to be transferred to the Invalides for burial next to his father. Janine remembered newsreels featuring SS soldiers in parade uniforms carrying the coffin. The Vichy propaganda machine had promoted the event as a great celebration of Franco-Austrian-German kinship and common history.

Paris was an occupied city with German signs positioned at every street corner. They now entered the government district with sandbags stacked high against official buildings and Nazi flags flying over every entrance. On the rue des Saussaies they pulled up in front of the old interior ministry that was now the Gestapo headquarters. Gendarmes ordered them off the bus and across a courtyard. An SS guard counted them, wrote down the tally, and counted again. Finally satisfied, he signed the transfer papers, kept the bottom sheet, and handed the stack back to the gendarme. Janine shook her head:

Liebe fuers Detail. Painstaking attention to detail. Sound in business, deadly in war.

Inside the building, smartly dressed German and French Gestapo agents moved purposefully. The men were handsome and the women attractive. Janine was separated from the others and led to an office on the second floor where a stout German woman in her late twenties dressed in civilian clothes waited. She was polite, wore a delicate perfume, and spoke good French. She told Janine that Oberrsturmbannfüher Karl Lindinger would interview her.

How civilized, Janine thought. *Like an appointment with my insurance broker.* While she waited Janine glanced at her arms. She had been compulsively scratching since her arrest and the skin was raw and bleeding from palm to elbow. She rolled down her sleeves—*might as well look good before he breaks my teeth.* Her cellmates had warned her about the Oberrsturmbannfüher. He was smart, spoke softly, and could be gratuitously vicious. They walked into his office and the secretary pointed at the chair facing the desk. Janine sat and regarded a man who wore a SS uniform, boots, and breeches. *The Nazi look*, she thought.

Lindinger closed the file on his desk and gave her a dark look.

"Sprechen sie deutche?"

"Yes, I speak German."

"How come?"

"I studied at Dusseldorf University."

"Did you learn anything?" he asked condescendingly.

"I did. German dentists are very good."

"We'll speak German, then," he said, glancing at his secretary who immediately headed for the door. Lindinger gave her shapely figure a proprietary glance. *His mistress*, Janine thought.

"Do you know who denounced you?" Lindinger asked.

"No. Why would anybody denounce me?"

"A dentist. Probably someone who wants to steal your patients," Lindinger said and added, "The champions in the denunciation game are doctors who accuse their colleagues of being Jewish. Dentists are rare."

Janine knew Lindinger was lying. A Résistance source inside the Toulouse police station had passed word that Prosper had been duped into talking by a detective dressed as a priest.

"This man tells us that you're the head of an escape line smuggling Anglo-American airmen to Spain."

"How would he know? He's a *dentist*," Janine said.

Lindinger appraised her and began rapid-fire questioning. What were the names of her contacts in Brussels, Lille, Paris, Lyon, and Marseille? He also asked about rendezvous locations in Perpignan and Barcelona. Janine responded that she had never been to those places, except Paris before the war. It helped that she was telling the truth. She did not know anyone in Lyon, Marseille, Perpignan, or Barcelona. After a while, Janine realized that a substantial amount of Lindinger's information was inaccurate. Although he knew about their contact in Spain, he placed the British consular attaché in Barcelona instead of Bilbao. Janine kept repeating that the French police had arrested the wrong dentist.

Lindinger then talked about Janine's parents. Her father had attempted to commit suicide; her mother had been deported to a camp in Germany. "And here you are. I hope it was all well worth it to you." He smiled, enjoying himself.

Janine hid the hurt and kept a blank face.

Lindinger went back to the file, turned a page, and tapped a finger on a line.

Janine tensed up—*here it comes.*

"Emma?" Lindinger asked.

"Yes."

"Your daughter? Like Emma Bovary," said Lindinger, elated to show off his knowledge of French literature.

Janine nodded. "Where is she?"

Lindinger looked at her. Suddenly friendly, concerned. "I'll ask you one question. You answer truthfully, I'll tell you where she is."

"Yes." Janine waited.

"Where do we find Adam Klaczko, a polish Jew member of the communist underground who goes by the name of Proust?"

Janine managed to keep her emotions in check. "I don't know who that is," she said, her face expressionless.

"There are many unpleasant ways to continue this conversation, Madame." Lindinger's voice rang out like cold steel.

"I know," Janine said.

And suddenly Lindinger looked amused and closed her file as if fed up with the melodrama of police work.

"Your daughter is in the Drancy internment camp. The two of you will be on the next convoy to a camp in Germany."

"You deport children now?"

"We have no choice. It's the same with Jews. We need adults for our factories, but the French government insists we take the children as well."

Lindinger took a last drag of his cigarette and buried it in the ashtray. The interview was over. The secretary appeared and escorted Janine out.

Lindinger watched the door close and picked up his telephone. "Get me Boucher."

He lit another cigarette as Boucher's voice came through the receiver.

"Boucher, you're a cretin."

Boucher came through protesting loudly.

"I just had her in my office!" Lindinger shouted. "This woman is smart and strong-willed. No question, she ran that escape line and it was idiotic of you to arrest her so publicly. Within hours every member of her organization had gone into hiding. You should have taken her at night after curfew and interrogated her right away. Whatever she'd tell us now is useless."

Boucher's voice could be heard through the receiver yelling: "The Toulouse Gestapo interrogated her!"

"French policemen should have arrested her!" Lindinger shouted in response. "But you don't trust your own force. That's why you used the milice and *we* pay the milice!"

Boucher kept protesting but Lindinger would not let him. "You had Turenne and you let him escape. We gave you that farmer in Brittany, but you didn't bother to make the arrest yourself and it turned into a debacle. We gave you Prosper Navarre and you wasted that information. You have failed at every step!"

Boucher's enraged voice could be heard through the receiver but again Lindinger cut him off. "One of your men was killed in Toulouse? So what? I lose men every day and you don't hear me snivel about it."

Boucher tried again, but Lindinger droned on. "You talk and talk while we Germans get things done! And that's why we are winning the war!"

Lindinger hung up, drew deeply on his cigarette, and blew the smoke at the telephone—*moron.*

The gesture spoke volumes.

34

JANINE WAS ON THE WAY to Drancy internment camp in the back of a black Citroën. They drove through Clichy, Montmartre, and the northeastern suburbs of Paris. They sped along while Janine brooded over her encounter with Lindinger. He was known for being a vicious interrogator but nothing vicious had occurred—*because he had gotten all he wanted out of her*. And now a loop of anxiety kept playing and replaying in her head. The only relief was the prospect of soon finding Emma and holding her in her arms. She should have been outraged and loudly protest her innocence when he asked if it was all worth it. She said nothing. He barely listened to her answers and went out of his way to show how bad his intelligence was. It was exactly the opposite. He was well informed. He knew about Proust. What else did he know? And the old worry came back with a vengeance: *Had the line been penetrated?*

The roar of engines distracted Janine. They were passing buses packed with civilians and escorted by police motorcycles. Janine could see children pressing their faces against the glass. A young boy waved feebly at her. He must have been three, four years old—*Jewish children, poor devils*, she thought. She waved back—*Emma could be on that bus*. And her mind swam back to those rumors of euthanasia programs she had heard during her time in Germany—*what will they do to those children?*

The Citroën was now approaching a U-shaped four-story building ringed with guard towers and encircled by a double fence of barbed wire. The windows were secured with iron bars and the glass had been painted cobalt blue. It looked like an improvised prison, which is exactly what it was. Janine knew that more than six thousand Jews and a few Résistants were confined here waiting for deportation to camps in the east—*and I'm about to join them.*

The Citroën was waved through the first checkpoint manned by the German military police, then a second one staffed by French gendarmes. The car pulled up in front of a low building and the Gestapo man in the front seat got out and escorted Janine inside. It was hot and the crowded room was thick with the smell of fear. Surly French gendarmes were processing men and women wearing yellow stars. The Gestapo man pushed Janine in front of him, raised his elbows, and held daintily onto the sleeves of his leather coat. He'd be damned if he touched anybody in there.

"Gestapo! Get out of my way!" he barked, parting the crowd in front of him on the way to the counter where he slapped down Janine's transfer papers.

"Datieren Sie das, unterschreiben Sie und stemplen Sie das!" *Date, sign, and stamp*, he ordered.

The gendarme dutifully complied and handed the bottom copy to the German who hurried out, convinced he had already been infected by several highly contagious diseases.

A policewoman snapped her fingers at Janine. "You wait there."

Janine stood with a group of bedraggled people and could hear the growl of an approaching diesel engine. The blue paint on the glass windowpane next to her had been scratched off in places and by leaning against the frame, she could see outside. The buses they had passed on the way were pulling over in the yard and immediately surrounded by French Gardes Mobiles holding up rifles and wearing helmets. A voice boomed from a loudspeaker:

"Children under age twelve move to the right, all other passengers move to the left."

The buses' heavy engines rumbled on, spewing fumes. People stepped out and Janine realized they were all women and children.

"Children under age twelve move to the right . . ." The disembodied voice repeated itself but the children did not want to leave their mothers. When the guards tried to lead them away, their mothers held onto them even more tightly. The voice coming from the loudspeaker now proved to belong to a police captain who stepped into Janine's line of vision. "Separate them!" he barked through his megaphone.

And the yard exploded into chaos. The Gardes Mobiles dove into the brawl, striking indiscriminately as they separated mothers from their children. The women still inside the buses now refused to get out. Gendarmes climbed through the back and flushed them out. The women scratched the gendarmes' faces, drawing blood, but the end result was never in doubt. The children were dragged away by their arms and feet, and infants wrenched away from their mothers.

Inside the facility, they heard the shouting and screaming but everyone remained silent, looking angrily at the ground. Janine noticed a couple of women wiping away tears—*they have gone through it all themselves and lost their own children*, she realized.

The captain blew his whistle again and Janine watched as the Gardes Mobiles surrounded the women and herded them back aboard the buses. The desperate clamor of the children left behind and the frantic screams of their mothers drowned out the noise of the engines. As the doors closed and the vehicles started moving, the women beat against the windows. Blood running from their pounding fists smeared the glass. But the buses kept rolling and soon were out of sight.

When the police captain who had overseen the whole operation walked into the room, Janine turned to face him.

"Capitaine!" As she approached, she could smell the alcohol on his breath. "What were you doing with those families? Have you lost your mind?"

"Shut up, you cunt!" He snapped at a gendarme and pointed at Janine. "Get that whore out of here!"

The gendarme pulled Janine away hissing. "Don't. This'll only make it worse for you."

As if in response the captain called out, "Make sure that slut is on the next train east!"

Shrugging off the guard's hold, Janine shouted back, "You people are worse than the Nazis!"

The captain raised a finger. "We're *better* than the Nazis," he said. "We get the job done right!"

The gendarme led Janine away, whispering, "There's nothing we can do. German orders. They want the adults deported first."

"Nothing you can do?" Janine turned on him. "Don't do it! Monsters! That's what you are!"

The gendarme opened a door and pushed her through. Low ceilinged with planks nailed over the windows, the next room was dark and fetid. At a long line of tables weary people watched gendarmes dump out the contents of their bags and suitcases, confiscating food, wine, cigarettes, and valuables, emptying wallets and grabbing checkbooks and savings certificates. When people protested, they were told that it all would be returned to them on the day of their departure.

A policewoman poked Janine with her baton.

"Where is your yellow star?"

"I'm not Jewish."

She snapped the papers out of Janine's hand. "Terrorist?"

"That's right."

"Where's your luggage?"

"I don't have any."

"Take off your jacket and blouse."

The policewoman checked Janine's pockets and the seams of her clothing and handed it all back. At one of the tables, three men wearing suits and chests full of medals were arguing with the guards.

"Jewish war veterans." The guard shrugged, following Janine's gaze. "They think their medals will protect them. They're fools, Jews are Jews."

"They fought for France," Janine said.

"So what? We all fought."

A gendarme ripped the medals off one man's chest and threw them into a barrel already full of previous encounters. When the man tried to slap him, three guards intervened and bludgeoned him until he fell bleeding to the floor.

Janine screamed, "Stop it!" and ran toward the still, bruised figure, but the policewoman caught her and dragged her to the door.

"You're on block five. Staircase three. That's where the non-Jews are. Stick to your own," the policewoman said, pushing her out the door.

Blinded by the sudden sunlight, Janine stumbled but caught herself and looked around to get her bearings—a courtyard surrounded by gray buildings crowded with people walking in small groups: men, women, elderly. Most wore yellow stars. Even on this hot day many were shivering. A few wore military blankets with their heads prodding through a hole in the middle.

A man peeled himself off the wall and balanced his tall frame on the balls of his feet. "Janine Dumas," he said.

"Who is asking?"

"I'm Jacquet, FTP. I was told to look out for you."

Janine stared at the man. He was in his forties, muscular with wide shoulders and a hard working-class face. He stuck out a hand and she shook it. It was rough as sandpaper.

"Who asked you to look out for me?"

"Someone you know. Goes by the name of Proust."

"Why should I trust you?"

"I had the honor of meeting Paul Turenne."

"Who's Turenne?"

"Last November when Paul Turenne had been arrested by les Renseignements Généraux, I picked him up," Jacquet said.

Paul was freed by the FTP in November. Janine's heart lifted. *Still, don't trust him.*

"How was he?"

"Badly beaten."

"How?"

Jacquet let out a sigh through tobacco-stained teeth. "A nerf de boeuf on the shins. Commissaire Boucher's work."

"And you freed him, how? With guns?" Janine asked.

"No guns," Jacquet said. "Razor blades. More efficient and quieter."

This matched the account of Turenne's rescue Janine had heard from Suzanne—*so this is the man who freed my uncle.*

Janine glanced at the French gendarmes on the roof manning machine guns. "Not a German in sight," she said.

"Nope."

"A proud nation, we are."

"There is a lot of hatred in this country. All the misfits and crooks that could never hope to rise to the top are now in power. They're out for revenge; and money, of course."

Janine glared at the building behind her. "They steal all they want from people's luggage."

"Yes and no one complains. Everyone is terrified of being deported and the gendarmes are the ones who draw up the lists."

"And their superiors let it happen?"

"They get a piece of the action. Their chief has just been awarded the Légion d'honneur for exceptional service to the nation. Every week, he pays a visit and leaves with suitcases filled with valuables."

Janine looked at the gray cinder block buildings around them. "What are those, flats?" Janine said.

"Used to be. It was built it in the thirties, one of the first low-cost tenements for working-class families," Jacquet said. "It was confiscated by the Nazis, and it's now divided into twenty-two staircases. When they're selected for deportation, they're moved to staircase one: 'Ready to deport.' One thousand per convoy."

"My daughter is here," Janine said. "Where do I find her?"

"Your daughter?" Jacquet shot her a look of disbelief. "You aren't Jewish."

"They arrested my whole family."

"How old is she?"

"Almost three."

"Why do you think she's here?"

"The Gestapo chief said so."

A shadow crossed Jacquet's face. "Come with me."

They crossed the yard, pushed a battered steel door marked with a red cross, and entered the camp infirmary. The smell of sickness was overwhelming with patients waiting on benches. Right behind, there was another room crammed with beds, all occupied. Two nurses and a doctor moved around, clearly overwrought.

Jacquet whispered to the doctor who wore a graying smock that must have been white at some point and a kippah on his thinning hair. The doctor glanced at Janine, took something out of a drawer, and slipped it to Jacquet.

Back in the yard, Jacquet deposited a piece of cloth in Janine's pocket. "Put it on when we get in," he muttered, steering between people as they walked toward another entrance.

Once inside Janine pulled out a white armband emblazoned with a red cross and slid it up her sleeve. Jacquet did the same.

"The camp is under French gendarmerie control, but the inside organization is left to the detainees," Jacquet explained as they moved along corridors lined with trash. "They're in charge of health and distribution of supplies. They do the best they can, but they aren't given much to do it with. Also, we live under the rules of collective responsibility. If a prisoner escapes, fifty people are punished. Informers are rewarded with food and promises of non-deportation. It's a very efficient system. Not only do these Vichy bastards carry out anti-Semitic legislation to the letter, but they also stop all aid coming in from the outside."

"What a shameful race we are," Janine said.

"No one is allowed to see the children left behind by deported parents," Jacquet continued. "Two Jewish nurses take care of them. There used to be three, but one committed suicide and the gendarmes won't allow a replacement. That's their way of preventing further suicides."

"You mean, because they know if they kill themselves, there'll be no one left to take care of the children?"

"That's what the gendarmes are counting on."

On top of a flight of stairs, guards checked their armbands. Although they hadn't seen a single child yet, they could hear them. Not cries but a low continuous moan. Jacquet opened a door and ushered Janine ahead of him.

"Oh my God," she cried.

The stench was unbearable and the sight horrifying—two hundred dull-eyed children packed into three rooms lying on filthy straw mattresses. Many suffered from diarrhea and buckets filled to the brim stood at the end of each row. Some children cried feebly, other simply lay in filth, sucking their thumbs. Janine walked among them and every time she spotted a kid a little older than the others, she crouched over and asked: "I'm looking for a little girl, her name is Emma. She has curly hair and brown eyes."

Not a single one answered. The nurses ignored her. When Jacquet spoke to them, they barely paused before shaking their heads.

Janine looked for Emma everywhere. Every morning she watched as new children were brought in by the police. Most came from Le Marais in Paris's 4th arrondissement—the Jewish district. At the end of the fifth day, Jacquet confronted her.

"Your daughter is not here. You lied to Lindinger, and he lied to you. That's his way of tormenting you."

Janine had come to the end of her courage. Emma was lost, her mother in a camp, her father probably dead. The pain from her torture. The infirmary doctor drained the pus, but he didn't have any antiseptic. When he poured pure alcohol over the wounds Janine fainted.

Hope became a memory of hope. Of all people, she thought of Mike. How good it had been to feel his interest. How glorious to dream of a better life with such a man—*not to be*. Janine began to give her food rations away. She kept to herself but listened to anyone who needed to talk. Rebecca, a primary school teacher, became a friend. Her husband had disappeared, and she had been arrested for being outside at an hour when Jews were not allowed in the street. She had been rushing to the pharmacy to get medication for her one-year-old son who had measles. The French cop who took her into custody didn't care. He brought her to the station and made sure she was in the police shuttle to Drancy that night. Luckily, Rebecca had learned that her neighbor had heard her son cry and was taking care of him. At least she knew where her child was, Janine thought. Then chided herself for envying her.

Food was scarce and hygiene conditions deplorable. Life in Drancy was awful, but nobody wanted to leave it. And money could make the difference between life and death. The camp had become the gendarmes' golden goose. Internees from wealthy families bribed them to smuggle in food. The guards charged fifty francs to mail a letter and one hundred to bring one in. An onion sold for fifty francs, a bread ration three hundred francs, one apple eighty francs, at a time when a primary school teacher's salary was less than two thousand francs a month.

"Or twenty-five apples," as Rebecca put it. And the gendarmerie was getting a lot more than money. "Remember Capitaine Lejeune, the one who stank of alcohol and met the buses?" Rebecca asked one day. "He has his own private harem. He keeps a couple of women in a room near the infirmary and visits them every afternoon. When he gets bored with one, he puts her on the next deportation train and gets a fresh one."

"That can't be," Janine said.

"Oh yes, and everybody knows. Radio London has promised to put him in front of a firing squad after the war."

The radio was their information lifeline. At night, when Janine was confined to the Aryan section of the camp populated by Résistance members and Amis des Juifs—friends of Jews who had been arrested sheltering Jews—they listened to a makeshift radio and heard reports of mass murders in concentration camps. Poland had become a slaughterhouse for Jews. Millions were being killed there in gas chambers. They even learned where they would soon be going, a place named Oświęcim-Brzezinka—Auschwitz-Birkenau.

A few days later Janine, Jacquet, and twenty-one Résistants found their names on a list of those selected for the next deportation train along with nine hundred and seventy-nine Jews. Many people sank into despair, but Janine felt nothing. Or rather, refused to feel anything. Giving up on hope was a relief—*I don't have to pretend to be strong anymore.*

A furious need for human contact had overcome her fellow deportees. In the days before deportation men and women who barely knew each other shared intimacies on cots or standing against walls. The breath of death was upon them, and they desperately wanted life. Janine's detachment was so profound, she joined the depravity. She ran into the infirmary doctor who had drained the pus on her breasts. He was still wearing his graying smock and kippah; she led him to a dark corner and slid her hand inside his pants. The man hesitated but he too was despondent and his arousal brutal. He lifted her skirt, hooked the crotch of her panties, and drove himself deep into her with punishing intensity. They did not stop when another couple walked by and, duly inspired, emulated them.

The quietness that came over her afterward felt liberating. There was nothing more to care for or protect. Janine had uprooted all the absurd pride remaining within her—*good riddance.*

35

PROUST PULLED HIS SNCF MAINTENANCE van up to the police control at Le Bourget train station with Mike and Robert sitting in the back. It was dark but the air was already hot and dripping with humidity.

"You're early," the gendarme said as he shone his flashlight on the clipboard Proust handed him.

"What's it to you? You pay for overtime?" Proust grumbled. "We start at daybreak. The krauts want everything fixed yesterday."

The gendarme ignored Proust. Railway workers were famously irascible, and they all hated les flics. He directed his light inside the van, stopping in turn on Mike and Robert's faces. They sat on crates and wore overalls stained with machine grease, and waved the guard off, shielding their eyes from the light.

"You want to take my picture?" Robert growled.

The gendarme switched off his light and handed the clipboard back.

"You all woke up on the wrong side of the bed this morning?"

"Yes, and every day this shitty war keeps going on."

The gendarme raised the gate. "The sun rises at 4:42 a.m. You won't have long to wait."

Proust waved him off. He *knew* what time the sun rose and that a convoy of buses from Drancy internment camp would roll in shortly after. The deportees would then be transferred to the train sitting on the tracks and in two and a half days the poor wretches would be in Poland. Proust nursed the engine into gear, but it creaked anyway.

Robert swore under his breath. He had taken the whole gearbox apart and rebuilt it with used spare parts, but it still rattled. He hated that sound. They had a seven-hundred-mile trip ahead of them. The van rolled into the rail yard to the switching tower with Proust keeping an eye glued to the rearview mirror.

"Fucking gendarmerie. They're already here."

Robert and Mike turned and watched a line of military trucks moving toward the gate. They grabbed their bags and rushed into the dark corrugated iron tower. As they climbed, the staircase rumbled beneath them like a scaffold. When they entered the control room at the top, the signalman was hanging his telephone.

"Good news. The Allies just landed in southern Italy," he said, thumbing up. The four men shook hands, celebrating quietly.

"They're in continental Europe," Robert said.

"And the Russians are on the outskirts of Smolensk. They'll be in Poland by the fall," Proust added.

Mike glanced at Proust—*always cheering for his team, this one.*

The telephone rattled. The signalman picked it up and listened. "The buses left Drancy," he reported, hanging up. "They'll be here in twenty minutes."

"Merde," Proust said. "They're early."

The tension in the room shot up. The job ahead of them was formidable and a few minutes could jeopardize the whole operation.

"Any way we could slow them down until daybreak?" Robert asked.

The man checked his watch and looked outside. It was still pitch-dark.

"I wish."

When Proust and Robert pulled binoculars out of their haversacks, the signalman produced a telescope, still in its leather sleeve.

"Maybe you can use this."

Mike's eyes lit up. "Très bon, merci." His American accent was thick as molasses. Proust thrust a finger against his lips and threw Mike a look—*don't fucking talk.*

Mike nodded—*okay, okay.* He liked to connect with people. It was second nature to him, but Proust was right. He pulled the telescope and the tripod out of their sleeves and began assembling the components. The signalman was pleased with the care with which Mike handled the device. "C'est de l'optique Zeiss," he explained, then continued in rapid French—Mike understood that the telescope belonged to his son who loved watching stars. Mike would have liked to ask how old his son was, but did not—no names, no talking. Look at one another as little as possible. The less he remembered the better. So he thanked the signalman with a wink, adjusted the finder scope, and focused on the gendarmerie trucks pulling over and Gardes Mobile jumping out the back.

Damn! It was still too dark! Even with the telescope he could only see shadows. Mike looked to the east where a hint of dawn was stretching across the horizon. They needed another half hour *at least.*

Preparation for this mission had gone smoothly. The British Consul in Bilbao had made sure they got the money and weapons they had requested. Mike had wanted four M42s submachine guns and a case of American grenades. He got the grenades but only two M42s, brought by special courier in a cello case on a flight from Casablanca to Lisbon and then smuggled through Spain and into France.

Mike had taught them how to take the weapon apart and clean it. It reminded Robert of the training before the Tunisian campaign. He had barely survived that one. At least this time they had a plan and success would all depend on grit and precision. And luck of course. Lots of luck.

While in Paris they had hidden in the apartment of a retired schoolteacher near the Place Denfert-Rochereau. His wife had been chirpy at first until she caught them cleaning weapons. The submachine guns were huge and the ammunition clips enormous, and there were all those grenades piled on her husband's favorite chair. She peeled her eyes away from the weaponry, made the sign of the cross, and busied herself in the kitchen. They barely saw her after that.

Through Résistance-Fer, Proust gathered the intelligence needed for the operation and the assurance that they would get all the help they needed on the ground. He also had grown infinitely curious about Mike, who upon learning about Janine's transfer to a camp in Poland had pushed the idea of attacking the train. "During transfer, always the best," he had said. "Same as in *The Great Train Robbery.*"

Only an American could think that way, Proust thought—*like a Western*. And that American didn't care about political affiliations; he just cared about winning the war. "You're focused and organized," he said to Mike. "You'd make a good communist."

Mike returned the compliment. "And you'd make a good capitalist. You know how to get the best out of people. You'd do well in America. You'd be a rich man in no time."

Proust chuckled—*me, a rich man? In America of all places!*

Robert spent his nights in a garage fine-tuning the SNCF van provided by Résistance-Fer. In a few short months, he had gone from snipping wires in a post office in Algiers to preparing to highjack a deportation train.

Witnessing Janine's arrest had deeply shaken Mike. Tossing and turning one night, he tried to anticipate all the things that could go wrong. There were many. This was a lot riskier than flying an airplane in combat.

The plan was to attack the train on an isolated segment of the line one hundred and twenty miles from Paris. A communist gendarme inside Drancy detainment camp had relayed instructions to

Jacquet. He was to stay with Janine and wear a hat so they could determine which car he and Janine had boarded.

And here they were. And it was still too dark to see much of anything.

Robert listened to the whine of engines in the distance. "Here they come," he said.

Paris city buses appeared, making a ponderous turn into the rail yard. Robert counted twenty-eight buses. The Gardes Mobiles were now positioned along the length of the platform as the vehicles pulled up parallel to the train. Capitaine de Gendarmerie Lejeune stepped forward and blew his whistle—nothing happened. The buses remained frozen in the semidarkness. Capitaine Lejeune shouted an order, and the Gardes Mobiles drew out their batons and moved toward the buses.

Robert and Mike exchanged a pained look as they listened to the sound of batons drumming against the sides of the buses. When the clatter subsided, the Capitaine blew his whistle again—still nothing. The buses might have been empty.

But these few minutes had been a godsend. The yellow sun timidly peeking over the horizon felt like a miracle. The men in the tower were now able to discern the shapes of people inside the buses. A few were standing and people began filing through the cabin and out of the vehicles. Soon the whole length of the platform was thick with people hauling bags and suitcases. The haunting human mass shuffled along in dreary silence. In the pallor of dawn even their faces looked gray.

Robert's own family flashed through his mind. "Men, women, and old people," he said.

"Find Janine," Proust snapped.

They focused on the crowd, searching among a thousand people who all looked alike in the dim light. Mike's telescope was too powerful. A face filled the entire eyepiece and he had to constantly check with his other eye to figure out what part of the crowd he was looking at.

"Merde."

The hat directive had been a mistake. Gendarmes were flipping hats off people's heads with their batons and laughing at the prisoners struggling to retrieve them.

Mike spotted a young woman with dark hair and raised a hopeful "Ha!"

"Found her?" Robert asked eagerly.

Mike looked again. "No."

Moving their gaze swiftly from group to group, they scrutinized the crowd, now being funneled toward the wagons.

"There is a guy with a huge bandage on his head," Robert said.

"Where?" Proust asked.

"Fifth bus from the right."

Proust aimed his binoculars and yes—there was a man stepping down from a bus. The white dressing over his head made him look taller.

"That's Jacquet. That's our man," Proust said.

"Janine's with him," Mike announced as her face filled his eyepiece. It was stunning to see her so close. Her visage was thin and pale but still beautiful. She got off the bus, glanced at the cattle cars, and said something to Jacquet, who smiled. He took her hand and led her sideways through the crowd.

"He was told to get on a car in the middle of the train," Proust said.

Suddenly Jacquet and Janine's progression was interrupted by gendarmes who pushed them toward the nearest box car.

"Car number eight," Proust said. "Not too bad."

As Robert watched the people being herded into the cattle cars, he homed in on a sign painted in yellow on the side of each: 20

CHEVAUX, 40 HOMMES—20 horses, 40 men. "How many people in each car?" he asked.

"Sixty," the signalman said.

Swinging his binoculars Robert focused on a small man in a suit and tie pacing nervously on a bridge overlooking the station.

He elbowed Proust. "Who's that?"

Proust handed the signalman his binoculars and pointed at the man.

The signalman *pfeued* in disgust. "That, my friend, is Jacques Denis, High Commissioner of Jewish Affairs. All deportation camps are under his authority and because he's an overzealous prick, he personally oversees every transfer."

The platform was nearly empty now. Red Cross workers were handing buckets of water to eager hands stretching out of the cars. Gendarmes moved behind them, padlocking the doors. On the bridge, Jacques Denis rubbed his hands and crossed his arms, looking satisfied.

"You see, he's done," the signalman said.

The empty buses were now leaving the area, and Proust, Robert, and Mike had a clear view of the entire train.

"The gendarmes are in the passengers' car at the end of the train?" Proust asked.

"Yes, thirty of them with a French commandant and two German officers from the Schutzpolizei," the signalman said. "When the train makes a stop, the gendarmes surround the cars. And they are not afraid to shoot. In March fifteen deportees escaped in Metz. Not a single one made it. Six were killed by the gendarmes, all shot in the back."

Proust pointed at the last car of the train.

"Who's in there?"

"No one. It's filled with food: eggs, cheese, fruits, vegetables, and meat. French authorities have to provide supplies for the trip. The Germans claim it's to feed the deportees during transport, but everyone knows it's for the Nazi officials at Auschwitz-Birkenau."

"Couldn't you blow up the tracks and stop the deportations?" Robert asked.

The signalman pulled on his mustache. "Our orders are to disrupt enemy supply lines and troop movements. People higher up see these deportations as a drain on the German war effort. Every train used to transport Jews is one not used to supply the Russian front or bring weapons on the Atlantic wall. They don't care what happens to the Jews."

36

INSIDE THE CATTLE CAR, JACQUET shoved people out of his way and secured the spot under the air vent for Janine and himself. The Wagon-ordner was a middle-aged French Jew who has been designated by the Germans as the prisoner in charge. He stood on a bale of hay and ordered them to spread it on the floor. This was their "bedding." The car was too small for all of them to lie down, so they sat, crumpled together as prickly dust from the hay settled on top of them.

A sharp whistle rang out and the train began to roll. A couple of women shook their heads on and on, whispering to themselves. A few cried. Men stared sightlessly ahead. Jacquet peeked through the air vent. Houses along the track displayed window boxes overflowing with geraniums and begonias, and in the gardens, white lilac was in full bloom. He slid down and sat beside Janine. She knew he was doing his best to protect her but felt it was pointless—*none of us will come out of this alive*.

The morning wore on. People settled in. A few even managed resigned smiles. The train passed through Aulnay-sous-Bois and Meaux. Then outside Chateau Thierry, it stopped. Jacquet looked out. They were on the edge of the Champagne region and remained there, sitting in the increasingly hot car. After a while the brakes unlocked and the train started again, moving *backward* this time. People looked at one another.

"We're returning to Paris," a woman cried.

Hope spread like a fever. Even the most apathetic raised their heads. They desperately wanted to believe they were going back and for almost an hour, hope was alive. Soon, they were in Meaux again and stopped outside the station. Everyone waited expectantly and then their hearts sank when they rolled forward again. After a few miles the train veered right, heading south.

"Anything's better than east," someone said. But there was a new sense of resignation in their faces. The convoy rolled on, slowing down and making stops of variable length along the way for no apparent reason. Jacquet knew that these stops and detours had a purpose. Railway workers were holding their train back. By intentionally sending another train on the same track, they forced the convoy to idle or back up, then loop around to rejoin its route. He assumed their convoy would be ambushed at some point. A futile endeavor, he thought. All previous attempts to free prisoners from deportation trains had failed.

Jacquet had worked for the French railways since 1919. He had trained as a mechanic and was sent to repair locomotives in shops from Paris to Strasbourg. He had married a locomotive engineer's daughter, and they had a baby girl. Those were the happiest years of his life, but the war changed everything. Due to their political affiliation, Jacquet and his wife were detained. When his wife died of influenza in prison, Jacquet dealt with his sorrow by enlisting in the military branch of the Communist party. As a precaution, he sent his daughter to live with her grandmother in the south. Jacquet missed her terribly and lived in constant fear of never seeing her again.

The month before, someone had broken under torture and given his name. In Drancy, he had been able to stay in contact with the Résistance and was told to wear a hat and make sure that he and Janine got into the same train car. Jacquet had seen how guards often flipped hats off detainees' heads as prisoners were expected to show respect and bare their heads in the gendarmes' presence. So Jacquet hit himself with a lead pipe, cutting a long gash on top of his skull, then asked the infirmary for gauze and bandages. The Jewish doctor wrapped Jacquet's head in a large white dressing shaped like a turban. Jacquet had not shared any of this with Janine. He didn't want to raise her hopes and resolved to inform her only as events unraveled.

By early afternoon, it was hot, and nature having taken its course, the stink inside the wagon was intense. They had also run out of water, and it did not matter how much they banged on the walls every time they stopped, the gendarmes would not open the doors. Finally, at Epernay station, the railway workers heard their cries and watered the cars with high-pressure hoses to lower the temperature inside. Then they snaked smaller hoses through the air vents and the deportees were able to refill their buckets. The train engineer ignored orders to depart and kept the engine idle until every car was replenished. The gendarmes stayed away. They did not mess with union workers.

After the train left Epernay, a fight broke out when men began to loosen the floorboards with a smuggled piece of metal. The idea was to escape by sliding under the car and landing on the track with the train still moving. The Wagon-ordner screamed for them to stop. "I'm responsible for this car! If you escape, they'll shoot me and everyone in this car will be punished."

The men kept working. Nails had to be pulled out one by one and every minute brought them closer to Germany. The Wagon-ordner kept arguing until one of the men grabbed him by the collar, slapped him hard, and began to strangle him.

"Now, you *will* shut up," he said in a harsh central European accent.

The Wagon-ordner's nose was bleeding profusely and although he fought back, he couldn't unlock the powerful hands around his neck. His face turned purple. People looked away when he began to suffocate.

"That's enough," Jacquet said from his corner.

The man turned to Jacquet and theatrically opened his hands wide, letting his victim go. The Wagon-ordner slid onto the floor, sucking air and coughing. He waved toward his attacker and spat: "Hungarian trash." A hard kick silenced him.

Germany was now less than one hour away. The locomotive puffed louder on the long climb up to the Champagne plateau. There was, Jacquet knew, a tunnel at the top and then flat terrain all the way to the German border at Novéant-sur-Moselle—a good place for an ambush, away from roads and invisible from the air. He clutched the handlebar on the side of the door and took Janine's arm. As they entered the tunnel the car plunged into darkness and the hammering of the wheels grew louder.

"Hold on tight," Jacquet said.

A second later, a crashing sound. The locomotive had hit something. People screamed as squeaking brakes sent them flying forward, piling on top of one another and the whole train grinding to a halt. A woman let out a long shriek and crawled out from under a heap of bruised passengers. Others moaned while disentangling themselves. And now they could hear sharp detonations rattling in the distance. *Machine guns*, Jacquet thought. He pulled himself up to look through the air vent but only saw darkness. And now louder blasts bounced off the tunnel walls. *Grenades.* He pulled Janine closer. "Hold on to me."

She shook her head, pushing away the hope, but she still latched on to Jacquet's arm and held it tight.

"They're coming to kill us," someone screamed.

The firing outside was continuous. Men were shouting. And Jacquet heard something new. He couldn't tell what it was at first and then: *Yes!* Footsteps on the gravel of the track getting closer. Someone was right outside. Then, the rasping sound of metal against metal—a crowbar popping off the lock. And the sweet rolling sound of the door sliding open and a wave of cool air rushing over them.

"Jacquet, are you here?"

"Yes." Jacquet pulled Janine toward the door.

"What about Emma?" she hissed, resisting his forward motion.

"Emma isn't on this train, damn it!" an angry Jacquet growled, grabbing Janine's waist and pulling her through the crowd toward the door.

"Stay inside. This is an order!" the Wagon-ordner hollered, shoving people back and attempting to slide the door closed.

Proust raised a flashlight with his fingers over the lens and terrified faces danced in the pinkish light along with the silhouette of the Wagon-ordner kicking blindly at anyone trying to crawl out through the narrow exit. Proust raised his gun. The muzzle emitted a small white flame, and a shot rang out. Blood gushed from the Wagon-ordner's forehead. Without a second's pause Jacquet, Janine, and several others stepped over his body and jumped down onto the track.

"Stay with me," Proust said, grabbing Jacquet's arm. Then he shouted into the throng. "Move to the head of the train. The gendarmes are in the back. Disperse into the countryside. Stay away from roads. At least you'll have a chance. There is none where you're going!"

Janine was pulled along between Proust and Jacquet. Flashes of gunfire illuminated the tunnel, and she made out two men covering the gendarmes' car in a hail of machine-gun fire. When one of them slung his weapon over his shoulder and began walking alongside the train, methodically popping locks with a crowbar, Janine could not believe her eyes. She knew that man. A name stumbled out of her confused mind—*Robert?*

A hand pulled her down. She crawled to the other side of the train and Jacquet and Proust led her deeper into the tunnel. Behind them Robert kept opening doors and shouting: "The guards are in the rear. Move toward the locomotive." He wanted to free as many deportees as possible, but it was more than a one-person job. "You!" He grabbed a man's arm and handed him the crowbar. "Open the cars ahead of you."

"Oui, monsieur."

Robert watched him unlock the next car, slide the door open, hand the crowbar to a man inside, and take off. The man threw away the crowbar and ran.

"Selfish bastards," Robert spat as he headed back fighting his way against a stream of deportees stampeding along the track. Those still locked inside the cars banged and yelled. Even worse, cars with open doors had people huddled in corners refusing to come out.

"Get out! You idiots!" Robert shouted. "They'll kill you all in Poland!"

Further ahead, Proust led Jacquet and Janine to a vault and aimed his light at rungs embedded into the rock leading up a ventilation shaft.

"Go," he said, giving Janine a rough boost upward. She began to climb with Jacquet behind her. When they had moved up, Proust climbed a few rungs to get a bird's-eye view of the tunnel. At the end of the train, the gendarmes' car had caught fire and every time rifles popped up from behind the windows a burst of machine-gun fire rang out and the rifles disappeared. Proust climbed back down, moved to the railway emergency telephone encased in the wall, and broke the glass. He tore off the receiver and the rotary dial box and threw the broken pieces onto the track.

Robert appeared next to him. "Are we done?" he asked.

Proust looked up at the empty shaft. Janine and Jacquet had reached the top. "Yes. Fireworks time," he said, pulling a flare out of his bag.

Robert cracked a match, lit the fuse, and threw it on top of a car. It blew up, spraying out orange fireworks.

Babam, babam! Two grenades exploded under the gendarmes' car.

"Go! Start the van," Proust yelled. "I'll wait for the American."

Robert hated to leave Mike behind but climbed up.

"Over here!" Proust called to Mike emerging from clouds of smoke.

"Where is Janine?" Mike asked.

"She's up already."

Mike took in a short breath. "You go. I'll close up," he said, slinging his machine gun over his shoulder.

Proust began to climb, and Mike followed. At the end of the train gendarmes were streaming out of their burning car. A megaphone blasted: "Get back aboard the train. All passengers must immediately return to their cars."

This announcement was followed by rifle shots. Bullets bounced off the tunnel walls, throwing the running deportees into panic. Some ran faster; others gave up, raised their hands, and climbed into the nearest wagon.

Halfway up the shaft Mike looked down and spotted two men crawling on their hands and knees fifty feet below. A gendarme caught up with them. When they turned on their backs and raised up their arms in defeat, the gendarme pushed his rifle against their foreheads and shot them, first one, then the other.

"Bastard," Mike whispered.

At the top of the ladder, Proust's hand pulled him into the light. They slid the tunnel access cover back in place and ran to the van parked a few yards away, its engine running. Robert moved from behind the wheel and dropped into the passenger seat. Proust took his place, depressed the clutch, and shifted into first gear.

"It's a slaughterhouse down there," Mike said, catching his breath.

"Some of them will make it," Proust replied.

"Not many."

"No. Not many."

Janine sat in the back next to Jacquet.

"Do you want to sit in front?" Robert asked. She shook her head.

"Hello," Mike said, gently touching her shoulder. "Remember me?"

The sight of Mike seemed to lessen Janine's despair. He had been on her mind and his sudden appearance bewildered her.

"I told you I'd come back for you," Mike said.

She stared at Mike and Robert. "What are you two doing here?"

"We saw you being arrested. We had to help out," Robert said.

The words felt absurd to Janine. These two were insane. The shock absorbers squealed as they bounced on the rutted access road and cut clean across a vineyard. The men's mouths were grim and set. Janine seemed dazed.

Janine turned to Jacquet and buried her face in his shoulder. There was an uneasy silence as they jerked up and down, hitting pothole after pothole. Then, Janine whispered to Jacquet, who turned to Robert and asked: "She wants to know if they released the body?"

"Whose body?" Robert asked.

"Her daughter Emma," Jacquet said. "She wants to know where she's buried."

Robert grabbed the handle on the back of his seat, and swaying with the van, spoke over the road noise, "Your daughter's safe."

"Emma's dead," Janine said.

Looking in the rearview mirror Proust shouted over the roar of the engine: "Your daughter was released to your concierge."

Janine sat upright. "When? Where is she?" she asked, her voice full of doubt and hope.

"They're in the Basque country. Suzanne found a safe house for them," Proust said.

Still doubting, Janine looked at Proust's face in the rearview mirror. "When?"

"Two weeks ago."

"Is she healthy?"

"Yes. Madame Raymonde has been taking care of her. She's asking for you, though."

Eyes widening with joy, Janine kept whispering. "Emma is alive."

They reached a paved road and the motion inside the van smoothed out. Janine kissed Jacquet and, stumbling across the floor, squeezed Proust's and Robert's shoulders. The van shook; she nearly lost her balance. Still, she kissed Mike's hand and held it against her cheek.

Mike smiled. "I know you wanted me back in the Air Force, but first we had to get you out of this mess."

"Thank you. Thank you all." Janine broke down, sobbing uncontrollably, but this time the men just smiled. They settled down in their seats as the van picked up speed. Their faces slack with relief, they passed cigarettes around. Even Proust's face softened a bit.

"Merde," he said.

They knew what he meant: Janine and Jacquet were safe. Emma was alive. Lots of danger ahead, but so far, they had pulled it off.

37

THEY DROVE SOUTH HEADING TOWARD the Basque country five hundred miles away. Proust expected the gendarmerie to keep highways under surveillance, so he took small roads and stayed away from towns.

"You know the region well." Robert was impressed.

"I don't," Proust said. "I studied the maps and memorized every road."

In the back, Jacquet was asleep. Next to him, Janine stared blankly ahead of her. Her anguish about Emma had abated, but she had replaced it with new anguish in the infernal merry-go-round of worries. Her mother was in a camp in Germany. Her father in a hospital, probably crippled for life, and too weak to survive another round of questioning. Turenne in Gibraltar, his condition uncertain. Mike beckoned her over, but she shook her head. She didn't want to be comforted. She didn't want to talk. She didn't want to be touched.

As night fell, they reached the southern Champagne region where they had a safe house for the night. Proust could not take the chance of turning on the headlights after curfew, so he drove slowly, leaning out over the steering wheel, staring into the gloom. He finally located a dirt road lined with chestnut trees. Ahead they could make out a mill spanning a river.

The miller, who had heard the engine, stepped into his courtyard. A thin, decisive man in his sixties, he introduced himself as Guy. His wife Lily stood in the doorway anxiously kneading her apron as her husband motioned the van inside the barn, where Jacquet and Proust helped him cover it with a tarpaulin. When they were done, they joined the others inside the house.

Guy filled glasses with wine, and everybody drank. When his wife noticed the bloodstains on Janine's dress, she took her hand and led her to a washroom behind the kitchen.

"Are you bleeding?" she asked.

"It's not my blood," Janine said.

Lily took the information and pushed it away. She fetched a towel, handed Janine a bar of soap, and mixed hot and cold water in a white enamel basin. "The washcloth is inside the towel," she said.

"Thank you." Janine began undressing, then hesitated. "Do you have any antiseptic?" she asked.

"Are you hurt?" Lily asked, a look of worry on her face.

"A little." Janine took off her brassiere and faced the old woman, who put her hand over her mouth.

"Mon Dieu," she murmured. The wounds on Janine's breasts shocked her. She crossed herself and, eyes reddening, said, "You wash and I'll get an antiseptic and a clean brassiere."

Janine hated the way she smelled and washed away the stink of prison the best she could. She was drying her face and arms when Lily returned with clothes, gauze, medicine, and a brand-new brassiere still wrapped in tissue paper. The best she had. She put on her glasses, unscrewed the bottle of disinfectant, and guided Janine under the lamp.

"Sorry, it will hurt," Lily said as she dabbed the antiseptic on Janine's ravaged nipples.

Janine clenched her teeth. "Go ahead. Pour it all over."

She's brave, Lily thought. *That stuff stings like the devil.*

It took all of Janine's will to clamp her jaw against the harrowing pain. After Lily finished administering the medicine, she applied gauze and then picked up the brassiere. "It's too large, but it's the only size I have."

"Let's fill the cups up with gauze. I always wanted a big bust," Janine whispered, trying to sound mischievous.

In the main room Guy refilled glasses as Robert, Mike, and Jacquet ogled the table set with their hosts' best china and silverware.

"I hope we aren't too much of an inconvenience," Proust said, following their glances.

"An inconvenience? Hardly. It's an honor, Monsieur. This is what we peasants do. We feed and hide those who fight for us," Guy responded.

Mike watched in awe as Janine appeared. She wore a dress too large for her but tightly belted around her waist. Hardship had tilled furrows and painted dark circles under her eyes—she was still beautiful, but also fragile and vulnerable. She gave him a half smile and tilted her head as to concede to life's absurdities. He pulled her chair out; she sat and patted his hand by way of saying thank you.

"Supper's ready," Lily said, gesturing at the table before rushing back to her stove.

"You aren't eating with us?" Jacquet asked, suddenly noting the number of place settings.

"Oh, we've had supper already. We live on the same timetable as the cows and chickens," Guy said, dropping into a chair beside the fireplace and reaching for his pipe.

Lily began to serve. She and the miller had clearly dug into their reserves to give them the best they had. After a salad of cucumbers and tomatoes, Lily asked, "I hope you like lamb?"

They protested—of course they *liked lamb*. Robert and Mike exchanged a look—*are we dreaming?* Jacquet caught the expression on their faces and chuckled.

Leg of lamb with green beans, potatoes, and parslied butter appeared. Mike, Robert, and Jacquet ate voraciously as Lily hovered around the table, keeping a close eye on her guests and refilling their plates.

Janine managed to swallow very little. *How quickly men adjust,* she thought. Jacquet had been in Drancy longer than she, but he was eating with a robust appetite. Men go through hell and starvation but when it's over, they put it out of their minds and fill up. Women don't forget so easily. She glanced at their hosts and suddenly fear gripped her belly as the Gestapo chief Lindinger's face flashed through her mind—*he would destroy these lovely people's lives in an instant.*

The morning violence still in him, Proust drank more than he ate. But after a few glasses he managed to unwind. Incredibly, the dinner ended with a rich caramel custard and a fifty-year-old Armagnac. The men rolled cigarettes, leaned back in their chairs, and watched the smoke gather around the dim petrol lamp hanging above the table. When Janine stood to help clear the table, Lily stopped her.

"After all you have been through, I'd never forgive myself if you lifted one finger in my house."

Janine thanked her and beckoned to Proust to follow her outside. The men watched as they walked out to a gazebo at the edge of the yard.

"Is there a problem?" Mike asked.

Jacquet waved him off. "Résistance business. The less you know, the better."

In the gazebo, Proust leaned against a pillar and crossed his arms. Janine sat on a bench and with a movement of the chin indicated the van in the barn and the men in the house. "Was it your idea to rescue me?"

"No. It was theirs," Proust said, meaning Robert and Mike. Then he added, "And the *Roast Beefs*."

"The British?"

"Right. You saved a lot of their aviators. They felt *obligated*."

"You were against it?"

"Yes. The risk was too high and someone else could replace you."

"So, why did you do it?"

"I owed Robert and Mike. This was a complex operation, they needed help." Taking another drag of his cigarette, Proust could feel the deep sense of anguish in Janine. "Why don't you tell me what's bothering you?" he asked.

Janine bit her lip, irked at being read so easily. "Several things," she said. "The Gestapo knows about you, even your real name—Adam Klaczko."

"Yes, we know," Proust said. "We had an informer in our ranks. He has been eliminated."

Janine was surprised. FTP operatives never, ever disclosed details of their actions to outsiders.

Proust knew what her worry was. That's why he had broken the rule.

"You've got an informer in your escape line, is that it?" he asked.

"Maybe."

"Then you've got a big problem."

Janine had never been able to determine who had betrayed Father Valencia, Loïc, Prosper, and the farmers in the mountains. At times she had thought there was a spy among them, but at other times she felt it was just bad luck. Somebody saw something and wrote a letter of denunciation. It happened all the time.

"Could Résistance-Fer watch people on the line for us?" Janine asked.

Proust took another drag and blew two clean streams of smoke out through his nose. "I'll ask them."

"Thank you," Janine said.

Inside the house, Mike wiped the bottom of his empty glass with his finger and licked it appreciatively.

"What do they call that stuff?"

"Armagnac." Robert handed his half-full glass to Mike. "Here, I've had enough."

"*I've had enough*," he repeated in a mocking tone. "You don't smoke, you don't drink, so I get all your leftovers."

"Lucky you," Robert said. "What I really miss is chocolate."

"Can't help you there," Mike said. A little buzzed, he pointed at Janine and Proust still deep in conversation.

"Look at her. On a death train this morning and already back in the fight."

Robert looked amused. He knew what was coming.

"How come men aren't all over her?" Mike asked.

"They probably are, but she ignores them. No time for that."

Mike cocked an eyebrow. He did not like *that* answer.

"And Janine's a certain type," Robert said. "Men are intimidated."

Mike clucked his tongue, annoyed. He *was* intimidated. She was at the same time tough and tender—handing out her cigarette so he could light his, touching his shoulder on her way to bed, kissing him on the lips as they parted, and also resolutely telling him to get back to the Air Force when he mentioned joining the Résistance.

"Falling in love?" Robert scoffed.

Mike leaned over. "You're pretty smitten with her yourself."

"I like her. I admire her," Robert said, scratching his chin with the back of his hand. "Not the same thing."

Mike sipped more Armagnac—*no it wasn't.* "I like a strong woman."

"You won't be disappointed," Robert said, his voice mocking.

Mike leaned back, reflecting on that, then gave Robert a soft punch on the shoulder.

"Nah, you have a thing for Nicole. I loved how she stole coffee for us."

"She is thoughtful and lovely," Robert said. The war had aroused in him feelings that surprised him—how sweet it had been to ride that bike through town with Nicole and feel so close to her. How anxious she was before he stole that car. He had never met a woman who cared about him that way. She was so alien to the life he had led. In Algeria, social position, religion, and family connections were paramount. She didn't care about any of it. She knew he was Jewish and that was fine with her—*she keeps saving our hides and behaves as if this was the most ordinary thing in the world.*

Lily had been up since before dawn preparing food for "my escapees" as she called them. The night before she had washed Janine's clothes, removed the bloodstains, and set everything to dry by the stove. Guy had gone to the village early and when Proust appeared yawning and pushing his shirttails down into his pants, he made room for him at the kitchen table. Lily poured Proust a bowl of hot chicory with milk.

"Most of the Jews on the train were recaptured during the night," Guy said. "Two companies of French gendarmerie, one from Reims and the other one from Chalons-sur-Marne, did the dirty work."

"Bastards," Proust growled. "How did they manage to move so fast?"

"They called for reinforcements on the track telephone."

"How? I disabled the one in the tunnel," Proust said. "The next telephone was ten miles away."

"One of the gendarmes was a long-distance runner. They say he ran the whole distance in less than one hour."

Proust let out a *pfeu* of disgust and drank in silence.

"The Schutzpolizei officers praised the action of the gendarmerie as a magnificent example of Franco-German collaboration," Guy said. "The collaborationist newspaper *L'OEUVRE* will be running an article condemning the cold-blooded murder of a Wagon-ordner by Communist assassins. It'll be on the front page."

The gendarmes were already setting up roadblocks. There was no time to waste. Lily fed everyone breakfast. Mike watched Janine, who was still having trouble eating but looked better in her freshly laundered clothes. Lily wrapped more food in newspapers that she handed to Janine with tears in her eyes. "Be careful, my children."

Proust took his convoluted route on backcountry roads and Robert and Jacquet joined him on the front seat. They traveled up on the hills and tension rose every time they spotted roadblocks on highways down below. In the back of the van, Mike had built a sort of berth out of crates and blankets and kept a bottle of water within reach. He had gestured for Janine to join him; she shook her head at first but eventually moved across on her hands and knees to lay next to him. As the day got warmer, they shared water, took off their sweaters, and swayed with the vehicle, their bare arms touching when the van took a curve. Mike dreaded that she'd edge away, but she never did. Her eyes were closed, and he wondered if she was feeling his touch or ignoring it.

Janine was very mindful of Mike's warmth and skin. Stricken with longing and ashamed of it. Three nights ago, she stood in a hallway copulating with a man she barely knew. *I'm ugly*, she thought, remembering the scabs on her breasts. *Stop whining*, she raged until falling asleep. When her head drifted onto Mike's shoulder, he wrapped his arm around her, and she settled in the hollow spot. The salty tang of his armpits soothed her and when remorse poked through her semiconsciousness, she pushed it off. Mike wondered if she was snuggling against him or if he was just wishing it. Then, lulled by the motion of the van and the elation of the moment, he too fell asleep.

In the front Robert and Jacquet had discovered a shared passion for fishing. As they drove alongside the rivers of central France, they discussed the fine points of hooking black bass, pike, and trout. Every time they crossed a bridge, they asked Proust to slow down so they could admire the patches of deep green water under low branches skimming the current.

"A perfect spot for trout," Robert would say.

"Small hooks with maggots. We'd score big time here," Jacquet would respond.

Proust had to smile. Those two were speaking with exaggerated normality. Visualizing as they talked. By reminiscing about life's simple pleasures, they pushed away the horror of the previous day.

It was past noon when Mike and Janine woke up. The van had stopped. The men were peeing off the side of a bridge with Jacquet and Robert extoling the river as perfect for fly-fishing. Nuzzled against Mike's chest, Janine asked: "Do you like fishing?"

"Not particularly. But I like the ocean and the beach."

"Emma loves the beach too," Janine said, sitting up. "Tomorrow, I'll have her with me."

Mike smiled but it was painful to watch the changing expression in Janine's face as lips trembling, eyes brimming with tears, she said: "I was convinced she was dead."

Mike lit a cigarette and handed it to her. She wiped her eyes, took a puff, and handed it back.

They reached Tours' railway station and Proust drove to the locomotive repair shop. They all got out of the van and stood there, suddenly shy at the thought of parting.

"The stationmaster will put you on the train to Bayonne. We're going back to Paris," Proust said, indicating Jacquet. "So, this is good-bye, comrades. And may I say that it has been an honor to fight at your side."

They shook hands and laughed, amazed at being alive and at the same time unable to express how good it felt—a hard parting of ways.

"Tell British Intelligence about us," Proust said. "The bigger the weapons, the harder we can fight."

"Will do," Mike said.

Janine held tight to Jacquet. She was reluctant to let him go. "I could never have survived this without you," she said into his shoulder.

Jacquet shook his head, brushing off the gratitude. "Only did what needed to be done . . ." He searched for words to express how grateful he was they had made it, but none came. Jacquet was a shy man, but the tenderness came through.

"Hug Emma for me. I've a daughter too. She lives in Toulouse, and I miss her every day," he said, wiping away a tear. Then, abruptly, he kissed Janine's cheek and strode away to catch up with Proust.

Janine watched him blend into the crowd of rail yard workers, wishing he would look back for a last good-bye. He did not.

The stationmaster led Robert, Mike, and Janine to a locker room where first-class train tickets and a suitcase filled with clothes were waiting. They were good suits, shirts, and ties for the men, and a navy swing dress for Janine. They dressed and packed their old personas away.

Mike opened his arms. "Looks like we're on our way to a wedding."

"We look rich. The Brits spared no expense," Robert said.

"It's safer," Janine said.

Police controls were less stringent in first class. The war had not shaken prejudices. Money still inspired deference. As they walked through the station Mike took Janine's arm. She was tall for a Frenchwoman, but Mike towered over her. She had forgotten how good it felt to have a handsome man at her side. For an instant her worries evaporated. She felt alive, almost happy.

They arrived in Bayonne the next morning. A postal van drove them deep into the Basque country. The farm stood at the edge of a village in the foothills of the Pyrenees. It was a typical Basque house with dark red shutters and wooden studs. As the postal van drove off, Madame Raymonde opened the door.

"Mommy!" Emma ran into her mother's arms. Janine scooped her up sideways to protect her wounded chest, then held her close, eyes filling with tears.

"Oh, I missed you, my baby," Janine said, holding her little girl's warm body close. She pressed her face against Emma's cheek and inhaled the soft soapy smell in the nape of her neck. Her flesh and blood, the best, most perfect part of herself. *Thank you, thank you, God, for protecting her.* She prayed instinctively as they kissed and hugged and spun around until Emma pushed herself away from her mother and looked into her face.

"You were gone too long, Mommy!" she said reproachfully.

"I know, sweetie, I'm sorry." Janine's eyes swam with tears.

With Emma back in her arms, Janine turned to Madame Raymonde and kissed her. Emma managed to wrap her arms around her mother and Madame Raymonde.

"I want a kiss sandwich," she said, giggling, and the two women kissed her on both cheeks at once.

And now Janine thanked God for the resilience of childhood. Holding her daughter, feeling her melt against her shoulder, but still with that small demanding streak within her.

"Mommy, I want you to see my room now!"

Janine headed up the staircase carrying Emma, laughing and tickling her. Only her daughter existed.

Mike watched them. *A mother and her child, the purest love there is*, he thought. The sight lifted him at first, then a bubble of sorrow broke inside him—his own mother holding him, her tenderness and the heartbreaking feel of abandonment after she had died. It was there, all at once, the deep affection he felt for Janine and the memory of his mother's love.

Janine and Emma took a bath together. They ate upstairs and talked and played. Since her mother's disappearance, Emma had been afraid to sleep alone. Madame Raymonde had set up a child-bed in her own room. Now Emma wanted to keep sleeping next to Madame Raymonde. Janine was saddened but did not object.

The evening air came in through an open window and Janine watched Emma sleep. In the quiet house the antique grandfather clock downstairs struck every fifteen minutes. Madame Raymonde turned over in her bed and coughed. Janine pulled up a chair and leaned forward, chin in her hands. Emma looked healthy and beautiful with her dark curly hair and long lashes. The room was so peaceful that for an instant Janine feared she was having a dream—no, the miracle was real.

Janine heard Robert going to his room and assumed that Mike was alone downstairs. Her heart thudded. She leaned back in her chair, her hands running up her thighs. She undid the top button of her blouse, cupped her breasts, and felt a tingling from her nipples. Still painful but bearable—nothing compared to the misery of the tortured women she had shared her cell with in Fresnes prison.

She felt a spike of shame—*they're in hell while I'm safe*. The black umbrella of guilt flipped open inside her—*all I can think about is that man downstairs*.

Emma mumbled in her sleep. "Go to bed, Mommy."

Janine kissed Emma's cheek and stood for another moment. The craving Mike had woken in her pushed the guilt away. She recognized the inevitability of what would come next—*I need him*. Yes, Mike was just passing through, but even for a moment life could be good. She *needed* to feel good. She loved how during the trip he had doted on her in ways no man ever had. And that face with the cleft in the middle of his chin, those moist lips always close to a smile, that big Irish nose. Janine smiled remembering girls at the lycée in Toulouse gossiping that men with big noses had big cocks. She wondered how his erection would feel in her hand.

She tiptoed down the stairs and found Mike sprawled asleep in an armchair. She crossed the room and could feel her bare feet leaving brief imprints on the cold tiles—*the trail to paradise*, she thought, poking fun at herself. Her dress brushed his arm, and she stood there looking at his chiseled face—*he's even more handsome when he sleeps*.

"Hello," Mike whispered, coiling his thumb and forefinger around her wrist. "How's Emma?"

"Asleep," Janine answered. "She sent me away."

"Good girl."

"Come," she said.

They walked down the hallway to her bedroom, closed the door, and stood facing each other in the semidarkness.

"Let me," Janine said.

She undid the buttons of his shirt and pressed her forehead against his chest. It was an odd gesture, as if she wanted to get close and push him away at the same time.

"We'll need to go slow."

"Of course."

But they did not. When Mike stepped forward to embrace her, she was already ahead of him, taking his head in her hands, raising her face for his kiss. His lips tasted of wine and tobacco, and she felt his tongue while his large hand ran up her leg. The desire was strong, the connection visceral.

Then she stopped his hands, bringing his fingers to her lips.

"I'm ugly," she said.

"What are you saying? You're beautiful."

"They hurt me," she whispered, her chin dipping toward her chest.

"Who hurt you?" Then, he understood and saw in Janine's eyes a fragility he had never seen before.

Still avoiding his eyes, Janine took off her blouse. "When they questioned me."

As she removed her brassiere, patches of gauze yellowed by antiseptic dropped off and instinctively she crossed her arms to hide the scabs and gruesome purple scars on her mangled nipples. Mike couldn't hide the anguish in his eyes. His reaction filled her with dread.

"You see, I am ugly," Janine said again, dropping her gaze.

"No, you're not," he whispered, raising her chin with a gentle hand. Eyes shining on the edge of tears, Mike asked, "Does it hurt to keep the bra off?"

"Yes."

"Let me put it back on, then," he said, taking the brassiere dangling from her hand.

"And you know how to do that?" she asked, her glance flirtatious now.

"A proficient man, I am."

Mike picked up the garment and passed her arms through the loops. After she had repositioned the gauze patches over her nipples, he expertly stretched the bra across her chest, leaned over, and hooked the straps.

"Snug as a bug."

Her eyes holding his, Janine slid her skirt down her hips. She did not let it reach the floor but held onto the waistband and stepped out of it, then laid it on a chair. She wasn't wearing panties.

"Take off your clothes," she said.

He unbuckled his belt, stepped out of his pants, and stood naked in front of her. He was strong and muscular. She reached between his legs and wrapped her hand around his erection. They caressed and kissed and took their time before moving to the bed. Her skin was the color of brown eggshells and quivered under his lips. The dark triangle between her legs was soft and fragrant. They were eager and found each other in ways that surprised them both. Their world shrank to touches, tastes, and smells.

"Mon amour," she murmured as she guided him inside her.

He took hold of her hips, anchoring her. The pleasure was intense, but it was the stunning tenderness that made them gasp.

"Oh, c'est bon!" Eyes closed, mouth open, she moved rhythmically astride him, her hands cupping her wounded breasts. It was unlike anything Mike had ever experienced. He was taking her *and* being taken, and the connection felt miraculous.

Janine shuddered, ecstasy coursing through her as Mike too was carried away on a tide of pleasure—la petite mort, *the little death.*

"I love you," Mike said.

Janine nodded—*I love you too.* She opened her eyes and saw that he was smiling.

They lay side by side listening as a summer shower broke outside and heavy drops plopped on the ground. A cool breeze came through the open window, swelling the curtains. Janine drew in a breath, filling her with a sense of contentment she had never imagined herself capable of experiencing again. And of course, the twinge of a doubt; there always was one. She had to be wary of her longing for this man who was just passing by, but she did not want to be wary. Could not be. Her heart wouldn't let her.

"I wanted you so much," she said.

"I've been dreaming of this moment ever since you checked my teeth in that hotel room in Toulouse to find out if I was a spy," Mike whispered.

She chuckled at the memory, then lowered her head onto his chest and settled her hand on his shoulder in a proprietary way—*I have what I want.*

They awoke already moving against each other. Outside, the rain had stopped. Janine's lips drifted down his chest and belly and her mouth took possession of him. He arched back, pleasure rising, but pulled her up to make love to her again. They improvised, moving from one precious moment to another. Touching, wanting, asking . . .

He whispered in her ear.

"With pleasure," she answered.

She rode up his chest and when her thighs arched over his face, she lowered herself to his mouth.

38

THE TRAIN ATTACK MADE THE headlines in the underground press. It showed for the second time in weeks that the Résistance could attack the enemy and free its own. Of the twenty-one Résistants on board the deportation train, only nine had been recaptured. Regrettably the Drancy signalman's station was searched and when the Zeiss telescope was found hidden there, the signalman was shot.

Lovemaking had become for Janine and Mike a way to shut out the war. This was not ordinary fucking. This was much more serious. Mike had never experienced such lust. The attraction was pure animal instinct. He needed to possess her even as he enjoyed being completely under her spell. The ring of her voice, the peppery smell of her skin, and that nonchalant way she had of walking around their room without any clothes on. She was so different, so unpredictable, so *French*. He watched her, marveling at the unbound passion they were experiencing.

Janine's feelings were laced with desperation. She was aware that the killings, the arrests, and her imprisonment had changed her. Her resolve was stronger than ever but worries never left her—she *felt* weak. She had nightmares about losing Emma and woke up stunned to be safe in bed. And now there was Mike with his tenderness and strength. So much about him felt foreign, but also wonderful and inspiring. The proficient tone of his voice, the way he caught her around the waist or picked her up and carried her to bed. And his joy when he drank, ate, and made love. For her, he was survival, her raison d'être, and of course she feared that it all could be taken away. She knew she couldn't live again as she had before. She couldn't bear the thought of being without him. One evening after making love, she propped up on an elbow and held Mike's head against her chest yearning to say: "I want you to stay with me and never go back to England," but she held herself back.

But the war had not forgotten them. News came from Résistance-Fer in Orleans. De Lacoste had been spotted in the station with a group of airmen. When the night train was canceled, de Lacoste stole a German Army ambulance, hid the airmen in the back, and drove off. Janine was furious. De Lacoste was behaving recklessly—*a man with a death wish, that's all we need.*

"He's cracking up. Happens with pilots," Mike said. "Take him out of the line for a while."

"He's one of our best escorts," Janine said.

Even more troublesome news came from Proust, who had informers inside the Renseignements Généraux in Paris. The Gestapo and the French police were looking for an American. The pro-Nazi parish priest in Toulouse had given a detailed description of Mike. The gendarme in the deportation train confirmed that one of the attackers looked Anglo-American. Robert was thought to be a Spanish Republican in his mid-twenties. More alarming, Commissaire Boucher had sent descriptions of two *terrorists*, as they were called, to police stations in the Basque and Bearn regions and posted rewards for their arrests. Proust sent word that Mike and Robert should be smuggled to Spain as soon as possible.

"Who is telling them they are here?" Janine asked. She picked a departure date but at the last minute decided that British airmen who had been in Pau for weeks should be given priority. The next day, she agonized about her decision. The Basques were famously tight lipped, but many in the area were aware of Mike and Robert's presence. An informer could be attracted by the reward their arrests would draw. If the Gestapo found them there, they would deport all the men and burn down every house in the village. Then Janine learned that the regiment of Austrian border guards patrolling the mountain paths was due to go on leave. A new contingent would arrive from Innsbruck to replace them. Guards were less efficient during rotations—*let's wait for that,* she decided, knowing it would give them a few more nights.

Robert was restless as usual and spent time with the Basque guides keeping track of German patrols' movements on the trails. He had not seen Nicole since the prison attack in Toulouse but knew she was now regularly shuttling airmen to Pau. He had also learned that Suzanne was training her to smuggle airmen on longer stretches from Limoges to Pau. This was riskier and Robert worried about her. He had had a lot of time to think since Algiers. Tunisia had been real combat, soldiers against soldiers, but this war here involving civilians with its constant spate of denunciations, arrests, torture, and executions sickened him. Nicole was in the thick of it and she was always on his mind, and perplexingly embodied his love for France. He needed to be with her, to cherish her, protect her, while night after night, he couldn't help feeling a pang of jealousy as he watched Janine and Mike disappear into their room.

Of course, those two had their own problems—lovers' problems. One night, when Mike had begun listing all the places he wanted to take Janine in America, she had drawn him to her until he had lost his train of thought. Afterward he realized that every time he attempted to discuss their future together, Janine found a way to distract him. Did she want such a future? She never asked about his family or ambitions or what they would do after the war. She only seemed to care that he was here with her now.

Mike knew she dreaded his return to combat. She was aware of how many allied aircraft were shot down every day and those numbers were climbing. He tried to humor her out of it.

"I've been downed twice. The odds of a third time are almost nil."

"You know that's not true."

"We had a mechanic on base who was running betting pools. The odds of being shot a third time were less than a thousand to one."

"Because so few survive being shot down twice."

"But I did. If I'm shot down again, I'll come right back here," Mike said, kissing the curve of her neck. "You'll never be able to get rid of me."

This made her angry. "Do you have to make a joke out of everything?"

They had their first fight. The emotions were intense, and it left them raw. Janine began to resent Mike. Passion begets dependence, and she held that against him. His extravagant optimism grated her. What was there to be so cheerful about? Millions were dead. People disappeared. Thousands were maimed or died every day. And he was so American: *He laughs too hard. He drinks too much. How can he be so sure the Allies will win the war?*

"If you were French, you'd be perfect," she told him one night.

"If I were French, you wouldn't give me the time of day," he answered.

She sighed but knew that there was truth to this.

"Papa Mike."

That's what Emma called Mike at breakfast the next morning. Janine froze, coming abruptly out of her sex-infused cloud. Mike had of course won her daughter over. He had found a guitar and every evening played songs for her. She couldn't stall anymore. Mike had to go. She couldn't let her daughter become attached to a man who might just be passing through. She picked a departure date and announced it to Mike and Robert.

She's getting rid of me. Mike was angry, and he worked up in his mind a forceful speech to convince her that she should take Emma and go to Spain with him. But eventually reason prevailed. He needed to return to combat, and no matter how he felt, she had to move him along.

Janine wished he had protested, if only a little—*he doesn't mind leaving, he's relieved in fact, he's looking forward to going back to his world.* She desperately needed the reassurance that their lovemaking meant as much to him as it did to her, and since he wasn't even questioning her decision, obviously it didn't.

Janine's feeling about Robert's departure was more straightforward. He was preparing his haversack one morning, when she sat down beside him. "The guides say you're like a goat on those trails."

"I was born in the mountains."

"We could use you here."

"Yes?"

"The Allies are bombing Germany around the clock, the British at night, the Americans during the day. The number of escapees keeps increasing. We need people who can get those men across the border. Helping ten aviators get back to England every month will be more useful than picking up a rifle and rejoining the army."

Robert had fallen in love with France, but not with the pervading civil war. He was also startled by the enigmatic attraction he felt for Nicole. Maybe he was fooling himself. They barely knew each other. And that was not all—he and Mike had gone through a lot together. They had been lucky. Why change that?

"Think about it," Janine said, feeling his hesitation. "Underground work is hard. You're alone. You can't trust anybody. And you're Jewish. If you were caught it'd be even worse for you."

"They can only kill me once."

Janine looked at Robert and nodded.

On their last night together Mike and Janine clung to one another and did not sleep. She felt a powerful current of life flowing as he took her but when it was over, she felt worse. She knew that she would never see him again. *She knew it.*

"I'll be back," Mike said.

Janine shook her head. "No promises, please." She leaned against his shoulder and let the tears flow.

Mike was exasperated by his failure to get through to her—*she doesn't trust me*. For the first time in his life, he was utterly comfortable with who he was and what he wanted—Janine was the love of his life. After the war they'd get married, have children, and build a life. Their being together had not happened by accident; the price had been paid and he wholeheartedly believed in their future together.

Eight men hiked up the mountain trail—the guide, Mike, Robert, and five airmen: two British, one American, one Canadian, and a Pole. The border with Spain was at the ridge, as crow flies, ten miles away.

"Look at that view," Robert said.

Mike was in a murderous mood. He didn't give a damn about the view. Three thousand feet below, the village looked tiny, and Janine's house was no more than a white and brown speck among the fields—*I was happy there. The happiest I've ever been.*

In the late afternoon, they reached a hamlet at the base of the big climb and the guide led them to a mountain inn. It was cool inside, almost empty but for a few locals playing cards. They took a table and a waitress brought over two brownish bottles that the guide stowed in his bag. Then, she filled their glasses with chilled white wine and stood by, bottle in hand, refilling glasses as soon as they were empty.

When the guide asked for the bill, she shook her head and with a glance indicated that one of the card players had taken care of it. The guide thanked him with a nod. The man raised two fingers in a V, scratched his head under his beret, and went back to his game.

When they walked out, Mike stepped beside their guide. "Everybody knows who we are," he said.

"We know our own," the guide said. "We can spot a foreigner a mile away. To the Germans, everyone's a foreigner."

The climb was hard. There was no moonlight, and they could barely see in front of them. They climbed and climbed, teetering on the edge of thousand-foot ravines and passing yards from German surveillance posts. Everyone was tense, they had heard the stories—men drowning in rivers bloated with spring rains, being caught a few feet from the frontier, or worst of all, breaking a leg and being left behind before the guide came back for a mercy killing. Thankfully, at every stop the guide passed the Armagnac.

At dawn they reached the crest trail marking the frontier. The guide put his finger on his lips indicating the need for silence. They didn't have long to wait. Four men of the Guardia Civil patrol appeared on bicycles on the narrow trail. Rifles slung over their shoulders, they rode carefully avoiding the potholes and pedaled away.

Crossing the trail where the guards had been, they descended from the hilltop. Several airmen began to run but the guide waved them down with a gesture—*you want to break a leg now?* Finally, in a green meadow the guide pulled out the Armagnac and passed it around.

"We're in Spain," he said.

The men shook hands but were too exhausted to celebrate. They sprawled on the grass, shoes off, nursing their blistered feet. Mike felt on edge. There was something to be angry at, but he wasn't sure what it was. The climb had been hard, he missed Janine, and something was up with Robert. They had barely exchanged a word all night.

Robert joined Mike and crouched down next to him.

"What's up?" Mike asked.

"I'm staying," Robert said.

"You're staying where?"

"In France. Janine asked me. She thinks I can help."

Mike's anger burst out as he blurred. "She didn't ask *me* to stay."

"You're a pilot. You'll get a new plane and get back in the fight; that's where *you* can help the most."

Mike realized they were about to separate. He was not ready for that. It felt wrong. "You climbed that goddamn mountain all night to tell me this now!"

"I just made up my mind."

"I don't like it," Mike said, lighting a cigarette to give himself time to think.

"You'll be fine," Robert said, his voice soft.

Mike pulled on his cigarette. Images flashed through his mind—Robert yanking him out of his burning plane, dragging him out of the station in Rome, killing Cossacks, blowing up that prison wall, and standing next to him in that tunnel spraying the Gendarmes' car with machine-gun fire.

"We're a hell of a team," Mike said, blowing smoke. "We should stay together."

"I can't be your copilot."

"We'll find you something in the US military."

"I'll be more useful here," Robert said.

He's right, Mike thought. Grudgingly, he said, "You'll be bored stiff without me."

"I will be. And you'll have to watch your own ass."

They looked away from each other. Mike felt a crushing emptiness. Robert was having second thoughts. He rubbed his chin with the back of his hand. This was harder than he had feared.

"So, that's it?" Mike asked.

Robert nodded. "It's the best thing to do."

Looking up, Mike was suddenly stricken by the magnificent surroundings. "Without you, I wouldn't see this," he said, opening his hands to indicate the lush valley dotted with tidy farms. "I wouldn't be here."

"We've been very lucky," Robert said.

"I would never have met Janine," he sighed. "That would have been a goddamn shame."

Robert chuckled. "You owe me, big-time."

Mike put out his half-smoked cigarette, got on his feet, and rubbed his face with both hands. "I'll miss you," Mike barked, clearing his throat.

"Same here," Robert said.

Together they stared down into the pastures below with the cows' bells ringing in the distance. The guide gave a signal, pointed at a farm down below, and the group got on its feet.

"Where will I find you after the war?" Mike asked.

"I like that town, Pau."

"The one with the palm trees and the funicular by the train station?

"That's it."

Still, they couldn't look at each other.

"I'll look you up," Mike said.

"What about you? You'll be in Chicago?"

"Yes."

"I'll look you up."

They laughed. Mike stuck out his hand; Robert shook it and at the last second, they hugged, brother to brother.

"Stay healthy," Mike said.

"You do the same."

Mike punched Robert clumsily on the shoulder and moved off. Robert stood watching Mike's big frame recede down the hill. When he caught up with the airmen and melded among them, Robert turned around and, shaking off the gloominess, climbed back toward France.

39

"IT'S RAINING AVIATORS." THAT WAS how a Dutch radio operator put it. Thursday, October 14, 1943, had been the bleakest day in the history of the US Air Force as sixty-two bombers were shot on a raid over Bavaria. With six hundred and fifty crew members either killed or on the run, escape lines in Holland, Belgium, and France were flooded with airmen and escorts striving to move them.

Robert had gotten a job as a bus driver on the Transports Palois Réunis. He worked the line from Pau to the Basque country, the very line he had travelled on with Mike and the perfect cover to smuggle aviators. With his lean body and pale complexion, he looked Basque, and his papers identified him as Robert Ybarra, born in Bayonne. To improve his cover, he had even learned a few sentences of the language.

When he was not driving his bus, Robert travelled all over the country to help with the onrush of airmen from "Black Thursday" as it was now called. He had arrived on Limoges that morning to collect three aviators hidden in the cellar of Suzanne's sister Charlotte. They were Americans members of a B-17 crew shot down over Alsace. The pilot, an Air Force major, had complained about bunking with enlisted men. He had also propositioned Charlotte.

"What did you do?" Robert asked.

"I quoted the tenth commandment: 'Thou shall not covet thy neighbor's wife.'"

"And it worked?"

"Like a charm. That's the thing about Americans. You pull out the Bible and they get back in line."

"Does it work with Brits too?"

"The Brits are too well-mannered to try anything."

And the major informed Robert in his heavily accented prep school French that at the next stop, he expected a private room and a bath.

"You'll be lucky to get hay in a barn and a fountain in the courtyard," Robert said.

The crewmen, who disliked their commanding officer, laughed when they heard Robert's words. On the train to Bordeaux, Robert followed procedure and scattered his aviators among several cars. "Sleep. Fake it if you have to," he said. "Don't make eye contact and don't talk." Train stations now displayed posters offering rewards for the identification of allied aviators. All it took was for one passenger to realize who that man was and call the German guards aboard the train. Robert sat on a jump seat at the end of a car. For the first time since Algiers, he was alone. Impersonating a fictional character had increased his isolation and darkened his mood. And he missed Mike.

A knock on the glass brought him back to the present. It was one of his airmen, looking grim.

"The major is practicing his French on passengers," the man hissed.

"Oh, fuck!" Robert hurried along the corridor.

Two cars down, the major stood in the center aisle, pointing out the window. "Maison," he articulated stiffly, pointing at a house.

A lady with a satchel on her lap repeated after him, "Maison." Around them passengers looked away, visibly distressed.

"Arrrbre," he said now, pointing at a grove of trees.

"Arbre," the lady corrected.

Insane behavior. Robert grabbed the major's elbow and dragged him to the end of the car. "Are you out of your fucking mind?" he whispered.

"I'm not taking orders from you, young man. Those people are perfectly harmless." As they entered the connecting area between cars, the major shoved him off and Robert lost it. He head-butted him, dragged him across, and opened the train door. The major managed to grab the handle on the side before Robert kicked him out. Wheels churning under him, legs pedaling in the air, the major starred at the nozzle of Robert's revolver aimed at his face.

"Who're you taking orders from?" Robert asked.

"You," the major hissed.

Robert gave his gun a whirl—*louder*.

"You," the major repeated. "I take orders *from you.*"

Robert straightened up and the man crawled back aboard. It was a miracle no one had reported them. Sometimes luck was with you and today it was. When the train came to a stop in Bordeaux, Robert spotted Lucile and two new girls waiting on the platform. "You try anything with those girls," he snarled at the major, "I'll find you on the trail to Spain and cut your balls off."

The airmen exited the cars with the major trailing behind. The girls smiled flirtatiously, took their arms, and led them away.

They're so young, risking so much, Robert thought.

A few hours later, he was on a night train to Paris to pick up four airmen brought by Suzanne from Belgium. It began to rain as they pulled into Paris's Austerlitz station, but Robert did not care. He and his airmen would be taking the next train south. This was his second trip to the capital, and he still hadn't so much as even stepped out into its streets.

He joined the crowd heading toward the French and German controls at the end of the platform and tried to distract himself from the danger ahead. A brunette in front of him reminded him of Nicole. She caught Robert's stare, rose up on her toes, and pointedly kissed her companion—*I'm taken.*

Robert felt his heart beat faster as he approached the control point where he managed to look as impatient as the people around him. The guard checked his papers, looked at him closely, passed the documents to the German guard who compared the ID picture to Robert's face and waved him through. *Ouf*—Robert exhaled in relief and headed for the Buffet de la gare where Suzanne should be sitting at a table with one escapee and the others at nearby tables. If Suzanne had two or three escapees at her table, it meant danger and Robert was to leave immediately. The Buffet was crowded. Robert ordered a chicory coffee at the bar and spotted Suzanne in her French railway conductor's uniform sharing a table with one young man. All was well. It was too risky for them to even acknowledge each other but he enjoyed her furtive smile as she rubbed her belly—*you were right, I'm pregnant*. The thought uplifted Robert. He glanced over at the well-endowed proprietress enthroned behind her cash register overseeing the activity in her establishment. The waiter slid a cup in front of him and whispered: "Les poulets arrivent."

Les poulets—chickens. Slang for cops. Cops are coming.

Robert hurried toward the door, but policemen rushed in, blocking all exits. A man wearing a double-breasted suit made his entrance. He scanned the room with obvious satisfaction and walked up to Suzanne. "Commissaire Renseignements Généraux. Bonjour, mademoiselle," he said.

A man who enjoys his position, Robert thought. And quite a performer as well, he amended, as the commissaire walked by an aviator staring into his cup, then spun around and pointed directly at the unfortunate man. "Vous, comment vous appelez-vous?"

The aviator did not understand that he had been asked his name and even if he had, he'd have responded in the wrong accent. Delighted with himself, the commissaire repeated his performance until he had rounded up four American airmen.

"Cognac!" the Commissaire barked, snapping his fingers at the barman who served him in a hurry while Suzanne was handcuffed and dragged away followed by the airmen.

Later, safely aboard the train to Pau, a despondent Robert found a spot in the corridor and leaned on the bar behind the glass window. Suzanne's arrest had been heart wrenching. They had not cuffed the airmen, only her. Janine had been right about the struggle of being in the Résistance. You have to control your rage and stay calm even when a close friend is being arrested right in front of you. Oh, God! Suzanne is pregnant and they will be interrogating her.

The train came to a stop in Pau. Robert walked among disembarking passengers and his mind swam back to Nicole and the day they had arrived there with Mike and Lucile. To his utter amazement, he spotted Nicole waiting in the crowd. The sight filled him with joy, then dread—*she's here to warn me. Someone else has been arrested.*

Robert stepped into the station expecting the worst, but Nicole just kissed him on both cheeks.

"Bonjour, Robert," she said.

"What's wrong?" he asked.

"Nothing is wrong. My train back to Toulouse is not until this afternoon and I heard you might be coming from Paris, so I decided to come get you."

Robert exhaled in relief, the knot gripping his gut unwinding slowly.

"I've got a job as a secretary in a freight company. I'll move to Pau at the end of the month," Nicole said.

"Good."

"Aren't you glad we'll be in the same town?" she asked.

Robert caught the pained look on her face and stopped in the middle of the hall, took Nicole in his arms, and kissed her, properly this time.

"Sorry, I'm dark today. Of course I'm happy."

"That's much better. I brought something for you," Nicole said, showing off her bag.

Robert looked at her, surprised. "What is it?"

"You'll see," she said, falling in step with him and taking his hand.

Together they crossed the avenue to the funicular. The car rose and Robert watched the mountains sparkling under the midday sun. He thought about Suzanne and said a silent prayer for her. As they exited on the Palais des Pyrenees, he glanced at Nicole—*she is so pretty and wonderful. I don't deserve her.*

They crossed the square and entered a hotel. Robert picked up his key from the hanging board and led Nicole upstairs. When they reached his floor, Nicole peered through the window overlooking the roof of a shed.

"In an emergency, you can slip into the courtyard that way."

Robert glanced at Nicole. She has hardened, he thought. The need to escape is now always on her mind—*God knows what she has been through shuttling airmen.* He unlocked the door and they walked into a spacious room with a double bed, a table, and two chairs.

"I got a large room for when I need to hide airmen," Robert said.

After he had shut the door, Nicole unzipped her bag and handed Robert a towel, a bar of soap, shaving cream, and a razor. "I felt so bad in Toulouse, when I didn't even have soap for you."

Robert looked at the towel and toiletries while Nicole was still unpacking, pulling out socks, pants, shirts, and underwear.

"What's all that?"

"They're my father's. He's a prisoner of war in Germany. He'd be glad to have you use them. I know you don't have much. So . . ."

Robert felt an odd burst of emotion. He was close to tears—*what's wrong with me?* He glanced at Nicole—no one had ever taken care of him in such a simple, intimate way. "That's very kind of you."

Nicole unfolded a pair of trousers and measured them against Robert's waist. "You're taller than my dad."

She pushed him toward the door. "Go get washed. I'll take down the hems."

The bathroom had a stall and a real shower, a rare thing in France, where most hotels featured bathtubs with capricious gas heaters and never enough hot water. Robert moved under the spray and raised his face to the warm stream. The soap smelled of palm oil. It felt good—*I was thinking of her, and she showed up.*

He came back into the room, his wet hair combed back from a face peppered with shaving nicks blotted with tiny pieces of toilet paper.

"That was a new blade I gave you," Nicole said.

"It wasn't that. It's . . . When I don't get much sleep I . . ." He forced a smile. "You know, my skin gets . . ."

She *did* know. Nicole had seen maquisards after they came back from missions. The strain and the tension made their skin break out and she wondered what ordeal Robert had had to deal with. She finished the hems, cut the thread with her teeth, and handed him the trousers.

"Try those."

Overcoming his shyness, Robert stepped out of his pants, took the ones she handed him, and put them on.

"Turn around."

He did and Nicole stepped back, considering. "The waist is loose." Miraculously, she fished a belt out the suitcase. "Here, this should help."

He slipped the belt through the loops. Now the pants fit perfectly. Nicole sat on the bed and considered his "look."

"Try them with this," she said, handing him a blue worker's shirt. After Robert had put it on, Nicole buttoned it while he pushed the tails down inside the pants. They stood face-to-face, her forehead inches from his lips. Robert wanted to kiss her but did not dare. Then, a knock at the door made them jump.

"It's me," Janine called.

Robert opened the door. Janine stepped in, kissed Nicole, and said, "I need to talk to Robert."

"I'm leaving," Nicole responded, already busy packing Robert's dirty clothes. "I'll wash them and bring them back."

"You don't have to do that," Robert protested.

"I want to. Be back in two weeks. That's when I start on my new job."

Nicole held the bag in her arms as if the contents were precious and left.

"What happened in Paris?" Janine asked, sitting on the edge of the bed.

Robert pulled up the chair and told her. Janine had already heard about Suzanne's arrest and wanted to know about the man in command.

Robert described a man in his forties, showing off for the whole café.

"A commissaire des Renseignements Généraux? How was he dressed?" Janine asked.

"Well," Robert said. "Double-breasted suit under a leather coat."

"Hair?"

"Shiny. Combed back with some kind of lotion."

"Anything else?"

"He had a shot of Cognac before he left."

"At ten in the morning?"

"Yes. Do you know who that is?" Robert asked.

"That's the man who tortured my uncle and arrested my parents and me," Janine said.

40

MIKE HAD BEEN IN A murderous mood ever since returning to England. He had learned his old unit had been transferred to Sicily and he couldn't wait to start fighting in southern Italy where he had been a POW—a revenge of sorts.

But the brass had other ideas. The sight of a returning airman had a tremendous impact on aviators' morale, so Mike was asked to brief airmen on escape and evasion, and he did. He showed airmen how to bleach the telltale nicotine stains off their fingers and stressed to always obey orders from their helpers. If captured, their helpers faced torture and execution while they would spend the rest of the war being fairly well treated in a POW camp ran by the Luftwaffe.

"Bring civilian shoes with you," he instructed. "Your military boots are a dead giveaway. It's the first thing your helpers will need to replace. Clothes are expensive and difficult to find on the black market, but large size shoes simply do not exist as there are few French and Belgian men who wear size twelve or larger. You'll have to walk many miles to reach Spain and a good pair of shoes might save your life."

And at every session at least one airman would ask, usually a pilot, about the chance of getting lucky with a hot French, Dutch, or Belgian girl working on the escape lines. Mike was annoyed and gave vague responses, but felt he was no better than them. He had lusted after Janine and still craved her every day. He missed the way she said "mon amour" in the clipped French way, linking the words—*Monamour*. To be desired by the woman you love was the most erotic feeling imaginable.

Being reminded of France made him more eager than ever to return to combat. After much badgering, he finally got a meeting with his old boss General Topor and that's when things went from bad to worse.

"I'm looking forward to rejoining my unit now based in Sicily, sir," Mike said.

"Won't happen. We're sending you home," Topor said.

"You can't be serious. I don't want to go home."

Topor pursed his lips. "O'Keefe, you've flown over fifty combat missions. You've been shot down over the North Sea, again in Tunisia, wounded, taken prisoner, and escaped. The Gestapo is looking for you all over France. It's time to go home."

"The war isn't over, sir."

"It is for you," Topor said tiredly. "It's the new Air Force policy directorate to not let rescued airmen return to combat."

"I don't give a fuck about your policy directorate!"

"Watch your language, Captain," Topor murmured sotto voce, rearranging papers, increasingly unhappy with the conversation.

And Mike lost his temper.

"The first time I tried to get to Spain, we spent our last night hiding in a farm north of the border," Mike said, pointing at Topor. "An informer had tipped the Germans and a Cossack battalion showed up. They shot the farmer, his sons, and our guide. They machined-gunned the livestock and torched the farm. Our contact in town, a café owner, had been arrested. I learned later that he was tortured to death."

Topor listened, his face impassible.

"Those people put their lives on the line so I could keep fighting. I owe them, sir!"

"I understand how you feel son," Topor sighed. "But I don't have a choice in the matter." And with finality, he closed the file on his desk. "We'll have your discharge papers ready in a few days."

Mike left the building seething. He walked into the first pub on his way, ordered a scotch, and drank it straight. When he tapped his glass for a refill, the barman asked to see his money and Mike paid. He now wore an American Air Force uniform, he wasn't one of "our boys flying to save Britain" anymore; he was a Yank. The United States was using England as a base to fight its own war against Germany and the large influx of rowdy American servicemen was not always welcomed. "Overpaid, oversexed, and over here" was how the British now referred to the Americans. Mike finished his drink, thanked the barman, and set his glass on the bar. Yes, things had changed, but his own feelings remained the same.

He went straight to the RAF recruiting office where he signed up to re-enlist. This was not unheard of. Many American pilots who had been in the RAF and then had joined the US Air Forces in the fall of 1942 had found it impossible to get used to American military procedures and requested to be transferred back to their original RAF unit. They were always welcomed.

"Glad to have you back, Captain," the British officer said. "It'll be official as soon as you're discharged from the US Air Force."

41

LOUIS WAS NO LONGER THE broken man who had jumped out of the Gestapo's window months ago. With nurse Nanette attending, Doctor Weiss had operated on Janine's father several times, affixing steel plates to reinforce healing bones. In a rare moment of candor, Weiss had talked in halting French about his own limp.

"Wounded in Verdun. Operated on by incompetent surgeon. I think of him during surgery. None of my patients will limp for the rest of their lives."

Nanette was still mourning her husband killed during an allied raid over Saint-Nazaire, but she had kept her grief private. She looked forward to surgery time, when she stood across the operating table, anticipating her boss's every need. She was his third hand and had the right instrument ready a fraction of second before he called for it—the right scalpel, traction device, or forceps. Weiss taught her how to cauterize blood vessels and this part of surgery became her domain. Because of the language barrier, he tutored her by showing. Once during a long operation, Nanette, who needed to hold a clamp perfectly still, felt a cramp rising up her arm. Weiss leaned over and with two fingers, gently rotated her wrist by half an inch, and the cramp disappeared. His touch resonated through her whole body, and as she maintained her hold, she hungered to be touched again.

The only annoyance Doctor Weiss ever showed was toward his limp that grew more pronounced as the day wore on. Nanette hated to watch such a handsome man sway unsteadily as he walked. One evening, after a long day of surgery, he left the hospital carrying an armful of books and a bag of tin cans. As he descended the main staircase, the twist of his hip threw him off balance and he dropped everything, with books and cans rumbling down toward the street. Nanette rushed to pick up his belongings and insisted on carrying them back to his apartment.

She was flattered when he invited her in for a bite of dinner. He owned a gramophone and while eating they listened to a Strauss violin concerto. The following week, he invited her again, and she stayed the night. Weiss was a generous lover. No one had ever touched her the way he did. She had sweet memories of her marriage days, but now realized that she and her young husband had fumbled a lot. Weiss was devotedly attentive to Nanette's needs and her timidity evaporated; she gave herself wholeheartedly to him. In bed, his limp disappeared, and he was the most handsome man she had ever seen. Weiss was as old as her father, but Nanette relished their difference in age. She loved surrendering to him in ways she could never have with a man her own age.

They could not be seen together outside of the hospital of course, so his apartment was their sanctuary. They had dinner, made love, and then lay silently side by side.

"What is there to talk about?" Weiss asked once in his rudimentary French. "All we have are painful memories and an uncertain future."

"Du bist die Liebe meines Lebens." *You're the love of my life*, she had learned to say to surprise him one evening after they had made love.

Lying in darkness, Weiss would recite Goethe's *Sommer* and Nanette would fall asleep lulled by the soft cadence of his voice.

"Der Sommer folgt. Es wachsen Tag und Hitze, und von den Auen dränget uns die Glut . . ."

In the daytime, Weiss was reserved to the point of surliness. They never exchanged side-glances loaded with meaning. All they seemed to share was a subtle melancholy. Although the hospital staff gossiped about everyone, Nanette trusted that no one suspected their relationship. A naive assumption, it would turn out to be.

All Saints' Day was a holiday. Most of the medical staff was off duty and the hospital crowded with visiting families. Nanette was filing charts when Weiss walked into his office and dropped his raincoat on the back of a chair. This struck her as odd—a raincoat on a sunny day like this? And why had he left it on a chair when he always hung his coat on a hanger? Then, Louis de Guilhem appeared in the hallway. He looked cheerful and opened his arms wide. "Look at me, no crutches."

"You're doing well," Nanette said.

"No choice. I've got this heartless drill sergeant who dragged me out of bed and forced me to get better."

Nanette had supervised Louis's rehabilitation. It had been a long road. After the removal of his arm and leg casts, Louis had gone through the misery of unlocking joints that had been frozen for months. Then, Nanette had come up with a regimen to rebuild his atrophied muscles. Finally, he had learned to walk again—at first, he stood on crutches, drenched with sweat, hands slippery on the handles, not daring to move. Then he took one step and another with Nanette encouraging him: "One more, just for me. One more . . ."

One lap around the bed the first day, two the next, and she had increased the distance every day after that. To distract Louis from his misery, Nanette talked. She was guarded but Louis picked up clues. She had been raised on a farm where her soul had been bruised by harsh poverty and an abusive father. With determination and hard work, she had graduated from nursing school. Her marriage had brought happiness that has been snatched away by the war. As weeks went by Nanette was effervescent at times. Louis guessed something good had happened to her. Her perkiness had lifted his spirits and helped his recovery.

Louis was also aware of what an exceptional human being his German doctor was. They had talked about World War I and realized they had fought on opposite sides of the battle of La Marne. Today was Louis's final appointment.

"Bonjour, Docteur," Louis said.

Weiss raised a finger. "Please excuse me for a moment."

The doctor disappeared into the hallway and Louis found himself alone in an office with a back door leading to the street. He picked up the raincoat from the back of the chair, put it on, and checking the pockets found coins and a few bills. Opening the side door, he went down a flight of stairs and just like that, he was in the street. He wanted to hurry but could move only so fast. He reached the boulevard and slipped into the holiday crowd, noticing that many people were carrying flowers.

It was All Saints', the day people honored their dead by bringing flowers to their graves.

Louis felt more alive than he had in years.

42

ROBERT LOOKED LIKE THE BUS driver he now was. A mustache squared his face under his black beret. Like the peasants standing around his bus with TRANSPORT PYRENEES RÉUNIS painted on the side, he only shaved on Sunday. Robert had learned that being cranky was an essential part of his job. He clapped his hands.

"M'sieurs, dames! You don't get on the bus in the next five minutes, we'll leave without you."

That got the wives in gear. They hustled their husbands who loaded sacks on top of the bus while the women lined up to get seats. Les grand-méres—the grandmothers had first pick. They climbed aboard and moved to the back where they found two young men with fair skin already ensconced—*city folks*, they determined, knowing exactly who they were.

Robert stopped a farmer climbing aboard with piglets in a burlap sack. "No, no." He pointed his thumb skyward. "Pigs go on the roof."

"You're letting the Boches inside," the farmer grunted, indicating the German guards waiting on the sidewalk.

"Why don't you speak a little louder?"

"My babies will catch cold up there."

"Give 'em a couple of aspirins and a glass of hot wine at bedtime."

The man headed for the roof. "I'll stay with my boys."

Robert was tense. The two "city folks" in the back were British aviators. They had spent the night in his room and before getting to the bus he had given them his usual lecture.

"Do not talk. Do not say 'merci' or 'excusez-moi.'"

Robert exaggerated the British accent—*ex-skew-ze-moi*—and the pilots nodded emphatically. When Robert was about to leave, he raised a finger, having forgotten something vitally important.

"Nod," he said. "Never say 'oui.'"

The older pilot smiled and said: "Nod."

"Très bien."

The bus was almost full when Robert spotted Nicole on the arm of an older gentleman. His heart drummed in his chest—*she shouldn't be here. It's dangerous.* Nicole wasn't moving to Pau until the end of the month. He knew, he had been counting the days. He cut through the crowd and embraced her. "What's wrong?"

"Nothing, I mean . . . ," Nicole said, indicating the man next to her. "He escaped."

It was Janine's father. "My God, Louis! How are you?"

Louis stared at Robert without recognition. Robert leaned over and whispered, "I stayed in your home with Mike the American pilot."

Understanding dawned on Louis' face. "You look like a Basque shepherd."

"That's the idea." Robert glanced at the German guards and whispered, "They sit behind me. Find a place in the back."

Louis nodded and took his place in line.

"Go. It's not safe," Robert said, kissing Nicole's cheeks. "When will you be back?"

"I start my new job in two weeks," Nicole said, looking longingly at him. Their encounters were always so brief. She watched Robert beckoning the German soldiers over. The two men picked up their rifles and climbed aboard the bus. Immediately her frustration turned to worry—*be careful, Robert, please.*

Robert started the engine and watched Nicole walk away. Just seeing her brought a joy that he never dreamt possible—*I want to marry her*. He smiled and, wrenching the large steering wheel, began the trip across town. They passed the Bernadotte garrison, which was now home to two thousand German troops. Then they rolled by the Château de Pau, crossed the Gave River, and headed for the mountains. He could hear the two guards behind him stretch and yawn. They were too old for combat and happy to get escort duty, but the unrelenting contempt of the French made them surly. Robert knew they were from Bavaria because at the end of each trip he took them for a glass of wine at the local café. Some passengers did not like his fraternizing with les Boches, but Robert ignored them. The Bavarians hadn't given him any trouble and he wanted to keep it that way. He also knew they would not hesitate to shoot him if they had to.

He leaned out over the wheel and surveyed the Jurançon vineyards carved like amphitheaters into the hills. It was harvesting time. Workers were picking grapes and dropping them into wicker baskets on their backs as they had done for centuries. Life looked so normal. Back in the bus, the men were fast asleep in the window seats, while the women leaned into the center aisle gossiping in fast paced patois. One passenger got off in Oloron, and five nuns in black robes and white cornets came aboard. They worked in hospices and hospitals all over the region and Robert saw them often. He shifted into gear, keeping an eye on the mirror that gave him a full view of the cabin. Only two of the nuns got seats and the other three had to stand in the aisle.

"Merde," he swore between his teeth.

The English pilots stood and offered their seats to the nuns. One of the German guards caught Robert looking in the mirror, turned around, and saw that one nun was still standing in the aisle. He wedged his rifle against the partition and stood up to give her his seat. She was young and shook her head—"Non, merci"—but the German insisted. She gave in and sat down behind Robert. Several women made gratifying comments and for once the German felt appreciated. He pulled out cigarettes and offered them around.

"Deutch cigaretten, gut."

This was no small gift. Tobacco was severely rationed. The men woke up in a hurry and shamelessly accepted the offerings. The women *pfeuued* at them—the gall of those boors.

Robert sensed trouble. His sweaty hands slipped on the steering wheel. He wiped them on his pants and watched the German hand out cigarettes to the British aviators who took them and nodded in thanks. Then the German rubbed the wheel of his cigarette lighter. A flame sprouted out and he moved around lighting cigarettes. One man held the German's wrist briefly, inhaled, and said, "Merci."

"Les cons." *Those morons*, Robert grumbled.

The German was now edging toward the British aviators. In a few seconds he would get a good look at them and notice the hands without calluses, the pale skin, the blond hair. Then he would rush back to the front, push his rifle against Robert's head, and order him to turn around, back to Pau and straight to German headquarters at the Bernadotte garrison.

"Et merde!" Robert shouted, swerving toward the grassy side of the road. The bus lurched, passengers swayed, and the standing German soldier and British aviator dropped on passengers' laps as the bus settled into a ditch. There were cries and some laughter. The guard, who had landed onto a nun's lap, got up red faced.

"Goddamn driving shaft!" Robert shouted, slamming the steering wheel and switching off the engine. "Everyone off the bus." He jumped down and raced along the bus to open the back door. The two Brits were the first out.

"This is no fucking time to be polite!" Robert whispered between clenched teeth.

Everyone disembarked. The women moved to the shade of a tree. The men congregated in small groups. Robert dragged out a toolbox, picked up a monkey wrench, and crawled under the bus. The driving shaft was fine, he had taken it apart and oiled it himself a couple of days earlier. He kept an eye on the feet of the people moving around. The two Brits wore the blue cloth sandals he had bought for them at the market that morning. German boots were moving in their direction when a pair of black leather shoes stepped between them.

"Gute deutsche Zigaretten, Dankeschoen."

It was Louis causing a diversion by thanking the soldiers for the cigarettes. The conversation continued about Munchen—Munich—and Robert lost track. He kept watching the new blue sandals, which were now surrounded by farmers' shoes. Robert could tell a farmer was passing a bottle of wine around.

Louis was peppering the Germans with questions. A photograph fell on the ground and the German picked it up. Good, Robert thought. He was showing off family pictures.

Robert banged on the shaft, greased up his hands appropriately, and crawled out. "Get the planks off the roof," he called.

The pig farmer handed down the planks. Heavy rains were a common occurrence in Southwest France; vehicles often got stuck in the mud and planks were kept on board for that eventuality. The men took up positions at the back of the bus. The Germans slung their rifles over their shoulders and joined the effort. His aviators were pushing too. Robert fired the engine and cranked it into gear. Mud sprayed from under the wheels, but when the men slid the planks under them, the bus got traction and the vehicle was back on the road.

"Everybody aboard," Robert shouted. The grandmothers climbed in first. Robert whipped his chin at the aviators.

"You two up there."

They scurried up the ladder to the bus roof to sit with the pig farmer. "Truly sorry," one of them whispered to Robert.

Now the bus stopped often to let out passengers at crossroads and without any more drama they reached the line terminus. Men retrieved their bags. The pig farmer stepped down carrying "his boys" and the British aviators were welcomed by two young women who led them away. Robert had his usual glass of wine with the guards and then he went to talk to la Patronne.

"I need a tandem bicycle," he said.

"Why not two bicycles?"

Robert jerked his chin toward Louis sitting at a table. "His legs aren't so good."

The patronne gave Louis a sidelong glance and lowered her voice. "He's the one I heard about, the one who was tortured?"

Robert looked at her but did not answer.

"I know, I shouldn't ask." She rubbed at her apron again. "The schoolteacher has a tandem. I'll get it for you."

Although Louis pushed on the pedals as hard as he could, Robert did most of the work. They rode between cornfields and pastures passing Basque farmhouses. When they reached the foothills, they got off and walked in companionable silence with Robert pushing the bicycle. Neither mentioned the bogus bus accident or how close they came to being caught. In late afternoon, they reached a village and Robert pointed at a farmhouse down by the river. "That's the house."

"Thank goodness," Louis responded.

Janine had worried all day, praying her father had made it to Pau and to Robert's bus. When she heard the clicking of bicycle wheels, she picked up Emma and ran out the door. Louis was getting off the tandem and eyes swelling, opened his arms. They approached each other tentatively, and the three of them stood pressed together for a long time.

"Bonjour, Pappy."

"Bonjour, Emma," Louis responded.

Madame Raymonde appeared, and Louis took her in his arms. Janine embraced Robert and wiped away her tears.

"Oh, Robert, I'm so grateful."

Night fell. The temperature dropped. They lit a fire and sat for dinner with the petrol lamp projecting shadows on the walls. Louis chewed carefully keeping a wary eye on his granddaughter. Emma clung to her mother and was not babbling the way he remembered. Louis recalled how one night he had cried in his cell, convinced he would never see his granddaughter again. But a miracle had occurred and here she was.

"Bonsoir, Pappy."

It was Emma's bedtime. The little girl kissed everyone around the table, even Robert, to whom she said: "Ta barbe pique." *Your beard stings.*

Louis watched Emma take her mother's hand as they headed for the stairs. There was gravity about his granddaughter that broke his heart.

"Have we lost our heads, do you think, fighting a war of resistance, civilians against soldiers?"

"No choice, unfortunately," Robert said.

Janine was back minutes later and sat next to her father.

"How is Emma?" Louis asked.

"I read her a story. She's fine."

"She recognized me. It's been over six months."

Janine poured herself some wine. "She asked when Grandma would be back."

"She'll be back," Louis said.

Janine turned the glass in her hand—*we hope.*

"Was Annie interrogated?" *Annie* was how father called her mother in their most tender times.

"Yes."

"Did they beat her?" Louis asked, taking Janine's hand.

A slight nod, almost imperceptible—*yes.* Janine gazed at her father and contemplated his growing bald spot and the deep wrinkles on the sides of his face—*he is so much older.*

"Do we know where Annie is?"

"Yes. She's in a concentration camp for female prisoners in northern Germany. It's called Ravensbruck. All deported French women are taken there."

43

"I'M A TRAIN CONDUCTOR!" SUZANNE INSISTED. She had no idea those men were allied aviators; she was told they were Dutch laborers on their way to Bordeaux to work on the Atlantic wall. Their documents were checked and stamped at the Belgian border. Yes, she had waited in the café with them to make sure they got on the right train to Bordeaux. No, she didn't talk to them.

"I don't speak Dutch and they didn't understand French."

Boucher knew she was lying, but she was of little importance to him. What was important was the arrest itself and the chance to demonstrate to Oberrsturmbannfüher Karl Lindinger that the French police were more efficient than their Gestapo counterparts. Besides, he considered it beneath him to torture a woman. He turned Suzanne over to them—*let them do the dirty work.*

French Gestapo agents had no qualms about interrogations musclées—they were determined to uncover the locations of safe houses used to hide aviators and the identity of the helpers who sheltered them.

Water boarding had no effect on Suzanne. When the beating grew more severe, she spewed out bogus addresses, and after a day of checking her tormentors came back even more enraged. They stripped her down, cuffed her to rings attached to the wall and took turns whipping her with leather belts. When she screamed she was pregnant, they hit harder. When blood and placenta oozed between her legs, they spit on her in disgust and left. A female prison guard helped Suzanne to a toilet where she washed the best she could, put her clothes back on, and cried, "They killed my baby."

She was then pushed into a cell crowded with male and female prisoners. Her conductor's uniform was stiff with brownish dry blood. A female inmate took one look at her, put a blanket on her shoulders and ordered a man off a bunk. Then, she helped Suzanne take his place. Men and women were usually kept apart, so Suzanne understood this was the end.

"Last station before the Mont Valérien?" Suzanne asked.

"Looks like it."

The Mont Valérien was an ancient fort in a Paris suburb with a courtyard used as a killing field and a beautiful view overlooking the Bois de Boulogne. Suzanne had always known this could happen but never really believed it would. How do you cope with this? *Well, I'm alive right now.*

She forced herself up. "Give me a hand," she said to the woman who had helped her. "Comrades," Suzanne called. She coughed and waved a weak hand as inmates looked up. "Did you hear the one about the two rabbis in Poland who are about to be shot?" Suzanne paused for effect. "When at the last minute the Germans decide to hang them, one rabbi says to the other: 'See, they're finished. They're running out of bullets.'"

A few prisoners chuckled. A man in the back mulled it over, then let out a loud guffaw that made everyone else laugh. Suzanne's bruised, swollen face lit up. She told another joke and got a bigger response. The jokes went on for a while but when the laughter died down, gloom settled over the cell once again.

Tomorrow at this hour, I'll be dead. Suzanne's battered body did not torment her anymore. *Does the proximity of death make my broken ribs hurt less?* She could not *imagine* being dead. When you look at the sky full of stars at night, you're watching the infinity of space, but as much as you try, you cannot conceive of it. It has to end somewhere. And if it does, what is behind it? It was the same with death. She was a Communist, and so didn't believe in God, but she couldn't help thinking—*there has to be something else.*

Well, she had been put on this earth for a reason—to fight for freedom and justice and she had done that. She mused on how sweet her life had been just days before: Cervantes, her fearless, gentle husband—she loved him so! And there was Charlotte, her beloved sister who had always supported her the best way she could—*she is going to be angry.* And Suzanne grieved for the pain she would cause to the extended family of her comrades with whom she shared the political beliefs that gave meaning to her life. She remembered someone saying that people went to church less to be with God than to be with each other. Political meetings were like that. You were there with your brothers and sisters and all together you part of something bigger than yourself.

The bleached dawn morning light filtering through felt like a betrayal. Suzanne could now make out her cellmates—rumpled clothes, wasted faces, they all looked old. A few caught her eye and smiled with a small nod of acknowledgment as if they knew her. Perhaps they were thanking her for the jokes—*well at least we had a few laughs.*

A knot of fear clenched Suzanne's belly as the footsteps of approaching guards resounded in the hall. A couple of men got up. A few exchanged furtive glances. Some looked anxious to get out of there. Others seemed to wish they could make themselves smaller. The metallic clank of the key turning in the lock made her shiver.

"All right, messieurs-dames," the guard said, pulling the door wide open. Slowly, the prisoners shuffled out of the cell. The guards led them along a hallway and down a flight of steps into a courtyard where two trucks waited—ten prisoners per truck. Suzanne managed to reach the truck last and sit next to the sentry—*grab a chance to jump out.*

The engines whined to life and the trucks rumbled out of the prison gate. Across the avenue, the owner of the bistro cranked out his awning. The script on the canvas fringe read: "Ici mieux qu'en face." *Better here than across the street.*

Ten poles in a single line. The prisoners seemed resigned, but Suzanne was not. She knew she was going to die but refused to accept it. She tried to brush off the dry blood on her dress and push a loose lock of hair behind her ear, but hands grabbed her wrists, and tied them to the rough wood of the pole. She saw the blindfold coming and shook her head.

"No! I want to see."

Her request was ignored. Suzanne heard the barking of an order and the shuffle of men aiming rifles. She became obsessed with the emptiness in her belly and wondered if she would hear the gunfire. She did. It was deafening. She smelled the gunpowder but felt nothing. They missed me, she decided.

It was her last thought.

44

THE ROOM WAS BLEAK AND DEPRESSING, like most rooms in hotels across from train stations in French provincial towns. The hunting scenes on the wallpaper had faded beyond recognition. The wooden headboard smelled of bee's wax and as for the bed, Janine knew that she would end up rolling into a sagging middle carved by generations of lone traveling salesmen. And then, there was the name: Hotel du Lion D'or, with a sign hanging above the entrance featuring a Golden Lion. A perfect embodiment for one of those plays on words the French loved so much. Au Lion d'Or sounded exactly like Au lit on dort—*in bed we sleep.*

Janine knew she wouldn't get much rest. It'd be another night away from her daughter. She opened a newspaper-wrapped package and arranged dark bread, sheep cheese, and ham on a metal plate. Then, she extracted a small bottle out of her satchel, flipped open the spring rubber top, and poured wine into a silver cup. This was Emma's cup, the traditional Godmother's gift on the day of christening. Janine lovingly rubbed the monogram engraved on its side and took a sip. She carried the cup everywhere for luck, even though she knew doing so was superstitious nonsense—*it just makes you miss Emma even more.* She sat on the bed and set her plate on the dark wooded table—*and now food will taste like beeswax.* She walked to the dresser, picked up the mirror on top, and set it on the table in front of her. This was her way to combat the haunting loneliness. She pretended there was someone else in the room. It was a ludicrous gimmick, but it helped her.

"You've got to eat," she told her reflection. "If Mike ever shows up again, you'll look like a sack of bones and how attractive will that be?" Listlessly she cut a slice of cheese. She had had no news from Mike since he had crossed into Spain. By now, he should be in the cockpit of a fighter aircraft escorting bombing raids over Germany. The average life span of a bomber crew, she knew, was seventeen missions, and survival was even lower for fighter pilots. Dozens were killed every week, stuck in burning planes spiraling into oblivion.

"What are his chances?" She had to stop kidding herself. Mike had been a gift from heaven, but he was gone and it suddenly occurred to her that if Mike were killed, no one would ever let her know. "Enough self pity!" she told the mirror while forking up a piece of cheese and chewing it methodically. A knock at the door made her jump. In one practiced movement, she grabbed her bag, opened the window, and started to climb out.

"It's Robert."

Janine jumped down from the sill, closed the window, and opened the door, revealing Robert and Proust behind him.

"What are you two doing here? It's risky, you know that."

"I dropped airmen at Charlotte's in Limoges. I was on the way back when he showed up," Robert explained.

"We need to talk," Proust said over Robert's shoulder. "Alone."

"How did you know where Robert was?" Janine asked.

"You asked Résistance-Fer to watch your helpers on the line. They told me."

Janine was in no mood for a meeting. Robert retreated into the darkness of the hallway and vanished down the staircase. Proust walked in and closed the door.

"Eating alone is what I hate the most."

Janine sat on the bed trying to ignore the box spring wheeze. "What do you want?"

Proust remained standing with his hands jammed in his coat pockets. "Suzanne was shot yesterday," he said flatly.

"I know. She was a very courageous woman." Janine's face turned somber. Suzanne's arrest and execution had broken her heart. "I'll stop in Limoges to see her sister Charlotte."

"I'm sure that'll help a lot," Proust said sarcastically. "Did you know Suzanne was pregnant?"

Janine whole body sagged. "No. I did not."

"This morning her husband Cervantes walked into the headquarters of the Renseignements Généraux and threw a grenade in the lobby. He killed three policemen, wounded five, and got away."

"Why are you telling me this?"

"We found out who denounced Suzanne."

Janine tensed up. "Someone we know?"

"No. It was the owner of the Buffet de la gare in Paris. Florentine Pellepoix is her name. Madame Pellepoix was paid a twenty-thousand-franc reward per airman and Suzanne brought in forty thousand. Apparently, she expected forty thousand francs per arrest and claimed she was owed another eighty thousand francs. She threw a fit in the police station and complained to everyone who would listen. That's how we heard about it." Proust pulled out his cigarettes but changed his mind and put them back in his pocket. "With the money she bought herself a fur coat from Lanvin. You get a discount if you buy early. Prices go up as you get close to Christmas."

"Smart woman."

"She has had several fittings because she keeps gaining weight. She must be the only one getting fat in the whole country. The coat is ready, and she'll be picking it up tomorrow."

Janine knew she would loathe what was coming.

"She's responsible for the death of Cervantes's wife and child. An eye for an eye," Proust said.

"What good will that do?"

"We need to put fear in the hearts of collaborators. A conspicuous reprisal will make people think twice about informing the police or writing denunciation letters." Proust clenched his teeth and added, "Govern by fear, that's what the Germans do, and it works."

From Janine, a long-suffering shrug. "No."

Proust gave her a certain look. "We're fighting a war," he said softly. "We've got to be as brutal as the enemy."

"Oh, don't give me that Bolshevik crap!" Janine snarled. "Besides, you don't need my approval."

"Suzanne was working for *you*," Proust said. "*You* need to show the people from Résistance-Fer who risked their lives for the cause that *you* will avenge them if they're betrayed."

"What good is vengeance?" Janine cried.

"It's a tool. A way to protect us and your people on the line." Proust leaned over and added, "We fight to win. If you didn't have the guts to do what's necessary, you should have stayed home filling cavities."

Janine sat up. That stung. She recoiled at the memory of the young German cold-blooded killing in Brittany. It still lived within her and now there would be another one.

"And Cervantes wants to do this?" she asked.

"It was his wife and child."

Janine exhaled deeply and without looking up, nodded.

Proust crossed his arms. "Is that a yes?"

"Yes," Janine replied.

Proust bowed in response. He turned around to leave but as he reached the door stopped and asked: "Did you ever find out if you had a mole in your line?"

"We're watching one escort," Janine said, not willing to share more.

"Stop watching. If you have doubts, liquidate him or her," Proust said.

"I need more than doubt."

"Liquidate who ever that is," Proust repeated. "If he's innocent, it's a tragic mistake. One more innocent life lost among millions. But if he's betraying the line and you don't make the hard choice; more of your people will be arrested, tortured, and shot."

Janine bit her lips, wishing simultaneously she were that cold blooded and feeling relief she was not. "Leave now. Please."

"Bon appétit," Proust said before closing the door behind himself.

A bone-weary Janine packed away her uneaten meal and drank some wine. When she heard a loud knock on the door, she glanced at the window but couldn't move. It was like Drancy the night before the train. Despair and surrender. She pulled a gun out of her bag and pushed it under her chin, nozzle up. She waited for men to crash the door but all she heard was a softer knock.

"It's Robert."

Oh, God, I'm losing my mind. She sprang up, slid the gun back in her bag, and opened the door. Robert stepped in and produced a half full bottle of Remy Martin Cognac from under his coat.

"What about a drink?" he said, his voice ringing with misery.

She caught the tension on his face. "What's wrong, Robert?"

He shook his head. "Suzanne's execution got to me, and I almost shot an American pilot on the way to Pau."

"I heard about it," Janine said. "His men reported him. He'll be court-marshaled back in England."

"That's big of them."

She looked at him with utmost fondness and patted the space next to her. Robert sat on the edge of the bed.

"My father said you had a close call with those British pilots in your bus."

"I drove into a ditch. It was a hell of a circus."

Her glance rested on him for a moment, feeling amused tenderness toward him, maybe more.

Robert uncorked the bottle. "We were lucky. Let's drink to that," he said, filling Emma's cup with cognac. The liquid had a lovely amber color and smelled fruity. "Santé." *To health.* He drank, refilled the cup, and handed it to Janine.

Why not? She swallowed it in one gulp. It was stronger than expected. Her eyes turned misty. "Ou là là!" Janine cried, waving her hand in front of her face.

Robert winced as the alcohol spread through him. He raised the bottle. "Why is this stuff so expensive? It's awful."

"You bought it."

"Hell no! I stole it from the bar downstairs."

He watched her guffaw, refilled the cup, and swallowed hard while reading the bottle's label. "That guy Remy found a way to get rid of his bad grapes. He stuck a fancy picture on the bottle and fools buy it."

"You don't have the right kind of palate, that's all."

"And you do?"

"I have an exquisite palate."

"A classy, educated lady with a palate."

"I am." Janine poured herself another shot and drank it down. Clumping the cup down on the table, she raised her chin and looked at Robert defiantly—*there.*

They grinned at each other, alcohol racing through their blood.

"A lady who drinks like a man." He smirked.

"Oh yeah?" she said. His words felt like a provocation that could not be left unanswered. Robert had woken a craving in her and the alcohol was melting her qualms away. She pulled Robert to her and kissed him. He was amazed but responded, and they fell sideways onto the bed.

Later, Robert could not remember if he had pulled or she had pushed, but she was the one who had crawled over him to switch the light off. He had buried his face in her neck as she unbuckled his belt. The room was cold, and they dove under the covers half undressed. The bedsprings whined. This was not soft love. He was inside her, then he wasn't. She knew how to please him and how to nudge him when she wanted to be caressed a certain way.

Robert's body was lean, his hair dark, and his skin chocolate brown, exactly like her husband. She made love to her dead husband and to Robert and relished being weighed down under both their bodies.

When he caught sight of Janine's face in a shaft of light, she looked happy and that felt like the most wonderful thing in the world. Their lovemaking was less a search for pleasure than a longing to alleviate the debilitating loneliness. Touch and be touched. Pure and simple survival.

At dawn the room was colder than ever, and they woke up still pressed against one another. Before they knew it, they were at it again.

"I'm weak." Janine's voice was bitter. "You understand that?"

"I do," Robert said, although he didn't. She was the strongest person he had ever met.

As the pace of their lovemaking quickened, she kept shaking her head as if trying to deny how good it felt. Then, her thighs clasped around his waist, and she cried out. He too cried out, and at that very moment, he thought of Nicole.

He had never felt so sad.

In the weeks that followed they behaved as if their night together had never happened. As time went on, Robert wished she would acknowledge their moment with a wink, a half-smile—*we both needed that.* She never did.

45

MADAME PELLEPOIX WAS SO ELEGANT in her mink coat, she felt like une actrice de cinema when she stepped out of the Lanvin fashion house on the rue du Faubourg Saint-Honoré. She looked rich and important. People would respect her now. No one would treat her like those people who had tried to cheat her out of her reward money. Thank God for Commissaire Boucher who had intervened and made sure she was properly paid. It was good to have powerful friends. She decided to walk to the Concorde and find a taxi there.

She passed the Brazilian Consulate and ignored the line of people waiting outside the visa section—*Foreigners get out*, she thought. *France for the French.* At the corner a policeman stopped traffic so she could cross the street. Everything was perfect. She heard steps behind her—*an admirer perhaps?* She glanced back but never saw the man who clasped his hand over her mouth. For an instant, she thought it was someone she knew playing the *who-am-I* guessing game. Then, she saw the flash of a razor and felt a cold nick across her throat.

"Mais enfin!" *For heaven's sake.*

He let her go. Outraged, Madame Pellepoix turned around but could only make out a man wearing a beret striding away—*another foreigner*, she thought as a gurgling sound made her look down where streams of blood were staining her brand-new coat—*the nerve of that man, someone will be punished for this!* She tried to scream but had no breath. Holding her throat with one hand, she extended her arm for balance and collapsed on the sidewalk like a broken marionette. The traffic cop rushed over, took one look, and threw up.

The blood squirting out of Madame Pellepoix's throat had now drenched her mink coat. Her feet and legs flapped wildly as her whole body jerked and shook in spasms as she died.

On the train back to Bayonne, Janine read in the underground newspaper *Le Franc Tireur*, an article describing the demise of Madame Pellepoix in gory detail. Suzanne's death had been avenged. Maybe it'll frighten off people thinking of betraying people for money, Janine thought. She folded the paper but still felt horrible about being connected to such horror. And she was more than connected; she had approved the assassination.

She had lost her bearings that night, even put a gun to her head. But Robert had shown up, made her laugh, and quenched the urges tormenting her. And it had felt good. She felt no remorse, it had been a purely physical moment and she needed it. They both needed it. Her affection for Robert was profound—*a truly kindhearted man, he is.*

The stream of rescued aviators smuggled to Spain and Gibraltar was now regular and funds arrived steadily from London. Janine knew that Mike was safely back in England, but there was something she felt bad about. Every time Mike had wanted to talk about their future together, she never let him. Every time he mentioned America or his family, she found a way to prevent him from envisioning their lives after the war.

Oh my love! Of course I want to be with you for the rest of my life. She talked to Mike at night when she could not sleep, often asking: "Did the eleven days we spent together mean anything to you?"

Ab oculis, a corde—*out of sight, out of mind*—loin des yeux, loin du coeur. It was true in all languages. Lovers had worried about this for thousands of years. In dark times she was convinced that for Mike she had just been a "roll in the hay" as the Americans love to say. When her mood improved, she believed the affair had been serious for them both. She knew that their intense loving had eased the pain she had endured since the beginning of the war.

He gave me hope.

46

MIKE WAS EAGER TO BE back in the cockpit of a fighter plane and kept badgering the US Air Force for his discharge papers. When they finally came General Topor made it clear he did not approve of Mike rejoining the RAF. He also mentioned that US military attaché wanted to talk to him.

What do they want from me? Mike wondered, feeling a worry gnawing at him as he took his papers and saluted. "Thank you, sir."

As he reached the door the general barked, "O'Keefe."

"Sir."

"You get yourself killed, I'll be royally pissed."

Mike looked back. Topor was already busy reading a file.

"I'll be fine, sir."

Topor waved him off with a flip of the hand.

With his papers in order and his RAF assignment forthcoming, Mike considered ignoring the summon from the US Embassy's military attaché's office. The order specified that he should wear a dress uniform and *not* shave or get a haircut. An odd directive that made him curious and this was only a prelude.

Everything that happened that day turned out to be unexpected. When he arrived for his appointment, an Embassy aide led him to the inner courtyard where a car waited for him. A few minutes later, he was deposited at the entrance of the Savoy, London's most exclusive hotel. Winston Churchill often took his cabinet there for lunch. When Mike entered the lobby, part of the mystery was solved. The Savoy had a dress code: suits and ties for the men, dresses for women. *Could have used a shave, though.*

"Captain O'Keefe?"

Mike turned around and shook the hand of a tall man in his fifties.

"James Harris. Good to meet you, Captain."

"Pleasure is mine, sir," Mike said, surprised that the military attaché did not wear a uniform.

Harris' grey eyes, serious behind steel rimmed glasses, did not miss much. He wore a well-tailored gray suit, a blue striped tie, and bulldog cufflinks. Not military, not even close. "Five o'clock, cocktail hour," he said.

The bar was all polished brass and dark oak. They sat in a booth with etched glass panels removed from the bustle of the room. Drinks arrived, although Mike did not remember ordering. Later he realized that their appearance was emblematic of this outfit. Things were *taken care of*—the message from the embassy, the car, the hotel, the drinks. There was a patrician feel to the proceedings that impressed Mike more than he cared to admit. It also gave him a clue. He had heard the rumors and decided to check his hunch.

"Harvard Law?" Mike asked, pronouncing it in the approved Boston manner.

"Close."

"Lawyer?"

"Banker."

Now Mike was sure. Harris was OSS, part of the newly established American Intelligence Service in which Ivy League lawyers, bankers, and businessmen went to war wearing starched shirts and three-piece suits.

"Am I talking to a member of the outfit Colonel Donovan is putting together?" Mike asked.

An almost imperceptible shrug from Harris. "No idea what you're talking about," he said.

Smooth. Definitely OSS, Mike thought. "So, what's up?"

Harris's eyes registered approval. He too valued the direct approach. "We don't want you back in the RAF."

"You want to send me home?"

Harris shook his head amused. "We want you back in France."

Mike sucked in his breath as gently as he could—*quiet down. Don't blow it.*

"Sell your soul to get back there, right?" Harris said with a sparkle in his eyes.

"What would I be doing?" Mike asked, trying to sound nonchalant.

"The old beaten path. Blowing up prisons, hijacking trains, smuggling allied pilots, hanging out with pretty French women."

"Anything you don't know about me?"

"We try to stay ahead of the curve."

Harris raised his glass and Mike joined him in a silent toast.

"The opening of a second front in France will happen soon and we need to school maquisards in the art of blowing up bridges and rail yards to disrupt German troop movements on the day of the invasion. That'll be a key part of your mission." Harris watched Mike's reaction and continued. "We're the eight-hundred-pound gorillas in this war. The British are our allies of course, but we want our own people on the ground. We're thinking about American interests long term. What happens once Germany is vanquished? How do we prevent France from sliding into civil war? Can we ward off a communist takeover in Europe? You've got a solid military record, you worked with the French Résistance, and they trust you." Harris took off his glasses and wiped them with his napkin. "You'll be reporting directly to me."

Mike fought thoughts racing through his brain—*Janine, Robert, Proust. Staying in the fight*. He glanced at Harris, who was waiting for an answer, eyebrows raised inquisitively.

"I'll need money and weapons," Mike said. As he spoke, he realized his life had just taken an unforeseen turn.

"Money's no problem," Harris said smoothly, seizing his advantage. "What exactly will you need?"

"Machine guns, plastic explosives, grenades, and ammunition. Also, medicine, blank ID papers, and civilian shoes sizes twelve and up."

"We'll get you UD M42 machine guns, a new weapon we supplied to the partisans in Crete. It's best for this kind of fighting." Harris took a sip of his drink and went on. "I understand you worked with that FTP man who goes by the name of Proust. Member of the French Communist Party. A skilled operative."

"He set up the train attack for us. I've a lot of respect for the Communists I've met. While we're on the subject, Proust mentioned that the Résistance badly needs mortars, submachine guns, and PIAT anti-tank weapons."

"They won't get them."

"Why not? Why are Tito's partisans in Yugoslavia getting better weapons than the French Résistance?"

"Strategic decision. If we send heavy weapons to the French Résistance, the Germans might react by sending in crack troops. We don't want elite SS divisions in place when we land in Western Europe. We'd rather have them on the Eastern front. Let the Russians have their fun with them."

Mike knew "strategic decision" was a lie. The allied brass didn't want French communists to be too well armed or too successful. Still, he gave it another try.

"The communists in the French Résistance fight hard. The better we arm them, the more they can help us," Mike said, leaning forward a bit.

From Harris, that tiny shrug again—*if it was just that simple.* He fixed Mike with an appraising stare and decided to give it to him straight. "Look, we'll invade next spring to liberate Western Europe with a combined allied forces of three million men. On the east, the Soviets have six and a half million soldiers storming into the heart of Europe and the harsh reality is Stalin's armies will defeat the Germans even if we never open a second front. It might take them another two or three years and a couple million more casualties, but ultimately, they will roll over the Nazis. The last thing we want is for the Red Army to reach the Atlantic. We'd end up with a European continent under Stalin."

A waiter glided up unbidden, with fresh drinks. Harris downed half of his before the waiter had disappeared, then he turned to Mike.

"A car will pick you up in the morning. Have your bags ready."

"When will I be leaving for France?"

"In a matter of days.

Mike finished his drink. "I'll be ready," he said, starting to rise.

Harris lifted his hand, indicating Mike should stay put. "Tell me about that Jewish fellow you escaped with in Italy. Where he is from?"

"Algeria."

"Did he ever mention being involved in underground activities before joining the French African Corps?"

"He mentioned seizing control of a post office in Algiers."

"The night before Torch landings?"

"That's what he said."

Harris smiled for the first time. "Next time you're together, tell him Bogart sends his regards."

"And he'll know what that means?"

"Oh, I think so. He's the one who came up with the nickname."

"Bogart sends his regards," Mike repeated. "I'll pass on the message."

Harris stood and solved the mystery of his sartorial orders. "Grow a mustache," he said. "And we've got a barber who will give you a French haircut and darken your hair."

Mike walked out of the Savoy bursting with anticipation and decided to walk. He needed to spend the energy fueling his elation. He'll be with Robert and Janine again.

"My God, Janine!" He could hear her voice: *Monamour!*

47

ROBERT WAS DRIVING HIS BUS back from the mountains. The day before he had taken one Canadian and two British airmen to Oloron and they were on their way to Spain. The Basque and Bearn country was now a key transit center for aviators waiting to be smuggled across the mountains. The underground was struggling to hide and feed men scattered in farms, cellars, apartments, and even a convent. *The war was comical at times,* Robert thought. Tight-fisted American accountants refused to finance the escape lines, which infuriated the British who were paying the bills. Hence, they insisted that Commonwealth aviators be smuggled first, so Americans were at the back of the line hidden in farms along the border.

Food on a French farm, even in wartime, was haute cuisine compared to army rations. Hiding was a lot less dangerous than air combat, and les cerises sur le gâteau—*the cherries on the cake*—the French women. Frenchmen were POWs in Germany and French girls were falling in love with Americans in spates. So, airmen who had once been desperate to get to Spain were perfectly happy to stay put. Robert, who had seen what the Cossacks did to farmers sheltering aviators, was eager to get them across the border as soon as possible. But when he showed up to get them, he had to deal with desperate French women crying as he took their amoureux away.

Robert now operated out of Pau. He liked that town; a place that a few months ago he didn't even know existed. People treated him as one of their own; his hotel room was comfortable, and he even ate well. He had made a deal with the Patron of Chez Francis, a black-market restaurant, and smuggled goods in his bus and in exchange got a couple of free meals a week.

All was well, but Robert did not trust it. His mind was a ping pong of worried thoughts. Nothing specific, just anguish deep inside. And there was Nicole. What had started as mere attraction was now full-blown love. She was set to start her job in Pau in a few days and Robert couldn't wait to be with her. Just thinking about her would get his mind feverish with anticipation. He was only a bus driver, but he knew he would do better. He was still a long way from the man he wanted to become, but he had drive and ambition. He could build a good life here with Nicole. Having ran away from a place he despised; he had found a new home.

48

DOWNED AIRMEN FLOODED THE LINES and de Lacoste was desperate. Since joining the Résistance he had had a few close calls but always managed to escape. A survivor to the core, he had smuggled Turenne out of Marseille and shot Detective Franjou in broad daylight in the middle of the crowded *place du Capitole* in Toulouse. But this time, he was running out of options. For nearly a week he had been stuck in Bordeaux with six aviators holed up in L'Hôpital psychiatrique de Cadillac in padded cells designed for the criminally insane. Some of the airmen were starting to feel a little insane themselves and causing trouble.

To make matters even worse, Lucile had arrived with five more escapees. Her contact was a Madame who ran a luxury brothel on the Quai des Chartrons. The lady had made a lot of money servicing German military for the last four years, but she now worried that the Nazis were losing the war. Fearful of how her activity would be looked upon after the war, she had joined the Résistance and started hiding Allied aviators.

The last de Lacoste had seen of Lucile was at the Poule d'Or in Pigale and he barely recognized her. Retirement from high-class prostitution and joining the line had had been good for her. She dressed simply, had shortened her red hair, and wore no makeup. She now was a mature woman exhilarated by her new freedom, but she was taken aback when she met de Lacoste. She remembered him as an always-elegant unflappable rogue. His clothes were soiled, his face unshaved, and eyes bloodshot. The nonchalant manner was gone.

He told Lucile that he had tried over and over to contact the Bordeaux underground and had gotten no response. He felt abandoned. "I've sent messages to this man Proust. He's FTP, he could help. He's not responding."

And Lucile was worried about her aviators. The girls at the brothel had discovered who they were and wanted to contribute to the war effort with "*freebieez for ze Yankees.*" But the girls drank a lot of champagne. They were silly and talkative and every night the place filled with U-Boats crewmen and Gestapo officers. The situation was quickly becoming untenable.

49

THE CABIN OF THE HALIFAX smelled of fuel, engine oil, and curiously, menthol. Mike found a path between crates anchored into nets and took a seat by the bomb bay. He was unshaven and the mustache he now sported made him look older. A French barber in Hampstead had given him a continental cut and darkened the hair sticking out from under his beret.

The flight Sergeant was a gangly kid with a friendly face and an Oklahoma accent. Nineteen, twenty at most. He shoved a stick of gum in his mouth and checked Mike's parachute. "Name's Dwayne. You French?" he asked.

In a whimsical mood, Mike answered, "Oui." Giving the word a Continental flourish.

"You understand English?"

Mike flipped his hand—*a little.*

The sergeant spoke loudly, articulating every word. He raised three fingers. "It'll be a three-hour flight." He said pointing at his watch. "You understand?"

"Oui."

The pilot, a tall man with the frame of a football player extricated himself from the cockpit, walked along the fuselage and sat beside Mike.

"A privilege to have you on board, Captain," he said, extending a hand that Mike shook. "Didn't recognize you at first. I attended your lecture on escape and evasion."

"Didn't bore you I hope."

Dwayne stared at Mike. "I'll be darned," he mumbled.

"I've got my dancing shoes with me." The pilot said, unzipping his leather jacket revealing the pair of wing tips hanging around his neck.

Dwayne grinned and showed off his own lace up Oxfords.

"Hope you don't get to use them tonight," Mike said.

The pilot chuckled, checked his watch, and stood. "We'll fly south for about two hundred nautical miles, past the coast of Brittany and then southeast. It'll be a straight line to the drop zone south of Orthez. I'll make one pass to drop those." He said pointing at the crates. "Then I'll make another pass to drop you. It's safer that way. Good luck, Captain."

As the pilot disappeared into the cockpit, Dwayne indicated the suitcase sitting at Mike's side.

"That goes with you?"

"Yes."

"I'll strap it to your leg. You'll want it to hang a few feet beneath you so it hits the ground first. The less weight when you land, the better."

"Done this before?" Mike asked.

"Yes, we started at the end of the summer, doing three drops a week . . ." Dwayne's voice trailed off and he looked away.

"Any mishaps?" Mike asked.

Dwayne chewed his gum a little faster and nodded reluctantly.

"You can tell me," Mike said.

"We had this French radio operator, a science teacher, a nice fellow. His English was good. He was curious about America; said he'd come and visit after the war. He wanted to see the Oklahoma oil fields. Hell, that'd be easy, they're all over the place."

"What happened?" Mike asked.

"We dropped him north of Lyon. His parachute didn't open."

Dwayne spat out his gum and whispered between clenched teeth. "Darn it. I checked it three times!"

The plane was taxiing now, gathering speed for takeoff.

Mike rubbed his unshaved chin—*don't you wish you hadn't asked.*

As the plane gained altitude, the temperature in the cabin dropped and the sergeant handed Mike a flask. "It'll keep you warm."

Mike shook his head. He was not cold. He felt as if all the systems in his body were running at higher speed. Even during his days in the RAF, he had never experienced such excitement. He knew he would never be in the cockpit of a fighter plane again and that was fine with him, he now itched for that other kind of war. At close range, nasty and thrilling, with buddies at your side. And afterward all you wanted was to embrace your friends and make love to your woman. In a few hours, he'll be back in that world—*unless the kid here screws up my parachute.*

Janine could not sleep. The message on the BBC broadcast had announced: "*The Irishman stopped drinking warm beer.*" Mike was on his way. She was reliving every kiss and caress of the summer. Her breasts were now healed, and she felt whole and lusty. The craving was so acute; her nipples were erect to the edge of pain. Crouched on her side with fists between her thighs, Janine's longing morphed into worry. The week before A-47 sky trooper flying from London to Lisbon had been shot down by the Luftwaffe over the Bay of Biscay, killing everyone on board. No, they'll bring him in a Halifax and none of them have been shot down during a supply mission—*well, not yet.* Above all, she was tormented by the vital, essential matter, "Is he coming back for me or because he's been ordered to?"

The sound of Dwayne's nasal voice woke Mike up. "Flying over the French coast, Captain."

Mike rubbed his face, stretched, and stood up to flap his arms. He breathed deeply, wrinkling his nose. He glanced back at the pile of crates.

Dwayne caught the glance, “Smell funny, right? Camphor and sulfa mainly, morphine also.”

Mike moved to the porthole encased in the back door. All he could see of nighttime France was an occasional light flickering here and there. He thought of the wounded airmen down there, and the Dutch, French, and Belgian nurses and doctors who were taking care of them. It often wasn't pretty. He had met a British pilot in Spain whose left arm had been mangled when his plane crashed. It had to be amputated without anesthesia. His rescuers had plied him with brandy and four men had held him on a kitchen table, rags stuffed in his mouth to muffle the screams for the procedure. But it had saved his life and that aviator thought himself lucky.

Dwayne manually cranked the bomb bay door open. Mike returned to his seat. Cold, wet air rushed through the cabin and the roar of the engine turned deafening. Mike took several deep breaths.

“French air.” Mike shouted, giving thumbs up.

Dwayne, who was not sure this was such a cause for celebration, returned the gesture. “Yep,” he said.

A light flashed above the cockpit door. Dwayne checked his watch and flashed five fingers—five minutes to the rendezvous point.

Seven thousand feet below, Robert was cold and cranky. A fine coat of snow covered the field in front of him. He walked in circles stomping the ground to keep warm. “When is the son-of-a-bitch gonna show up?” He growled. He had arrived at the rendezvous with a group of underground men and watched them position red lanterns one hundred yards apart and build up piles of wood at the edges of the forest. The night had turned bitterly cold and it started snowing again. Robert hated to wait, hated to stay in one place. His mind was dizzy with awareness of the danger of their situation. Informers were everywhere—one tip to the Milice or the Gestapo and they would all be caught in the open.

The hum of an engine bursting out from behind a hill took him by surprise. A frenzy of activity stirred up around him. Red signal lanterns turned on. Bonfires along the drop zone lit. Robert smelled the heady stink of wet wood doused in grain alcohol. The roar above his head and the heavy shadow of the Halifax felt like a miracle. Robert was bowled over by the sight and overwhelmed by gratitude. They were *not* alone. They had Allies, friends that showed up when they said they would.

The underground men flashed a message in Morse code. Like a friendly beast, the Halifax circled lazily above them and came back so low Robert lost sight of her between the trees. The pilot returned the Morse code, lights shone inside the aircraft and white aureoles popped into the sky. It took Robert a moment to realize those were parachutes. Men ran across the field unhooking crates from the collapsing white silk. The plane disappeared and Robert worried for a minute but soon the growing rumble of its engine was back. The Halifax approached. Robert could see two men in the bomb bay. The rectangle of light was obscured for an instant as one of them jumped and his parachute opened. The one who remained in the aircraft waved at Robert. It felt like being saluted by someone from outer space. Then, the plane rose, and the bomb bay closed, shutting off the light. The aircraft's gray belly turned cold and remote as it faded into the clouds.

"Goddamn it!"

That was a familiar voice. Mike had hit the ground and was being dragged along the frozen field by a surface wind. Robert ran toward him and seizing armfuls of parachute silk, bundling it against his chest.

"Robert?" Mike asked in a loud whisper.

"Of course."

Mike freed himself from the parachute straps and untied the suitcase roped to his feet. His grin could have lit up the night. "Come here, you asshole!"

They hugged like bears, laughing and dancing around. Robert took Mike's head in his hands and stared at his face.

"Look at that mustache! You are ugly."

They laughed again, bellowing so loudly that the maquisards wrapping Mike's parachute darted them uneasy looks.

"That case stays with me." Mike said pointing at the leather suitcase on the ground. The men nodded and moved off to retrieve the remaining crates and load them on horse carts lined up at the edge of the field. Others began shoveling dirt into a trench.

"What are they doing?" Mike asked.

"Burying the parachutes."

"Can't they re-use the silk?"

"And be caught with a shirt made from an American parachute?"

Mike swore. A few weeks in England and he had already lost his edge. He followed Robert, his feet sinking through the snow piled over blankets of leaves. They reached a dirt path with two bicycles propped against a tree.

"Not a fucking bicycle again?" Mike protested. "I've still got blisters from last time."

"My Cadillac is in the shop."

Mike put his arm around Robert's neck.

"I've got money, weapons, medicine, radios, and tons of fake IDs. I'm back! Tell the truth: This war was boring without me?"

"Yeah, I had no one to bail out of trouble. Did you bring chocolate?"

"Would I forget a thing like that?" Mike dug into his overcoat and handed Robert two bars of chocolate in shiny blue and gold wrapping.

"Swiss?"

"For you, only the best."

Robert tied Mike's suitcase on the back of his bicycle. The maquisards were moving off, supplies hidden under hay on the horse carts.

"How's Janine?" Mike asked.

"She's well. You came back for her?"

"Came back for you."

"I knew it."

"I'm in love with that woman, you know."

Robert felt a stab of shame remembering the night at the Lion D'Or. The French had a word for it: *Un moment d'égarement*—a moment of confusion—yes, you lost your head but you should be forgiven. All that sweetness and groping in the dark had felt so right at the time and felt so wrong now. But then Janine acted as if nothing had happened—*if she doesn't feel remorse why should I?*

Robert unwrapped a bar of chocolate, broke off two squares and let them melt in his mouth, sighing with pleasure.

Mike pushed on the pedals, then dropping into the saddle, he announced. "My ass hurts already."

It was still dark when they reached the farm. Janine stood in the lighted doorway. She wore a freshly ironed dress. Her hair was pinned up high. She had dabbed a little rouge on her cheeks. There was burning aliveness in her eyes. Mike propped his bicycle against the wall and embraced her so fiercely, he lifted her off the ground.

"God, I've missed you!" he said, twirling around and kissing her.

"Let me down, you animal," she protested even as she snuggled into his arms. When he finally did, she grinned and touched his mustache.

"Look at you! Dark hair, a mustache, you look French!"

"A real improvement huh?"

"*Absolument.* The more French the better."

She held his head with both hands and kissed him hard on the mouth. They were behaving like an old married couple that had been apart for a while and happy to be reunited.

Robert brought the bicycles inside. Stirred by sudden shyness he tried not to watch them. Janine had helped Mike take off his coat and then his jacket. She was now appraising him.

"You're wearing a lot of sweaters," she said, padding the bulk on his shoulders.

"Hey, it was freezing on that plane." He removed one sweater after another, piling them on top of a chair. Janine puffed out her cheeks mimicking chubbiness.

"You've gained weight."

"No one gets fat on English food."

She pointed at his belt. "How many pairs of pants are you wearing?"

"Two," Mike answered, adding with a grin. "And three pairs of British army issue long woolen underpants. Want to check them out?"

Janine let loose the clear pealing laugh Robert had not heard in months. Mike put a hand on Janine's waist and kissed her forehead. The simple ordinariness of the gesture pierced Robert's heart. He missed Nicole and felt a stab of loneliness so sharp; he looked down to hide the envy on his face.

Janine took up a petrol lamp and led Mike away. "Good night, Robert."

"Good night," Robert answered. He picked up a blanket and lay down on a cot by the fireplace. The flames had long since died down, but the logs still radiated an incandescent glow. There were still two or three hours until dawn, but he knew he would not sleep. He stared at the ceiling and brooded about Nicole. She was, he knew, taking aviators from Limoges to Pau that very night—her first overnight transfer. A wave of dread raced through him. He could see her face clearly in his mind, determined and beautiful. *Please Nicole, be careful.* The thoughts churned through his mind in a constant loop.

50

BUILDUP FOR THE ALLIED LANDING INTENSIFIED. OSS planes dropped arms and ammunitions every night. Robert joined Mike who was training the men of the Maquis on UD M 42 machine guns supplied by the OSS. "High Standard Manufacturing Company in Hartford Connecticut" was the name on the barrel—*Hartford, Connecticut! Where the fuck is that?* Robert wondered.

This was the first time the French Résistance received armaments shipped from the United States. The crates were opened and the maquisards watched in awe. They had friends in faraway places that sent brand new weapons and ammunition. They were grateful.

At the end of the session, Mike crouched down beside Robert. His blue eyes twinkling as he lit a cigarette. "I've got to remind them to keep their weapons clean. Don't want them jamming in the middle of the fight."

"Right," Robert said. Mike had lectured them about the M42's low tolerance for dirt until they wanted to punch him. "Maybe you should tell them one more time."

"You *are* an asshole."

"Well, you *are* a little anxious because they are using *American* weapons for the first time," Robert said. "You're worried they'll screw up. National pride on the line."

"I never liked you, Robert. You know that."

"That's what I love about you Americans. You aren't scared of the enemy, but you're terrified of fucking up."

"And the French aren't?"

"The French *expect* to fuck up. Then they have to rely on their ability to improvise: System D—Systeme démerde."

"De-merde?" Mike repeated. "Get out of the shit?"

"Exactly."

"No System D with me. Those assholes are gonna be so well trained, they'll terrify entire fucking Waffen SS divisions."

Mike's certainty was contagious. Robert was looking forward to actual combat, fighting the real war.

51

PROUST HAD RECEIVED DE LACOSTE'S cry for help and after much badgering Résistance Fer finally managed to smuggle the airmen and their escorts aboard a freight car hauling coastal battery guns bound for Hendaye on the Spanish border. Lucile, de Lacoste, and the eleven airmen stood swaying in the crowded car and when the train edged out of the station, everyone let out a sigh.

The relief was premature. A few miles out of town disaster struck—the train stopped, the freight car door slid opened, and SS men pulled the aviators out.

"Amerikanische und Britische Bomber Crews!" *American and British bomber crews!* The SS officer shouted as his men punched and kicked.

"Murderers! Women, children, old-people killers! Forty thousand Bürger getötet in Hamburg!" *Forty thousand civilians killed in raids over Hamburg!* the SS officer screamed. Then, he listed city names.

His soldiers answered, "Ja, ja . . . ," raising their hands. "Bitte ich," fighting among themselves to be chosen.

"Hamburg, Bremen, Kassel, Mainz, Pforzheim . . . ," the officer called, picking the men with families in those cities.

The chosen lined up machine guns at the ready while the airmen pleaded, "Geneva Convention. Prisoner of war, Geneva Convention . . ."

"Schiessen!" *Fire!*

Blood spurted out of the aviator's bodies as they dropped. Within seconds, eleven allied airmen were dead.

De Lacoste and Lucile were taken to Bordeaux Gestapo's headquarters for interrogation. De Lacoste took his beatings bravely, but the water torture broke him. His lungs were on fire. He knew he couldn't take another session. He had to do what he had promised himself to never do again—give them a little. Well, maybe more than a little, but save himself to save others. Everybody makes compromises at some point in their lives. The war in France would be over soon and he would be a hero. He had to be clever and strike a bargain. When his tormentor pulled his head out of the water de Lacoste yelled, "I want to speak with Oberrsturmbannfüher Lindinger!"

The man looked astounded that de Lacoste knew the name of the Gestapo chief. "Does he know who you are?"

"Yes."

When his interrogators left de Lacoste collapsed: "Merde, merde!" Then, thinking fast, he regained his composure—*I've done this before.* He thought gloomily about his girlfriend who had been arrested in Lille two years before. He had been powerless, like today. But there were ways to make it look right. It had to be carefully done of course—*I'll be fine.*

It was morning when Lucile was escorted down a hallway to a bench next to the building back door. Her face was swollen and bruised. Her fingers were the worst with bloody sockets where her nails had once been. The pain was excruciating, but she was proud of herself. She had been a prostitute since she was sixteen; pleasing men was second nature to her, but not this time! She had not told them anything. De Lacoste was brought over and sat next to her. Both his eyes were black and dry blood caked his ears and nose. He managed a wink and indicated the guards—*fuck them.*

"They'll take us to the Fort du Ha prison to be interrogated again," he said.

Minutes later they were led outside and pushed into a large Renault with one man behind the wheel and two more in the back. Lucile and de Lacoste sat in the foldaway facing them.

The streets of Bordeaux teemed with people, trams, buses, and bicycles and the car made slow progress through traffic. They reached the edge of town where a flea market crowded both sides of the street. As they wheeled through the intersection a truck appeared coming right at them. The driver jumped on the brakes a second too late and broadsided them sending the Renault into a spin. When they finally came to a stop, the Gestapo men burst out of the car and shouted at the truck driver who now stood on the footboard of his cabin and argued back. De Lacoste and Lucile saw their chance. They bolted out and sprinted away. A gunshot cracked. Lucile stumbled and fell. De Lacoste raced toward the flea market with a Gestapo man in close pursuit. Blood spreading on the side of her skirt, Lucile managed to crawl on her hands and knees, but the second Gestapo man ran over and dragged her back to the car.

De Lacoste sprinted into an alley lined with stalls. Behind him, his pursuer fired his gun into the air and shouted at people to get out of the way. But de Lacoste was fast. When the Gestapo man reached the edge of the market, he fruitlessly looked in every direction and was furious. Shoving bystanders aside and spewing his rage, he stomped back to the car.

52

THE WAVE OF ARRESTS STARTED IMMEDIATELY. On a fishing boat off Saint-Jean-de-Luz, the Basque captain and his crew watched a Kriegsmarine cutter settle in their wake and shadow them all the way to port. French police boarded the vessel the moment she docked. They shoved aside the protesting captain, rushed down to the cargo hold, and reappeared pushing frightened allied aviators in front of them. The police cuffed the captain and his crew and turned them over to the Gestapo waiting on the dock.

In Hendaye, the driver steered his Refineria de Petròleo truck toward the Spanish border as he had done several times this month. Less than one hundred yards from the frontier, a French guard stepped out and raised his arm. The moment the rig pulled over, one guard opened the driver's door while another climbed through the passenger side and kicked the driver out. The beating began the moment he hit the ground. On the other side, a wounded airman screamed in pain as a German officer dragged him from behind the seats.

Robert had resumed smuggling airmen and today his mind was wild with anticipation. Nicole had started her job in Pau and tonight they would celebrate with a dinner at Chez Francis, a black-market restaurant. Upon learning the allied invasion was imminent, Mike was back in the city, but as he stepped out of the funicular and on the Palais des Pyrenées the grim intrusion of the war put a damper on his spirit. A Gestapo car followed by truck filled with Feldgendarmes turned into the rue Henri IV and stopped in front of the hotel where Robert had a room and many allied airmen had been sheltered. An SS officer blew his whistle. The convoy stopped. Feldgendarmes jumped off the truck and surrounded the building while Gestapo agents stormed inside.

Minutes later, the Gestapo men reappeared pushing men and women with their hands above their heads. Mike spotted three young men, obviously allied aviators, and at the back of the line, Nicole and Madame Gaillac, the hotel owner.

"Oh fuck!" Mike knew the Gestapo's next stop would be the bus terminal. He ran and reached the station just as Robert's bus was pulling into its slot. The door opened and the two German guards stepped out. Mike knocked on Robert's side window. "Gestapo on the way," he said.

"Merde." Robert slid out the driver's side and led Mike to a side street as the Gestapo car rolled over the corner. The SS officer blew his whistle. Feldgendarmes jumped off the truck and surrounded the bus.

Later that evening Robert led Mike down the steps to Francis's black-market restaurant. The place was full. When he saw them, Francis hurried out of his kitchen and hustled them into his supply room.

"They're looking for you, Robert," he said, wiping his hands on his apron, his eyes on Mike.

"He's with us," Robert said.

No other introduction necessary. Mike and Francis shook hands.

"Nicole and Madame Gaillac have been arrested," Robert said.

"I heard," Francis said, miming a telephone with his thumb and fingers. "They've been taken to Gestapo headquarters."

"Where is that?" Robert asked.

"The villa St. Albert on the avenue Trespoey," Francis said; then, jerking his head toward the dining room, added, "I've got to take care of my customers." And he left.

The supply room was crowded with boxes. Two bicycles hung on hooks. Mike leaned against the wall and slid down to a crouch. Robert paced the room, thoughts racing through his mind—very bad thoughts.

"We'll find a way," Mike said.

Robert looked unsure but nodded. The door swung open. Francis edged in with rolled up cots, a bottle stuck under his arm and food on a tray. He set the tray and the bottle on a crate. "Curfew starts in two hours. Stay here and get out of town in the morning." And he was gone.

Mike took some food and handed the plate to Robert who shook his head. "They're beating Nicole up, right now."

"We'll find out when she's transferred and we'll pick her up."

Robert bit his lips—*right.*

They unrolled the cots and lay down. Francis was finishing the service in the dining room. Customers were leaving. They heard him close his kitchen and climb the stairs to his apartment above.

Mike fell asleep but Robert did not. He had had many bad nights before. The night in Sedjanne after being wounded in Tunisia had been bad. This was worse. Far worse. What those bastards were doing to her—*là maintenant*—at that very moment.

Mike woke up to a thumping noise. It was Robert carrying a bicycle out of the room. Mike got up, picked the other bicycle and followed.

"Where are you going?" he asked, as he caught up with Robert.

"I'll be back."

"It's curfew."

Robert didn't respond. They climbed on their bicycles and rode through deserted streets avoiding French police patrols. Soon, they reached the elegant Tudor mansion where the Gestapo was housed. They took stock. The place was quiet with no guards in sight.

"The cells are in the basement," Robert said.

Mike nodded. It looked easy.

"Let's storm the place and get her out," Robert said, eyes blazing.

Mike pointed at the searchlights bolted to the façade and to narrow openings flanking the doors. "Those are machine-gun slits. We make a move and the whole place lights up like a Christmas tree. They'll radio the garrison and in five minutes we'll have truckloads of SS to deal with."

"I'll take my chances," Robert said.

"Like hell you will. Best to strike during transfers. You know that."

Robert shook his head.

"Get on your bike," Mike said.

Robert darted Mike a look and reluctantly climbed back on his bike.

Robert was woken up by the phone ringing in his kitchen. Francis answered, talked briefly, hung up, and stepped into the room. "Nicole and Madame Gaillac will be moved to Toulouse this afternoon."

"How do you know?" Robert asked.

Francis hesitated—*you shouldn't ask but* . . . "There is a Swiss national who works as a German translator for the Gestapo. He's one of my best customers."

Mike sat up. "How will they move them?"

"By car to the station and then by train. That's how they transferred Prosper."

"How many guards?"

"Two."

"We'll need weapons," Robert said.

Francis looked hard at Robert. "Are you sure about this?"

Mike sat up. "Yes. He's sure."

Francis provided breakfast and two Sten Mark submachine guns in burlap bags. They sat on boxes, ate, and took the weapons apart.

"Shoot the guards and the driver. Get behind the wheel and drive off with Nicole and Madame Gaillac in the back," Robert recited.

"A simple plan," Mike said.

"It'll work better if I'm alone."

Mike laughed. "You aren't doing this alone."

"I want to be alone."

"No," Mike said.

"It's personal."

"Getting me out of a burning plane was personal too."

"I don't need you," Robert said with an insolent smile.

"A firefight with two women in the backseat of the car. One bad move, everybody is dead. I take care of the guards; you handle the driver."

Words that stirred the soul about the blood tie between them came to Mike, but he knew Robert wouldn't go for that crap. "Well pal, you're stuck with me until the end of this goddamn war," is what he said.

"Lucky me." Robert stood and began pacing again.

Mike watched him. "Sit down. I'd like to eat my breakfast in peace."

They arrived early, ordered lemonades at the Café de la Gare and sat at a table overlooking the station entrance. The main hall was crowded with people traveling for Easter celebrations. The train to Toulouse had been idling on the quay for several minutes when a Gestapo Citroen appeared up the street. The barman was drying a glass with a cloth. He held it up to the light and almost dropped it as he watched Mike and Robert pull Sten Mark submachine guns out of their haversacks, snap magazines in place, and shroud the weapons in burlap bags. Fingers on triggers, they walked out of the café, burlap bags hanging at their sides. The Citroen rolled past them and stopped by the station's entrance.

Two Feldgendarmes exited with Nicole and Madame Gaillac cuffed at the wrists. They had been beaten; their faces were swollen with alarming bruises around the eyes. Nicole turned toward the café as if she *knew* Robert would be there. She shook her head—*no don't do it!* Then she looked up toward the avenue.

Robert followed her gaze: An army truck was rolling down the hill and soon entered the station courtyard. Feldgendarmes jumped out and took up positions. And now Nicole and Madame Gaillac were marched toward the main hall.

"We'll grab them on the quay," Robert said.

Mike followed Robert through the café's back door. When they stepped onto the platform Nicole and Madame Gaillac were less than thirty feet away. But now the Feldgendarmes herded passengers forward and the two women and their guards were immersed in a sea of civilians.

"Merde," Robert said, shaking with rage.

And they watched Nicole and Madame Gaillac being escorted aboard the waiting train.

53

THE BARMAN HAD BEEN TELLING the story all-day and started over for the benefit of new customers. Janine sat at the bar staring into her cup of ersatz coffee.

"The truck came from the rue de la République. I heard the tires screeching; I looked out and bang!" he said, slapping his hands. "The truck slammed into the Renault."

Janine sipped her coffee, wincing at the taste.

"First two men jumped out of the car," the barman went on. "Then a woman and a man got out of the back. And by God! They ran like devils. I never heard the shot, but the woman fell in the middle of the street. I thought she had slipped but the side of her dress was all bloody."

"What happened to the man who escaped?" a customer asked.

"Like an arrow, *pfutt*, gone. He disappeared into the crowd."

"No one went after him?"

"The Gestapo man did. But he lost him in the market. He was furious when he came back."

Janine looked up from her coffee. "He was angry?"

The barman turned to Janine, delighted by the new interest in his tale. "Yes. He was yelling in German. Pushing people out of his way. I couldn't understand what he was saying, but he was not happy."

"And the woman was dead?"

"Oh, no. She was alive. One of the boche dragged her back to the car and dropped her in the trunk."

"In the trunk?" Janine asked.

"I guess they didn't want have her bleeding all over the seats." The barman hung his head. "We could hear her scream, but they didn't care. Dropped her in there like a bag of dirty laundry."

Janine had heard similar accounts in the cafes she had already visited that day. Details varied but everyone agreed that the car had stopped in the middle of the intersection and the truck was responsible for the accident. There was confusion about who had escaped. Some saw one man run away, others saw two. A few even believed that a man had been shot, not a woman.

"And what did the driver of the truck do?" Janine asked now.

The barman opened his hands with a shrug. "He just stood there."

"Was his truck damaged?"

"The front bumper was bashed in, and the headlights were broken. There was lots of glass on the pavement."

"And the police never came?"

"Oh yes, but they took their time. When they showed up everyone was gone. They asked a few questions to write their report, you know. They threw sawdust on the blood, got a pail of water from the charcuterie, and washed it away. That was it."

"The truck driver was French?" Janine asked.

"Of course."

"You talked to him?"

"No. I mean we all stayed away."

"Was there a company name on the side of the truck?"

"Construction, something . . ." The man seemed suddenly doubtful.

"No," the waitress cleaning tables chimed in. "There was no name on the truck."

Elbow on the bar, the picture of weary boredom, Janine rested her chin on her hand. "It was the truck driver's fault, right? He didn't respect the right of way."

The barman nodded thoughtfully. "I guess so."

"So, this guy hit a Gestapo car with Germans on board. He must have been worried, no?" Janine asked.

The barman shrugged; he did not remember anything more. The waitress came over wiping her hands on her apron.

"The truck driver just stood in the middle of the street. He looked kind of stupid. When the Germans drove off with the woman in their trunk, he climbed into his truck and left."

Janine dropped coins on the zinc-topped bar, left the café and hurried around the corner. Her head spinning, she leaned over and vomited in the gutter, trembling with each helpless spasm.

"Are you all right, Madame?" a passerby asked anxiously.

"Too much ersatz coffee."

"You shouldn't drink that crap. It's poison."

Pumping air into her lungs, Janine wiped her mouth with a handkerchief and began to walk. Her mind was spinning—they shot the woman but lost the man. The car stopped in the middle of the intersection. The truck driver drove off without getting a police report. The trucking company would need one for the insurance. The Gestapo agent who lost the man threw a fit when he came back—*bad actors always overact.*

Now, she was sure. The accident was a set up—*they shot Lucile to make the man's escape more believable.* Janine's worse fears had come to pass. In the last few days, a record number of members of the network had been arrested. There was only one person who could have provided the intelligence required for an operation carried out simultaneously by the French Police, the Gestapo, and the German Navy. After months of searching and anguish, the answer was finally clear.

De Lacoste was their traitor.

54

CHARLOTTE MOURNED HER SISTER AND ran her shop the best she could. With the holiday season coming up her customers were in good spirits, and it was agony to appear cheerful. The evenings were excruciating, and the weather fit her mood—dark early and freezing rain. She had made dinner for herself but had no appetite and pushed her plate aside. Three British aviators who had hidden in her cellar had left that morning. They had shaken her hand at length, saying, "Merci, Madame." One of them had even managed to declare in his high school French that he and his comrades would come back after the war and take her to dinner at the best restaurant in town. "Après la guerre." *After the war.* People talked about it all the time. *Will it ever be over?* The arrests and constant worrying exhausted her, her mind working overtime, fabricating fears and feeding the irrational belief that worrying thwarted peril.

A tap at the window gave her a jolt. She sprang up and hurried to the door. It was de Lacoste, who made a face and childishly rubbed his nose on the other side of the windowpane. When she opened the door, cold damp air blew in with him.

"What ever happened to sweet French weather? This is worse than England," he said.

Tonight, anyone who could allay her crippling solitude was welcome. She kissed him and spotted bruises on his face and cuts on his neck.

"What happened to you?" she asked.

De Lacoste sighed, signaling that he had been through a hard time but was not ready to talk about it yet. He had been smart not to give Charlotte's name to the Gestapo. "I heard about your sister. I'm sorry," he said.

Charlotte nodded a thank-you. De Lacoste blew on his hands and pointed at the food on the table. "Do you have enough?"

"Yes, sit down."

He winced as he sat, the physical pain making his eyes swim. "I need to lay low for a few days."

She made him a plate and poured wine. De Lacoste ate slowly. He had trouble chewing and swallowing was difficult too.

"Tell me what happened," Charlotte asked, when he'd put down his fork.

De Lacoste told Charlotte about the airmen massacre and the night in Gestapo headquarters in Bordeaux. His eyes welled as he described Lucile being shot. "They beat her up. They pulled out her nails with pliers, but she did not talk," he said, wiping his eyes. "The Gestapo is after me. I need to talk to Janine. Do you know where she is?"

"No," Charlotte said. *He shouldn't ask me that*, she thought, feeling discomfort knotting her gut.

"I know I shouldn't ask . . . ," he said, picking up on her inquietude, "but how do you get in touch with her when you need to?"

Charlotte kept her calm. "I send a post card to city hall in Toulouse. They pin it on the board with the local announcements." Then, filling up his glass, she added, "I'll send a message for you tomorrow. Meanwhile stay here and rest," Charlotte said almost tenderly.

"You don't mind having me here for a few days?"

"Of course not. You know I enjoy your company."

De Lacoste drank. "This is good wine," he said, raising his glass.

Charlotte's shop was closed on Mondays. She usually slept late but today she woke up early and anxious. The house was quiet. De Lacoste was asleep in the basement. Restive, she cleaned her shop and vigorously mopped the floor. She felt better and was almost done when a knock on the glass door made her turn. It was the postman, who held a blue telegram in his hand. Her heart jumped. Telegrams were always bad news. She opened the door and took it. Realizing the man was waiting for his tip, she stepped to the cash register, handed him a coin, and waited until he was gone before tearing the envelope open. With trembling fingers, she unfolded the wire that read:

CANCEL VACATION. ARISTOCRAT CONTAGIOUS.

Charlotte felt sweat pouring down her back. This was from Janine. The alias referred to a name with an aristocratic "de" as a prefix and it meant: "De Lacoste works for the Gestapo. Go into hiding."

The sound of water running in the kitchen startled her—*Oh God! He's up.* Slipping through the jingling bead curtain into her kitchen, she mumbled a bonjour to de Lacoste, who cheerfully wished her a good morning. She headed for the WC and locked herself inside. There, she tore the telegram into pieces and flushed it down the toilet. One shred of blue paper kept coming back up. She flushed the toilet three times until it was gone.

"Well, *girl*," she whispered. "You didn't like your life yesterday and today it's worse." Charlotte listened to de Lacoste in the kitchen and stood there trying to contain her terror. Finally, she stepped out and managed to look cheerful. "Feeling better?" she asked.

"A little bit. Lots of nightmares, though."

"The shop is closed today, but I want you to stay downstairs. It's safer," Charlotte said.

De Lacoste gave Charlotte an amused glance and just stood there. His nonchalance did it. All at once fear and rage rose within her—*you contemptible snitch!* she thought. And as sudden hatred infused her with strength, she snapped: "Go downstairs now!"

De Lacoste flinched. "Yes, yes," he said, heading for the cellar and pulling the door closed behind him.

Minutes later, Charlotte was up in her room. There she packed a small suitcase, tied a rope to the handle, and opened her window. Cocking her ear to the sounds coming from the kitchen, she lowered the suitcase to the passageway one floor below.

That's done. But when she raced down the stairs and found de Lacoste standing by the sink filling his water carafe, she broke into a sweat. The rope holding her suitcase was dangling loosely behind the windowpane, right in front of him.

"Where are you going?" he asked, turning to face her.

Calm down, he hasn't seen it. "To the post office," she said. "To send the postcard to Janine as you asked. And I've got to get supplies for the shop. I'll be out all day. Stay downstairs."

"Can you get me some cigarettes?"

"If the line is not too long. Otherwise I'll try tomorrow."

"Thank you." After a second de Lacoste asked: "You're my friend, right?"

"Of course I am," Charlotte said. Controlling her loathing, she stepped forward and kissed him on both cheeks. "Get some rest. This war is far from over. You're needed back on the line."

"You're right." De Lacoste picked up his carafe and headed for the cellar. Charlotte listened to the steps creaking as he descended and wiped her forehead drenched with sweat—*she loathed that man.*

The suitcase was there at the end of the rope next to the garbage bins. Holding her purse and suitcase, she pushed her bicycle and squeezed between the reeking bins. When she reached the sidewalk, the baker crossed the street to help her with the door.

"They're watching your shop," he whispered. "Don't have any more visitors for a while."

"Who's watching?" Charlotte asked.

"Two men moved into the empty apartment above my shop. I heard their phone ring last night. They're from the police."

Charlotte secured her suitcase on the luggage rack while striving not to glance up at the windows above the bakery.

"How do you know they're from the police?"

"Who else could get a telephone line? They wear suits and they are not friendly."

"Merci," she said, climbing onto her bicycle.

"I'll watch your shop while you're gone," he said.

He knows I'm running away, Charlotte thought, pushing on the pedals. Who would have thought? She had always assumed the baker was a Vichy sympathizer.

At the post office, Charlotte didn't mail any postcard, but sent a coded telegram to a beauty supply distributor in Bayonne telling Janine that de Lacoste was in her cellar and that policemen were watching the shop. She knew people from the Résistance would turn up to take de Lacoste away, but worried about the cops across the street and wondered what Suzanne would do in this predicament. "*Be bold, it always works*," her fearless sister used to say. The thought cheered up Charlotte and she knew what to do. After checking her suitcase at the railway station consigne, she rode on to the Gestapo headquarters on the rue George-Sand. When she got off her bicycle, the guards stepped out of their sentry box and approached her with curiosity. French civilians did not visit the Sicherheitspolizei offices willingly. When she showed them the document identifying her as the wife of a French SS, they helped her wedge her bicycle into the rack.

A German secretary ushered Charlotte into the Sturmbannführer's office. He stood up from behind his desk and crossed the room to kiss Charlotte's hand. He was a chubby man, with a round face and a friendly manner. Charlotte wasn't fooled. She knew the man could be ruthless.

"Always a pleasure to see you, Madame," he said.

"Thank you, Sturmbannführer," Charlotte said, wiping off a tear while thinking—*don't overdo it.*

"War is hard on families," the Sturmbannführer said, watching her. "How can I help?"

"I am . . . concerned . . . ," Charlotte said, shrugging as if to dismiss her own worries. "There are men watching my shop from an apartment across the street."

"Who are they?"

"I don't know. I guess they are people who hate me because my husband serves in the German military."

The Sturmbannführer, who had been hoping for information about enemies of the Reich, circled back to his chair, nodding thoughtfully. "I'll make sure we investigate, Madame," he said.

He won't bother. Charlotte took in a short breath and said: "In Lyon, last January, terrorists threw a bomb inside the house of a French officer serving in the Legion of French Volunteers against Bolshevism. His wife and three children burned to death."

The Sturmbannführer tilted his head, looking pained.

"It's probably nothing," Charlotte said. "I'm sorry to have bothered you."

"You didn't bother me," he said stiffly. "We always take care of our own, Madame."

"Thank you, Sturmbannführer." Charlotte turned to go, but the officer's voice stopped her.

"May I ask you a question?"

Oh God, what? "Of course."

"We keep receiving information about women sheltering allied aviators. Women talk in beauty shops. Do you ever hear anything of the kind?"

"Everyone knows about my husband," Charlotte said with a rueful smile. "I'm the last person they would tell."

"Right, of course. Thank you. We'll take care of your little problem."

"Thank you, Sturmbannführer." Stunned by her own gall, Charlotte headed for the door, her skin burning from chest to chin.

55

UPON LEARNING DE LACOSTE WAS in Charlotte's cellar, Janine, Mike, and Robert caught the first train to Limoges. They had to act quickly. De Lacoste was a skilled operative who worked with British Intelligence and there was the possibility he might be made privy to the codenames announcing the Allied invasion. So, they urgently needed to take him out of action before he could share any strategic information with the Nazis.

André, their contact in the local underground, awaited them at the station. Cautious, vigilant, and young—he was in his twenties—he received up-to-the-minute information from Résistance contacts all over town. Today was market day. The streets were crowded with shoppers but there wasn't much to buy—mainly secondhand clothing, wooden soled shoes, and resharpened razor blades. After almost five years of war, everything was worn out or patched up. The four of them sat on the terrace of a café overlooking Charlotte's street.

Since Nicole's arrest, Robert was a changed man. At his darkest hour, he sneered at his romantic delusions—*Getting married, having children, settled down in Pau, what was I thinking?* His dreams had seeped away, leaving behind intense rage and penetrating sadness.

"Nicole is all I can think about," he had told Mike, who felt deeply for his friend and worried about his spirit. He needed Robert's wiliness and quick thinking. What was coming would be ugly. It was an elaborate operation—overpower the cops across the street, take de Lacoste to an empty warehouse, interrogate him, shoot him. So many things could go wrong. And they'd need to watch over Janine, who insisted on being involved.

Janine felt responsible for the deaths of Loïc and Prosper. They had been arrested *after* de Lacoste had delivered groups of airmen to them. And Karl Lindinger, head of the Gestapo in Paris, had played her like a marionette. Pretending to be misinformed to protect de Lacoste, who was working for him. It had all been right in front of her nose all along. She had questioned de Lacoste's reckless behavior at some point, but ultimately dismissed it because he had gotten Turenne out of Marseille.

"That's what a double agent does," Mike told her. "He earns trust from all sides."

But Proust's words still echoed in Janine's head. "If you have doubts eliminate him. If you don't have the guts to do what's necessary, you should have stayed home filling cavities." Guilt infested Janine's soul and she was determined to handle de Lacoste's execution herself.

On the other side of town, commissaire Boucher stepped down from the Tour's shuttle. He was in good spirits. Today he would decapitate a major Résistance organization. It had all started with a tip from a barman working in a high-class brothel off the Champs-Élysées that Gestapo chief Lindinger visited once a week. He had a regular there, a shorthaired brunette who dressed in a man's tuxedo. Boucher had dispatched Lenoir, who watched Lindinger having short, intense conversations at the bar with a man who always seemed eager to please. The Gestapo chief was never satisfied; nothing he heard was ever good enough. Lenoir knew the routine. This was Lindinger's main informant.

They investigated and learned his name was de Lacoste. His papers were in order, including his *ausweis* pass, which allowed him to work and travel all over the country. This was unusual—*ausweis* were not easily obtainable. From then on, Boucher had de Lacoste followed, rotating the inspectors on his tail. They watched him shuttle allied airmen from Paris to the Spanish border. They lost him briefly after his escape from the Gestapo in Bordeaux, but he was soon spotted boarding a train in the provincial station of Libourne. After that interesting interlude they trailed him to a beauty shop in Limoges and Boucher learned that it belonged to Suzanne's sister, the train conductor he had arrested at the Austerlitz station in Paris. The sister was also part of the escape line. It made sense; Résistance was often a family affair. And now de Lacoste was staying put nursing his wounds. Classic police work—watch and wait and strike at the right time. Boucher had Lenoir and Lazare watching from an apartment across the street from Charlotte's shop. A telephone line had been installed and Boucher was in constant contact with his team. The day before informers reported that the Limoges underground was mobilizing for some kind of action. That told Boucher an intervention was expected at any moment. It was all falling into place beautifully and this time Boucher intended to personally supervise the dismantling of this major escape line.

Boucher's mood turned when he marched out of the station. He had asked for the local Renseignements Généraux office to send a car and there was none. He stomped into the Café de la Gare, flashed his policeman's identification to the patron, grabbed the telephone on the bar, and barked into the receiver.

"Get me the Renseignements Généraux." The connection was established and Boucher listened to the crackling double ring: *Drr-riiing, drrriiing . . .*

The phone was picked up and the policeman who answered was *désolé*—sorry. The chef had an emergency; he apologized. Yes, of course, he knew who Commissaire Boucher was. He suggested he take a taxi.

Boucher swore and hung up.

Behind the bar, the patron busied himself drying a glass with a cloth. "Five centimes for the call," he said.

Boucher threw a coin on the counter and walked out. There were no taxis at the stand, not even a velo-taxi. He had to walk. He guessed the local commissaire had figured an operation against the Résistance was in the making and had made himself scarce—another one who was terrified of hearing his name on the BBC. *Cowards, all of them.*

In the bar, the patron kept an eye on Boucher from across the street and picked up the phone.

By the market, Janine looked at Mike and Robert and pushed her hands down on the sides on her armchair—*shall we?* As they were about to stand, horns blared and a camouflaged green Kübelwagen, followed by a military truck, roared into the street. They remained in their seats and along with everyone on the terrace, craned their necks to watch the convoy pulling up in front of Charlotte's beauty salon. German soldiers jumped out and rushed past the people queuing outside the boulangerie and into the building. Minutes later, they reappeared, shoving two men in front of them. Their shirts were ripped, and their faces swollen. Both protested loudly and flashed their ID cards.

"*Policier français!*" one of them shouted, but the soldiers kicked both flics onboard the truck.

Janine, who had learned of the police surveillance in a message from Charlotte, nodded briskly. *Thank you, Charlotte.*

A teenage boy on a bicycle pulled over, whispered to André, and wheeled off.

"A commissaire from Paris is in town. We're watching him," André said.

Mike leaned toward Janine. "This is getting more dangerous by the minute. Stay put. We'll get de Lacoste and go from there."

"I want to question him myself," Janine said, her voice hard.

Minutes later, Mike watched Robert shatter a glass pane on Charlotte's back door, snake his arm through, and open the lock. As they entered the kitchen, Robert switched on the light and moved to the sink while Mike hid in the hallway.

"Charlotte, is that you?" de Lacoste called from the cellar.

"She isn't here. Come on up!" Robert shouted as he turned on the faucet and listened to footsteps climbing the staircase. When he heard the cellar door creak open, he leaned over to wash his face.

De Lacoste stepped into the kitchen holding a Luger handgun. "Who are you?"

"Robert. You smuggled me across France, remember?"

Recognizing him, de Lacoste asked, "What are you doing here? German soldiers were across the street a few minutes ago."

"I know. We're here to get you out."

Robert dried his face with a dishcloth. "Put that gun down," he said, smoothly sliding brass knuckles over his right hand.

De Lacoste clipped on the safety lock and pushed the Luger into his waistband. "You scared me," he said.

"Get your things," Robert said. "Only what fits on a bicycle rack."

Eyes darting around, anxiety palpable, de Lacoste did not move. "Where is Charlotte?" he asked.

"She's gone. This place is not safe anymore," Robert said, maintaining a soothing tone of voice.

Mike entered the kitchen, and de Lacoste jumped. "Who are you?"

"We met in Limoges, remember?"

De Lacoste stared at Mike, distrust all over his face.

"Charlotte has been denounced. Let's go," Robert said.

"You didn't shake my hand when I came in," de Lacoste said.

"I was washing up. Let's go, you're in danger!" Robert whispered angrily.

De Lacoste lunged forward, kicking Mike in the groin. Whipping around, he then propelled himself headfirst into Robert's chest. The blow paralyzed Mike, but Robert moved sideways and buried a brass-knuckled fist deep into de Lacoste's side. They heard the sickening sound of his ribs breaking. De Lacoste cried out and went for his gun, but Robert was faster. He grabbed the Luger, threw it in the sink, and pushed de Lacoste against the wall.

"You son of a bitch!" Robert spat, dragging him toward the cellar. "Go downstairs."

"You said this place is not safe?" de Lacoste cried, grimacing in pain as he stumbled down the stairs.

Robert turned to a mortified Mike, still trying to catch his breath.

"Get Janine," Robert said.

At the Renseignements Généraux's office, Boucher marched between the desks, threatening everyone and getting nowhere. The commissaire had taken their only automobile, and they didn't know when he would be back. Boucher let fly a string of invectives, promising punishments and demotions. He grabbed a telephone and barked a number to the operator. The connection was swift, then it rang and rang, and no one answered. The operator came back on the line, but Boucher told her to let it ring. She protested and disconnected. A furious Boucher slammed the phone down. "Where the fuck are Lenoir and Lazare?" he shouted. "Somebody get me a car!"

Timidly, a milicien mentioned he had a two-door Juvaquatre at home—a car so small that people called it a motorcycle with doors. It was humiliating, but Boucher swallowed his pride. "Go get it," he said.

In Charlotte's basement, de Lacoste was now tied down to a chair with his wrists and ankles secured with electrical wire. Legs could be seen hurrying past the casement window. A shot would be heard in the street. He had to be killed quietly. Robert sat on the stairs. Mike leaned against the wall. Janine stood in front of de Lacoste.

"When they caught you in Lille in 1941, the bathtub torture was like drowning over and over again, right?"

De Lacoste winced at the memory. "It was awful."

"You broke down, didn't you?"

"No, I did not! I played them," de Lacoste said. "They caught me taking photographs of coastal defense positions north of Cherbourg. I had to be smart," he continued, brimming with righteous indignation.

Janine exhaled softly. "Lindinger was the head of the Gestapo in Lille at the time. You gave him Louise, your girlfriend, the nurse. They found the wounded Canadian pilot she had been taking care of in her attic."

"She was denounced. I had nothing to do with it!" de Lacoste protested.

"When you joined the line, you'd been working for the Gestapo for what? A year?"

"I was not working for them. I was playing them!"

"The Belgian escape line through Lyon and Marseille was decimated at the end of '41. You betrayed them, right?"

De Lacoste shrugged. "I only confirmed what Lindinger already knew."

"The heads of the networks were all executed."

"I didn't know that."

"You gave Turenne to the Gestapo. They tipped the French Police, and he was arrested in Pigale."

"That wasn't from me! I tried to save Turenne that night. I only gave them little people."

"Like Prosper, the café owner in Pau," Janine continued.

"I had to feed them something from time to time."

"You also denounced Loïc."

De Lacoste shrugged again. "Loïc hated me. I had no choice."

"All the men from his village were deported. Half of them are probably dead by now."

"I know it's terrible," de Lacoste said, his face bowed.

Janine looked away, disgusted. "What about Nicole and Madame Gaillard? You feel bad for them too?"

"They're unimportant. What are they going to do to them?"

"They have been deported to Germany."

De Lacoste rolled his eyes. "Why? Those Nazis shouldn't have wasted time on them."

"They also shot Father Valencia, the Basque boat captain, and the truck driver who smuggled wounded airmen."

De Lacoste now looked annoyed at so much overkill. "I know I've made mistakes. But I did the best I could. That's what people do in war."

"In Bordeaux, you sacrificed Lucile to make your escape more believable."

"She was just wounded. She is in the Fort Du Ha prison infirmary," de Lacoste said.

Janine glanced at Mike and Robert and turned back to de Lacoste. "You feel better now that you've told me everything."

De Lacoste heaved a sigh. "Yes. It's a big weight off my chest." Then he looked at Janine, suddenly realizing the implications of this fact.

"You won't kill me, right?" de Lacoste asked, his voice vibrant with hope as he caught Mike twisting a dishcloth into a rope. "It's so fucking unfair!"

"You wanted to make it right, but you couldn't," Janine said.

"Exactly," de Lacoste said, crying as he watched Mike wrap the dishcloth around his neck.

Mike slid a broomstick into the loop, and Janine stepped closer. Mike looked at her and said, "Let me do it."

"No." Janine took ahold of the broomstick and tightened the dishcloth. She recoiled at the sight of the fresh scars on de Lacoste's neck, souvenirs of his beating in Bordeaux. Eyes filling, she forced herself to think about Loïc, Prosper, and all the others—*do it for them.* De Lacoste's body vibrated with convulsive groans. His larynx cracked but he was still alive. And suddenly the strength left her. She struggled to hold onto the broomstick.

Mike pushed her aside and took over. "Go! Please."

Wiping tears, Janine climbed up the stairs and walked out.

Mike fastened the grip. Eyes open wide, de Lacoste was resigned to dying but his body went into wild spasms fighting for life anyway. After the longest time, he finally went limp.

Robert raised his gun as he heard footsteps in the kitchen. It was André. "Got word that the flic has left the prefecture with a milicien. They're coming this way," he said. He caught sight of the scene below, and he climbed back up, eager to get out of there.

The Juvaquatre stopped in front of the hair salon. Boucher bolted out and ran into the building across the street. He was back minutes later, his face purple with rage.

"Come with me!" he told the milicien waiting by his car.

The man protested, but Boucher dragged him along. They moved through the door adjacent to the salon, along the corridor, across the kitchen, and moments later they were in the cellar staring at de Lacoste's contorted face.

"Now, that's one handsome man," Boucher said.

A hammer-like sound made them look up. The cellar door had slammed shut above them. The milicien raced up the steps. They could hear heavy furniture been pushed against the door.

"Open the fucking door!" He raised his gun and fired at the lock. When Boucher joined him, they slammed their weight against the door. It did not budge.

Out in the street, the people queuing in front of the boulangerie stepped back, obeying a man holding a gun. A second man crawled on the sidewalk and broke the casement window with his elbow.

In the cellar Boucher and the milicien heard the tingling sounds of broken glass and then a *thump* on the dirt floor.

"What was that?" the milicien asked.

"Get down!" Boucher shouted.

There was another *thump* and this time they both saw what made it. An olive-colored, lemon-shaped object with a vertical groove pattern lay primly in the middle of the room.

"Down! God damn it!" Boucher shouted while diving behind a rusting tub.

Across the street, the baker was serving customers when a double explosion rocked the street. The boulangerie's window slid down like a sheet of ice and a cloud of smoke gushed out of the casement windows.

In the cellar de Lacoste's body, still tied to his chair, had been blown across the room. Boucher shoved the tub away, tried to sit up, and fell back. His right shoulder, arm, and leg were riddled with grenade fragments and bleeding.

The milicien was dead. He hung by one leg, a foot caught between two steps. His blood dripped steadily, making puddles on the dusty wooden boards.

Mike, Robert, Janine, and André stood at the end of the street astride their bicycles watching the firemen uncoil their hoses. They climbed onto the saddles, pushed on the pedals, and rode away.

56

SINCE NICOLE'S ARREST, ROBERT'S SUNNY personality had disappeared. Heartbroken and sullen he had turned into a shadow of his former self. Nicole and Madame Gaillac were put aboard the train in Pau but didn't get off in Tarbes or Toulouse. If they were in a Gestapo jail, they would have found out by now.

"Robert is angry. I worry about him," Janine said.

"He'll be fine," Mike said, knowing full well that Robert was nowhere near being fine. The previous week they had been ordered to sabotage a rail line south of Bordeaux. Once there, they were stopped by a local Résistance chef who decided to confiscate their weapons and explosives. It was *son secteur*—his district—and he made it clear, not politely, "Nothing happens here without my permission."

Mike explained they were on the same side, fighting a common enemy, and following orders from London. The man was not impressed. His maquis had been fighting alone for three years, he had lost a lot of comrades, and he did not take orders from anybody, especially someone in *London*. When he ordered his men to start collecting the explosives, Robert lost his temper. He grabbed the chief, shoved a revolver against his throat, and shouted: "Keep away from the stuff or I'll blow your head off!"

The maquisards raised their weapons. Mike armed his Sten. It was touch and go for a few seconds. Then, Mike looked at the Résistance chief in the eyes and asked if they were ready to shoot an American officer. Ultimately the man gave in, but Mike knew if he had not been there, Robert would have been shot.

With the allied landings imminent, everyone was on edge. One evening after dinner, Janine looked at Robert sitting silently by the fireplace and signaled to Mike—*go to bed.* Mike nodded and headed for the bedroom. Janine pulled her chair next to Robert, leaned over, and kissed him on the cheek. He looked at her, startled. She had his attention.

"Robert, over two hundred thousand French men and women have been sent to camps in Poland and Germany. Nicole and my mother are among them. We heard Lucile has been deported as well. This war will end, and they will come back."

"Last week, at St. Michel prison in Toulouse, the SS machine-gunned all the political prisoners," Robert said.

"They were all men," Janine said. "Nicole was not among them."

"Nicole has been executed or died during interrogation," Robert said.

Janine took Robert's hand and raised her face to his, eyes shining, close to tears. "You don't know, Robert. We don't know. You have to believe she's alive and will come back. We have to be like Mike. He's convinced that we will all survive and win the war."

"I know. I can't stand it," Robert said.

"It gets on my nerves, too," she said, squeezing his hand. "But he's right. Hope is better."

Robert nodded. Janine watched him trying to agree with her, wanting to believe her but not succeeding.

That night a coded message from the BBC announced the allied landing in Normandy and a mobilization of all networks. The Résistance's primary mission was now to prevent German reinforcements from reaching the landing zone.

Within days Mike and the maquis were ready for a major offensive. The target was a German Infantry Regiment headed for

Normandy and the Deutsche Reichsbahn train scheduled to pick them up. Mike had wanted to attack the column and the train at separate locations but there had not been enough time to arrange two operations. Instead, radio messages and couriers had been sent and maquisards and guerrillero veterans of the Spanish Civil War from all over the region had swarmed to this station, the only place where they could rendezvous at short notice.

Mike and Robert stood in a cemetery overlooking the train station surrounded by vineyards and sunflower fields. It had rained during the night, but the morning was glorious. The quiet of their perch was deceiving. Just below them one hundred and fifty maquisards waited.

A feeling of foreboding tearing at his nerves, Mike turned, looking for distraction. The landscape caught his eye. "This is a beautiful spot."

"It's a cemetery."

"Yeah, but look at the fields and the river sparkling out there. It's all so peaceful."

"A poet you are."

"If the need ever arises, get me a spot out there under the trees," Mike said, indicating a line of graves.

"I'll do my best."

Mike picked up the wine bottle set on the tombstone next to them. He took a gulp and handed it to Robert, who shook his head.

"How can you drink this stuff early in the morning?"

"Keeps me focused," Mike said.

"Good to know," Robert said, his face shadowed with melancholy.

Sharing Robert's misery, Mike ached for his friend and fought the sorrow rising in his chest. He rubbed his face and then in command of himself again extracted a cigarette from his breast pocket and turned toward the wall to light it.

Robert liked how Mike cupped his hands to shield the flame as he drew in the smoke. *A simple gesture, well executed*, he thought, apprais-ing his buddy. Comes from a rich family. He could have had an easy war but volunteered instead. And now he comes back to France to fight among us and be with the woman he loves—*a class act.*

Mike stubbed out his cigarette and made the sign of the cross. *The Hail Mary with the farmers in the mountains*, Robert remem-bered. He had envied Mike's flair that night. How he had been able to reach out to those folks and restore their confidence.

So, a prayer. Robert lowered his head determined to pray too. He had never thought of himself as religious but now he asked God to spare Nicole. "Don't let them break her teeth, burn her breasts, or submit her to that awful bathtub torture. She's one of your better cre-ations." And now images of Nicole drifted toward him. She came to him in colors—aquamarine blouse, hazel eyes, auburn hair, and that tiny gold cross on a chain around her neck. How she blushed when she had something serious to say and how small tears seeped from the corners of her eyes when she laughed too hard.

"Enough," Robert muttered. He felt no fear and looked for-ward to combat. It kept him from obsessing about Nicole—a dev-il's bargain.

Every German they killed or captured today would not fight the Allies in Normandy or have to be fought again on the way to Berlin. Like all armies in retreat, the Nazis were dangerous wounded preda-tors, destroying everything in their path. Before leaving Tulle, a small town south of Limoges, 2nd SS Panzer Division Das Reich hung ninety-nine civilian men from lampposts and balconies to punish the local population for helping the Résistance.

Robert could now see the maquisards getting into positions. They were young and painfully thin. Their Bret guns appeared enormous in their hands. As teenagers they had seen their parents devastated by the collapse of the French army and had spent years sending packages to their fathers and brothers in POW camps in Germany. They needed to expunge the humiliation and craved for their share of this war.

Robert heard footsteps, picked up his gun, but set it down as Cervantes's frame appeared. Since losing his wife Suzanne and his unborn child, Cervantes always volunteered for the most dangerous missions.

"Buenos días, señores," he said, shaking their hands.

"Lots of Spaniards here today," Robert said.

"Yes. Guerrilleros españoles fighting for France." Thousands of Spanish Republicans who had escaped Franco's regime had joined the French Résistance.

Mike raised the wine bottle. Cervantes hoisted it up and took a gulp. "Goddamn German efficiency," he said, wiping his mouth. "Just like during the Aragon offensive. Always on time. The column's right behind those hills," he said, pointing to the west. "And the train crossed the Tarn River half an hour ago. They'll both be at the station *exactly* on schedule."

"We're here to welcome them," Robert said.

From their vantage point Mike and Robert could see the first vehicles in the column appear on the west side of town just as the steam from the locomotive rose from a valley on the north.

"Fait attention à ton cul," Robert said as he and Cervantes picked up their weapons and headed for the station.

"Watch your own ass," Mike grunted, shifting his Bret gun over his shoulder and proceeding in the opposite direction toward the one hundred and twenty maquis men positioned alongside the German column's path.

The train slowed as it approached the station. At first, it all went according to plan. Robert, Cervantes, and two Résistance-Fer engineers ran along the embankment and deftly managed to climb aboard the locomotive. They overpowered the German engineers and French ones brought the train to a stop. On the west side maquis guns began cracking. Orders were to fire at will until the enemy had surrendered. The Germans caught in the crossfire spread out on both sides of the road, their progression halted.

The whole operation started to unravel when the maquis unit hidden behind the embankment did not move. Their mission was to rush across the track and take over the whole train, but they remained hidden. Fighting collaborators and miliciens was one thing; facing the German army was another.

"They're scared," Robert said. He climbed on the tender and shouted, "Attack now!"

Cervantes waved his arms, bawling. "Come over, you motherfuckers!"

The train was now idling outside the station. French engineers on the footplate were shoveling coal into the firebox and spinning the handwheel to reverse steam and roll *away* from the German column, but the maquis men were still lying motionless on the embankment.

"Those cowards! I'll go get them!" Cervantes jumped off the locomotive and raced across the track.

Just then Robert spotted tarpaulins flying off a flatbed wagon exposing troops manning artillery pieces and heavy machine guns.

"Come back!" Robert shouted.

Cervantes was still running, waving and shouting, "Come over! Now!" And the maquis men were finally climbing up the embankment.

Bruur—Bruur.

Machine-gun fire cracked. Cervantes was cut down in a hail of bullets. And foolishly, the maquis men were now rushing across the track. Their timing was terrible. Most were mowed down before reaching the train. The others retreated, falling back into the ditches.

"Merde, merde!" Robert screamed. Now the artillery on the flatbed was bombarding the maquisards surrounding the German column. Wehrmacht troops aboard the train exited the cars and swarmed toward the locomotive.

"Bastards coming at us!" the French engineer shouted.

Although Robert and the Résistance-Fer men on the tender tried to keep the Germans at bay with sustained fire, they kept coming. Some on the roof were jumping from wagon to wagon. Robert and the engineers raised their hands, waiting to be shot, but the Germans just shoved them onto the floor. These were not SS but Wehrmacht troops who still believed in taking prisoners, and the German engineers quickly retook control of the locomotive.

Outside the station, Mike and his Résistance men positioned on buildings overlooking the road were facing intensified gunfire. The German troops were seasoned fighters and their aim accurate. Casualties mounted quickly on the Résistance side.

And now a platoon of SS troopers was rushing to the head of the column next to an open truck armed with mortar tubes mounted on its sides. Gunners aboard the truck lobbed shells blasting maquis machine-gun positions. One hundred yards from the station, the SS broke ranks and sprinted toward the train, waving and shouting at the soldiers manning the artillery pieces. The firing stopped briefly while the SS ran past the locomotive and climbed aboard the cars.

The pause in firing provided an opportunity. Mike and his men rushed into the breach, but now the locomotive was moving again. The train lurched forward, puffing through the station and ramming through the maquisards' line, artillery pieces blasting.

Feeling the movement, Robert tried to crawl off and jump, but he was pulled back and kicked hard. Bloody and half conscious, his head leaning outside the tender, he spotted a Spanish guerrillero crawling along the track holding sticks of dynamite. Pinned down by sustained fire, he dug through the gravel, stuck the dynamite under the rail, and lit the fuses with his cigarette.

Robert shuttered.

"No pasarán!" the guerrillero shouted as the explosion blasted him to pieces. Twisted rail segments spun into the air, annihilating the track.

The German engineer pulled on the brakes. The train shook and fiery sparks flew off the wheels, but the locomotive managed to stop a few feet from the severed track. Provided this last opportunity, Mike and his battalion of machine gunners made a desperate attempt to retake control of the locomotive. They rushed ahead under fire, but the engineers had already reversed direction. The train was now rolling back out of the station. A furious roar arose from the column of enraged German soldiers who shouted at the locomotive to halt. But the train kept moving and picking up speed, rolling backward toward Normandy. With the hope of rescue steaming away, the commander of the German column raised a white flag.

"Fuck, fuck, fuck!" Mike screamed as he watched the smoke from the locomotive fade in the distance. "Robert is on that train!"

57

MIKE BLAMED HIMSELF FOR ROBERT'S CAPTURE. Janine, burdened with her own guilt, was unable to soothe him. She had asked Robert to join the Résistance. If it wasn't for her, he would be at home with his family in Algeria.

"I should have stayed with him," Mike said.

"You would have been caught," Janine said.

"No. I'd have pulled back when the maquis didn't attack the train."

"Why didn't he?" Janine asked.

"He was heartbroken about Nicole." Mike looked down, then up. "And the rage got to him."

Janine, who had worried about Robert's anger, took Mike in her arms and kissed him. "Mike, my love, we both miss Robert. He was our closest friend."

"Don't talk about him as if he were dead."

They didn't make love that night. Mike was unwilling to be comforted and Janine was struggling with feelings about Robert she couldn't share.

A few days later, news came that the Germans were rounding up Basque prisoners for interrogation and sending them to a camp in Alsace. It was a sliver of hope.

"Robert's papers say he's Basque," Mike said. "He knows the region like the back of his hand. He speaks the language."

"He speaks a few words," Janine said, keeping her thoughts to herself—*a Résistant who is also Jewish. What are his chances?*

"He'll make it, I know he will."

"Stop saying that!" she said, her eyes filling with tears. "Robert is dead."

And the war in France was coming to an end. The Allies had broken German resistance in Normandy and were now fanning across France. In Toulouse, at Sainte Marie's hospital, the German medical staff was ordered to evacuate. That evening, Nanette rushed to Weiss's apartment.

"I'm going with you," she said. "I'm like you. It makes no difference to me if the patients are French or German."

Weiss's face filled with sorrow. "My little Nanette, I'm a German officer of a soon-to-be-defeated army. There is no future for us anywhere."

"I love you. These last months have been the happiest in my life." And leaning against his shoulder she whispered, "Ich denke Dir wenn mir der Sonne schimmer vom Meere strahlt."

Weiss looked away, his blue eyes shining with tears. Nanette had memorized the opening verses of one of his favorite Goethe poems. *I think of you when I see the sun glimmer reflected from the sea.*

"It's curfew time. You must go, Liebling," he said, taking her in his arms.

"So, after tomorrow, I will never see you again?" she said.

"No. You will not. We should be thankful for our time together."

"Then, we will make love one last time."

"I fear it will be even more difficult for us afterward."

"Oh, you're so German!" she sneered as she led him to the bedroom.

Weiss didn't resist. *Liebe macht blind*—love makes you blind. He relished her, caressed her, kissed her, and for a few hours, they managed not to think—just *feel*, and *be felt.*

All wars end in chaos, and this one was no exception. After Toulouse was liberated, Janine, Mike, Louis, Emma, and Madame Raymonde returned to the city to find that the milice had plundered the apartment, so they struggled to make the place livable again while around them the need for revenge had swept the nation. *Résistants de la dernière heure*—Résistants of the last hour—as everyone called them, were the worst. The closer someone had come to collaborating with the enemy, the more vociferous they were. Over ten thousand collaborators, policemen, and miliciens were summarily executed in wild purges—*Epuration sauvage*, as it was called. Boucher was shot in his hospital bed, Lenoir executed in the street, and Lazare lynched by an angry mob. Everyone had to account for his or her actions during the war, and young women suspected of having slept with the enemy were primary targets.

Nanette was terrified that Louis de Guilhem would not answer her call for help. Hiding in the damp cellar of her building, her thoughts ran in a dizzying circle of hope and despair: *He's forgotten about me. No, he wrote to thank me. He said he would visit me at the hospital as soon as the Germans were gone.* She had little food left, too much time to think, and she could not face her fellow countrymen. Not after what they had done to her. An orderly who had seen Nanette slip into Doctor Weiss's building had denounced her—*collaboration horizontale*—horizontal collaboration. She had been a German doctor's whore.

Armed civilians dragged her and two other nurses to the Place du Capitole. Surrounded by an ugly crowd, a chubby Frenchman wearing shorts and a dirty undershirt made salacious jokes and shaved their heads. People spat on the girls as they were escorted to an open truck filled with other *tondues*—shorn women. Swastikas were daubed on their naked skulls and, so adorned, they were paraded through the streets of Toulouse. After being released from the miserable cortege, Nanette returned to her tiny apartment. Her door was broken, and the place had been vandalized. Petrified, she retreated to her cellar and only came out at night to get water and forage for food in trash cans.

It was a hot day and Louis was drenched with sweat as he and Mike hurried along the street checking house numbers. That morning, he had found Nanette's letter under a pile of mail and journals. Now, on Nanette's street, Louis checked the envelope in his hand and pointed at a door.

As they hurried inside, the concierge stepped out of her lodge and stood in their way. "Messieurs?" she called, asserting her authority. Her arrogance wilted when she spotted Louis's FFI armband and Mike's officer's uniform.

"Where is the cellar?" Louis asked.

The concierge pointed at a door behind the trash bins. Louis pulled out an army flashlight. Mike shoved the bins out of the way, and they rushed down the spiraling stone steps leading to a corridor lined with padlocked doors.

"Nanette, where are you?" Louis shouted.

The concierge who had followed them yelled, "She's gone. She was a German officer's whore."

Mike pointed at her. "You, out!" he shouted. The concierge mumbled a protest but retreated up the steps.

Louis shook the padlocks and checked the space under the doors. "Nanette, come out, you're safe. We'll protect you," he called, raising his flashlight to illuminate a dark patch of flies swarming on the ceiling. Lowering the beam, he noticed the door below did not have a padlock.

"Over here," he called.

Mike and Louis strained against the door, pushing away a heavy trunk and scraping the floor on the other side. Finally, they managed to slide inside. Louis's flashlight shone on rumpled blankets on top of a makeshift cot.

"She was here," he said, shifting the light to milk bottles half filled with water and empty tin cans swarming with flies. "*Oh mon dieu!*" he cried, lifting his flashlight.

Mike looked up and recoiled. "No!"

Nanette's body hung from the bars of the cellar's window, the back of her gray shaved skull drooping at an unnatural slant.

Louis climbed on the trunk and loosened the noose while Mike lifted the body. Then they laid Nanette on the cot; her face was acutely pale. Purple bruises from the rope sullied her neck.

"She was the nurse who took care of you?" Mike said.

"Yes," Louis said, caressing Nanette's shaved head. "I had given up. She saved me."

Louis made the sign of the cross and whispered a prayer. Mike raised the light and looked closely at Nanette's face.

"It's impossible," he muttered.

"What?"

"This woman was the nurse on the Red Cross train from Limoges. She showed me how to remove the tobacco stains from my fingers. She told me her husband had been killed in an allied bombing raid."

"Where? What town?"

Mike looked up, trying to remember. "Saint-Nazaire?"

"That's her," Louis said. "That's where she was from."

Nanette's eyes were still open. Louis gently closed them, and the two men stood in stunned silence.

"She saved us both," Mike said.

"Yes." Louis sighed and wiped back a tear. "But we are too late to save her."

Louis and Janine did their best to resume their practices and rebuild their lives while grieving for their friends and loved ones who might or might not still be alive.

"I despise hope," Janine told Mike one morning.

But they went on and worked and hoped anyway. Louis, who thought he could have saved Nanette if he had gone through that pile of mail earlier, now obsessively checked the mail drop. And that morning, he heard the concierge outside, and saw an envelope fall out of the drop. He picked it up, stared at the markings, and walked into the kitchen where Janine and Mike were having breakfast.

"It's from Nicole," he said.

They looked up, Janine's face full of hope. "She's alive."

The three of them stared at a sealed envelope addressed to Robert in neat womanly handwriting. On the back was written: NICOLE ORMIERES, GARE DE DIJON, FRANCE.

Her finger gently rubbing under the word *Robert* on the envelope, Janine asked, "Should we open it?"

"Of course," Mike said. "We need to find her."

Janine slid her forefinger under the flap and ripped the envelope open.

Robert, mon chéri,

Madame Gaillac and I are aboard a deportation train standing in the train station in Dijon. A woman from the French Red Cross gave me pen and paper and promised to mail this letter.

First of all, I love you. I close my eyes and remember your handsome face and how happy you have made me, and that memory keeps me going. After we left Pau (you scared me that day at the train station but now I'm glad I saw you and Mike), the Gestapo took us to Toulouse and then put us with other prisoners on a train going north. We have been on this ghost train, as we call it, ever since. The Jewish women among us taught me about the Torah and the High Holy Days. It is a beautiful religion; if you want me to become Jewish when we get married, it will be fine with me. I told this to Madame Gaillac and we both cried laughing thinking how upset my mother would be.

In the last two weeks we've moved only a few kilometers a day or not at all. The Résistance is blowing up the tracks and we have to stop until they are repaired.

The Feldgendarmes are making the Red Cross ladies leave. I must go. Please, mon amour, do not take too many risks and remember how much I love you.

I kiss you with all my heart.

Your Nicole

"I should go to Dijon," Mike said.

Louis glanced at the postmark and shook his head. "This letter was mailed last month." He sighed. "Who knows where she is now?"

A week later, Janine received a message from the Résistance-Fer. Nicole's train left Dijon station on the afternoon of August 26, 1944, and crossed the border on the first of September. Nicole was aboard the last deportation train to reach Germany.

58

MIKE REQUESTED A TELEPHONE LINE to be in direct contact with the OSS in Paris but was turned down: *Telephones are reserved for high-ranking French officials, monsieur.* So, Mike pulled strings with his Résistance friends in the Postes, télégraphes, et téléphones worker's union, got a line, and began to receive intelligence reports.

Accounts of Robert's whereabouts remained obscure. He had not been hung or shot like thousands of maquisards captured in combat, but the news was as ominous. He likely had been shipped to Natzweiler-Struthof, a concentration camp in the heart of the Alsatian forest—one of the Nazis' most brutal. The weather there was sizzling hot in summer and bitterly cold in winter. Most prisoners died of exposure within months of arrival.

Life in the Toulouse apartment had returned to a semblance of normality. Mike was now an established member of the household and one morning at breakfast, Emma called him Papa. Janine started to intervene, but Louis stopped her with a look—*let it be.* Emma had made up her mind—Mike was her Papa. On outings, when she grew tired and wanted to be carried, Mike hoisted her onto his shoulders and trotted along imitating a horse, eliciting enthusiastic giggles. He spoke English to her, and she learned quickly. She had entered into her fourth year and could say: *Thank you*, *please*, and her favorite word: *again*. He played the piano and they sang "Twinkle, Twinkle, Little Star." Janine worried about the attachment, even deplored it at times—*he's using Emma to show off how wonderful he is.*

Truth was, Janine was terrified of losing Mike. To the casual eye they seemed to lead a happy existence, but the war had not ended for them. In many ways peace was worse. They had learned that gangrene had spread on Turenne's legs and Janine's uncle was now in a hospital in Britain recovering from a double amputation. Their lives were overshadowed by the cruelty of hope about the fate of Janine's mother, Robert, Nicole, Lucile, Madame Gaillard, and all their friends who had simply disappeared.

The phone came in handy. Mike learned that female deportees aboard the last deportation train to Germany had ended up in Ravensbrück. So, Nicole, Madame Gaillard, and Anna were all in the same camp.

Janine tried her best to come to terms with Mike's determination to find Robert—*he needs to do this; I should respect that.*

When the French First Army under the command of US Sixth Army Group reached Natzweiler-Struthof, they found the camp empty. It took some doing but Mike convinced Bogart to let him travel to Alsace.

"You are not going to Germany!" Janine cried when she heard.

"It's not Germany, it's Alsace."

"It's been integrated into the Reich for the past four years. It is Germany. And it will not be safe. I know the Germans. They will fight to the last man, woman, and child."

"I'll be under US military protection," Mike said.

"I don't want you to go."

"I'll only be gone for four days."

They didn't sleep in the same bed that night but the next morning, Janine held onto him, her anguish visceral. "Just come back."

"I will."

"You won't find him," Janine said.

"I've got to try."

She *pfeued* him, moved away, and immediately pulled him back. "Go," she said, meaning: *I hate you with all your silly hopes.*

Natzweiler-Struthof camp was a collection of wooden buildings in the foothills of the Vosges Mountains. British Military Intelligence was looking for four British SOE female field agents who had been interned there. They had ordered the exhumation of the one hundred and fifty bodies of the men and women executed before the camp's closing. Mike spent two days looking for a male with a left hipbone fractured by a bullet—a gruesome task that brought no result. But the trip was not useless. British Intelligence directed Mike to a French Alsatian Résistance member who had escaped Natzweiler-Struthof and had managed to find his way through the Vosges Mountains, running for days under icy rain.

Although he was in appalling condition in a military hospital, the Alsatian was conscious, and he remembered Robert. He told Mike that Robert had cannily claimed to be Basque and so received the better treatment reserved for valuable prisoners. The Nazis were fanatical about hunting down soldiers who had deserted to Spain. Robert and the other Basques had come up with tales of SS officers who had paid handsomely to be smuggled through the Spanish Basque country to Portugal where they boarded ships to South America. Since none of the other Basques admitted speaking French, Robert had found himself the de facto translator as they came up with the compelling stories that kept them alive. Mike shivered imagining Robert pretending to speak the whole language based on the few sentences he knew. But the ruse had kept him away from the firing squads. The Alsatian confirmed that Robert and the Basques had been shipped to Germany for further questioning.

Mike returned to Toulouse looking forward to sharing the hopeful news, but only Louis was interested. In the few days he had been gone Janine had grown more withdrawn. At night their intimacy was as intense as ever, but in the morning, the wall was raised again, and the distance remained. Something was wrong, very wrong. Mike considered talking to Louis, but he too had retreated into silence, forever trying to guess from the war news the distance between the advancing Red Army and the camp of Ravensbrück, where his wife might still be alive.

After the Allies crossed into Germany in the middle of December, Mike worked overtime reading reports and interrogating contacts. One night Janine was awakened by the sound of Mike's voice on the telephone. She had had enough.

"Hang up that phone!" she cried, stepping into the room.

Mike looked up and put his hand over the receiver.

Janine stood there, shivering in her nightgown. "Do you really believe Robert is still alive?" she asked.

"Yes, I do. He's a survivor."

"Ever the optimistic American!" Janine spat. "Being clever is useless in a concentration camp."

"That's not what I hear," Mike said, pointing at his phone. Remembering one such person was on the line, Mike spoke into the receiver, but his interlocutor was gone.

Janine broke down. "Robert is dead," she cried. "They're all dead. My mother, Lucile, Nicole, and Madame Gaillac. Death is all that comes out of Germany. Death in gas chambers, hangings, and mass murder of prisoners of war."

Mike knew it was true. Reports from Soviet troops of gas chambers at Auschwitz had been derided as Communist propaganda, but Mike had seen a report from a British medical unit describing another camp where they had found tens of thousands of pairs of discarded children's shoes. Genocide on a massive scale was being conducted in the East.

"We have been fighting this war for four years. Now it's over," Janine said. "And I need you to be here with me."

Mike stood to take Janine in his arms, but she stepped back. "What's the matter?" he asked. "You don't love me anymore? What is it that you are *not* telling me?" he insisted.

"Méle toi de tes affaires." *Mind your own business.*

"Everything about *you* is my business."

That did it! Janine grabbed files, papers, books, even the Bakelite telephone, and threw it all at him. She was prodigiously angry. Angry about how easy it was to hate the man you loved, angry for being in love, angry for her helpless need for reassurance and support. She had been self-dependent all her life, but now she needed him.

"You want me to stop searching for Robert?" Mike asked.

"Yes! But you never will. I know you; you never give up!"

Mike again reached out for her. "Come here, my love."

"No, no, no!" she cried. As he caught her, she hit him with the flat of her hands. When he finally managed to cradle her in his arms, she burst into tears and pushed her head against his chest, sobbing helplessly.

"Please, tell me what's wrong." And suddenly it came to him. "Oh my God! You're pregnant!" He leaned back and looked into her face. "That's what it is, isn't it?"

Janine muttered between sobs. "Yes."

"That's wonderful!" Mike cried. A bolt of pure joy ran through him. He slid his arms under her knees and lifted her, laughing and twirling around the room. "Now you'll have to marry me," he announced. "You've got no choice. No child out of wedlock for you!

No, ma'am. You're Catholic! Hell, we're both Catholics. We'll have a big church wedding!"

"I will not marry you until *you* decide this war is over," she said, sliding out of his arms.

Mike thought about that and grinned. "Okay."

"If you go on another mission and don't come back, I will not have your child," Janine said. "I will not be a single mother again!" And she stood there reliving her abortion when she was sixteen and how awful it had been.

"Sweetie, I'll always be there," Mike said, reaching for her.

"Don't touch me." And she marched out, slamming the door behind her.

Mike was overwhelmed by elation and despair in equal parts—*I love this woman. I'll be a father. I've got to take care of her. What if she is right and Robert is dead?* Then the pain shot back, stinging deeper—*I can't abandon Robert.* Mike could not shake the violent certitude that Robert was holding out somewhere, fighting to stay alive and needing his help.

The war hardened with casualties mounting on all sides. At home, Mike kept a steady middle course between the need to reassure Janine and his determination to find Robert. Emma was blossoming and bringing much-needed joy to the family. She was full of energy and spoke French and English indifferently, at times switching languages in mid-sentence. She called Mike "Papa" and Janine "Mommy."

Janine experienced the early stage of pregnancy with conflicting emotions. One day she was overjoyed and hoped for a boy with the round Irish face of his father. Then, just as quickly, she was convinced that this pregnancy was a mistake. How could she trust such a stubborn, irresponsible man? A Frenchman, she could read, but

Mike was still a mystery to her—*c'est un Americain. They exaggerate their sentiments. Oh yes, he loved her. He kept saying it. Trying to convince himself perhaps? The truth is, he's only staying until he finds Robert. No, no! Learning I was pregnant made him truly happy.*

The German winter counteroffensive in the Ardennes had failed and Allied armies were now moving deep into Germany. Mike was far from the battle line and communication was difficult. Then, a messenger showed up at the Toulouse apartment and handed Mike a dispatch from Bogart. "Your telephone line is out of order. Get on the first train to Paris."

Janine froze at the news. She did not want him to go. Mike showed her the dispatch. "I'm going to Paris, not Berlin. If it's a dangerous mission, I'll say no and resign."

"You promise."

"I promise."

Janine kissed him and withdrew. She did not trust him.

Mike arrived in Paris's Austerlitz station the next day, took the metro, and got off at the Concorde station. He had developed a cold on the train and was rattled by stress. As he walked up the avenue, snowflakes twirled in the wind. OSS headquarters was at 80 Champs-Élysées, but Bogart had arranged to meet at the bar at Claridge's hotel, three doors down. Mike had made up his mind—*I'll resign from the OSS today. That's what Janine wants. We're going to be parents. I'll take her to America.* Then, he sneered at this simplicity—*she'll fight me about that. What else is new?*

Claridge's lobby was crowded. Mike made his way past the ornate art deco bar and spotted Bogart waving him over. The man had aged perceptively, his suit sagging off his now much thinner body.

"Good to see you, Captain." His smile was the same.

"Good to see you, sir."

They shook hands and sat down. Mike had prepared a sentence to announce his resignation—*do it now*, he thought, but a waiter brought drinks. Bogart raised his glass, and he simply said, "We found him."

Mike held his breath—unable to hope. *Don't jinx it.*

"We found your friend Robert. He's in poor health but he's alive," Bogart said, taking another swig of scotch. "He's in a sub camp of Dachau near Stuttgart."

"Are you getting him out?"

Bogart shook his head ever so slightly. "The camp is in the area controlled by the Third Army commanded by General Patton. The man is obsessed with diseases and has ordered for all displaced persons to be quarantined to prevent epidemics. No exceptions. Going through official channels would take too long. Robert would be dead by then."

Mike's face darkened. He leaned over and growled, "Don't tell me we're gonna let him die out there."

"I'm not," Bogart said, pushing a thick brown envelope across the table.

"What's this?"

"Documents." Bogart nodded. "To get him out."

Anger melting, all thoughts of retirement gone, Mike stared at Bogart. He'd never have expected this WASP bottom-line intelligence chief to show such compassion.

"This won't be easy," Bogart said. "Patton's orders are strict. No one comes out, but we've got someone inside the camp who will help you." Then, tapping on the envelope, he added, "You've got maps and passes here and the proper identification to get through the British, French, and American lines. And you'll both get uniforms: American captain for you, French lieutenant for her."

"Her? You mean Janine?"

Bogart nodded. "She'll be identified as an FFI chieftain. That'll be useful when dealing with French army commanders."

"I need someone who can drive," Mike said.

"Janine got her license in '38 and she speaks German."

Mike leaned back in his chair. This was Bogart. He never gave you a choice. "You talked to her?"

"Last night, on *your* telephone. Seems the line's been repaired."

Mike wanted to say that Janine was pregnant, but what was the point? This was going to happen the way Bogart wanted it, or not at all.

"And she agreed to do this?"

"Oh yes. I explained the situation and she said yes right away. Actually, I doubt she would let you go without her."

That woman is a piece of work, Mike thought.

"We got you an ambulance," Bogart continued. "And vouchers to requisition gasoline from the armed forces along the way."

"An ambulance?"

"As I said, your friend Robert is in poor health. Most of the men coming out of the camps cannot sit for any period of time."

It was a terrible image, but Mike dismissed it—*Robert is alive, God damn it!*

Bogart stood and extended his hand. "Janine is taking the night train. Time is of the essence, you understand."

"I do, sir."

Mike stuck the envelope under his arm, took Bogart's hand, and shook it hard. His cold was gone. "Thank you, sir," he said before hurrying away.

59

THE OSS HAD PROVIDED A KRANKENKRAFTWAGEN, a Mercedes-Benz L1500E ambulance captured by the Allies during the Normandy invasion. It was a white boxy two-door van with frosted side windows and red crosses on the body and roof. An American mechanic showed Mike how to work the gearbox and together they went through the checklist of onboard necessities: four extra cans of gasoline, two new spare tires, a toolbox, a set of spark plugs, and a medical kit. And also, a 9mm Sten submachine gun and two 9mm Browning P.35's with ammunition.

A tailor fitted Mike for a natty 8th Air Force Captain's tunic with sterling silver pilot's wings. Mike was again officially part of the US military, and he felt it was befitting to wear it on his last mission of the war.

He woke early, shaved, dressed in his new kit, and headed for his bank on the Place Vendôme. He stopped there first, walked to Van Cleef & Arpels, made his purchase, and continued to the Austerlitz station where he reserved a table at the station restaurant.

He was standing on the platform when Janine stepped down from the train. Her British-issued khaki dress and jacket with a French lieutenant's insignia and FFI armband suited her. Her face was smooth and full—*the glow of pregnancy*, Mike thought, his heart skipping a beat.

"Don't tell me you've always had a weakness for women in uniform," Janine said.

"Even weaker when you wear nothing at all."

Janine chuckled and took his arm.

"Did you sleep on the train?" he asked.

"All night. Like a baby," she said. "I'm hungry."

"Ah, I thought of that."

Sitting in the restaurant, Mike watched Janine devour tartines of buttered bread and strawberry jam. When she was finally satiated, Mike glanced at their waiter, who brought over two flutes of champagne.

"To us," Mike said, raising his glass.

"And Robert," Janine answered, tapping her glass with his but barely wetting her lips. Mike drank his wine, then flipped open a tiny blue velvet box featuring a diamond ring. "Janine Dumas, will you marry me?" he asked.

"It's beautiful," Janine said. Then, she gave her usual answer, "As soon as you have resigned from the OSS."

"We'll get Robert back and I'll file to be discharged."

"Then I will be your wife." Janine held Mike's cheek and kissed him on the lips. "You've got a big heart," she said, admiring the ring. "I love that about you." Then she put the ring back in the box and handed it to Mike, who leaned over and put it in the pocket of *her* uniform.

"We'll get a big house, with a garden, lots of room for children and dogs," Mike said, raising his glass. "More champagne?"

"I'm pregnant."

"To our new baby," Mike said, drinking it down. Then, the specter of what lay ahead of them cut through his euphoria—*she's expecting. This is a dangerous mission.* "I wish you didn't have to be part of this."

"I want to be. I gave up on Robert, but you did not. You're better than me. Thank God for that."

A taxi took them to the garage where a mess cook had packed thermoses of coffee, sandwiches, and bottles of mineral water for their journey. The mechanic checked the ambulance one last time and gave it a thumbs-up.

"It's a sixteen-hour drive," Mike said as they wheeled into the street. "We'll get there before dawn."

Janine had not been in Paris since her incarceration at Fresnes prison. Driving through the nineteenth arrondissement, the sight triggered bleak memories. They now were following the route the Gestapo had taken on the way to Drancy and images of children being brutally separated from their mothers flashed through her mind. To shake off the memories, she began a positive litany—she was in love with the man sitting beside her and carrying his child. In a few hours Robert would be with them and the war was coming to an end.

"We'll cross into Germany by nightfall," Mike said.

Germany. Just saying the word filled them with dread. The krauts, les boches, the Huns, and all their wars and the killings and the misery they had brought to the world. The towns and villages they passed still bore scars from combat. Mike focused on driving while Janine checked the documents in the envelope Bogart had given them.

In the Champagne region, the countryside reminded Mike of their escape down the hillside after the train attack—being in the tunnel, freeing all those people, climbing up the air vents—*damn, we got lucky that day.*

Janine had fallen asleep. "The mother of my child," Mike whispered. His heart filled with gratitude, but a sudden fear burned through his mind. A dark thought, out of character but vibrant—*if something happens to me, this child will be all that's left of me.* But his confident side soon prevailed—*lighten up*. Farther down the road, a sign pointed toward the Word War One battlefield of Verdun. *Dad fought there and here I am.*

Janine woke up and Mike felt she should drive during daylight hours, so they switched places. She was a good driver, focused and watchful of the road ahead, whispering to herself at times—*wet pavement, watch out.* In a light drizzle she used the windshield wipers sparingly, just what was necessary.

They stopped at one roadblock after another. Gendarmes gawked at Janine's lieutenant's stripes, checked their papers, and waved them on. They shared sandwiches and drank coffee. Night fell and Mike took back the wheel outside Strasbourg. Soon, they reached the Rhine and stared at Germany on the other side. Not a single light, a dark sinister landmass emanating evil. The border was a brightly lit, heavily staffed roadblock. American and British soldiers flanked French customs officers. Their documents were checked more carefully this time. First the French examined them, then the Americans; finally, a British officer came over. He noted Mike's uniform. "US Air Force? What bloody hell are you doing here? It's no garden party out there." Then, flipping through the documents, his attitude changed dramatically. "1940, RAF?" He handed back the papers and saluted, smartly. "Have a safe trip, Saar."

And they rolled into Germany. The border town was silent. Not a soul, not a light. They sat straight up, scrutinizing the streets lined with half-timbered houses, some heavily damaged, others untouched. Janine checked the documents and pointed at a road sign.

"Oberkirch," she said.

Mike swerved into a country road as it started to snow—thick, feathery stuff fluttering down from a low sky. He leaned forward, staring through the swath that the wipers cut across the windshield. The night was oppressive.

"How does it feel to be back in Germany?" he asked.

"Not good."

"You studied in Dusseldorf. How was that?"

"For most of it, it was one of the best years of my life."

"So, you liked the Germans?"

"The ones I studied with, yes. They were good people. Then came Kristallnacht. Burned buildings. People bloodied and dragged out of their stores and homes." Janine recoiled and went on. "It was dreadful being surrounded by so much hatred. Watching them strut with their Nazi salute, angry and mean, itching to go to war."

Her memories were mirrored in the terrain—hardened snow blanketed muddy roads widened by tank tracks. At the next roadblock, a French sergeant glared at Janine's uniform. "Qu'est-ce-qu'elle fout là cette femme?" *What the hell is this woman doing here?* He snatched their papers and cranked up his field telephone. He read from the sauf-conduit and grimaced, moving the receiver away from his ear. Clearly the person at the other end was yelling at him. After a few "oui, Capitaines," he hung up and handed the documents back to Janine with a Gallic *pfeu.*

They drove through pitch darkness. The ambulance's blue painted headlights illuminated less than fifty feet of the snowy road ahead of them. The jerry cans of gasoline inside the van exuded an acrid smell that made them queasy and forced them to keep the windows rolled down with outside temperatures below freezing. The Krankenkraftwagen was a thirsty beast and Mike had to stop often to refill the tanks. Each time, he kept the engine running.

"Turn it off and it might never start again," he told Janine.

The OSS office had provided an itinerary they had been instructed to follow to the letter to avoid combat zones. So they looped around a lot with Janine illuminating the map on her lap with a flashlight.

At a roadblock manned by French and American soldiers of the 7th Army, an American officer ordered their jerry cans refilled and warned them about marauding enemy soldiers.

"Are you armed?" he asked.

"We are," Mike responded.

"SS units are deserting all over the place," the officer said. "They're dangerous. If you run into them, don't ask questions. Shoot first."

The previous summer, Mike had insisted that Janine learn to fire a Sten gun. She had agreed reluctantly but had turned out to be an excellent marksman.

"A soft touch does wonders for accuracy," Mike had marveled.

"Dentist's hands." She had smiled.

Janine pulled her Sten from behind her seat, armed it, and wedged it in the door compartment. They went on through bombed villages, burned farms, and acres of tree trunks hacked by artillery. After so many hours staring into the darkness, their bloodshot eyes stung. Janine stared at road signs. Mike caught the dread in her eyes.

"Are you all right?" he asked.

"Yes, watch the road. We're getting close."

A little before four o'clock in the morning, Janine spotted a signboard with snow piled on its upper edge. Peering closer she could see the letters: DISPLACED PERSONS CAMP.

"Turn here!" Janine cried, pointing.

They had almost missed it. Mike stepped on the brakes, the vehicle slid sideways, but he managed to swerve into the side road.

"They hid the camp in a forest," Janine said, apprehension heavy in her voice.

Mike glanced at her and was suddenly angry with himself—*how could I bring her here? I'm a fool.*

Shock absorbers whined on the uneven pavement. They dreaded what was ahead of them—a *concentration camp*, the epicenter of Nazi horror.

"It'll be worse than you can imagine," Janine said. Her voice had turned into a murmur. She was talking to herself, trying to prepare for what was coming. "A lot worse."

"We'll get Robert and get out," Mike said.

Now, lights filtered between the trees and a huge compound appeared behind fences and guard towers with lights illuminating the perimeter. Menacing and ominous, it seemed to belong to another world. But here it was, a night's drive from their home—*a death camp*.

"Oh, God!" Mike said as an overpowering stench filled the car. They rolled up their windows in a hurry and Janine put a hand over her mouth, fighting nausea. Mike wiped a tear from his eye.

Now, they could make out sentries by the gate, standing near burning bonfires in tin drums. The American soldiers motioned for Mike to roll down his window. When he did, he understood the fires covered the stink with the smell of green wood and gasoline. Mike handed over their documents, which were passed along to the officer on duty. The sentries were young. They walked around the ambulance, eyeing its occupants with curiosity. They had not seen a healthy woman in a long time and this one was a looker. One of them pointed at Janine's armband.

"What does 'FFI' stand for?" he asked.

"French Forces of the Interior."

"French Résistance?"

"Yes."

The soldier nodded. "We've got a lot of French in here. Also, Poles, Czechs, Yugoslavs, Dutch, Russians."

Janine indicated the high towers. "They aren't prisoners anymore. Why the fences?"

"They want to get out, but we've got to make sure they ain't sick first," the soldier said.

The officer in the sentry box read their documents and spoke on the telephone. Janine and Mike looked through the barbed wire and could see shadows drifting between buildings. The officer stepped out and handed the papers back to Mike.

"Your medic is waiting for you. Barrack eleven. You don't want to stay too long, Captain; it's not healthy in there."

"Don't plan to."

Mike shifted the ambulance into gear and the guards opened the gate. They rolled between barracks and could see men and women, all painfully thin, wearing army fatigues over stripped pajamas. They moved slowly or watched them drive by with dull eyes.

A medic waited in front of a barrack with a white "11" painted next to the door. Mike pulled over and let the engine run. Reaching behind the seat, he grabbed a bundle of clothes tied with strings. When he opened the door, the terrible smell flooded in.

"Better if you wait in the vehicle, ma'am," the medic said.

Janine didn't argue. She watched Mike follow the medic inside the barracks and worked to control a sudden panic. The silence frightened her, and she dreaded that smell—a disinfectant with a whiff of something else. Rotting flesh, the putrid stink of gangrene, that's what it was. She stared at the barrack's entrance, willing Mike to reappear. A dull sound made her jump—inmates were carrying bodies on stretchers to a wheeled cart. Every time they loaded one, there was a *thump*. When Janine had counted six *thumps*, the men tilted up the cart and wheeled it away in the darkness.

Janine pushed the door open and threw up. Then, she grabbed a bottle, rinsed her mouth, spat out the water, and closed the door.

The men in striped pajamas and army fatigues returned with their now empty cart. At long last a square of light flashed as the barrack's door opened and closed. The medic led the way with Mike stumping along behind him carrying a child in his arms. It was dark but as they passed in front of the headlights Janine could see that the clothes were way too big for him. *He couldn't find Robert. He took a child instead.*

The medic opened the driver's-side door and Mike gently lowered the child onto the middle seat.

"Bonjour, Janine," a familiar voice murmured.

"My God . . ." Janine blanched. It felt like a spear piercing her heart. "Oh, Robert."

"Never thought . . . I'd see you again," Robert mumbled. His eyes looked enormous. Ugly scabs dotted his bald skull.

Mike slid behind the wheel and handed Janine a medic's cap with a red cross on its side. "Put that on his head."

Janine caressed Robert's sunken cheek and set the hat on his head.

"We're taking you home," she said gently.

Robert closed his eyes.

"Make sure they see the armband," the medic said. "Keep him hydrated, that's the main thing."

Janine repositioned Robert to expose the Red Cross band on his sleeve with PETTY OFFICER 2ND CLASS stenciled above it.

Mike gunned the engine. "Robert, we're slipping you out of here. I know it's hard, but you must keep your eyes open when we go through the gate."

"I understand," Robert said.

Janine looked at Mike in alarm—*no way we'll be able to fool those guards.*

"Give me a cigarette," Robert murmured.

"You smoke now?" Mike asked.

"Camouflage," Robert growled.

Mike felt like a fool—*he's still sharp*. He lit a cigarette and wedged it between Robert's chapped lips. As they rolled away, Janine heard another body being dumped onto the cart. Mike drove slowly. Far to the east, they could see the faint pallor of dawn—*damn, not daylight. We don't want daylight.*

Robert saw it too. "Step on it," he said.

When they turned into the road leading to the main gate Janine squared her shoulders. Robert squinted as the smoke from his cigarette drifted into his eyes. He forced his head up and tried to straighten his back. When they pulled up at the gate and the sentries stepped out of their box, the ambulance engine suddenly sputtered.

"Clutch," Robert said.

Mike had released the clutch pedal too soon and the engine was stalling.

"Please, God," Janine whispered.

Mike slammed the gear into neutral, stepped on the clutch, and revived the engine.

Robert grunted.

The sentries beamed their flashlights inside the ambulance, glanced at the medic puffing on his cigarette, but were more interested in Janine's lovely figure. Eager to distract them, Janine lowered her window.

"Where are you from, soldier?" she asked.

"Detroit, Michigan, ma'am," the sentry answered.

"Motor City," Janine said, smiling. "And the Great Lakes?"

"Yeah, Great Lakes and fresh air," the sentry said, wincing at the smell in the air. "Better than here."

"I hope you all go home soon," Janine said.

"We hope so too, ma'am. We don't like it here."

Mike lit a cigarette, inhaled deeply, and revved the engine. Not hard, just enough to tell the sentries—*get on with it, will ya.*

"Wait a minute!" An older guard stepped out of the sentry box and opened the rear door of the ambulance. Janine made sure Robert stayed upright between them. They listened as the guard rattled the stretchers and checked the equipment case filled with medical supplies. Finally, he closed the door and knocked on the roof.

Mike watched the gate rise in front of them. As they wheeled through, Janine caught Robert's cigarette falling from his lips.

"Need to lie down," Robert gasped, coughing.

"Two more minutes," Mike said.

Tears running down his emaciated face, Robert made a valiant effort. Janine put a hand on his chest and held him back while Mike drove, keeping an eye on the gate in the rearview mirror. They took a turn, then another, and when the camp was no longer visible, he pulled over.

Janine stepped out. Between the trees, she could still see flashes of the bonfires in the tin drums. She opened the back door while Mike carried Robert around and laid him on one of the stretchers.

"Dankeschoen," Robert murmured.

Janine climbed beside him, covered him with blankets, and poured out some water into a cup. Robert closed his eyes, meaning—*not thirsty*.

"You've got to drink," Janine insisted. She lifted Robert's head and helped him take a sip. He had a hard time swallowing but managed a little.

When Mike got underway again, Janine checked the medical instrument case. She found the hypodermic syringe set and pulled it aside. Switching on her flashlight, she checked Robert's arms—no flesh, just skin and bones. She rubbed the inside of his elbow looking for a vein, then bit her lip in frustration and closed the medical case.

"I was hoping to put an IV in him," she said as she crawled back into the passenger's seat. "But there's nowhere to put it."

"Did he drink?"

"A little."

Mike lowered the visor to shield his eyes from the rising sun. Janine was silent for a while but finally asked, "How was it in the barracks?"

Mike sucked air between his teeth. "It was hell . . ." How could he attempt to describe the abomination? "Living corpses with big eyes stacked up on wooden bunks," he finally said. "I couldn't tell who was dead, who was alive."

"Children?" Janine asked.

"No. I asked. All gassed on arrival."

Janine stared at the road for a moment and then turned back, stretched her arm, and touched Robert's head.

"We'll be home tonight, sweetheart. You'll be fine, we'll take good care of you," she said in a reassuring voice as if talking to a child.

Mike calculated they could drive another fifty miles before refilling the tank. Around 6:00 a.m they crossed lines of US Army tanks and infantry patrols moving toward the front. This was reassuring. Mike felt tension fading from his arms and shoulders. He glanced at Janine in the passenger seat and at Robert in the back. They were both asleep. These were the two people he cared most for in the world, and he was taking them home.

There was another place he'd like to take them. He imagined stepping off a train at Chicago's Union Station along with Janine, Emma, and Robert and introducing them to his family waiting on the platform. Mike snapped out of his reverie and checked the gauge. The ambulance needed fuel. They had just crossed paths with an

Allied battalion moving toward the battle line. It was safe to pull over and Mike let the ambulance drift to a bare patch of ground on the side of the road.

Janine heard voices and woke up with a start. The driver's seat was empty, but she could see Mike in the side-view mirror holding a jerry can up against the tank's nozzle.

"Stay away!" Mike shouted.

"Kamerad," a German voice responded.

Janine turned to the driver's-side-view mirror—a handful of SS men had appeared at the edge of the wood—no helmets, torn uniforms; a couple held bayonets in their fists. Janine watched Mike drop the jerry can and she heard soldiers rush toward him. Mike's gun fired twice. Bodies slammed into the side of the ambulance.

"What's happening?" Robert cried, waking.

"Deserters," Janine cried, pulling a burlap bag from under the seat.

"Give me a weapon," Robert said.

Janine pushed an ammunition clip into the Browning and slid the gun on the floor of the ambulance. Robert padded around and found it. Janine armed the Sten just as her door swung open.

Brrrp.

She fired point-blank into the man's chest and watched him stagger, then drop like a stone.

Heavy pounding on the rear of the ambulance made her turn. The back doors flew open, and a tall SS man leaned inside shouting at Robert, "Gib mir die Waffe!" *Give me that gun!*

Robert's wobbly fingers managed to push off the safety catch and squeeze the trigger. The weapon crackled. The bullet hit the embroidered SS logo on the man's jacket lapel. He grabbed his neck, blood spurting between his fingers, then turned and stumbled away.

Janine sprang out of the ambulance and rushed to Mike, who was down on his knees struggling with an SS trying to pry the Browning pistol out of his hands.

She raised her weapon and screamed. "Hor auf! Haende hoch!" *Stop it! Hands up!*

The Nazi was fighting hard. He wanted that gun, almost had it. Janine danced around the struggling men trying to find a clear line of fire and finally stepped up close and aimed directly at the SS man's head.

Brrrp.

Blood gushing from his temple, the Nazi spun around and floundered against the ambulance. Janine pushed him off and crouched down beside Mike, who was laying on the ground clutching his side.

"He stabbed me," Mike said, blood trickling from the corner of his mouth. "Shoot them," he mumbled.

Janine stood and the three SS men raised their arms in surrender.

"Kamerad!" one said.

Another one pulled photographs out of his breast pockets. "Children, drei Kinder, Frau . . . war zerstoert."

"Essen." *Food*, said another one.

Janine held her gun level and stepped toward them.

Brrrp.

The cracking of the bullets and the vibration of the weapon in her hands was exhilarating. Two of the men rolled in the ditch, their bodies twitching as they died. The third one was still alive, his mouth sucking for air. Janine squeezed the trigger again and finished him off.

Robert was keeping an eye on the wounded SS man still walking in circles, blood pouring out of his throat. He aimed at the man's head, fired and missed, then fell back on his stretcher, spent.

Janine raced back to the ambulance and with strength she didn't know she possessed, grabbed Mike under his arms and dragged him around the vehicle, leaving a nasty trail of blood in the dirt.

"Move over," she ordered Robert.

Robert struggled to make room and watched Janine turn Mike around to lift his heavy frame. She wedged him on the side of the ambulance, climbed aboard, and attempted to pull him up.

"Push on your legs, darling," she said.

Mike groaned and pushed up. Janine laid him down on the stretcher next to Robert. She flipped the medical kit open and tore up Mike's shirt, unveiling an ugly wound just below his rib cage.

Blood was gushing with the rhythm of Mike's heartbeat. Jabbering endearment and encouragement, Janine painted the wound with iodine, but the blood washed it away. She needed to apply a pressure dressing.

"Mike, darling, I need you to move to the side," she said.

Mike did not answer.

"Janine," Robert whispered, laying a weak hand on her arm.

"Not now!"

Janine tried to move Mike, but his body was slippery with blood and the stretcher kept sliding under him. She pulled out an ammonia inhalant and popped it under his nose. Mike's eyelids flickered.

"Please, Mike . . . ," she said softly.

"I'll help you," Robert whispered as he managed to slide his skeletal arms under Mike's chest and together, they rolled Mike onto his side. Janine pressed an adhesive compress over the wound until the hemorrhaging stopped. Holding it tight, she secured the wrap with bandages.

"Help me turn him over," she whispered.

Robert didn't have much more to give. But they managed to push Mike over on his back and Janine secured the bandages around Mike's chest.

"Thank you, Robert," Janine said. She kissed Mike's forehead and crawled out of the ambulance.

Robert's eyes filled with tears as he heard the back door slam shut and Janine behind the wheel shifting the engine back into gear. They wheeled around the wounded SS man now crawling blindly on his hands and knees. The tires screeched and they were back on the road heading west.

The ambulance bumped around. Robert strained to budge and managed to turn on his side and kiss Mike's forehead. Then he laid back and cried, keeping to himself the terrible truth he had known for several minutes.

Mike was dead.

60

AS JANINE DROVE FARTHER AWAY from the front, military roadblocks became less stringent. Security officers peeked in the back of the ambulance and figured the two men lying there were done for. They were intrigued by the attractive woman staring sightlessly through the windshield with that fixed look borne out of intense suffering, but they asked no questions and waved her through.

Around 8:30 a.m., Janine pulled into a checkpoint manned by British military. The officer in charge checked her documents and gave an order. An olive drab Bedford QLD refueling truck pulled over and men busied themselves, filling the ambulance's tank and jerry cans. The officer tapped on her window and handed Janine a mug of tea. It was hot and sweet. She wrapped her hands around the cup and for an instant felt an odd happiness.

She could hear the rushing sound of air filling the tires with short bursts. A faint smell of engine oil and gasoline drifted inside the cabin. She watched as a young mechanic wearing oil-stained overalls popped the hood. He had a friendly face and dark brown hair. Janine's husband had had hair like that. She squeezed the mug hard and forced the memory away. She felt no guilt about the men she had killed that morning, no remorse, not even the slightest unease. It had been the proper thing to do, like drinking tea, driving an ambulance, or draining an abscess.

The mechanic closed the hood and weighing on it, locked it.

"All set to go, miss," the officer said.

"Thank you," Janine said, handing him her empty mug. She started the engine and as it caught, she remembered Mike telling her to never turn it off, even during refueling—*wrong about that, my love.*

Mike's funeral mass, celebrated at Sainte-Étienne cathedral in Toulouse, was attended by more than two thousand people. Latecomers stood in the square and listened to the mass through loudspeakers. Every Résistance organization was represented, from the FTP communists to the Gaullists to the guerrilleros españoles. Even those who had never met Mike mourned his loss. He was more than an American ally; he had been part of the Résistance, he was one of their own.

Dressed in black wearing a hat with a black-netted veil, Janine stood between her father and Jacquet, who had traveled all night to be there. Jacquet's presence had made Janine's heart swell with gratitude, and she had asked him to stand at her side. Bogart stood in the next row. The organ was playing. She stared at Mike's coffin wrapped in an American flag. At least this time there was a coffin. Her husband's plane had exploded on impact and no remains were ever found. The war years were a quagmire in Janine's head. Everything she had fought for felt futile. All her actions had only brought misery. A Bach sonata filled the church. She had chosen that piece because Mike had loved it, but the music did not touch her. She felt almost indifferent. She knew from experience that the feeling of emptiness would not last and soon be replaced by debilitating sorrow. The ceremony ended and Proust, Louis, Jacquet, and Bogart carried the casket outside where the large assembly stood at attention and saluted when a military band played "The Star-Spangled Banner."

After the crowds at the church, Janine was glad the burial at the cemetery on a hill above the train station would be a private affair. Taps were played and two Air Force officers removed the flag from the casket and meticulously folded it, before Bogart presented it to Janine.

"On behalf of the President of the United States, the United States Air Force, and a grateful nation, please accept this flag as a symbol of our appreciation for your loved one's honorable and faithful service."

Honorable and faithful. Janine was infinitely proud of Mike and even prouder to have been loved by such a remarkable man. She watched the coffin being lowered into the grave and felt empty—empty of warmth, empty of life. There would be no big house with a garden and lots of room for children and dogs. No large bed to sleep in, no lovemaking. No drinking wine by the fireplace at night and coffee in bed in the morning. No singing and piano playing. And most of all, no magnificent presence as he walked into a room and lifted her in his arms, that glorious feeling of loving and being loved.

Mourners began to disassemble. Bogart went around and shook hands. He knew everyone's name—Louis, Proust, Jacquet, Charlotte—and greeted them individually. Nobody spoke much. Most were blinking back tears.

Janine still stood at the edge of the grave staring at Mike's coffin. Down there was the love of her life—the father of her unborn child, the man who could soothe her, infuriate her, and always make her laugh. *I'm nothing without you.* She brought her fingers to her lips and blew Mike a kiss.

Jacquet stood silent next to her. Janine wrapped her arms around him, seeking the comfort he had once brought. Today there was none to be had.

And now Bogart was at Janine's side. She barely listened as he offered his sympathy and thanked her for all the Allied airmen she had saved. Then he produced a letter and handed it to her.

"This is from Mike's father," he said.

Janine took the envelope, which showed the seals and the marking of the City of Chicago. It had been addressed to the American Embassy in Paris and bore her name. It was a piece of Mike. She held the letter close against her heart.

"If you decide to answer," Bogart said, "contact my office and we will forward your letter to him."

Janine nodded, stepped away, and opened the envelope.

Dear Janine,

I hope you will forgive me for addressing you by your first name. Mike told us so much about you in his letters that I feel I already know you. He said that you were planning to get married and from that moment on you became the daughter he had chosen for me. He was overjoyed by the prospect of being your husband and the father of your child.

But tragedy has struck, and Mike's loss is as awful a shock for you as it has been for all of us. We are trying to carry on as best we can, but life will never be quite the same again. Please accept our deepest sympathy and be assured that the entire O'Keefe family welcomes you with open arms.

I am, of course, concerned about your well-being and that of my first grandchild. I want you to know that whatever I can do for you will be done gladly.

There are many things we would like to know, especially about you, your daughter Emma, and your parents. Please, write to us and keep us informed about your family and the birth.

God be with you, my child.

Thomas O'Keefe

Janine wrote back. She thanked Mike's father for his letter and expressed her condolences for the death of his son. She recounted how Mike had saved her life during the war by rescuing her from a deportation train. She quoted Emma, who used to call his son Papa Mike, and mentioned that they were all praying for the return of her mother who was in a camp in Germany. She thanked him for his offer to help. Her pregnancy was progressing normally. She expected to give birth by the end of the summer and would keep him informed.

She was too numb to cry and sleepwalked through the following days. When she found the velvet box containing Mike's engagement ring in the jacket pocket of her uniform, she didn't look at the diamond or reminisce about the marriage proposal; she dropped the ring in a drawer and closed it with her hip. This was the second time she had lost the love of her life; the second time she carried a child who would never see his father. Happiness was a forgotten sensation for her, a sentiment for other people.

That fateful day, on that German road, Janine had pulled over a few miles down. Mike had never looked more handsome. She had known he was dead the instant she opened the back door.

"He's with God now," Robert had said, shivering as Janine's pain ran through him, adding to his own.

She had crawled between the stretchers and taken Mike in her arms and squeezed as hard as she could. She recalled kissing Mike, whose mouth was still warm, then kissed him again, her lips pursed hard with despair. Robert had turned away and cried. Janine wanted to shout but did not.

She was behind the wheel again, empty and numb, driving in a state of watchful misery but determined to bring Robert to safety.

She wished she did not have a daughter to take care of or a father to console. Mike had left a gaping hole, and she did not want to live alongside that hole.

They tried to hide Mike's death from Emma, but the little girl knew something bad had happened and kept asking for Papa Mike. Janine told her that he was visiting his family and would be back, hoping she would forget about him. She did not and would often slip into Mike's office in Grandma's old room and sit in his chair holding her doll. Janine was heartsick when one afternoon, she heard Emma hum a lullaby and count to a hundred in English.

Emma's questioning remained relentless, and the lies became unbearable so, finally, Janine took her daughter on her lap, brushed a lock of hair behind her ear, kissed her several times, and told her the truth.

"Sweetie, Papa Mike has gone to heaven," she said.

"Like my real daddy?" Emma asked.

"Yes."

"Papa Mike will not come back?"

"No."

"I will never see Papa Mike again?"

"No, sweetie."

Emma clung to Janine's blouse and cried. Mother and daughter slept in the same bed that night and several nights after that. Emma never again set foot inside Mike's office. She stopped talking and would only answer questions by nodding or shaking her head. She also reverted to thumb-sucking.

Janine was gnawed by guilt. Every time a man walked into the apartment, Emma disappeared. Janine understood that her daughter didn't want another Papa. Her grandfather was the only man that she could bear to be with, and Louis took it upon himself to replace both of Emma's fathers. It was not easy. Emma refused to be carried on his shoulders and when he tried to play the piano, she shook her head and closed the lid.

Numbness was what Janine felt most of all. Nightmares tormented her. A vision kept recurring. In it, Mike was still alive and her husband, who had miraculously survived his plane crash, came home from a POW camp. The situation was awkward and comical, but Emma loved it, running from one father to the other—*Father* and *Papa Mike*. Waking up was unbearable. She tried to push back the hood of grief but could not. She told Proust, who had moved to Toulouse and visited often, that she expected to learn of her mother's death after the liberation of the camps.

Janine stopped listening to the news filled with stories of camp survivors dying by the tens of thousands as they were marched from camp to camp. Louis attended his patients, prayed for his wife, and found a way to comfort his granddaughter by reading her French fairy tales. Emma particularly liked *Cendrillon* and *La Belle au bois dormant*. The two of them sat side by side every night after dinner, Emma with her thumb in her mouth, her grandfather reading with his arm loosely wrapped around her shoulders.

And then, there was Robert, wasting away in Toulouse's Sainte Marie's hospital. He had lost more than half of his body weight and was not expected to survive. Janine fought daily with the doctors and when they prescribed morphine for end-of-life care, she took Robert out of the hospital and installed him in the grandmother's room that had been Mike's office. When she attempted to remove the crucifix over the bed, Robert waved her off.

"Jesus was a Jew," he growled. His wasted muscles made every movement painful, so he spent his days immobile in semidarkness. Janine reviewed the scarce medical literature on the treatment of malnutrition and consulted with a retired *médecin* colonial who had attended survivors of the Armenian genocide in Syria in 1917. She read every Red Cross bulletin coming out of Poland and Germany. Information was sparse and often contradictory. Camp survivors were dying because they were fed too fast or given the wrong food. The truth was that no one knew how to treat chronically starved people. Doctors, medics, and nurses all over Europe were learning as they went along. Proust came to the apartment every day after work. Robert was having trouble opening his mouth, so Proust and Janine took turns spoon-feeding him. It was slow and difficult. A fungus had grown under Robert's esophagus and swallowing made his whole body shake with excruciating pain. Often, he refused all food and became delirious.

"Did I tell you to bury me beside Mike in the cemetery on a hill above the train station?" he'd slur through his nearly closed mouth.

"Yes, you did."

"We attacked the German train from there. You know where that is?"

"I do."

The weather was getting warmer, but Robert was always cold. His mind wandered. "Why doesn't Nicole come see me?" he would ask.

"Nicole was arrested before the Normandy landings, Robert," Proust would respond.

"Ah, yes." Then the fog would descend again. "Tell her to come tomorrow."

Robert badly needed protein but was unable to chew, so Janine squeezed the blood from chopped raw lamb and tried feeding him with a medicine dropper. Robert vomited up most of what he swallowed, grew irritable, and threw her out of the room. Then she heard that camp survivors seemed to be tolerating cooked chicken blood. Louis managed to get a live chicken from a farmer as payment for dental work. Madame Raymonde killed the bird, collected the blood, and cooked it in a frying pan, making *sanguettes*—thin blood crepes, which Robert seemed to tolerate. The slight improvement only brought darker thoughts.

"J'en ai marre de vivre." *I've had it with life*, Robert told Proust.

If Robert died, Mike's ultimate sacrifice would have been in vain, and Janine was determined to save him. She had entered her fourth month of pregnancy, her belly was beginning to swell, and she decided to take advantage of her condition—*he might do it for me*. She waited until the early evening when Robert was enjoying the breeze of the warm spring air through the open window.

"Are you sleeping?" Janine asked.

"No," he answered, his eyes still closed.

Janine sat on the edge of his bed and took Robert's hand. "You know Mike is dead?" she asked gently.

"Yes. I was there."

He's sharper than usual today. Good. Janine sucked in her breath. "I'm pregnant, Robert. I'm pregnant with Mike's child."

Robert opened one dark, bloodshot eye, and looked at her. "That's good," he said, closing his eye again.

"Mike will be with us through his child."

The thin smile flickered on Robert's lips, intent on some private revenge on the war.

"I will need your help, Robert."

He let out a small breath—*how?*

"When Mike's child grows up, he'll need a father," Janine said.

Robert opened both eyes. Janine could see him struggle with the enormity of what she was asking. "I can't." And with a pleading look, said—*let me die, please*.

Janine squeezed Robert's hand. Her eyes filled with tears. "Robert, I will need you. I *need* you to live. Do you understand?"

Every muscle and ligament tightened in Robert's scrawny neck—*don't ask me that.* He couldn't endure the physical pain anymore.

"I'll try," he finally whispered.

"Thank you." Janine kissed his hand. He took it back, darting her a dark, feverish glance. He was angry.

"Leave me alone," he said.

"I love you, Robert."

"Go away."

Robert didn't lose his temper anymore, but it was heartbreaking to watch him twist in pain as he forced himself to swallow food and water. He had resigned himself to *not* dying but resented the hell out of it—no relief, no closure, no peace to look forward to. And he needed lots of breaks.

"Let me rest," he'd say.

"Yes," Proust, who had taken over the feedings, would answer.

They had a routine. When Robert was tired, Proust stopped the feeding and let him sleep for half an hour, then he would wake him up and feed him again.

It went on for days, with Proust, Janine, and Louis taking turns to feed Robert. They had ups and downs. Sometimes he was able to keep the food down, other times not. Eventually they noticed shades of pink returning to his face. A few days later, he became more alert, even asking Proust for chocolate. Janine froze when she heard of the request.

"Oh God! Did you give him any?"

"No. I'm trying to get some on the black market."

"Don't! Chocolate is poison to starved bodies. It's too rich to tolerate. When they liberated the camps, American medics could not understand why so many inmates died within hours of their arrival, and why they lived longer in camps liberated by the British. Finally, they realized that chocolate was the first food American soldiers handed the survivors. The Red Cross spread the word, and they stopped the practice."

At last, Robert became strong enough to feed himself, but then a brand-new torment set in. Robert began eating obsessively. This stage of recovery was neither triumphant nor joyful. He did not talk. He did not move. He simply ate. One Sunday, the sky was blue, the air soft and warm, and Janine told Robert they were going outside.

Why would I want to do that? He did not ask.

Later, as they stepped out of the apartment, Robert froze at a rumbling noise coming from below. It was the elevator churning up to their floor. *I'm not getting into that thing.* The fear of enclosed space overwhelmed Robert. He broke into a sweat as Janine slid the metal curtain shut behind them and the machinery clanged above them. But the floors glided by smoothly—*It's all right. It's all right. Not so bad.*

They walked across the lobby and into the street, where people were moving so fast Robert froze again. But Janine held his arm, and they walked to a bench in the Place du Capitole.

Seated, Robert looked around in awe. "I had forgotten about colors," he said. "Everything was gray there, even the snow."

Children ran by holding balloons. Janine followed them with her gaze and Robert watched the emotion on her face. "If it weren't for me, Mike would be sitting next to you right now," Robert said.

"I don't want to hear that kind of talk from you ever!" Janine said. "You understand?"

"That's the truth, though."

Janine fought to contain the sadness gripping her. "This is no one's fault, Robert. Why am I alive while Loïc and Suzanne are dead? It's the war, Robert. That's the way it is."

"Mike died while rescuing me," Robert said.

"Mike was killed in the war. You've got to let him go as I am trying to."

They sat in silence for a minute, then, "I'll take care of you and the children," Robert said.

Janine looked up, her face glowing with all the tenderness she felt for him.

"I promised you," he insisted. "You asked."

Janine took Robert's arm and kissed his cheek. "You remember that?"

"Of course I remember!" he answered, adamant. "'I will need your help. When Mike's child grows up, he'll need a father,' you said."

Janine closed her eyes, working up the courage. "Robert, I said that because I wanted you to live."

As the understanding dawned, Robert stared at Janine. "You don't want me to be a father to Mike's son?"

"You'll be his uncle," Janine said, tightening her grip around his arm. "I wanted you to fight, Robert, and here you are. You're recovering," she continued urgently. "Look, it's a beautiful day."

Robert's face had turned to stone. "The truth is, you don't need me at all," he said, looking away.

Janine took his arm and laid her head on his shoulder. "I will always need you, Robert."

Her words hung in the air. A tear welled at the corner of Robert's eye, and he wiped it away. The sun was warm, and he felt almost healthy. He would not be this child's father, but he was alive.

"I'm glad you didn't let me die," he finally said. "You lying bitch."

They looked away from one another and for the first time in a long time, they smiled.

When the telephone rang one morning, *Mike's telephone*, as they tried not to call it, Janine picked it up and listened to a male voice with a Swiss accent. "Yes," she said. "I'm her daughter."

Louis sat up, Robert put down his paper, and they both looked at Janine still on the phone.

"Thank you very much." Janine hung up the receiver and clasped her hands. "Mother, Nicole, and Lucile are alive," she said.

"Annie's alive," Louis said, his voice cracking, tears starting. He pushed on the table and stood from his chair.

"Whom were you talking to?" Robert asked.

"An official from the Swiss Red Cross," Janine said. "They transferred a group of Frenchwomen from a camp in Germany to Switzerland. A woman who knew my mother was in that group. She told the Red Cross that Mother, Nicole, and Lucile were alive when she left the camp two days ago. She also said they could hear Russian tanks and artillery a few miles away."

Robert ran a hand over his face. "Nicole," he whispered. He had never been so afraid to hope.

Louis took Janine in his arms. Father and daughter embraced and began crying uncontrollably, clinging to each other like castaways.

61

GERMAN FORCES SURRENDERED ON MAY 7. Newspapers announced that fifteen million prisoners of war and camp survivors would soon be the repatriated. When news came that the first French contingent was expected to arrive in Paris within days, Janine managed to obtain train tickets for Robert and herself. They also needed official entry documents for the repatriation centers, but Parisian bureaucrats had already restored the habit of ignoring requests from the provinces. So Janine went back into war mode and had the papers made. They were exact replicas of those issued by the Ministère des prisonniers, déportés et réfugiés with all the right stamps and signatures, produced by the same expert who used to make *ausweis.*

Janine and Robert stayed in a hotel on the rue de Sèvres. They got up early every morning and walked to the Orsay train station repatriation center, where they secured spots behind fences in the main hall. For three days they watched French POWs disembark as the Marseillaise blasted through the loudspeakers. Then, on the fourth day, a wave of whispering hissed through the crowd. "Survivors from Buchenwald."

"That's for us," Robert said. Janine took his arm, and he felt all the hopes and fears in her grip. There was a scattering of applause when the train came to a stop, but it died quickly as a group of emaciated men shuffled into the station. Their heads were shaved and many still wore the blue and white striped uniforms of the camps. They moved in clusters, their faces spectral in the station's unforgiving light. The arrival hall remained eerily silent but for the clattering of wooden clogs on the pavement. Robert's jaw tightened as memories stormed his mind. These men had the vacant look of his Basque friends, just before they died.

"Monsieur le Maire. Monsieur Hébreard!" Janine shouted.

A thin man of indeterminate age turned toward her.

"Who's he?" Robert asked.

"The mayor of a village in Brittany where Loïc was caught. All the men were deported after they found allied airmen hidden in the school."

The mayor approached the fence. "Madame Janine?" he asked, recognition flooding his face.

"Yes," Janine said. "Can we help you?"

"What happened to Loïc?" he asked.

Janine shook her head. "They killed him."

The mayor nodded as if he had expected that answer.

"What about the men from your village?" Janine asked.

The mayor turned to indicate the group of skeletal men waiting for him.

"They took seventeen of us. We're eight now."

"Oh, Monsieur Hébreard. I'm so sorry," Janine said. "I'm here hoping to find my mother, Anna de Guilhem."

"The women were at Ravensbrück." The mayor raised his arms slightly as if in apology. He rejoined his companions and like a close-knit family, they shuffled away.

Janine and Robert spent the rest of the day watching trains pull into the station and thousands of emaciated men shuffle by. Suffering had a face and a smell. Every convoy brought a sharp stink of unwashed humanity.

"Next train is from Ravensbrück. Women only," someone said.

Janine and Robert tensed up. Anna and Nicole could be on that train. And the first group of women appeared, some in their striped camp uniform, others wearing army fatigues. All painfully thin, many with scarves over their cropped hair. A group walked by, trailed by three women who were obviously being shunned by the others. Robert realized that one of the stragglers was Lucile, the beautiful girl who left prostitution to join the line and had been shot and wounded in Bordeaux while de Lacoste escaped. She was no longer young or pretty and her red hair was cropped short. On crutches, but walking with the grace of a tall, wounded bird.

"Lucile!" Robert called.

As she approached the barrier the other women in her group began to chant: "La pute, la puuuute!" *The whore, the whoooore!*

"Robert, is that you?" Lucile asked, ignoring her tormentors.

Robert leaned over and kissed her. "I'm so happy to see you."

"Nicole talked about you so often. She's still alive . . . at least I think so."

"*Bon,*" Robert murmured, experiencing an instant of happiness, before the curtain of worry descended again. "When did you last see her?"

"Last week. We were scattered after that."

"Have you seen my mother, Anna de Guilhem?" Janine asked.

"You're her daughter! Oh my God! She's a wonderful woman, your mother," Lucile said, her eyes shining. "She saved us! I don't know where she is. We were separated when we left Ravensbrück."

The hall was filling with deportees piling up behind Lucile, pushing her forward. "Where can I find you?" she cried.

"The Lutetia hotel," Robert shouted. "Tell them members of your Résistance network are waiting for you there."

Lucile turned around and called, "What happened to Suzanne?

Robert shook his head. "Shot at the Mont-Valérien."

"Those swine!" Lucile yelled. And she moved on, hobbling on her crutches, her head bobbing above the crowd.

A five-star hotel on the boulevard Raspail, the Lutetia had been during the war the headquarters for the Abwehr, the German counterintelligence service, and this was where camp survivors were now being taken.

Janine and Robert crossed the rue de Sèvres where people stood behind fences lining the path to the hotel's entrance. The sidewalks were crowded with poster boards displaying messages from families looking for survivors—handwritten notes pinned next to photographs of healthy-looking men and women.

"If they're still alive, they look nothing like those pictures," Robert said.

Just then, a green and white platform bus labeled TRANSPORT EN COMMUN DE LA RÉGION PARISIENNE pulled up to the curb. The crowd behind the barriers began to shout and wave photographs when one by one camp survivors hobbled down from the bus. All were gaunt and hollow eyed and startled by the cries of the crowd, not understanding why people were shouting or what they wanted. Some caught on and stopped, studied a photograph, shook their head, and moved to the next person's photograph. Others walked on staring blindly ahead. Boy Scouts, their forearms locked into a seat position, carried those too weak to walk. Many deportees were sobbing from joy and exhaustion.

Janine and Robert watched hoping to recognize a face. When night fell, they learned there would be no more buses until the morning. They showed their passes and entered the hotel. Inside, the scene was surreal. Gaunt camp survivors eating in the Lutetia's elegant dining room decorated in the style of a luxurious 1920s ocean liner. They found Lucile alone at a table and joined her. She had secured her crutches against her chair and leaned back, taking in the crystal chandeliers and the sleek art deco furniture.

"This place is exactly as it was," she marveled. "I had a Wednesday here, a high-ranking civil servant. Very polite," she said, mimicking his prissy manners. "We would have dinner here first, then go to his room. There, he was less polite."

Janine and Robert watched Lucile chew carefully like someone who understood the importance of food.

"I had forgotten about plates," Lucile said, delicately spinning one around. "So pretty. The hotel has a special menu for deportees. I'm allowed mashed potatoes, ground meat, and fruits." She took another bite, then turned to Janine. "Your mother spoke German and worked in the camp's administration, so she was able to keep Nicole and me away from the steel mills. It was so cold in winter, metal stuck to your fingers and peeled off your skin. It'd get infected and that was the end of you." She wiped her mouth with her napkin and resumed talking, faster now. "Men have always liked me. Also, I have red hair," she said, touching her bare skull. "I did. I mean I do. A general from the Luftwaffe here in Paris told me that in German folk tales red hair is the mark of beastly sexual desire."

Janine and Robert exchanged a look, fearing what was to come.

"So I found myself a *Berufsverbrecher*, a German career criminal, one of those who ran the camp," Lucile said. "Mine was in charge of the kitchens. I gave him love; he gave me food." Lucile glanced at the women deportees at other tables. "That's why they call me the whore—*the whoooooore*. They're jealous because I found a way . . ." She paused briefly. "My *Berufsverbrecher* wasn't so bad, and the food he gave me helped the four of us survive." She shrugged. "The Russians hung him the day after they arrived. I guess he was bad to other people. Not to me, not too much . . ." Her voice trailed off as if she could not begin to describe what an attractive woman had to do to survive in a death camp.

The next morning Janine went back to the Orsay train station and Robert stood outside the Lutetia with families crowded behind the barriers. Lucile was in his mind. The war had a way of weeding out imposters, but she had figured out how to survive and help her friends. He knew from his time at Natzweiler-Struthof that caring for others helped you hold out. He had not been able to talk about his ordeal, but Lucile had, on her first night back. That took real courage.

Cheers pulled him out of his thoughts. A bus filled with women turned around the corner, with another behind.

"They're from Ravensbrück," an official said. "They arrived at Le Bourget airport."

Robert drew in a sharp breath. Most of the camp survivors came by train. Only the ones in poor health, he knew, were flown in. The roar of arriving buses sent his heart thumping. His longing for Nicole so intense, every muscle in his body knotted up.

The buses pulled in front of the hotel, but the women inside remained in their seats. They had lived in fear for too long; Robert knew they would not budge until ordered.

"Terminus!" the conductor shouted, trying his best to sound cheerful. Passengers began to stand. Robert moved along the first bus, peering through the windows—*she isn't here.* He moved to the second bus—*she isn't here either!* Then he felt his throat tighten as he spotted a thin figure walking up the aisle. The woman wore a hat and the usual camp's striped uniform. He could not see her face but there was something familiar about the way she tilted her head. Robert walked alongside the bus as she made her way to the platform. Then he rapped on the glass and called, "Nicole!"

The woman startled and squinted at him through the window. "Robert, is that you?" She brought her fingers to her lips, then with emotion so intense that she could barely walk, she lurched down the aisle and Robert caught her as she descended the platform.

"Lock your arms around my neck, my love," Robert said. Tears welling, he kissed her forehead, stumbling and catching himself as he carried her.

"You're here for me," Nicole said, choking. "Oh, Robert, I'm so happy they didn't kill you."

"Oui, ma chérie, it's all fine, now," he said, talking through his tears and carrying her up the hotel front steps to the entrance where a nurse held the door open.

Her face was thin, and her hair cropped short, but her eyes were sparkling with joy. "Robert, you're so handsome. I'm so happy, mon amour."

She felt so light in his arms, Robert was afraid to hurt her. "Tout va bien. Tout va bien."—*Everything's fine, everything's fine*, he kept repeating as he brought her to the ground-floor infirmary where a nurse helped him lower her into a wheelchair.

"We'll give her a bath and new clothes," the nurse said. "Then, she'll get a room."

Robert leaned over, kissed Nicole's forehead, and watched the nurse wheel her away. Then, hands shaking, he just stood there, lost. Orphaned children rescued from the camps had taken over the hotel lobby. The boys played hide-and-seek. The girls jumped rope. They did not talk or make noise. They moved around like furtive shadows. Tiny twin boys with short white-blond hair and emaciated faces hop-scotched on a course chalked onto the hardwood floor. With their clothes flapping over their wizened limbs, to Robert they looked like angels.

A doctor exited the infirmary and asked Robert if he had been vaccinated. Yes, of course. That was one of the conditions for being admitted into the hotel.

"Good. Since you'll be with her, I want you disinfected twice a day."

Robert nodded. "How is she?" he asked.

"She has joint pain, and she may become delirious at times, but we'll keep her hydrated and that'll help with the fever. But the kidneys . . ." A shadow crossed his face. "They all have terrible kidneys. Still, she's got good veins and we've being able to put an IV in her. So . . ."

"When can she go home?"

"Are you a relative?"

"She's my wife," Robert lied.

The doctor looked at Robert, pondering how much hope he should give this man. "Soon, hopefully," he said.

When Nicole was rolled out of the infirmary, Robert hurried over, but the twin boys beat him to her. Nicole's face brightened when she saw them. She slid her thin arms from under the blanket and put her hands around their shoulders. "Meine lieben Kinder," she said, kissing them.

"Nicole, Nicole! Wir lieben Dich, Nicole," the children kept saying as they tightened the blanket over Nicole's chest.

"I hid them for over two months," Nicole said. "Twins, you know, they had to be kept away from the doctors."

"Wir moechten beir Dir bleiben," the boys said, holding Nicole's hands.

"They want to stay with me," Nicole translated.

The nurse leaned toward the boys. "You have your own room, children. Nicole needs to rest."

The boys did not understand and turned to Nicole.

"Kinder spiet," she whispered in their ears.

The boys obeyed immediately. They kissed Nicole's cheeks and went back to their game.

Nicole's fourth-floor room was beautifully appointed. The bed was large, with side tables and crystal lamps. The window had a view of the poplar tree on the Square Boucicaut and Le Bon Marché department store. Nicole lay in bed propped on pillows, an IV dripping steadily into her arm. She watched Robert.

"You were in the camps!" she said. "You're so much thinner."

"I was," Robert said reluctantly. "But I was freed early. I'm all fine now. Tell me about you."

"Oh, Robert, I dreamt about you waiting for me so many times," Nicole said, her face lighting up. "I thought it'd happen at the train station in Pau but here in Paris, it's even better. I'd never been on an airplane before." Nicole raised her head briefly, then fell back onto the pillow. "Look at this place. It has its own private bathroom." She looked amused for an instant. "Come out of the camps and you get a room in a luxury hotel. Who would have thought?"

"There is more," Robert said. "At night you'll be able to see the lights of the Eiffel Tower. And when you get stronger, we'll go to the Bon Marché across the street. Every deportee is given a free set of clothes there."

"Oh, Robert, I thought about you every day," Nicole said, her voice suffused with emotion. "It helped me so much, especially during the winter. It was so cold, and we were so hungry." She stopped talking and suddenly blurted out, "I turned twenty last month. We have to celebrate."

"Happy birthday, sweetie!" Robert said, kissing her hot, dry lips. "We'll go out for dinner. Paris has so many restaurants, it's unbelievable."

"Black market restaurants, like chez Francis in Pau, where you wanted to take me?" she asked, a loose grin spreading over her face. For an instant Nicole looked as young as she actually was. Robert caressed her cheek; she nuzzled against his hand and fell asleep.

The nurse who came to change the IV bottles told Robert that Nicole was being given water, nutrients, and a mild sedative that explained her continuous sleepiness.

"Keep talking to her," the nurse said.

"Does she hear me?" he asked.

"Yes, it reassures her. Your voice will keep the nightmares away. You're her husband?"

"Yes. We got married just before she was arrested," Robert answered, expanding the lie, making it realer, as if it would hasten Nicole's recovery.

The nurse urged him to go down to the dining room and get something to eat. He said he would but instead he drank lemonade and talked to his sleeping Nicole.

"We'll find an apartment in Pau with a view of the mountains. The government is offering former Résistants employment in the police force. I'll take the job for a few months until I find something better. In the meantime, we'll have enough money to get us through . . ."

"I love your voice . . . ," Nicole murmured, her eyes still closed. "Tell me more."

So, Robert told her about his family and the place where he grew up. He said that his mother would be upset because Nicole was not Jewish but that his father would not care and would love her like a daughter. In the half-light, with her smooth forehead and high cheekbones, Nicole had the face of an angel. The brutality of the camps still vivid in his mind, Robert wondered: How did she survive? She was unbroken, her humor and spirit stronger than ever. Nicole was being rehydrated and fed intravenously. She was having trouble talking, but that was because of the medication.

The room grew dark. Nicole was tossing her head on the pillow. At times her face was strained with anguish and she looked like a different person. Robert took her hand; it was cold and slippery. With his thumb, he gently brushed the tattoo on her arm. The touch woke her up. She looked at Robert and as if by magic her face became young again.

"Come to bed with me," she said.

Robert took off his shoes and lay down beside her. Nicole nudged against him. She looked profoundly happy.

"Do you know what happened to Anna, Janine's mother?" Robert asked.

"We were separated but I think she died of typhus. She was a wonderful woman, she helped me with the children. Oh, Robert, what they did to those poor children."

"Like the ones downstairs."

"Yes. I hid them. They're from Lithuania. Doctors did bad things to twins." She stopped talking, then a minute later asked fretfully, "Where am I?"

"You're in a hotel in Paris. Do you want me to carry you to the window so you can see the lights of the Eiffel Tower?"

"Later," Nicole said, searching for his hand and holding on to it. "You have to promise me something."

"Of course."

"Don't let them say that during the war everyone was a hero," she said with unexpected force. "There were a lot of French Jews and Résistance women in the camps. They all told the same story. They all had been denounced by French people."

Robert was surprised by the vehemence in her voice. He tried to be soothing. "Ma chérie, the war is over. We're together. All that doesn't matter anymore."

Nicole shook her head. It *did* matter to her, but then, she closed her eyes, and her breathing became regular. Just as she seemed asleep, she began talking again. "I'm happy," she said, smiling, her eyes still closed. "The man I love was waiting for me."

Later, she stared at him as if wanting to engrave the image of his face in her mind. "Your eyes have sparkles of green in their middles. Green and brown eyes, my lover has . . ."

"You'll feel better soon," Robert said. "I'll feed you the way they fed me. Meat juice every day, then milk, and eggs. It'll be easier. You already have an IV. You're way ahead of me."

"Oh, good," she whispered, falling back to sleep.

Night was falling. The rotating light of the Eiffel Tower flashed over the roofs of Paris. Robert had moved back to his chair and taken Nicole's hand. She breathed a deep sigh. He leaned over and kissed her forehead.

"Merci, Robert, mon amour," she whispered.

She closed her eyes and Robert felt an abrupt stillness descend over them.

"Nicole!" Fear sucked the air from the room. Gutted, he crawled onto the bed and took Nicole in his arms. "Please, please, my love," he begged.

But he knew life had left her. The room was quiet. He kissed her again and again, combed back a drenched lock of hair from her forehead, and rocked her gently for the longest time. It was pitch-dark outside when he finally leaned on his back and let the tears stream down his face.

"Après la guerre." *After the war.* There would be no such thing for him. He held Nicole's hand, and the pain kept growing. All day they had been planning their future and now the crushing loneliness engulfed him. The overwhelming urge to *not live* was back, as strong as in that bed in Toulouse. And Robert saw the dead of his war all over again—American soldiers in the port of Algiers. Eli on the Sedjanne battlefield. His Africa Corps comrades massacred in the desert. The hangings in the camps and the relentless firing squads. And Mike's face calm and peaceful as he died in that ambulance. The visions were so real that it seemed like just another nightmare when he heard the door open and two women walked into the room. The nurses, he assumed. Robert got off the bed.

"Bonsoir, Robert," said an old woman wearing the striped camp jacket under an army coat. Her face was seamed and her smile unsteady.

"Bonsoir, Anna," Robert said, recognizing Janine's mother, who looked twenty years older than when he last saw her. Janine stood behind her.

Anna embraced Robert and kissed him on both cheeks. For an instant she seemed joyful, but glancing over his shoulder, an infinite sadness darkened her face.

Robert tried to draw in a breath but couldn't. His chest was too full. "She died a few minutes ago," he said.

Janine took Robert in her arms; she held him tightly and they both cried.

Anna knelt beside the bed and took Nicole's hand. "I thought that if she made it out of the camp she'd survive," she said, wiping back tears. "She was so strong, so funny. She sang every night to the children. She invented games for them. She made them laugh. She shared the little food she had with them. I told her she badly needed it for herself, but she shared it anyway." Anna paused for a moment and added, "And you were always in her mind. She talked about how lonely her life had been and then she'd say: 'And then I met Robert!'"

Nicole was buried in the Bagneux cemetery in the southern suburb of Paris. Madame Gaillac, the hotel owner, never came back and was thought to have died during the march out of the camp. Two weeks later, the doctors released Lucile and Anna and, along with Janine and Robert, they took the train for Toulouse.

62

ROBERT MOVED BACK TO PAU and took the job as a police inspector in les Renseignements Généraux as he had told Nicole he would. This was the very same police organization that had fought so hard against the Résistance. The service had been purged and new blood with solid war credentials was in demand. The French provisional government was worried that the colossal number of weapons parachuted by the Allies could be used for a political insurgency. So Robert spent his days in dark cellars and caches under pigsties where they unearthed crates filled with machine guns and ammunitions.

Every morning, his first thought was for Nicole. He still wore her father's clothes. This was the worst part of the day, when the loneliness was most acute. He knew his heartbreak would take time to heal but one afternoon while ridding the funicular he had taken so many times with Nicole, a flicker of gratefulness went through him. He had been luckier than most. He had had the chance to say good-bye to the woman he loved. Her last words still reverberated through him: "*Merci, Robert, mon amour*." Nicole was at peace when she took her last breath—*at least that*. One thing the war had taught him was to rise up and meet the hardships life threw at you. And when the funicular reached the top and the doors opened, he knew what to do.

He visited Toulouse the following Sunday and Anna organized a picnic on the bank of the Garonne. Blankets were laid on the grass and despite the ever-present rationing, they had managed to bring food for everyone and plenty of wine. Janine had grown very pregnant, and Robert felt at peace sitting next to her. They watched Emma and her grandfather by the river's edge. Louis picked up a piece of slate and skipped it. The stone bounced on the water and Emma jumped up and down, delighted. Anna joined them and tried her luck but failed miserably. Emma rushed to her grandmother with open arms and consoled her with a kiss.

"Emma started talking again," Robert said.

"Yes." Janine nodded. "The day my mother came back."

Robert spotted Proust and Lucile descending a flight of stairs. Proust held a bag and carried a folding chair. They moved carefully with Lucile holding tight to Proust's arm.

"Proust has been helping Lucile, I hear," Robert said.

"Yes. She had surgery to remove a bullet fragment in her hip."

Lucile still had a birdlike look, but her hair was growing back as red as ever. She kissed Janine and Robert while Proust set the chair and helped Lucile ease into it. Louis and Anna joined them. They uncorked bottles of dry white Jurançon. Proust filled the glasses and Robert passed them over. Lucile raised hers and declared, "Szczescie jest pomiedzy ustami i brzegiem kielicha."

They drank and Proust translated, "'Happiness is between the lips and the rim of a glass.' Lucile learned Polish in the camps and now she wants to open a bar."

"That's what retired hookers do!" Lucile said. "A café near the stadium where you all come for drinks after football games."

"They play rugby around here," Robert said.

"Rugby, then," Lucile rectified happily.

When Lucile and Anna began to unpack the food, Robert led Janine away and helped her sit under the shade of a tree.

"How are you feeling?" he asked.

"Good." Janine put a hand on her belly. "You'd think I was having twins. I'm twice as big as when I was expecting Emma."

"He's a big boy," Robert said.

"Or a huge girl."

Staggering under the weight of conflicting emotions, Robert decided this was the moment. He asked Janine to marry him. Janine's face filled with tenderness. She took his hand and raised it to her lips.

"Robert, I will not let you spend the rest of your life trying to make up for Mike's death. He wouldn't want that."

"How do you know?"

"You are *not* in love with me, Robert!" Janine said. "You and I lost the people we loved. We can't replace them with each other."

"Maybe that's what they'd want us to do."

"You have a good heart, Robert," Janine said, her voice threatening to break. "But you need to think of yourself. Sometimes being selfish is the most generous thing you can be."

Robert smiled bravely. "I despise selfish people."

Janine dismissed that with a kiss. "We've both been truly in love, Robert—you with Nicole, me with Mike. We should be grateful. Losing them broke our hearts but it's much, much better than if we had never known them."

"Better to be heartbroken than never to have loved?" he asked bitingly.

"Stop brooding, Robert. You'll meet a good woman, and you'll fall in love again."

Robert took a ragged breath and stared blindly at the Garonne River. At that instant he loathed Janine, who wouldn't let him try to repair the past.

"You're my dearest friend, Robert," Janine said as she nudged close to him. "And you deserve a woman who will love you completely.

I can't fall in love again." She slid her hand inside his and their fingers intertwined. "I'm broken."

"Don't say that."

Janine patted her belly and indicated Emma playing by the river. "I'll give my love to them," she said. "The men I fall in love with all die."

63

JANINE'S BABY BOY WAS BORN on the third of September. Lucile, Proust, and Robert rushed to the hospital. Lucile had regained most of her grace and poise. Her red hair was growing back, and her face showed hints of her former beauty. The men had dressed up for the occasion and each held a bouquet of flowers. They all followed a nurse wearing a Catholic nun's habit and a white cornette. She knocked on a door, peeked inside, and opened it wide. A radiant Janine lay in a bed. Anna sat at her side. Her hair had grown in too, soft salt-and-pepper waves.

"How's the prince?" Lucile asked, leaning over the cradle as Robert and Proust handed out their bouquets to Anna.

"He's the loudest child in the ward," Janine said.

"He's a big boy," Proust said.

"Three kilos and seven hundred grams," Anna said. "A little over eight pounds. The nurses haven't seen such a big baby since before the war."

Robert joined Proust and Lucile at the cradle. The baby slept with his fists closed tight. He had a full head of strawberry blond hair.

"Look at that hair!" Lucile said.

"He's got more than you and me," Anna laughed.

Robert was quiet. He held out his index finger to the baby, who grabbed it and looked up. He had blue eyes. Robert wanted to smile but couldn't. The baby let go; Robert straightened up and stared out the window.

"You can say it, Robert. It's all right," Janine said.

Robert hesitated but said what they were all thinking. "He looks exactly like Mike."

"He's even got freckles," Janine said.

Faces unsteady, they all looked away, stricken with sadness from hearing Mike's name. Footsteps in the corridor broke the tension. A white-coated doctor appeared at the door.

"Madame Dumas, there is a gentleman in the lobby who asks for you. We can't understand what he's saying but he's handing out these." The doctor pulled a cigar out of his breast pocket. "This is a Montecristo, a very expensive Cuban cigar."

"Merde." Robert rushed into the corridor.

A large man with a red face and a full head of white hair was addressing the nun at the reception desk. He spoke English, enunciating every word and pointing at his own chest.

"I am here to see my grandson. I come from Chica-go, America. Madame Janine Dumas is the mother. You are Catholic, I am Catholic too."

The nun only understood *Catholic*, but she liked that.

"Mr. O'Keefe?" Robert asked, approaching with his hand extended.

"Yes." The man turned around and faced Robert. "Thank goodness! You speak English?"

"I'm Robert. I was a friend of your son's."

Thomas O'Keefe pumped Robert's hand and then pulled him into a hug. "Mike talked about you in his letters. It's good to finally meet you."

Thomas O'Keefe moved to a chair to pick up the huge bouquet of flowers he had parked there. "Robert, will you take me to see my grandson?"

Robert led Thomas O'Keefe along. As they approached Janine's room the doctor was just leaving.

"Merci pour le cigare," he said.

That much French, Thomas O'Keefe could muster. "Have another one," he said, planting another cigar in the doctor's shirt pocket.

Visiting hospital patients was something Thomas O'Keefe knew how to do. First, he handed the flowers to Janine, then asked after her health and assured her in a booming voice that she was the most beautiful young mother he had ever seen. He then paid his respects to Anna. He did not need to be told that she was Janine's mother; he simply knew. He kissed Lucile, then shook hands with Proust and gave him a cigar.

"I have four children, but this is my first grandson," he said, leaning over the cradle. "May I?" he asked.

"Of course," Janine answered.

Thomas O'Keefe took the baby out of the cradle and lifted him up. "Strong and gentle this boy is," he said, cradling him expertly against his shoulder. Eyes brimming, he turned to the bed and added, "Thank you, Janine, you've made me a very happy man."

Then, rocking the baby, Thomas O'Keefe cried like only a true Irishman can.

After a few days with Janine, her family, and his new grandson, Thomas O'Keefe devoted himself to learning every detail of Mike's war. Robert took him to the garden of the church where they blew up the prison wall. He asked to see the place where Mike had parachuted from the Halifax and insisted on crossing the Pyrenees on foot, just as his son had. But when he asked to see the farm where the Cossacks attacked them, Robert shook his head. He couldn't go back there. "Bad memories," he said.

"You saved Mike's life that night."

Robert looked squarely at him. "We saved each other."

Thomas O'Keefe saw the emotion in Robert's face and took his arm. "Please forgive me, Robert. I'm just an old man who misses his son."

"I wouldn't be alive if it weren't for Mike, sir," Robert said, fighting tears. "He got me out of a death camp, and he didn't have to."

Robert poured out his heart, telling Thomas O'Keefe how Mike had rescued him. "I was with the Basques. We were five, then three, and the last two died the day the Nazis abandoned the camp. Then the Americans arrived but they couldn't help me. I couldn't even swallow water. I was dying but it felt good just to hear their voices. It was like hearing the Americans in Algiers." Robert stopped and wiped a tear with the back of his hand. "I was lying on that bunk. The end was near, and I was fine with it. And in the middle of the night, out of the fog, there's this guy shaking my shoulder and speaking French. 'Robert, comment ça va?' *Robert, how are you?* It was Mike. He picked me up and carried me out. I thought I was hallucinating. Then he slid me onto the front seat of an ambulance and there was Janine right there. That's when I believed it was real." Robert shook his head and continued. "And then at a refueling stop, Mike was killed by rogue SS men."

Thomas O'Keefe slid his hand onto the back of Robert's neck and gently rested his forehead against his. "I know all that, Robert. I read the OSS report. And Mike was right to come get you. I would have done the same thing. You don't leave a comrade behind. And *you* didn't either. Mike would have died in Tunisia if you had not hauled him out of his plane."

"He told you that?"

"He wrote me about it."

Something passed between them. Robert's heart lightened for the first time since Mike's death. If Mike's father forgave him, perhaps he could forgive himself.

"I want to take my son back to America," O'Keefe said. "Mike needs to get home, you understand that?"

Robert responded that he did.

They visited the Bourdés cemetery overlooking the train station and Robert led Thomas O'Keefe to his son's resting place. The old man rubbed Mike's engraved name on the headstone. When he went down on his knees, Robert stepped away. Thomas O'Keefe talked to his son for a long time. Then he walked back to the gate, brushing the earth off his trousers.

"Mike asked to be buried here?"

"Yes, he did."

Thomas O'Keefe took a long sweeping look at the countryside. "And this is where you set up the ambush?"

"Yes. It had rained the night before. It was lush and very green."

"A beautiful sight?"

"It was."

"Did Mike say something about that?"

"Yes." Robert was surprised by the question. "He talked about how peaceful and serene it was." Robert paused. "He made a joke. 'If something happens get me a spot in the shade.' He meant under the trees."

Thomas O'Keefe walked away looking at the scenery. When he came back to where Robert waited, he spoke gently.

"France is Mike's home. I understand that now. He should lie where his heart is," he said.

Thomas O'Keefe never mentioned taking his son's body home again.

EPILOGUE

MY FATHER WAS EIGHTY-FOUR AND AILING. That winter, when his health took a turn for the worse, my brother and I and our families rushed to be with him and my mother in the family home, outside Pau, in the foothills of the Pyrenees.

Our arrival gave him strength. His spirits lifted and he felt better. A year earlier he had broken his hip and now ambled along with a walker. Le machin—the contraption, he called it. He fought hard for his independence and still managed to move in and out of the house by himself. Weather permitting, he sat in his chair on the terrace facing the mountains and the trails to Spain—this was his spot. He paid little attention to the TV news except when the war in Iraq was mentioned. One evening an American anchorman in Washington concluded his report by saying: "And now, in silence, the photographs of the twenty-eight American servicemen and -women who lost their lives in Iraq this week." The screen turned black, and names and pictures began fading in and out.

"Aides-moi tu veux?" *Give me a hand, will you?* Dad said.

I helped him up. He took off the University of Chicago hat my son had sent him and stood at attention watching the faces of the American soldiers flashing on the screen. When the segment ended, he put his hat back on and said in that loud voice people develop when they become hard of hearing: "Ces soldats ressemblent exactement à leurs grands-pères." *Those soldiers look exactly like their grandfathers.*

Then he grabbed his walker and shuffled out onto the terrace. I went over to help him, but he waved me off and managed a smooth transition from walker to chair. He looked at the mountains, clasped his hands under his chin, and closed his eyes. He had told me that he thought often about his comrades in the Résistance and the allied airmen he had met. He cared deeply about the Americans, and now I knew he was praying for their grandchildren dying in Iraq.

My father died four months later. Family, friends, and neighbors attended the funeral in the village cemetery. The local rabbi wrapped the coffin in a blue and white flag emblazoned with the Star of David. Prayers were said in Hebrew and in French.

A couple of veterans from the French Vietnam war had driven through the region that morning and picked up the few remaining survivors of my father's Résistance network, including a couple in their eighties or nineties. The man had a slight Polish accent and his wife had stunning green eyes. She had aged but this was the woman who used to own the Café des Sports and kiss my father every time we came in.

I noticed an old woman stepping out of a car with Toulouse license plates. Her face was wrinkled, and her white hair was cropped short. Her son hurried around the car to help her, but she was already on the move. He had a square jaw, a full head of thick white hair, and a brick complexion that reminded me of a young Bill Clinton.

The woman was surprisingly energetic for her age. She spotted the Polish man and his wife and moved toward them with open arms. The three of them kissed, held hands, and looked into each other's eyes, sharing a moment of emotion as they turned to my father's coffin. Her son, who had hung back, joined them. The Polish man embraced him and raised his hand two feet high, indicating that the last time he saw him, that's how tall he was. His wife kissed him several times, leaned back, and complimented his mother on what a handsome son she had.

Other friends and old comrades joined them. Tears were wiped with the back of hands. Memories were shared and they lamented that they now only saw each other at funerals—c'est la vie.

The man with the Polish accent held the French colors over my father's coffin as it was lowered into the ground. He was ninety-six years old. When I thanked him for coming despite his advanced age, he protested, "I could not let Robert go without holding the flag for him."

Then I noticed the wiry lady heading for the burial mound and her son catching up with her. She stood at the edge of the grave, looked down at my father's coffin, brought her fingers to her lips, and blew him a kiss.

Los Angeles, August 12, 2024

ACKNOWLEDGMENTS

Much gratitude to my literary agents Peter Benedek, Byrd Leavel, Lily Dolin, and Sophie Baker for their continued support, work, and encouragement. Thank you to Lyz O'Keefe and Sarina Simon, who both read every draft of this novel; Lori Weintraub, Tim Disney, and Bill Whitaker, for their valuable insights; and Ann Berman and Emi Ikkanda, for their editorial guidance.

My heartfelt thanks to Claire Wachtel, Barbara Berger, Juliana Nador, Kristin Mandaglio, and all the people at Union Square & Co. It is a true joy to work with you.

And thank you to all those writers whose work inspired me: Elif Shafak, Jennifer Egan, David Benioff, Anthony Doerr, Mary Karr, Anne Tyler, Elizabeth Strout, Alan Furst, Tim O'Brien, Sebastian Faulks, Julian Barnes, Anne Tyler, and Ian McEwan, to name a few.

READER'S DISCUSSION GUIDE

1. Janine and Loïc have a serious disagreement in the first chapter of the novel. What is her moral dilemma? Identify key moments in the story when you agreed with her judgment and others when you did not. How does she resolve this dissonance and how did it change her?
2. Janine studied dentistry in Germany right before the war. What else did she learn there in addition to dentistry?
3. What it is that happened in Janine's life that led her to join the Résistance? What was it in her character and her life that made her choose this extraordinary path?
4. Why did Robert, who lived safely in Algeria, decide to enlist? If you had been in his situation, would you have done the same thing?
5. Were you surprise to read how the French police fought the Résistance? Did you feel there was some rationale in Commissaire Boucher believing that this was the beginning of a new era with a united Europe led by Germany?
6. What motivated Suzanne and her sister Charlotte to join the Résistance? Were you surprised to learn that resistance was often a family affair?
7. Why did Mike join the RAF when the US was reluctant to get involved in the war? Did his upbringing propel him to join? Was it in part to escape his father's world? How would you gauge his relationship with his father?

8. What were Churchill's reasons for ordering the British navy to sink the French fleet at Mers-el-Kébir, killing 1,300 French sailors? Do you think he was justified?
9. Did you agree with Robert when he felt his regiment was sent to Tunisia as cannon fodder?
10. Mike and Robert come from radically different worlds. What do they have in common? What was the base of their undying friendship? What did Janine have in common with them? And how were their motivations different?
11. Janine and Proust are at opposite ends of the political spectrum. He is ruthless and she is trying not to be. What in their lives caused them to have these beliefs and make those choices? Who did you agree with? What leads them to become closer at the end of the novel?
12. Why did the Italian nuns hide wounded Jewish prisoners from German doctors? Was it purely their religious beliefs?
13. What about de Lacoste? Do you believe that he honestly tried his best?
14. Motherhood is a recuring theme in this novel. Janine is determined to never be a single mother again. Why did she eventually change her mind?
15. What did Mike feel when he saw Janine with her daughter? Why did he have these feelings and how did they affect his behavior?
16. Were you surprised by Lazare's behavior with Prosper?
17. Marguerite is a Frenchwoman who decided to work for the Gestapo. Could you justify her decision? Did it make sense to you?
18. Do you agree with Mike that if Proust had come to America he would have been a rich man?

19. Nurse Nanette fell in love with a German surgeon. Did you approve of the relationship? Did you have any sympathy for Doctor Weiss?
20. How did you feel about Thomas O'Keefe? How would you describe his relationship with his son, Mike?
21. Mike and Robert in their own private ways were in love with the same woman. How did their attraction differ?

The President

OF THE UNITED STATES OF AMERICA

has directed me to express to

ROBERT PITON

the gratitude and appreciation of the American people for gallant service in assisting the escape of Allied soldiers from the enemy

Dwight D. Eisenhower

DWIGHT D. EISENHOWER
General of the Army
Commanding General United States Forces European Theater

Recognition from President Dwight D. Eisenhower to Robert Pitoun (spelled Piton here) for service to the Allied cause during World War II.

By the KING'S Order the name of

Monsieur Robert Piton,

was placed on record on

26 November, 1946,

as commended for brave conduct.
I am charged to express His Majesty's
high appreciation of the service rendered.

C. R. Attlee

Prime Minister and First Lord
of the Treasury

Commendation from King George VI, signed by Prime Minister Clement Attlee, to Robert Pitoun (spelled Piton here) for brave conduct during World War II.

DÉCISION N° 79

Le Général DE GAULLE, Président du Gouvernement Provisoire de la République Française, Chef des Armées.

CITE A L'ORDRE DU REGIMENT

PITON Robert . F.F.C. -

" Agent du réseau d'évasion " BOURGOGNE " depuis le mois de Mars 1944, a participé d'un façon extrêmement active à l'évacuation des aviateurs anglais et américains tombés sur le sol français durant l'occupation allemande.

" S'est chargé du convoyage en voiture des parachutistes alliés qui lui étaient amenés à PAU et qu'il conduisait jusqu'au-delà de la zone interdite où il les remettait à des guides surs qui leur faisaient passer les Pyrénées.

" Environ 80 Aviateurs ont pu, grâce à ses soins, regagner l'Angleterre.

" Exemple vivant de la résistance de la jeunesse française à l'envahisseur. "

CETTE CITATION COMPORTE L'ATTRIBUTION DE LA CROIX DE GUERRE 1939 AVEC

E T O I L E D E B R O N Z E

PARIS, le 8 Mars 1946.

Le Général DE GAULLE, Président du Gouvernement Provisoire de la République Française, Chef des Armées.
P.O. Le Général JUIN,
Chef d'Etat-Major Général de la Défense Nationale
***signé :* JUIN**

PRÉSIDENCE
DU GOUVERNEMENT PROVISOIRE
DE LA RÉPUBLIQUE FRANÇAISE

MINISTÈRE DE LA GUERRE
FRANCE COMBATTANTE

PARIS, le 5 Décembre 1946.

Référence à Rappeler:
334/ 15.686/JC-ST

COPIE CERTIFIÉE CONFORME

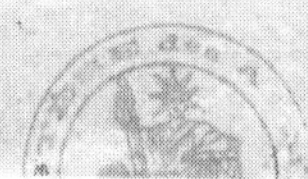

LE CAPITAINE BOILEAU

La Croix de Guerre awarded by General De Gaulle to Robert Pitoun (spelled Piton here).

ABOUT THE AUTHOR

Jean-Yves Pitoun is a screenwriter and director in France and the US. He's known for *American Cuisine, Word of Honor, Haute Pierre*, and *Interventions*. This is his debut novel. Pitoun lives in both Los Angeles and Southwest France. He can be reached at pitounjy@gmail.com.